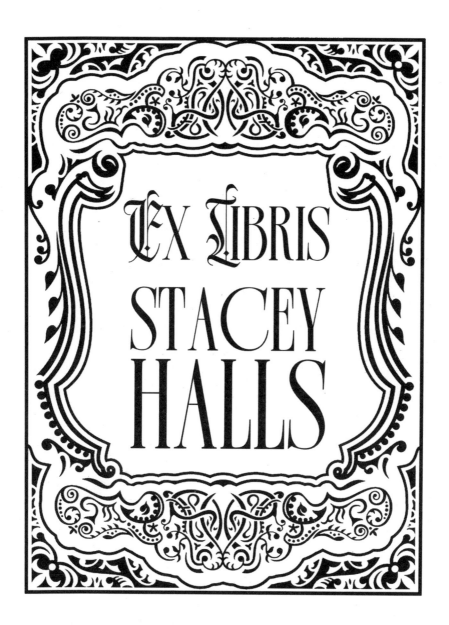

Ex Libris

STACEY HALLS

THE HOUSE HOLD

ABOUT THE AUTHOR

Stacey Halls' first novel *The Familiars* was the bestselling debut novel of 2019, won a Betty Trask Award and was shortlisted for a British Book Award. Her second *The Foundling* and third *Mrs England* were also *Sunday Times* bestsellers. In 2022 she won the Women's Prize Futures Award. *The Household* is her fourth novel.

www.staceyhalls.com
 @stacey_halls
 @staceyhallsauthor

THE HOUSE HOLD

STACEY HALLS

MANILLA
PRESS

First published in the UK in 2024 by
MANILLA PRESS
An imprint of Zaffre Publishing Group
A Bonnier Books UK company
4th Floor, Victoria House, Bloomsbury Square,
London, WC1B 4DA
Owned by Bonnier Books
Sveavägen 56, Stockholm, Sweden

A CIP catalogue record for this book is
available from the British Library.

Hardback ISBN: 978–1–83877–681–7
Export ISBN: 978–1–83877–848–4

Also available as an ebook and an audiobook

1 3 5 7 9 10 8 6 4 2

Typeset in Dante by EnvyDesign Ltd
Printed and bound in Great Britain by Clays Ltd, Elcograf S.p.A.

Manilla Press is an imprint of Zaffre Publishing Group
A Bonnier Books UK company
www.bonnierbooks.co.uk

For Keith

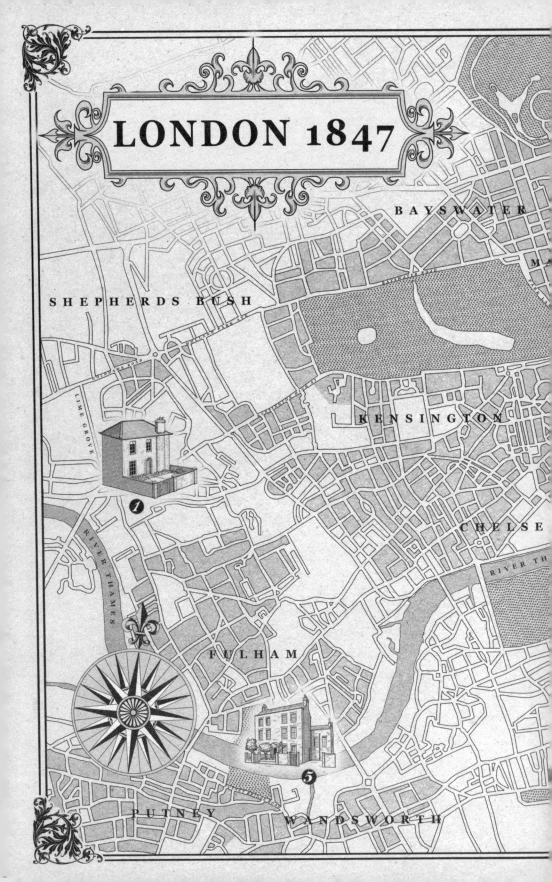

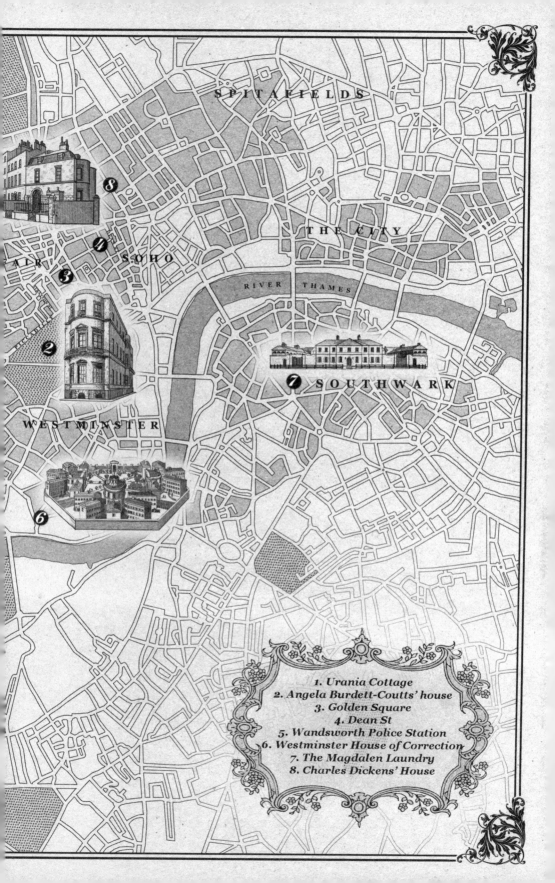

SPITALFIELDS

THE CITY

FAIR

SOHO

RIVER THAMES

WESTMINSTER

SOUTHWARK

1. Urania Cottage
2. Angela Burdett-Coutts' house
3. Golden Square
4. Dean St
5. Wandsworth Police Station
6. Westminster House of Correction
7. The Magdalen Laundry
8. Charles Dickens' House

CONTENTS

Rising is a thing unknown. It cannot be. It is all descent.
Lectures on Female Prostitution (1842)
Ralph Wardlaw

There is a lady in this town who from the window of her house has seen such as you going past at night, and has felt her heart bleed at the sight. She is what is called a great lady, but she has looked after you with compassion as being of her own sex and nature, and the thought of such fallen women has troubled her in her bed. She has resolved to open at her own expense a place of refuge near London for a small number of females . . . and to make a HOME for them.

Appeal to Fallen Women (1847)
Charles Dickens

'Martha wants,' she said to Ham, 'to go to London.'
'Why to London?' returned Ham.
They both spoke as if she were ill; in a soft, suppressed tone that was plainly heard, although it hardly rose above a whisper.
'Better there than here,' said a third voice aloud – Martha's, though she did not move. 'No one knows me there. Everybody knows me here.'
Then Martha arose, and gathering her shawl about her, covering her face with it, and weeping aloud, went slowly to the door. She stopped a moment before going out, as if she would have uttered something or turned back, but no word passed her lips. Making the same low, dreary, wretched moaning in her shawl, she went away.

David Copperfield (1849–1850)
Charles Dickens

CHAPTER 1

The White Cockatoo

Martha is quite alone in the house. Another girl, Mrs Holdsworth said at breakfast, will arrive before supper. It is a dull morning in mid-November, and she lights a lamp because she can. It whirs and spits as she carries it from room to room, familiarising herself with the layout of the house – or the cottage, as Mrs Holdsworth calls it, though there is little of a cottage's modesty about it. The rooms are large, the ceilings high and airy. The staircase has a smooth walnut handrail. Outside, there is a white-painted wash-house, a wide lawn and an orchard. The garden is dead and dreary. There are no dwellings either side, and beyond the back fence, a dozen cows graze placidly, paying no mind to the grey-brick house or its residents. In the distance, brickfields and nurseries mark the flat land like pox. Yesterday, on Martha's journey here, the early darkness acted as a blindfold. She has no idea where Shepherd's Bush is, only that London is near enough.

Mrs Holdsworth has gone to the post office at the end of the lane. Martha heard the street door close, the key turn in the lock, the smart tread of her boots on the path. The sound is ordinary to her; she is quite used to being shut inside places. What she is not used to is the silence, for at the Magdalen Hospital, even the dead of night was broken with coughs and sniffs and sneezes, with bodies rearranging themselves. Here at Urania Cottage, the quiet descends like a woollen helmet. Things that ought not to make noise do: chairs creak; sashes shudder; candles sputter in the draughts. Martha cannot remember the last time she was absolutely alone, and finds herself unsettled by it.

She stands in the bedroom – *her* bedroom, which she will share with two others. The shades are down, and the dim lamp casts a gloomy pall over the furniture: brass beds, a shelf lined with books, a medicine cabinet and washstand. Beneath each of the beds is a brand-new chamber pot. The fireplace stands empty, to be used only in times of sickness, so the room is cold, but Martha does not notice. She puts her thumbnail to her teeth, as is her habit, and chews.

For the time being, Martha and Mrs Holdsworth, the matron, are the sole occupants, and last night passed an awkward evening in the parlour. Martha spent most of it letting down the nightdress Mrs Holdsworth gave her, and making a fine mess of it. She has always been poor at sewing, despite her mother's talent, and knows she must improve.

Mrs Holdsworth collected Martha herself from the Magdalen Hospital at Blackfriars, as though she were an important parcel. As they journeyed through the streets, London grew darker, like a great lamp turning down, and Martha was aware that a part of her life was ending, another beginning.

She spent a year at the Magdalen laundry, washing, pressing, ironing, and the burns on her hands have faded to a tapestry of faint scars. The man who recruited her to Urania Cottage – Mr Dickens, who seemed to glimmer with the energy of a child – saw her hands and asked what she would make of becoming a servant. She replied that she was not afraid of labour and then somehow found herself revealing that it stilled her mind. He appeared to like this and made a note of it on pale-blue paper edged with gold.

The parlour is at the front of the house. Martha goes downstairs with her lamp and stands in the doorway, looking in. Richly furnished in shades of plum and grape, it is too grand a room to remain in for long without touching something. A crimson oilcloth covers the central table, and sermons are framed on the walls. It is rather a challenge to be left alone with all these luxuries: the calfskin books, the drawers groaning with silver plate, the snowy pillowcases. Martha finds herself obsessively assessing the value of things, for everything at Urania Cottage is brand new, from the wallpaper to the little pouches of dried lavender in the fresh pine drawers. Everything has its own distinct smell of wealth and promise.

A thought occurs: what if her first morning alone here is a test? The most dependable of people might be tempted to slip a candlestick up a sleeve. She shuts herself out of the room, polishing the door-knob with a handkerchief.

The night before, by the fire, after a quiet supper of chops and fried potatoes, Martha asked Mrs Holdsworth if she was allowed to write to her sisters. Her older sister, Mary, works as a pastry-cook in a shop near Oxford Street; her younger sister, Emily, is a housemaid in Reading, not far from where they grew up. She has not spoken to either of them in more than a year; at the Magdalen, she'd been too proud to send her address to Mary, too ashamed to share it with Emily.

'Of course,' Mrs Holdsworth replied, looking up from her mending. 'I ought to have told you sooner that you may write to whomever you wish, though all outgoing and incoming correspondence will be read by me. You may use the stationery in the dining room and ask me for stamps.'

Martha copied two identical notes, keeping them brief, and was purposefully vague about where she had lived for the last twelve months. If she had allowed herself to think about how concerned they might have been, how they might have tried to find her, she would have hesitated to write at all, and so she passed the notes to Mrs Holdsworth before she could change her mind.

She goes now to the kitchen, the humblest of all the rooms, and the one she feels most at home in. She pulls a chair from the large, scrubbed table and sits on her hands, looking into the larder, where the shelves are neatly ordered, stacked with clean new jars and pots not yet smeared with fingerprints. Beside the larder is the scullery, which is as cold as an icebox. Just outside the kitchen, in the hall, a door beneath the stairs leads to the cellar, where wine, beer and coal are kept. Mrs Holdsworth wears the keys like a talisman at her waist. Though Urania Cottage gives the appearance of an ordinary house, so much of it is fastened away from curious fingers: the linen cupboard, the stamps, the cellar. There are drawers that do not open, doors that remain locked. It reminds Martha of a doll's house, of a staged domestic life where, upon closer inspection, the fire is a pile of ribbons and the windows are pasted shut.

The house, she was promised, is the first clean page in a

new book for girls like her, who wish to begin their lives again. Even now, Martha does not fully believe in such charity. There is bound to be a catch, a price she will be obliged to pay at some point.

Glancing around the kitchen at the china she unpacked last night, at the custard glasses and the meat screen, the new-fangled beetle-trap crouching like a toad beside the range, the row of neat aprons hanging like question marks on pegs, the sense of new beginnings, the pressure to succeed, threatens to overwhelm her. With nobody else here, she feels like a ghost.

She has the urge to make noise, to leave her mark on the house, to prove that she is real, if only to herself. Remembering the delivery from the grocer that is yet to be unpacked, she goes through to the scullery and draws from a box a small copper tea-kettle. An enormous cream dresser covers the wall behind the door, and she places the kettle in the centre of an empty shelf and stares at it. She takes it down again, wiping away the smears her fingers have made on the polished surface with her apron. Then she replaces it, wipes her fingers again, and begins stacking the jars.

❦

In the first-floor drawing room of a large house off Piccadilly, a tall, exquisitely dressed woman places a porcelain cockatoo on a perch before the window and looks out at the bleak day.

In the park across the street, the trees are bare, but the thoroughfare below has no season. At midnight and high noon, in the dead of winter and the closed fist of summer, it is thronged with carts and carriages, animals and people. In France, she missed the clatter and peal of wheels and hooves, the proximity of life on the other side of the sash. She arrived home a little over an hour ago, and is still wearing the layer of grease and grime she has acquired from travelling.

'Miss Angela,' her companion, Hannah Brown, calls from the tiny sitting room next door, 'Mr Faraday has invited you to be a dinner guest at the Royal Institute on Saturday week.'

The sitting room is Angela's favourite in the house. The walls are lined with books, and from a gilt frame above the chimney-breast, her father gazes down as Mrs Brown works diligently through the piles of correspondence that arrived while they were away.

Mrs Brown calls again. 'He would also be grateful for the recipe for Mrs Wild's oyster and vermicelli soup.'

'I should think Mrs Wild would be flattered to give it,' Angela replies without moving from the vast window. The cockatoo was a present from a friend, and she uses it ironically to mark her comings and goings. Its presence on the perch signals that she is in London.

'And St Stephen's infant school should like to know if you might fund a magic lantern and slides for their New Year's Day feast.'

'I don't see why not. Tell them yes.'

Angela watches the fluid street below. If London has a colour, she thinks, it is brown. Paris is pale grey.

'Anything yet from the duke?' she asks, trying to sound careless.

'Not since Dover. Were you expecting something?'

The doorbell chimes in the depths of the hall.

'No, no. I rather hoped – never mind. I ought to bathe. And you ought to rest.'

But she knows the older woman will not. Mrs Brown has

been with her since Angela was a girl of thirteen, about to embark on her first tour with her mother. The three of them completed a circuitous route of Europe, absorbing paintings in Munich, sculptures in Lausanne and volcanoes in Naples. On her return to London two years later, Angela was barely recognisable from the reed-like creature who once sank into the upholstery in her mother's friends' drawing rooms. Almost two decades have since passed, and though Angela's lesson-books were given away long ago, Mrs Brown remains, with the addition of her husband, the retired doctor William Brown, who had accepted that Angela came like a dowry with his wife.

The Browns live in an apartment at the top of Angela's mansion on Stratton Street. They are more like devoted parents than servants, bickering in Angela's presence, and neglecting to tell one another all manner of things, but generally very agreeable to live with. Agreeable for Angela, at least, who is good-natured and attentive to their needs. Her own parents died nearly four years ago, and the Browns occupy the chasm they left quite comfortably. Dr Brown delivers letters for Angela and helps with the wine delivery. More often than not, he can be found wandering the shops off Regent Street, searching for a mechanism for his watch or dining with generals at his club. Mrs Brown spends most of her time with Angela. In another life, she might have been a tenant farmer, with her sturdy disposition, her flagrant disregard for weather and temperature. Her skill is containing and sealing off Angela's feelings, no matter how stormy. She is the thermometer to Angela's mercury.

When the Browns take the occasional trip without Angela, her home feels very empty indeed. It is far too large for one person, so she often fills it with friends and acquaintances and acquaintances of friends, and several times a week serves dinner for twelve. The bells are always ringing, the silver rotating, and the constant procession of boots have worn the steps smooth. The house, four storeys of brown brick with more windows than anybody might bother themselves to count, is like an extension of Piccadilly below it: a bustling inn on a busy highway.

The Stratton Street mansion was left to Angela by her grandmother, Lady St Albans, along with a sum so extraordinary the figures appeared at first glance to roll across the page like ball bearings. On a hot, dusty August day, Angela stood with her family in a darkened room in Furnival's Inn as her father's lawyer read the terms of Lady St Albans' will. Angela was made the sole heiress of her estate: a decision so controversial that the broadsheets fell over themselves to announce it. Her five older siblings received nothing, two aunts nought and her mother only a small amount, for Lady St Albans was Angela's grandfather's second wife and not a blood relation to the family. Nor was she accepted by them. Lady St Albans' desire was that Angela, the youngest bud on the family tree, received everything: half a million pounds, an income of fifty thousand a year, plus a half-share in the bank Coutts and Co., the family firm Angela's grandfather founded, not to mention all her jewellery, property, stocks, shares and securities. One condition of the will was that she take on her maternal grandfather's name, Coutts, becoming Angela Burdett-Coutts. As the years passed she found herself dropping the Burdett, for having had two names most of her life, three felt like too many to carry, and so she began dashing off her letters as Angela Coutts, and others followed suit.

The newspapers screamed that the bequeathment made her the richest woman in London. An image was formed in her likeness, conjured from ink and paper: glamorous, attractive, dripping with diamonds, suitors falling at her feet. What they and the rest of the nation would not accept, though, was Angela as herself: sensible, private, entirely unostentatious. But mostly she was a young woman grieving for her grandmother, of whom she was dearly fond. The visits to Lady St Albans' country house at Highgate, where she kept pigs, and where at Christmas Angela would pick firs and holly from the garden; the trips to the coast, where they would take rooms overlooking the sea; the nights at the theatre; the horse rides on the heath – all of it had come to an end at the same time that Angela was forced to emerge into the public gaze, in which she had no interest, and which she would discover came with a heavy tax no banker's draft could resolve.

Angela adjusts the cockatoo and brushes an imaginary speck of dust from its tail. The maids have been in this morning, and the bird is immaculate. Sitting level with passing omnibuses, Angela often comes face to face with curious gazes peering through the dusty glass. On one occasion, a gentleman from Putney wrote to the mistress at Stratton Street to enquire of the bird's authenticity. He had a bet with his friend who thought it an ornament, and Angela was sorry to disappoint him.

'I think I'll have more coffee,' she says, too quietly for Mrs Brown to hear.

The older woman appears in the doorway, clutching a pale-blue letter. 'The house at Shepherd's Bush is finally ready, and Mr Dickens invites you to view it. He is "regretfully busy",' she reads aloud, 'but "trusts everything will be to your liking".'

'Perhaps I will visit this week. I'll take my bath now.'

Mrs Brown retreats to the bureau beneath the window, and at the same time Stockton, the footman, appears in the drawing room. He performs a shallow bow and passes her a card.

'Beg pardon, miss,' he announces. 'I told the gentleman you were resting but he insisted it was urgent.'

'Parkinson,' she says, taking up the card. 'I wonder what he wants?'

But her body knows. A knot tightens somewhere inside her, and when Stockton leaves to fetch him, she automatically closes her eyes and breathes deeply. She hurries to the little sitting room.

'Mr Parkinson is here. He told Stockton it was urgent,' says Angela. It is all she needs to say.

'We don't know it concerns *him*,' Mrs Brown returns with authority. 'Every time the lawyer comes, you think it will be about that, and it almost never is. He likely has some papers for you.'

Angela glances at her father's picture above the chimney-breast. She does not like the portrait, which is mostly darkness; he is almost in profile, with half his face in shadow, and she wills him to turn and look at her. Her mother she misses dearly, but there was something about being the youngest and a girl that made her feel like a Christmas present to her father. Her mother had the same smile for all her children; her father's was especially for her.

Parkinson is waiting for them. A nondescript man, he might be anywhere between forty and sixty, and has barely aged in the years Angela has known him.

'Miss Burdett-Coutts,' he says, taking her hand in his. Parkinson is one of the few remaining people who call her by her full name, out of respect for her father, which she respects in him. 'Thank you for agreeing to see me. I trust your time in France was enjoyable?'

Angela withdraws her hand and pulls her mantle closer. 'Very, thank you, Mr Parkinson. The Jardin de Tuileries is beautiful in the frost.'

'Indeed. My sincerest apologies for calling so soon after you arrived home, but it is necessary for me to alert you to—'

'Has he been released?'

Parkinson's face darkens. 'I am afraid so.'

Angela straightens her sleeves and exhales through pursed lips. 'I felt it, as soon as I came back. I felt it.' She shoots a troubled look at Mrs Brown, who reaches for her as if she is a girl of thirteen again.

'I am sorry, dear.' Holding her tightly, Mrs Brown rubs Angela's arm before turning to face the lawyer. 'Do you know *why*, Parkinson? It is far too early, is it not?'

'Yes. He realised there was a chance of release if he claimed bankruptcy, and so he successfully petitioned the court. His pardon was granted at the beginning of the week.'

'This week! I wouldn't have come home if I knew. I would have stayed in France. When did you find out?'

'The chief commissioner delivered the news himself, not an hour ago, at the office. I came directly.'

Angela glances instinctively towards the window. 'When?' she asks.

'He will be freed from Clerkenwell prison in the morning.'

There is a heavy pause as they absorb this.

'Have you had any correspondence from him?' Parkinson asks.

Angela glances at Mrs Brown, who replies: 'Nothing for some months.'

'Do pass anything to me, Mrs Brown. He may enlighten us to his plans.'

'He was supposed to have four years!' Angela cries. 'I cannot understand why they let him out again. How can the law serve him and not me, whom he lives to torment? How is it just, when his release makes me a prisoner?'

'I am so very sorry, miss.'

'I will never be free of him, will I, Parkinson? I cannot imagine a day when I will ever be rid of Richard Dunn.'

Mrs Brown clutches at her arm, her own cheeks indignantly pink as she shakes her head. 'It isn't right, you know. It isn't right at all, how that man worms his way through loopholes and weaknesses. The law ought to be harder on him.'

'I fully agree with you, Mrs Brown.'

Dr Brown appears at the drawing-room door. 'What's all this?'

'Richard Dunn,' Mrs Brown spits, 'has been released from prison once again.'

'No! It can't be. Parkinson?'

'I'm afraid Mrs Brown is correct.'

'Then the law truly is an ass. My dear' – he addresses Angela – 'do not be disheartened. He shan't come within ten yards of you if I have anything to do with it.' He shifts his gaze to Parkinson. 'Ballard will resume his post? I presume you have already sent for him?'

'I shall send a note to the police station at once.'

'You may write it here,' the doctor commands. 'And I shall take it to the station myself.'

※

An hour later, in the bath, Angela washes herself unhappily as some of her most unpleasant memories come flooding back. This year marks not only a decade since her inheritance – a gift that came with a curse. Shortly after that hot day at Furnival's Inn, her father forwarded two letters from a man named Richard Dunn to Angela, which declared his love so freely that her father wrongly assumed she had found a lover. Bemused and even a little flattered, Angela presumed they had been written by a madman and forgot all about it.

Some weeks later, Angela went with Mrs Brown to take the waters at Harrogate. A day or so after they arrived, Angela found a calling card in her hotel room, and recognised the name instantly. She enquired with a porter and was thoroughly chilled to learn that Dunn had booked the room opposite hers.

It was then that their hellish game of cat and mouse began. A slim, tall, moderately successful barrister twenty or so years older than herself, Dunn was undeterred when Angela removed herself and her belongings from the Queen's Hotel and found rooms across town. Within an hour, another letter fluttered onto the doormat. She threw it on the fire and braved a walk through the mineral wells with Mrs Brown, but on their second circuit of the flower-beds, Dunn appeared at her elbow, and for the rest of her stay, not a day passed in which he did not make himself known.

The man was not discouraged by her coldness or the harsh manner she showed him, and so, not wanting to worry her parents, she wrote to Edward Marjoribanks, a senior partner at Coutts & Co. and a dear friend of her father's, who advised her to apply for protection from the local magistrate. A policeman, the dependable Ballard, was dispatched from London to the North Riding and, armed with the magistrate's warrant, arrested Dunn one cold, sunny morning in the street outside the house. Though it seemed a drastic step, she was relieved, for a part of her feared he would turn violent; there was something about his smooth, even-tempered exterior that deeply frightened her. She watched from an upper window as he cursed and swore at Ballard and, on seeing her, cried that she was a whore, shouting with such vitriol she was left trembling. The whole experience was so unpleasant that she did not stay in Yorkshire to see him fined.

But Dunn did not pay. Instead, he was sent to prison for a little over a month, during which time Angela returned to London and her parents. She was twenty-three years old.

Of course, Dunn did not dissolve away, as Angela had hoped. Shut inside her rooms in Harrogate, uneasy and frustrated at the disruption he had caused in her otherwise smooth life, she only ever imagined it was temporary. She could never have dreamt what would follow: a decade of looking over her shoulder, of fear pricking her skin.

Dunn's furious cries return to her whenever she throws his letters in the fire and watches them flare and curl. Parkinson has asked her to hand all correspondence to him, but she can barely stand to know that something Dunn has touched is in her house. Though left unopened, his letters call out to her with threat and malice, his words scored through the paper like scars.

The bath-water cools, and she forces her thoughts away from Dunn and instead thinks of the duke, who is at home in London. If Dunn is to be released tomorrow, she ought to visit her friend tonight, though her bones ache so, and no matter how much she soaps herself, she cannot clean the dusty road from her skin. It is already growing dark, and in the morning the doorbell will chime, and the little tray in the hall will fill with cards, and Richard Dunn will pass through the prison gates a free man, and turn his clear, steady gaze upon her.

※

At the Westminster House of Correction, almost as soon as the morning gun is fired, the door of cell number six bursts open.

'Get up,' barks the turnkey, an unpleasant woman with a perpetual grey sheen, like turned meat. 'Tracey wants yer.'

It is an hour before dawn and very cold. In the top bunk, two girls rub their eyes and peer at the grim halo offered by the warden's lamp. Josephine rises first, causing the damp chill of the cell to penetrate their woollen nest. Her bed-mate makes a noise of complaint.

'Where's the other'n?' The turnkey stands on the threshold, her currant-like eyes narrowed beneath a grubby mobcap.

'Here,' Josephine replies through a great yawn, sliding her head down her shoulder to indicate Annie.

The turnkey lifts her head suspiciously but makes no effort to move further into the room. 'Get up, the pair of yer. Tracey wants a word.'

Had the dismal wintry light risen with them, it would have revealed a brick room no larger than four feet by ten, with two slim beds stacked against the wall adjacent to the door. Below the window, which is covered with bars and set too high in the wall to look out, a low stool perches before a desk so frail it might as well be made from splints. A Bible sits untouched on its surface. The desk is superfluous to Josephine and Annie's needs; they are poor readers and even worse writers, and neither has been sent a scrap of mail.

The two of them drop like stones from the top berth and put on their rough dresses and boots. The early hour and the darkness have stolen any curiosity about why the governor might like to see them. Silently, they follow the turnkey to the vast and empty oakum room, where in half an hour hundreds of women will sit side by side, picking tar-coated rope into threads.

Lanterns illuminate a curious scene. The prison governor, Augustus Tracey, a tall, slender man with silver hair piled like ashes on his head, is leaning against the platform with his long legs crossed. Before him, grouped on the first and second row of benches, are five of their fellow inmates, some of them known to Josephine and Annie. Barrels and baskets of rope crouch against the dark walls like stowaways. In the pre-dawn light, the scene appears not unlike a prayer group aboard a ship.

'That be all, sir?' asks the turnkey.

Tracey thanks her and she closes the great doors. In the passage beyond, the inmates can be heard shuffling to the washing cells.

'Please,' says Tracey, indicating that the new arrivals should take a seat on the low benches before him. Josephine sees the governor's eyes flick to the thick scar that runs through both her lips towards her jawline. Just as quickly, he looks away. They settle closely beside a small, rickety-looking girl, and Tracey distributes a pile of papers, one to each of them. In the poor light, they peer and frown at the close print, and a rough voice speaks up from the front.

'Can't read, sir.'

The voice belongs to a young woman sitting on the front bench, whose reddish-gold hair frizzes beneath her cap.

'Ah,' said Tracey. 'Thank you, Miss—'

'Walker, sir.'

'Miss Walker. No matter. It was always my intention to read the address to you. These copies are for you to revisit in your free time.'

Josephine yawns and looks around at the painted iron pillars, at the misshapen baskets where endless serpents of rope await them. She is serving a sentence of six months, and in thirteen days will be released. This is her first time in prison, and she has not minded it, but only because of Annie. Quick, warm, brilliant Annie, with her soft hands, her giant, gentle heart, her slick tongue. Some stroke of divinity placed Josephine in Annie's cell on that first morning, and though they didn't meet until their work was completed and supper eaten in the chilly dining hall, by nightfall Josephine was in love. Annie seemed instantly like a friend, and from that day on they have barely been parted. For more than five months, they have worked, prayed, eaten and exercised beside one another, earning red stars for their diligence. At night, they share a bunk and cover each other's mouths with their hands. At the close of the first week, they scratched their prison numbers into the brick where their mattress met the damp wall, and there they remain, inscribed forever.

The strength of her feeling is so that Josephine finds she does not want to rejoin the outside world. Beyond the safety of the prison walls lies chaos and threat. Here, they have everything they need; outside, they have nothing. Annie is due to be released in five days, but she has asked to stay so that she may leave with Josephine. As far as Josephine is concerned, she herself would stay another year, two, five, as long as she could be with Annie. Tothill Fields, or the Westminster House of Correction, is a dreadful place: biting cold in winter, stifling in summer. The wardens are as vicious as the rats that scurry through the airless corridors. The inmates are haunted, crazy, desperate. The blankets are thin; the work is tedious and makes cat's meat of their hands. But they are able to sit close by one another, and in the silence, Josephine can daydream about what life will be like with her love. She would withstand all of it a thousand times over for Annie.

'Doubtless you are all intrigued as to why you've been summoned from your beds,' says Tracey over the sniffs and yawns. A pool of blank stares meet him; of course, he has never slept in a prison bed and supposes them comfortable enough to be summoned from.

'All of you are facing release in the coming weeks, and there is an opportunity, for those of you who are interested, for when that day arrives. A friend of mine has opened a house not far from here, for women like yourselves, who wish to continue their journey of repentance away from the situations and temptations they have left behind.'

In the pause that follows, one woman asks: 'What's repentance?'

With long fingers, Tracey shifts the lantern an inch away from him. 'Repentance? Ah, making amends.'

'Needlework?'

'No,' he says. 'The opportunity is a place within this house, not far from London, the purpose of which is to help women who have fallen. There, you will live in each other's company, train in service and eventually – eventually,' he repeats for emphasis, 'go abroad and begin new lives in a distant country.'

Half a dozen faces cloud with suspicion. 'You're transporting us?'

'*No. No.*' Tracey shakes his head, as if wondering how to begin again.

'What is it then?'

'Listen carefully. You, the seven of you before me, are all in possession of red stars on your armbands.'

Several hands reach automatically to touch the crudely sewn patches that distinguish them from their cellmates.

'You are good workers, and your behaviour sets you apart from your peers. You, above six hundred others who pass through here every year, have the potential to reform. You have the potential to change the direction of your lives. The virtuous inclinations within you have been noticed, not only by myself but by the wardens, and have elevated you to be chosen as candidates for this new venture. There is no cost to your-selves. There is only gain.'

'But what is it?' asks the first red-headed girl. 'Not another prison?'

'It is a home. A place of refuge. The sort of happy, comfort-able place some of you may not have known in your short lives. I have been assured that there you will be treated with the utmost kindness. You will learn how to keep house, so that one day you may keep your own. You will learn many things it is good and useful to know. You will be trained for service, and once you have proved yourself in ways moral and prac-tical, your passage will be paid to a new country as *émigrées*, not prisoners. You will enter this new land as free women, free to work, to marry, have families of your own. The possibilities are limitless.'

In the great dark room, the women are quiet and thoughtful. Josephine's smallest finger finds Annie's and curls around it.

CHAPTER 2

The Oakum Room

Jean Holdsworth shifts her basket onto her left arm to hold open the white-painted gate for the young woman following her. The girl looks several years younger than she is and holds her shawl in a fist beneath her chin as if against a fierce wind.

Mrs Holdsworth, herself in her early fifties, is dressed in half-mourning. In January, she will be able to put away the grey and lavender and return to ordinary colours, which now seem as unusual and garish as the garments the girls living at the cottage are expected to wear: raspberry poplin, lilac satin, bold checks in blues and greens. They seem to her more suited to a night at the theatre than a refuge for fallen women, too closely aligned with their pasts than their futures. The fabric has been bought from a draper in the Tottenham Court Road, and there is no mistaking the expense. She has raised her concern to the committee about the practicality of the gowns when the girls are to be taught housework: simple fabrics in browns and blacks would be more appropriate.

But her suggestions have been dismissed. Not being one to take no for an answer, Mrs Holdsworth argued that the budget would be better served in the linen cupboards or even on a maid; for four pounds, they could have two young girls from the village do the laundry and cooking. When this was waved away, she played her final card and made the point that such expensive outfits might tempt the young thieves among them. But she swiftly learnt that the committee wish her to be forceful only with the residents.

The dresses are only part of her initial doubts. How the girls' religious needs are to be served has not yet been arranged. The committee has decided they will not leave the house for any reason, including to go to church, and so a chaplain will be found. Mrs Holdsworth mildly suggested that the girls, of whom she is in sole charge, might be liable to become flighty if they are obliged to stay indoors at all hours. She was then reassured that the girls will not *wish* to go outdoors with all the chores and lesson-books and sewing available to them, as well as the endless supply of coal. The committee is convinced that by simply removing them from the metropolis, with all its vices and opportunities for sin, the girls will transform as if by magic into meek, fluffy church mice.

Mrs Holdsworth asked if they would be permitted to exercise in the garden.

'Of course they may exercise in the garden!' somebody retorted. 'This is no prison.'

'Sirs, if you please,' said Mrs Holdsworth. 'There is a danger of the girls finding life here . . .' She groped about for an appropriate word and settled eventually on: 'dull.'

'My dear Mrs Holdsworth—'

'Let her speak.'

'I only mean to say that these girls will have only recently been awarded their liberty. They will come voluntarily, and to find their freedom restricted once again . . . it will be off-putting, to say the least. I can't predict how many will remain if that is the case. In my opinion, I should be amazed if any last until Christmas.'

Her warm Paisley burr allows her to tell the truth with minimal offence.

In late October, all but one member of the governors' committee of Urania Cottage gathered around a polished table in the dining room at Devonshire Terrace, engulfed in a low-hanging fog of tobacco. As well as Mrs Holdsworth, the company comprised Mr Dickens, a clergyman, two prison governors, an educationalist and Dr Brown. Angela Burdett-Coutts, who had invited Mrs Holdsworth, was not present, and Mrs Holdsworth was mightily disappointed. She knew she ought to find comfort in the fact of there being another woman on the committee: a rare thing. But appealing directly to Miss Coutts is on a par with a lowly court official requesting an audience with the Queen. In the familiar masculine environment of whiskers and brandy, Mrs Holdsworth felt her old, tough skin form like a suit of armour. With the exception of the prison governors, not one of these men has actually worked in a prison or workhouse. Still, Mrs Holdsworth knows their type. In her working life, she has come across many boards and committees who are more familiar with the thick carpets and flock wallpaper of the governor's quarters than the wards and sickrooms below.

For this situation, she left a good job as superintendent of the lying-in ward at Bridewell House of Correction. The position of matron at Urania Cottage was not one she found and applied for herself; she was invited to do so in a letter, written on pale-blue paper, handed to her personally by the governor at Bridewell, a man named Sharpe. Mr Dickens's note was flattering, but she was not overcome by it. Of course she was familiar with his novels, but she has no time for such things. He was a friend of Sharpe's, and after some gentle persuasion, she found herself in the governor's house, sitting across from them both. It appeared that Sharpe wished for her to take the job almost as much as his friend, and so she agreed, as to refuse would have felt like turning down a favour. And she was ready for a change of scenery, a change of routine. Since her husband died seven years before and she shut up the house at Greenwich, she has not stayed in a position longer than two years, and that time was approaching. A quiet house in the country, a small group of inmates, whom she would come to know intimately: it was just what she needed, though she knew the chaos and crush of the city prisons would call to her again.

On this November afternoon, she and the young woman bundle themselves inside the cottage, and she senses at once that the downstairs fires have gone out. She looks in the parlour and the dining-cum-schoolroom, then calls for Martha. A moment later, the tall young woman appears in the passage to the kitchen.

'Martha, have you not kept an eye on the fires? Don't tell me the range has gone out.'

Martha's face replies for her. Then she turns her quiet, grey gaze on the young woman standing in the gloom of the passageway, clutching her shawl.

Mrs Holdsworth sighs. 'This is Polly. Polly, meet Martha, our first resident.'

The girls eye one another warily. Polly looks dreadful. Her dress is thin, the cuffs and collar frayed and worn, and the shawl wrapped around her shoulders offers little warmth. Violet smudges beneath her eyes make her appear very white, and her brown hair is dull and stringy. Mrs Holdsworth asks Martha to show Polly to her bedroom while she fetches her clothes and timetable, and the two girls go upstairs, Polly's canvas bag bouncing against her skirts.

The linen, outdoor clothes, bonnets and boots are kept locked in two large presses on the landing, for which Mrs Holdsworth keeps the key on a silk belt. Loading her arms with cotton and wool and taking a set of stays from the heap on the shelf, she is at once reminded of bones and the pork she has forgotten to order from the butcher. She thinks for the hundredth time how badly she needs a deputy.

In the back bedroom, Martha is sitting on her bed, Polly standing beside hers, still clutching her bag. Mrs Holdsworth sewed it at eleven o'clock the previous evening, having remembered a minute after blowing out her candle; she worked from her blankets with tired eyes.

There is an awkwardness between the two girls, with them being forbidden to discuss so many things: where they have come from, why they are here. What they have left. A dozen portcullises of conversation remain fastened, and effort must be made to find an opening. It will be easier, she thinks, when more arrive and there is no want of things to do.

'Here are towels, linen, an apron and a dress. You may adjust it after supper,' she says, passing the bundle to Polly, who reaches for it, her shabby sleeves rolling down to reveal yellowing bandages at each wrist, bronzed with rusty stains. Colour flares instantly up her neck, invading her cheeks. Martha turns respectfully away as Polly quickly covers her arms.

'There is mutton broth on the stove,' says Mrs Holdsworth, after a moment's hesitation. 'Martha, would you make the fires up again? And this time keep them burning.'

⚸

'I been thinking, we could go hop-picking in the summer. I done it once with my cousin, years ago. Kent, it was. We walked from her house all the way there. Miles! We slept outside every night.'

They are walking around the prison yard in the rain. The prisoners are expected to exercise in all weathers, and are given no extra layers to do so, though the temperature is barely warmer indoors. The rain does not bother Josephine. Far worse is how, with no fire, their damp, chilly dresses never thoroughly dry, and by evening their very bones are cold.

Annie is not listening to her and says: 'Australia sounds warm, don't it? It has to be if it's the other side of the world. Whatever we have, they have it upside-down. If it rains here, it's sunny there.'

Since Governor Tracey told them of Urania Cottage the previous morning, it is all Annie has talked about. That night in bed, by the dying stub of a candle, she frowned at the close, black little words on the paper Tracey had given them, written by his friend, who had signed himself *their* friend. Neither she nor Josephine can read well, but she stared and stared anyway, as though if she peered hard enough, she would unlock the mystery of the words.

'I was talking about Kent, you goose,' says Josephine.

'I know you was,' Annie replies. 'It made me think of warm places.'

'Kent ain't that far away.'

They complete another circuit. Josephine knows that Annie wants them to go to the cottage, the home for fallen women. Is she a fallen woman? The term sounds to her quite grand. Each time Annie has talked of it, Josephine has gently steered the subject away to other avenues of possibility. She does not believe for a moment that the women who go to live at the house will have the same liberty as those who leave the prison. The place sounds to her like a no man's land, a purgatory between the House of Correction and freedom. But Annie is interested, and there is something about this that worries Josephine. It is not the fact there will be other girls there or that it is outside of London; it is that they will not be able to be free with one another. Their love, a living thing, will have to be trapped like a mouse beneath a teacup for as long as they live in the house. This does not appear to have occurred to Annie.

'I shouldn't care to live anywhere but England,' Josephine says.

'Why not?'

'Because you live here.'

That morning, at breakfast, Annie remarked that she had never left London. She asked Josephine about the places she had lived with her family. Her father was a gravedigger and the Nashes moved all over – Kensal Green and Norwood and Bow, close enough to not be true countryside, but quiet and dull all the same. Josephine answered honestly. She has no wish to leave London, which she feels is the very heart of the universe, where the gutters run with blood and the largest road is the river. The London she knows is so far from the damp stone cottages of her childhood, her father lying on the rag rug, mud crusting his fingernails, drinking stewed tea as the fire sank into itself. All her siblings are dead, picked off like coals collapsing into the grate. Her mother was gone long before them.

The city is cruel but not heartless; it always offers a step to sit on, a secret corner to tuck oneself inside. There are thousands of people working thousands of jobs, fine parks and wide streets in which rich and poor may walk side by side. In London, a cat may look on a king.

And Annie is a Londoner, born above a Soho pawnbroker's into the sort of large, loving family that Josephine envies. Annie's siblings scattered into service, labour, child-rearing. Her mother, a charwoman, was sick and lived with Annie's older sister Maud. Annie sent money when she could, but after a sizeable doctor's bill, she took it upon herself to relieve the household she worked for of a few items of laundry: a couple of chemises, a petticoat or two she did not think would be missed. They were. Mr and Mrs Howard of Charlotte Street attended the court hearing and watched passively from the gallery as their maid was sentenced to a nine-month term at the Westminster House of Correction. There was nobody to pay another doctor. Annie's mother died, and the family splintered like kindling.

'One thing about it,' says Annie, as though their conversation never ceased, and in a way it hasn't, 'is we wouldn't have to find board.'

Josephine hasn't thought of this and feels something inside her sit up. She accepts that their options, if they must be honourable, are limited. A laundry is the most likely place they will find work, though these days work is hard to come by. There are too many young women like them looking in the city and more arriving each day. Annie appears to have no knowledge of this, having been fortunate in her situations. Now, without a reference and with a mark against her character, she will no longer be welcome in the tall cream houses she'd come to know. If they find themselves in the laundries – Bethnal Green, perhaps, or Cambridge Heath – Josephine wonders how long Annie will tolerate the scalding and plunging, the steam and the sweat and the burns.

Later, when they lie in the top bunk, fitted snugly into one another, with the perilous slats cracking beneath them, something is troubling Josephine. 'I don't understand why we was chose,' she tells Annie, running a finger down the round of her cheek.

'Me either,' says Annie.

'They must have been watching us close. I hope not too close,' Josephine adds wickedly. She pushes her nose into Annie's neck. Somehow she smells better than anything else.

'Twelve days,' she says when Annie is quiet. They are whispering, as talk is forbidden after lock-up. They have learnt to do everything quietly. Annie's hand finds hers in the dark.

'We must give Tracey our answer in the morning.'

Josephine says nothing. The letter Tracey read spoke of distant countries. The colonies, he called them. Not a single land but a group of them, further than the limits of their imaginations. It is like trying to picture a new colour.

'I think we do it, Jo. Together.'

'The bit about becoming the faithful wives of honest men . . .' Josephine cannot keep the uncertainty from her voice.

'They can't force marriage on us. They can't force nothing

on us. Where better to start again, Jo, but somewhere far, far away?' She traces the outline of Josephine's fingers. 'How about I make you a promise? We don't get on a ship nowhere unless you want to. And if you ain't ever ready, we don't go.'

Josephine is silent again, and Annie puts her face even closer, so that their foreheads are almost touching, and their breath becomes one.

'If you don't like it, we'll come back to London. I think you will, though.'

Josephine frowns. 'I don't know why they chose Sarah Brigham,' she says. 'I should hate to live with her.'

Annie laughs. 'She ain't going – she told me so today. I don't think none of them are.'

This only justifies Josephine's reservations.

Sometimes she allows herself a fantasy: they are sitting either side of a fire on a wintry afternoon. The sky is darkening at the window, and Annie's feet rest on Josephine's lap as she hums tunelessly. The cottage they inhabit is a vague approximation of all the ones she has lived in, only this one is warm and well lit, with evidence of their life together all around it.

Annie waits in stillness, and finally, Josephine sighs.

'Tell him yes.'

'Really?' Annie's smile spreads through the darkness.

'Yes. We'll do it. We'll go.'

As soon as they tell Tracey, everything happens quickly. There is a meeting at the governor's house, an incongruous dwelling in the centre of the prison grounds, with winter pansies colouring the sills and a brass door-knocker that shines like a flame amid all the bleakness. Their first meeting, which they take together, is with Tracey and one of the founders of Urania Cottage, a slim and lively man named Mr Dickens. The second is a more intensive session alone with the same man.

Josephine answers his questions honestly. She is taken aback slightly at how interested he is in her past; her calm, dark gaze meets his levelly, though his eyes flick now and again to her scar. He writes everything she says on blue paper, and by the end of their session, his fingers are stained with ink. He speaks at length of the house, and it is as though he has dropped a picture into her mind, because she finds she is able to carry it from the room and examine it almost like a memory.

They are measured for new dresses and told they will be met outside the prison on the day of their release. They are asked not to speak with anybody they might recognise at the gates or to tell anybody where they are going. At once, the days shorten; the hours spent working, in chapel, exercising, hurtle towards the unknowable. Josephine is more nervous than she cares to admit. There is a blank space in her mind where the future lies, and though she has little to keep her in England and everything to leave for, the finality of it all frightens her.

She is absorbed in her thoughts one morning in the oakum room, a few days before their release. By now, her hands work independently, though her skin weeps where the sores open day after day, and little blistery rashes come and go. Another thing she hasn't told Annie is that she has no desire to be a servant, no wish to make beds and cook meals all day long.

The benches in the oakum room have no backs and force the women's spines to curl like ammonites. Even at midday, the light is poor, clinging to the high and narrow windows as though clamouring to get back out. The air is thick with dust and tow from the ropes, floating in a haze before them. The new girls often cry when their necks hurt and their eyes sting. Most are there a week or two, then vanish; some are on their sixth, seventh, eighth term, as though Tothill Fields is a hotel they return to at leisure. Above the platform, a painted sign declares PRISONERS ARE NOT TO SPEAK TO EACH OTHER. The room is quiet but never silent, punctuated every few seconds with a sigh, a sneeze, a cough. Now it is November, the infirmary is full, and the morgue waits below like a baby bird with its beak open.

At the edge of Josephine's vision is a disturbance. A superintendent enters the room and speaks with a warden, who gets down from the wooden viewing platform and strides through the benches. Josephine returns to the junk gathered in her apron and is rearranging the hook tied above her knee when something makes her look up.

Blinking as dust settles in her eyes, she watches Annie rise from the bench behind, a dozen places to the left, and follow the warden to the front of the room. The brick floor is coated with fibres, and Josephine notices how they stir five, ten, fifteen yards in Annie's wake, whirring and pooling before her own feet. The superintendent is speaking in a low voice to Annie, who is nodding.

'Eyes down,' another matron barks in her direction, prowling the platform like a mastiff.

Josephine picks again at the junk in her lap, but her fingers look strange, as though they don't belong to her. She lowers her cap and sees Annie follow the warden to the large double doors leading to the corridor.

'I said eyes down.'

But Josephine is not listening, because at that moment Annie looks quickly back into the crowd of hunched women, indistinguishable in their blue and white dresses and mobcaps, and her eyes find Josephine's. Later, Josephine will replay this scene over and over, because she thinks she has seen uncertainty, even fear, in Annie's glance.

It is only much later that Josephine will realise it was neither of those, and that she didn't in fact know Annie Ledbury, prisoner 847, at all.

When the second pale-blue letter arrives at Stratton Street, Angela knows she must go to Shepherd's Bush. She has been home almost a week, and in that time has attended the theatre, an assembly, a dinner and a ball. One has visited and she has paid a call on another. The bulk of the correspondence that missed her in Paris has been dealt with, friends' books she borrowed while travelling returned, and gifts distributed. When she is at home, she cannot sit for long; in bed, with the sheets warmed by the bed-pan, sleep eludes her.

She has let the cottage, with which she was so absorbed before her departure, sink into the silt of her mind. The girls have already begun arriving, and she has not seen the house in its full ensemble, with the windows dressed and the sheets pressed and on the beds. She has been putting it off and is too busy to examine why, though she knows that part of it is that, now it is finished, she does not really know what role she is to play there, other than as a sort of visitor. Behind the scenes, off stage, her contribution is clear: she pays for the groceries and medicine and linen and soap and all the other things that must be found in a household. She has no wish for the girls to feel awkward in her presence or for them to stop their duties in order to sit and drink tea with her. She does not know what topics they will discuss, cannot imagine what they could have in common. Far easier to sign a banker's draft and be done with it.

But of course, she cannot say any of this to her friend Charles without seeming unfeeling and ungracious, and so, go she must.

Angela and Mrs Brown bid good morning to Constable Ballard, who occupies his usual station atop the flight of stairs leading to the street door, and will accompany them to Middlesex. Ballard is a civil, ginger-whiskered man in his late forties; short in height, mild-mannered and with an air of gentility, though he was born a cobbler's son in Leicestershire. He has protected Angela at intervals over the years; bittersweet intervals, for she regrets the need of him but feels better when he is there.

In return for his protection she shows an interest in his life, and remembers to ask after his wife and three daughters, and even his two old cats, which were kittens when they met. It has been some time since he was here last, but the kitchen staff at Stratton Street remember how he likes his cocoa, and Mrs Wild the cook sends up warm bags of sand for his pockets. Ballard knows Dunn in every guise, and as long as he is here, Angela knows she is safe, though he does draw more attention to her home. Occasionally, passers-by ask what his business is at Stratton Street, imagining a scandalous crime has taken place.

It is a cold, pink morning when Angela sets out in the carriage with Mrs Brown and Ballard for Shepherd's Bush. The laurels in Kensington Gardens steam in the winter sunshine, and she finds herself sitting forwards, looking through the window at the torrent of faces passing by. Mrs Brown has brought a bag of nuts to crack and suck as they travel. When the carriage reaches the south side of Hyde Park and passes the cavalry barracks, where her father used to take her as a girl, Angela finally exhales.

When her father was alive, the whole unpleasant business with Dunn was nightmarish and yet bearable. He dealt with the lawyers; he squared with Dunn in the street; he kept the worst from her mother. It was he who accompanied her to the private chapel on Albemarle Street after Dunn followed her to St George's. It was he who insisted she have a senior footman shadow her wherever she went. At first she resisted, because it meant having to give up her walks in Kensington Gardens, where servants were not allowed. But her father was a force even Angela was occasionally intimidated by. For her twenty-sixth birthday, her parents took her to a hotel in Norwood, where on the Sunday morning, the footman recognised Dunn in the congregation. Wearing his Sunday best, her father pursued him down the aisle and away through parkland, returning to his wife and daughter breathless but victorious. They managed to laugh about it, and even Angela saw the humorous side when they recounted the tale to their friends. Her father somehow made Dunn seem more of a pest than a threat, like a fly or a roach he was more than capable of squashing.

For a long time, her parents were there to rouse her from the clammy, suffocating darkness that often descended upon her as easily as if she were a child writhing in her bedclothes, dreaming of monsters. Dunn's intrusion in her life was horrid, but they were there, stationed in the house on St James's Place, not five minutes' walk from her home.

Then, just as suddenly, they were not. Her mother went first, her father a little over a week later. On the day of their joint funeral, St James turned black, as if a snowstorm of soot had landed on every brim and collar. The loss of her mother had been dreadful, but her father going so soon afterwards was a shock she has still not come to terms with. She wishes she had told him how badly she needed him to stay alive for her. She wishes he could know that she has not married, because it would be like settling for a tin necklace, when diamonds is all she has known. Part of her still feels to blame for not sitting every minute at his bedside as he slowly starved himself through grief over her mother, for not trying hard enough with the porridge and cream. He could never resist her tantrums; if she had shown him one, he might have been sitting in his chair by the fire instead of hanging above it, wearing a distant smile.

Since her protector deserted her, Dunn has loomed larger than ever, and now she must face him alone.

The carriage finally gathers speed on Kensington Gore, and Angela settles back in her seat, finding a stray nut shell beneath her heel and grinding it into the floor.

Her first impression of Urania Cottage is that it is a rather dull suburban villa. Its size is adequate for a modest family, but Angela cannot see how a dozen girls plus a matron will live here. A low-pitched, hipped roof sits beneath a flat, grey sky, and above the front door a semicircular fan-light sends a dim glow into the pale morning. The flower-beds beneath the downstairs windows lie bare and lifeless, and there are no friendly lamps or faces at the windows. One of the upstairs sashes is open, and she gazes up for a moment as smoke unwinds from a chimney. A more ordinary home it could not be, but she supposes this was a considered choice by her friend Charles, who is the most thorough and deliberate man she has ever met.

'Good morning, Miss Coutts, Mrs Brown,' says Mrs Holdsworth, opening the street door wide. 'And who is this?'

Angela blinks. 'This is Constable Ballard. He is accompanying me on a business matter. He will remain outside the house, if that is agreeable to you.'

Mrs Holdsworth frowns. 'I'm afraid it isn't,' she says. 'A constable standing on the doorstep will attract the wrong attention. You may come inside, sir.'

'But surely nobody comes down this lane?'

Mrs Holdsworth says nothing, and Angela sighs.

'Very well. Ballard, could you wait in the carriage? I shan't be too long.'

The man gives a single nod and goes back through the gate.

Mrs Holdsworth lets them in, already weary, as though she might ask Angela and Mrs Brown to mind the girls while she does something more valuable with her time. There are three of them in the house now, and Angela is introduced to them in the kitchen as they prepare the tea-tray to take into the parlour. They, too, are pinched-looking and tired, smudged with coal and smeared with flour. They barely greet her, glancing at where she stands in the doorway before resuming their task, as though she is only the knife-grinder. There is an unmistakeable tension in the air.

Mrs Holdsworth asks her to lead the way back to the parlour and tells her in the gloomy passage that a girl left them that morning after breakfast. She had arrived only two nights ago and said that she found the house too quiet, the work too dull.

Angela is astonished. 'Too dull? Did she not know what she would find here?'

'I believe she did,' Mrs Holdsworth replies, directing Angela to a chair before the hearth. 'And of course, she did not really give it any time at all. She was on laundry duty yesterday, and I did explain to her that she wouldn't be doing it every day and that work is done on a rota, but of course she wasn't interested and went on her merry way.'

'Where did she go?' Angela asks as the other girls drift in with the tea things.

'She said she has an aunt in Lee Green.'

'How very concerning,' says Mrs Brown.

Angela finds herself a little in awe of Mrs Holdsworth, who she knows has worked in men's prisons as well as women's. She reminds Angela of a governess her sisters used to have, who was too formidable for them to even complain about in private.

Mrs Holdsworth pours the tea, and the girls arrange themselves. Their posture is poor, their gazes direct, even brazen, like cats, Angela thinks. After a moment or two of silence, Angela realises she is expected to speak.

'I hope you are all settling in well,' she says, but it comes out flat and insincere. She is suddenly intensely aware of her own appearance, from her rabbit-fur boots on her feet to the patches of eczema that have stained her neck most of her life. Angela puts a hand to it automatically and withdraws it again.

She has not asked a question, and so nobody speaks. One of

the girls appears brighter and more alert than the others, who seem rather squalid, particularly the small girl with the bandaged wrists and violet shadows beneath her eyes. All of them share a wariness that Angela doubts will ever leave them, no matter how skilled they become at baking soufflés and getting stains out of tablecloths.

'How do you like life at Urania Cottage?' She directs the question at the bright one, who is regarding her with warm grey eyes.

'I like it very much, miss,' she replies.

'And what is your name?'

'Martha.'

'You were the first to arrive?'

'Yes, miss.'

Mrs Holdsworth stifles a yawn, catches Mrs Brown's eye and gives an appeasing smile. The house, Angela notices, is spotless.

'Mrs Holdsworth, you used to work at a prison,' Angela says.

'I did.'

'My father was a passionate reformer of the prisons. You must find it very different here.'

'I am familiar with your father's admirable work,' Mrs Holdsworth replies. 'I confess that I—'

A distinct hammering at the door. A beat of silence as all the women in the room, in an unguarded moment of curiosity, look at one another.

Mrs Holdsworth gets quickly to her feet, and they all wait for voices in the hall. Within seconds, there is a squawk of protest, Martha's name is called, and into the room bursts a young woman.

She is two- or three-and-twenty, plainly dressed, with Martha's nose. Her cheeks burn red with cold. Martha leaps from her chair. In a blur of skirts and arms, the two women are embracing with such urgency and passion the women seated cannot help but be moved by it.

'Mary! Oh, Mary.' Martha wipes her face and embraces the other girl again.

'Oh, Martha! You – oh, I could turn the air blue. Where have you *been*? Oh, you *goose*.' She holds Martha before her at arm's length and crushes her once more. 'I could strike you. I ought to strike you.'

The newcomer is entirely unaware of present company; it is as though she and Martha are the only two in the room. Mrs Holdsworth has followed Mary into the parlour like a storm-cloud and closes the door firmly, as though to avoid disturbing the rest of the empty house.

'Who on earth do you call yourself, and what on earth do you make of barging in here?' she demands, barely concealing her rage.

'Oh,' says Mary, noticing for the first time the astonished little group assembled on chairs. 'Have I come at a bad time? I'm Martha's sister. I got her letter, and so I came.'

'I shouldn't care if you were the Queen of Sheba. You'll not come marching in here without an invitation.'

'But I was invited. At least, Martha told me where she was. Oh, Martha, I thought it couldn't be real. Let me look at you.'

'I am sorry, Miss Coutts,' Mrs Holdsworth says, though Angela is amused, and Mrs Brown appears delighted.

'A happy reunion!' Mrs Brown brings her hands together. 'Have the two of you been apart for long?'

'More than a year,' says Martha.

The older girl cannot remove her eyes or her hands from her sister. 'I thought you were dead, Martha, I really did.'

'No, only – well,' says Martha, 'never mind all that. I'm here now.'

'I'm so glad you wrote. There's so much to tell you. Well, only one thing that matters, really – sorry, would you mind if I sat a moment? Thank you, thank you.' She takes the seat Mrs Holdsworth has vacated, unties the strings of her bonnet and throws it back as the others look on in astonishment.

Mrs Holdsworth is incredulous. 'Well, if you are staying, I suppose I'll fetch further refreshment. Miss Coutts, I apologise sincerely for the—'

Angela puts up a gloved hand. 'We must make the young lady comfortable.'

Oblivious to them both, Mary reaches again for Martha's hands. 'Oh, Martha, it's really you.'

'It *is* really me. I wrote to Emily as well,' Martha goes on. 'Is she well, do you know?'

'Oh, Martha, I don't know how to say it.'

There is the faintest tinkle of china as Angela sets down her saucer. Martha's features transform from joy to alarm. 'What is it, Mary?'

Mary places her elbows on her knees and her face in her hands. Just as quickly, she recovers herself and sits up straight, rearranging her expression and looking determinedly at Martha.

'She disappeared, too. At the start of this year, she just—' Mary holds up her hands. 'She left the house she was working at, gave no address, told no one where she was going. She didn't write to me, and we didn't know where you were, so she couldn't have told you either. I haven't heard from her since February.'

There is a heavy silence, broken only by the pop and click of the fire, which is struggling in Martha's neglect.

'Well, where could she be?' Martha asks.

The others turn in unison to Mary, like faces in a broken mirror.

'I don't know,' says Mary, pained. 'She's vanished. I can't tell you how dreadful it's been for me this year, with both of you gone and me not knowing where to find you.'

'I'm sorry, Mary.'

'It's a good thing Mama isn't here. I never thought I'd say it, but it's true. She'd skin me for not looking after you two.'

'How can you say such a thing? You mustn't blame yourself, especially not on my account. What happened was no one's fault.'

'Well, I do. I ought to have kept the family together. Besides, what did happen? Thank you,' Mary says, accepting a cup of tea from Mrs Holdsworth, who appears to have warmed slightly towards her. 'What is this place?' She looks about at the room, the other girls.

'It's a home for girls who have fallen on hard times,' says Mrs Holdsworth.

Mary looks at her sister with true compassion and takes her hand. 'And where were you before?'

'One of our rules at Urania Cottage is to never disclose personal histories,' Mrs Holdsworth cuts in. 'The rule does not extend to family members; however, I'll thank you not to talk about it in front of the others. You'll have many things to discuss, I'm sure, and I can loan you the use of the dining room next door for the purpose, if Miss Coutts has no objection.' She glances at Angela in the easy chair.

'Of course not, Mrs Holdsworth.'

Mrs Holdsworth nods, then turns to the sisters. 'I'll remind you, though, Martha, that private conversations with family members are not permitted at Urania Cottage, and I'm obliged to chaperone. You may have half an hour, and then I'm afraid I must get on. Mary, you're welcome to stay for dinner. Lucinda is making a warm white soup. Miss Coutts, Mrs Brown, perhaps you would do the honour of joining us? Or might you prefer to dine when the girls are more established in their culinary skills?'

Angela smiles. 'Thank you, Mrs Holdsworth. We'd like very much to stay.'

CHAPTER 3

Middlesex

Annie does not return to cell number six that night and is not in the oakum room come morning. As the women queue outside, Josephine shivers with the bone-cold chill that has drenched her since the previous day. Somebody asks where Annie is, and she pretends she hasn't heard. At the front of the queue, she takes her pound-and-a-half and says to the warden: 'I'd like to see Governor Tracey.'

The warden sneers. 'I'd like a set of gold teeth.'

'Tell him it's about the cottage.'

'What cottage?'

Another warden looks up from scooping junk out of baskets. 'What about it?'

'I need to speak with him.'

'That's what you need,' says the first, nodding at the hateful twists of tow and tar. 'Now move along.'

'Please. I need to speak with him.'

The warden pushes her onwards, but when every woman has been dealt her junk and the benches are full, Josephine sees her slip out. There are other workrooms at Tothill: straw-plaiting, where the inmates make bonnets for lunatics, knitting and laundry. At breakfast, Josephine asked the women she knows from these other rooms if they had seen Annie, and all of them said no. She spent the whole night waiting for the sound of boots approaching their cell.

Tracey does not come to her until the following evening. By then, a new cellmate has joined her and has slept a night beneath Josephine in her old bed. She asked Josephine's name, but Josephine remained beneath the blanket, facing the wall, and made no reply.

'Suit yourself,' said the woman, whose name is Bertha. Bertha snored all night, and the weak slats protested loudly when she turned in the dark. The pallet still smells of Annie, and Josephine did not sleep until shortly before the gun.

When the door screeches open, still she does not move. And when Tracey begins speaking to her, addressing her back, she interrupts him, turning halfway. 'Where's Annie?' She has thought this question so many times in the last two days, the words stuffed inside her mind like wads of newsprint, stamped over and over.

There is a beat of surprised silence. 'Miss Ledbury reached the end of her sentence,' Tracey replies.

Josephine turns fully and pushes herself upright. He is holding a lamp and peering at her. 'I know that,' she says slowly. 'She was staying in with me until we could go. You said she could stay.'

Tracey's dark eyes are puzzled. 'Annie asked to leave.'

Another stretch of silence. Josephine has the queer

46

sensation of an icy pail being tipped down her back. 'When?' she asks thickly.

A frown knits Tracey's impressive brow together. 'During your final interview with Mr Dickens. You didn't know?' When she does not reply, he says: 'You wished to speak to me about the cottage?'

Her lips are parted, as though she might speak, but she finds she is trembling violently.

'Governor,' says Bertha from below, 'may I raise with you a matter that concerns my own good self and the day of my own departure, which—'

'Will that be all, Miss Nash?'

When she makes no response he sweeps from the room, taking the light with him.

As Bertha mutters beneath her, Josephine's head finds the cold pillow. Her lips are still parted, but of course there is nothing else to say.

Two days before Josephine's release, a package is waiting in her cell after supper. Bertha notices it first and takes a candle over.

'What's this?' she says, lifting a label attached to a brown paper parcel tied with string.

Josephine is exhausted and wonders if she can summon the energy to climb to her bed. Another day has passed, the same as the one before – gruel, rope, benches, bread, prayer, silence. There have been more attempts at conversation from Bertha, who, undeterred by Josephine's disinterest, witters on about a bad landlord and a sister in Stepney.

'That ain't my name, so it must be for you.'

Josephine accepts it without interest. It is heavy and soft, like a coat left out in the rain.

'Well, ain't you gonna open it?'

With deliberate slowness, she slips the string over the parcel's shoulder, traces the cool, smooth brown with a finger. Footsteps quicken in the passage; she freezes for a moment, but they continue on.

A slash of pink, like a mouth opening. Josephine's own lips part in response as Bertha brings the candle closer and, with it, her own sour smell. The paper begins to bleed with colour, opening like a bud in the cell as a dress comes to life before their eyes. It shakes off its wrapper and seems to rise before them as if from a long sleep, stretching an arm, folding the other across its stomach with a sigh. And the colour itself: pink, but a singular pink, not a delicate rose but warm and bold, friendly, like Annie's tongue. Josephine clutches the dress tightly to her chest.

'What a fine bunch of rags,' Bertha declares. 'Who's sent you that? And what's this?'

Her cellmate stoops again, and Josephine accepts from her a folded cream letter with only a handful of words inside. Neither she nor her cellmate can read them. Josephine crushes the note inside her stays.

She never finds out what it says. Two days later, she undresses for the final time and gives her garments back to the prison. The rich cream paper falls to the floor, and an orderly sweeps it up in an instant. Josephine steps into her new dress. The gown is an obscenity to the prison staff, who shake their heads and jeer at her. It shines bright like a lantern when Josephine finally, after so many months, steps beneath the arch alone into the pearly November morning and takes a breath.

There, a small band of people wait for news of those inside or for inmates to come out. A crossing-sweeper works beneath the prison wall, whistling as he goes. A ribbon of white sky runs above, and the ground is sugared with frost. Josephine surveys the shabby crowd and searches beyond, to the end of the street, where the buildings are covered by scaffolds and the pounding of construction beats behind her eyes. Distantly, a dog barks.

And then, like a mirror catching the sun: a flash of sand-coloured hair, the edge of a cloak retreating. The everyday noises combine to create one single high, piercing note as Josephine stares hard and realises she is holding her breath.

'Josephine Nash?'

A woman in grey stands before her, her shoulders warm beneath a thick woollen mantle edged with silk, her dark hair streaked with iron. Josephine wrenches her attention back.

'I am Mrs Holdsworth, the matron at Urania Cottage. I'll take you there, if you are happy to proceed?'

Josephine waits for Mrs Holdsworth's eyes to be drawn to her scar, but they remain fixed on hers.

Then Mrs Holdsworth does something unexpected: she takes hold of Josephine's arm to guide her across the street and into the cab. Josephine is surprised to find herself allowing it, noticing the way their wrists entwine, how deathly white her hand is protruding from the raspberry poplin. Mrs Holdsworth helps Josephine into the carriage and speaks to the driver, joining her a moment later and closing the door.

They ride in silence through the cold, mired streets of Westminster, then through fields and market gardens and smoky brick yards, and Josephine falls asleep. When the cab crawls to a stop in a quiet lane, she wakes to find a blanket on her knees. A small basket of food at her feet remains untouched.

The two women climb out, and Josephine follows Mrs Holdsworth through a little gate and up a path towards a handsome brick house. She is unable to notice much of anything, as there is such a pain in her head she feels as though it might split open, though she is dimly aware of a cool shadowy hall, with warmth lapping in from two doorways, and a flight of stairs so high she thinks she might never manage it, her bones are so tired, her feet so cold. She has the vague impression of a young woman coming to one of the doorways, filling it with a handsome dress the colour of wet autumn grass, a bow at her throat. Through another doorway, another girl sits at a large, polished table with an open book in front of her, her pale, heart-shaped face turned to look into the hall.

Like a child, she climbs the stairs behind Mrs Holdsworth, stumbling in her long skirts, taking them in one hand, the banister in the other. She is led to a room at the top of the stairs with three beds. Mrs Holdsworth explains which is hers and points out the little cabinet for her things beside it and the press and drawers she will share with the others. Josephine does not look at these or at the view of the bare garden. She only stands at the foot of the bed with her hands on the brass rail, encased in misery so abject the matron stands in awkward silence, before eventually giving her privacy, and gently closing the door.

Parkinson's chambers are situated in a damp little corner of Furnival's Inn, a warren of buildings in the city that are home to the Inns of Chancery. Angela arrives on a blustery morning to find that Parkinson is out. She tells the clerk she wishes to wait and is shown into his office. Ballard stands outside in the cramped passage with his back to the wall. Some attentive office boy has kept a low fire going, and she takes herself towards it, warming her gloves before the flames and looking around.

The chief atmosphere is one of gloom, which she has always found to be the case in lawyers' offices. The corners are black as midnight even at midday, the windows fastened to the fog, and icy gusts that push their way through stubborn cracks around the window send case-papers scattering like roosting pigeons. A lamp burns low on the large desk, which is stained here and there with ink and ancient wax.

Parkinson was only briefly her father's lawyer; for most of her life it had been Marjoribanks, now a dear friend of Angela's. Marjoribanks was very fond of her when she was a girl, bringing her dolls and nuts at Christmas. At home, Christmas was always a magical affair, with parties and presents and chandeliers twinkling throughout the house, and extravagant sets for the plays Angela put on with her sisters. The three Christmases since her parents' deaths have been as sociable as ever, with Angela hurling herself into a current of assemblies and dinners, leaning on the hospitality of others in an attempt to forget her parents' absence. It brings her such joy to see children tumbling about her friends' homes and gathering about their coat-tails at church.

But on all three occasions, she has woken in varying states of grief. Last year, it coated her lightly, like the first frost, but the year before, she was encased in it, entombed, so that it was like waking in a coffin of her own melancholy. Nothing she did that day could thaw it, and she went home early to relieve the tears that had formed in her eyes when the children began to sing. Watching them play and laugh had set up a confused pain in her chest, and she thought about it with curiosity in the following days. She did not regret her childlessness; children were beguiling, exotic creatures that she enjoyed but did not wish to have, rather like pineapples. She could only imagine that the painful feeling came from the grief of no longer being a child herself, and from longing for those innocent days. Nevertheless, her fourth Christmas without her parents is approaching, and she is almost certain she will go abroad.

Almost an hour has passed when Parkinson appears, bringing a cold draught with him. He is apologetic, explaining that his client wished to show him the South Eastern Railway depot, and then a dogcart overturned on Cheapside.

'Mr Parkinson, I am uneasy,' Angela begins when they are seated. Parkinson prefers the narrow sill beneath the window to his large, comfortable chair, and the white gloss is smooth with wear. 'Richard Dunn has been out of prison a week, and I have seen neither hide nor hair of him. Nor has Constable Ballard. He has not approached me in any of the usual places. He hasn't followed me, to my knowledge. I have been out on foot, in the carriage, to the park, the theatre . . . I don't know where he is. Ballard asked at the Gloucester across the road if anybody fitting his description is staying there, but nobody is. He has kept watch over the windows opposite – nothing.'

The last time Dunn was freed, he took a room at the hotel on Stratton Street overlooking Angela's home. She was ignorant to it, until one of the maids commented to another that a curious man appeared to be watching the house; several times, she had seen him peering between the curtains of a window in

the eaves, too high for Ballard to see or notice. The news travelled swiftly upstairs. Ballard marched over to the Gloucester,
but Dunn pointed out that without a warrant from the magistrate, the constable could make no arrest. Dunn refused to
leave his room, and when Ballard finally left, so did he.

'A happy result,' says Parkinson cheerily. 'Perhaps he has
lost interest in his quarry.'

It is troubling to Angela that Parkinson can believe this.
If he has made the suggestion because he is tired of the situation, of course she is, too – more tired and worn-down than she
ever thought possible.

'I doubt that is the case, Mr Parkinson,' she replies levelly.

'You've had no correspondence?'

'Mrs Brown says not.'

'Then enjoy your freedom.' He remains perched on the sill
with his arms folded.

'He would not have petitioned bankruptcy if he did not
have a design,' Angela replies, trying to hide her irritation.
'There is a reason he wished to come out of prison.'

'Prisons are unpleasant places. He is an opportunist, to be
sure. But you cannot be absolutely certain that his reasons
concern you.'

'Of course they do. Perhaps not directly – perhaps he hasn't
a plan – but he will certainly continue his pursuit of me. People
like Dunn don't merely forget or lose interest.'

'Some do, when their luck runs out.'

Angela rearranges her hands in her lap, runs her tongue
across the back of her teeth. 'Mr Parkinson, his luck has not run
out. He has just been released from prison. I would say that
indicates his luck is very much in.'

She has gone too far; Parkinson's expression closes. 'Well,' he says, 'you are familiar with the course of action by now. Any letters are to be sent to me. Any sightings, alert me at once, and we shall pursue the usual avenues.'

'The usual avenues have led us here! The usual avenues are failing to protect me or to bring this nightmarish situation to a close. Dunn is a madman. Are there no places in asylums for him? Can that avenue be explored?'

Parkinson makes a weak face. 'Lunacy is difficult to prove.'

'In men, perhaps.' She is white with fury. 'Mr Parkinson, this must be the last time. We must find a way to put him in prison once and for all, without him being able to slither out through some archaic legal loophole. This time he claimed bankruptcy; is anybody actually *sure* he is bankrupt? Has anybody seen where he lives and how he pays for it? Did he give an address?'

'He would face a very serious charge if his claim was fraudulent.'

'More serious than harassing a woman for ten years, I dare say.'

Parkinson rearranges some papers on his desk. 'I shouldn't be unduly distressed, miss.'

'What if he breaks into my house? What if he kills me, Mr Parkinson?'

'The law does not concern itself with what-ifs.'

Often, Angela feels as though she is fighting her way out of a box. Red legal seals glare like warning lamps from Parkinson's desk, which is busy with solid, confident things sure of their place: blotters, writing paper, heavy books and sealing wax. Glass-fronted cabinets crowd the walls, showcasing their knowledge. She is surrounded by evidence of the law being adhered to and carried out in every case but hers. A thousand precedents, a hundred thousand clauses, two hundred lawyers working in this inn alone – yet nothing, apparently, that can remove Richard Dunn from her life once and for all. Angela does not know how many clients a lawyer like Parkinson has. She is in awe of the fact that her situation, so large and real and life-altering, is something that he is able to detach himself from. It is staggering to her that her trials are only a small fraction of his job, tidied into a folder, squared into a bill.

She thanks him and journeys home with the carriage-curtain drawn over the glass, sealing herself in darkness.

><

On her first morning at Urania Cottage, Josephine wakes with the quiet, gentle rising of her roommates Martha and Polly. The inside of the window is slick with condensation, but her feet find a rag rug on the floor, and to her surprise, the water Polly brings up to wash with is warm. They clean themselves and dress in near silence. Polly seems shy, but Martha is serene, moving fluidly, her gaze meeting Josephine's now and then with kindness over the morning prayers.

They assemble at the kitchen table for porridge and then repair to the schoolroom for lessons. Mrs Holdsworth gives Josephine a slate and asks her to copy the alphabet from the board, but the letters cramp and slide in her vision. Josephine will not admit this, and painstakingly attempts to move them from the board to her slate with her chalk. Mrs Holdsworth tasks her instead with writing one letter at a time and then erasing it, all the way to Z. Josephine traces *A*, with its sharp symmetry, and *J*, like a smudge of coal on a cheek, or a feather. She writes them alternately, erasing them with the square of sacking each time, until their ghostly scars are seared on the slate.

She writes faster and faster, the quick, pleasing sound of chalk on slate reaching a staccato, until she presses so hard that the chalk snaps. Mrs Holdsworth takes the slate from her hands, and she turns her head to the window, looking out onto the cold garden. A blackbird dances along the fence, peering between the bare boughs and branches as though searching for something. Josephine notices how the fingers of the apple trees reach towards the top of the fence in an attempt to escape.

'Josephine?' The voice reaches her from some distant place, like the bottom of a well.

'Josephine.'

She cannot remember the last time she saw a view from a window. It has been months since she last watched clouds pass, unobstructed by bars.

'Miss Nash.'

She wrests her attention from the garden. Mrs Holdsworth stands with her back to the fire, her hands on her hips, elbows pointing at angles from her waist. Josephine has forgotten the question or has not heard it; her mind feels like a sluice, muddy and stagnant and choked with debris. Mrs Holdsworth sighs and says: 'You may go and help Martha in the kitchen.'

There, Martha is pressed against the large, scrubbed table, deftly removing the veins from a lump of suet. She has the long fingers of a musician, and Josephine watches from the doorway, thinking how the fat might well be an instrument, so absorbed is she in her task. She appears to know exactly what she is doing, as though she has been preparing food in this house her whole life. She looks up, and Josephine feels her hackles lower.

56

'I'm to help you,' she announces, stepping down into the room.

'I'm making roly-poly pudding,' says Martha. 'Have you made it before?'

Josephine shakes her head. 'What is it?'

'A tedious dessert that requires three hours' labour, but I *will* master it this time.'

Already, Josephine has noticed how Martha speaks a little finer than the others and uses words she herself does not know. She ties an apron, and Martha shows her how to remove the veins and membranes from the rind. The process is not unlike picking apart the tow at Tothill Fields, and when Josephine begins, Martha says: 'Oh, you have done it before.'

'No,' says Josephine.

Martha looks quizzically at her, amused. 'Then you would make a fine butcher.'

Josephine lowers her eyes, and Martha pauses for a moment, before resuming her task. They work together in silence, and every so often a girl comes into the kitchen for this or that, throwing out a remark on her way through to the scullery or the cellar. Martha replies in her easy manner, and Josephine is grateful that she does not attempt conversation. The other girls talk too loudly, too often. They are frequently admonished, at mealtimes for speaking while eating, for breaking away from their chores, resting on their knees, dustpan in hand, to laugh and exchange gossip. Polly is the odd one out. She is silent, watchful, melancholy, like somebody who has just received bad news.

When the suet is shredded, Martha shows Josephine how to mix in the flour and sets a little bowl of cold water close by.

'How much should I put in?' asks Josephine.

57

'As much as if you were making bread.'

None of the Nash family homes had ovens, and so they cooked their bread at the nearest bakehouse. It was Josephine's job to bring it home, and she used to carry it in both arms, like a new baby in a linen cloth. They had to wait until her father returned from work before they could eat it, and she could hardly bear to see his dirty hands fold the pure white slices into his mouth.

When Josephine hesitates, Martha adds the water herself and Josephine stirs, lulled by the rhythm of the spoon against the bowl. Josephine is astonished by how well they are provided for here. In the larder, there is hardly room on the shelves for the mice among fresh butter, jewel-coloured jams, jars of rich cocoa. At breakfast, the table groans with food that she and her siblings would have fought over: golden crusts, sunny butter, smooth, warm eggs. At Tothill, her appetite shrunk to a grain; here it is awakening, and her senses are keen as a hound's, her nose and taste buds overwhelmed with fragrant flavours.

Martha flours the table and throws down the dough as though it might bounce. 'Now we roll,' she says, handing Josephine a wooden pin. They smear the pastry with strawberry jam, pushing it gently to the edges, and Martha rolls it up like a carpet. Jam oozes from the edges, and Martha gathers it up with a spoon and offers it to Josephine.

'What do I do with it?'

'You can eat it. If you like.'

Josephine brings the spoon to her lips, and though it is winter outside, she is at once in a bright field in June, searching for strawberries in the hedgerows. Her wrists are stained, and she can feel the juice running down towards her elbows.

Now, in this wintry kitchen, the jam tastes so good that she has the fleeting urge to cry. Martha does not watch her, makes no remark. She sets about soaking and flouring a cloth to cook the pudding in, and Josephine washes the spoon in silence.

❦

The next day is the first of advent, and Mrs Holdsworth sends the girls out in pairs to gather greenery for garlands. With a basket each and sewing scissors, Josephine and Martha go together to the bushes in the lane with instructions not to move beyond the sight of the house. Martha has had the fore-sight to take a pair of leather gloves from the gardening shed. She gives one to Josephine and keeps one for herself, and they work in preoccupied silence. Martha's basket fills more quickly than Josephine's. Soon it is full, and she kneels on her apron and begins to sort the greenery into little piles.

'What a shame there's no holly bushes,' she says. 'A garland without holly isn't much of one at all.'

'We might find one,' says Josephine.

'Mrs Holdsworth said we weren't to go out of sight of the windows.'

Josephine's eyes search down the lane. 'I'll go. You stay here.'

'You won't go far?'

Josephine has not seen Martha uncertain until now.

'I won't.'

'Take my glove,' says Martha, passing Josephine her re-maining one.

The lane they are situated on sits between two highways, both going west. In the distance, a figure approaches from the north. Josephine waits, facing the house and looking sideways as if crossing the road, and eventually a stovepipe hat and blue wool coat come into focus.

'Good day, miss.'

A constable is an unexpected sight in the farmland of Middlesex. He does not stop to make enquiries but smiles pleasantly, then turns into Urania Cottage. The gate chirps, and a moment later, three smart raps ring out from the street door.

The winter sun is bright, the hall too dark to reveal who answers, but the door closes firmly behind him, and once again the scene is still. Josephine watches the windows of the house for a minute longer and then walks on, finding a gap in-between two gorse bushes and sliding through sideways with her basket into the field beyond. Mud sucks at her boots and spatters her hem as she strides towards the far side and a promising looking copse in the north-easterly corner.

She will find holly for Martha. She will seek out the sharp, glossy leaves and glistening berries, because she knows what it is to want something that hurts.

Constable Frank Holdsworth sets his hat on the kitchen table and pulls out a seat. He thanks the young woman who pours him tea from the pot, thanks her again when she pushes the milk jug towards him, avoiding his eye. She vanishes into the scullery as his mother appears with a currant loaf, looking tired and harassed but not dissatisfied. He notices, too, how her chignon is braided with thick streaks of silver and is no longer the shiny chestnut of his childhood. With a flap of her hands, she sends the kitchen girl, whose name is

Polly, to help with the cleaning upstairs. Polly hangs up her apron and washes her hands, and finally the kitchen is theirs, though distant thumps and voices permeate from the rest of the house where the others go about their chores. A chicken carcass simmers in a pot on the stove, and the room is warm and fragrant.

Frank has always known his mother to be in motion. He has glimmers of memory, in which her face is never present; he can only recall her back bent over the range, the twist of her hair above flagstones, the fire. So it is no surprise to him that the house is a hive of energy, the type of house he feels at home in. He was expecting another institution or a small-scale work-house – the sort of grey, hopeless places his mother thrives in – but Urania Cottage is a real home. Today, he is an ordinary son visiting his mother.

He tries to remember the last time he sat across from her, a pot of tea between them. Since she left the little house at Greenwich, she has had no home at all, only spare rooms in institutions. For many years, there has been no door to let himself in at, no fire at which to take off his boots, no chair in which he might spend the night. Of course he may not stay here, at a house for fallen women, but as long as he is permitted to visit and offer a hand about the place, he will enjoy the comfort of the house and the normality of it.

'No Mr Dickens today?' he asks, finishing his first cup and pouring a second.

To his dismay, he has not been able to boast to his colleagues at the section-house that his mother is working for one of the most eminent writers alive. Neither would he mind telling the pretty girl at the cookshop where he buys his morning roll. But his mother has made it doubly clear that her work, her employers (including a very rich heiress who supposedly lent money to the Queen), the house and everything concerning it is a secret he must take to the grave.

They have no other family members, nobody who asked for their forwarding address. The handful of friends and neighbours from Greenwich considered it a great shame when she gave up the house to go and work in a prison, and she was grateful for their sympathies. But privately, she told Frank she was not sorry to leave that part of her life behind. For many years, she lived happily, busily, as a wife and mother, and so it was a shock to be left alone, watching her husband's life insurance run down on coal and food and other things she could pay for herself if she found work. Being the daughter of a farmer had taught Jean Holdsworth that life, with its intervals of fortune and sorrow, comes in seasons, that spring follows even the bitterest of winters, and it was a lesson she had passed on to Frank.

'He won't be here today,' she replies. 'He was here last night till ten making up his book. I almost forgot to lock the beer cupboard.'

Frank pitches forwards slightly. 'He writes here?'

'No, he keeps a sort of ledger of the girls, their past lives and so on. I don't know what it is.'

'I dare say you're the last person in London to read his novels.'

'I dare say I'm not. Not in this house.'

She cuts her son a second slice of cake. She takes none herself.

'What sort of governor is he?' Frank asks, mouth full.

Mrs Holdsworth sighs. 'Exacting. He visits every room, and woe betide if a cushion is out of place or a curtain not hanging as it should be. Enough about that. Tell me how things are at Wandsworth.'

'Never a dull moment, that's for certain.'

There is the soft sound of boots on flagstone, and he looks up and sees the girl from earlier hesitating on the threshold.

'What is it, Polly?' asks Mrs Holdsworth.

The girl glances at Frank, and her knuckles tighten around the handle of the broom she is holding. 'The candle box is empty upstairs.'

Mrs Holdsworth stands and fumbles with the set of keys at her belt. 'This opens the cellar. Return them to me at once and show me how many you've taken.'

Polly turns and is gone.

'It will do them no harm to know we have a visiting policeman,' Mrs Holdsworth says drily, returning to the table. 'Not that most of them have any respect for the law.'

Frank is not in the least surprised.

It frightened him at first to be scratched and spat and pawed at by women. It was a shock to find out that they could be rude and foul-mouthed, as aggressive as riled-up navvies when they got going. He encountered the worst cases in some of the most violently depressing parts of the city during his constable training – places he has no wish to ever think about again, let alone visit. Still, he does not encounter many women of that kind at Wandsworth, where the most common cases are house breaks and toll collectors reporting debts. For more than a year, Frank has been eyeing a transfer to the Thames Division for the hint of glamour and piracy it affords, but he has done nothing about it.

More boots in the passage. Two girls appear in wraps and bonnets, their cheeks pink. One of them is holding out her hands, which are bleeding, ribboned with scarlet scratches. Blood drips languidly, splashing the kitchen floor.

'Josephine, whatever have you done?'

'She was picking holly for the garlands, Mrs H.' The other girl glances at the constable sitting at the table and turns white.

Alarmed, Frank sits a little straighter.

'Is it Emily?' she asks him.

'I'm sorry, miss?' Frank returns.

His mother intervenes. 'He's nothing to do with all that. This is my son, Frank. Martha, fetch a cloth from the scullery.'

Josephine seems unbothered by the fuss and blood. She allows her hands to be bandaged by Mrs Holdsworth, picks up her basket and leads Martha from the kitchen.

'Never a moment's peace,' Mrs Holdsworth says to nobody in particular when they are gone.

Frank wonders why his mother gives the illusion of resenting her work, when they both know she enjoys it immensely.

'Who was it that the tall one mentioned? Emily?'

His mother is on her feet again, stirring the stock, wiping down a jar with her apron. 'Martha's younger sister is missing.'

'Missing from where?'

'I don't know the ins and outs of it. Martha's older sister came to give her the news. By all accounts, she's vanished from her situation in some house out in Reading. I don't recall all the details, but it's concerning, to say the least. Martha is understandably worried, though of course . . .' She returns to the table, sweeping cake crumbs with a brisk palm. 'Well.' She straightens and glances at the passage, lowering her voice. 'All these girls have disappeared to some extent. Perhaps their families don't know where they are or what happened to them.

Perhaps they don't want to know. Martha's sister could well have joined their number.'

'If you mean . . .'

'I think you know what I mean. One poor decision can lead to a lifetime of pain and God only knows what else.'

'The girl ought to be found, though,' says Frank.

'She might not want to be. Martha herself was . . . I'm getting carried away.' She shakes her head and gathers the plates up with a clatter.

Frank knows it's time he left. He thanks his mother for the tea and cake, and with a spoon pokes the chicken on the range. On his way out, he glances into the grander rooms at the front of the house, whose doorways are ajar, offering glimpses into unknowable worlds.

He has not noticed the figure waiting for him in the gloom at the bottom of the stairs, standing as tall and still as a coat-stand. She takes his wrist, and he almost cries out, reaching instinctively for his rattle, and is drenched with shame when he realises it is the freckled girl from earlier, who brought in half a hedgerow in a basket. Her hands are still cold.

'Good grief.' He laughs, putting on his hat. 'You gave me a fright.'

'Sir.' Her voice is low and urgent, confidential. 'I don't know what business you have here, but I wonder if you can help me.'

He glances towards the back of the house. 'I wonder that myself. The truth is, miss, I'm not sure. I heard about your sister. I'm very sorry about it, but I don't know how I might help.'

'Please, sir. Mrs Holdsworth will kill me if she knows I'm even speaking to you, but I don't know who else to ask. If I leave this house, I won't be welcomed back again, but if I stay, I shan't find her. So what should I do?'

'Miss . . .'

'Gelder.' She pulls a much-worried note from her apron pocket. 'I was sent this, this week – from the housekeeper where Emily was maid. She said Emily left in February with no forwarding address. Look, it's short, don't you think?'

Frank glances at the few lines. The tone is curt, dismissive. 'She was last in Reading I believe?'

Martha nods.

'Has the superintendent been informed?'

'I don't know, truthfully. She is only sixteen.'

His mother has told him that all the young women in the house fell into criminality in one way or another. He finds this difficult to believe of Martha, who could easily be a governess or the daughter of a clergyman – and also of Polly, who is as timid and unobtrusive as a servant.

'Well, the local station house is the place to start. Though if she disappeared in February, they ought to have been informed straightaway, really, so as to begin the search. It will be difficult now, with so much time passed.' On seeing her face, he adds: 'If you were to write to them and register her missing, if she is not already, that would be the best place to begin. I can help you write something, if you like.'

He hopes his voice does not betray the knowledge that the police have no time to look for women who disappear. Some go over bridges; some end up in situations so unfortunate that death would be a blessing. What people find hardest to take is that so many of them go willingly, but perhaps this young woman would understand that better than most.

He lifts his hat to Martha and wishes her good day, striding quickly down the garden path and forgetting her by the time he has boarded the omnibus, not because she has not moved him, but because letting go of tragedy and anguish is almost a reflex by now. He has had to learn it, just as he learnt how to clean his boots and plot his beat; if he took on the worries of every troubled soul as his own, he would have gone mad some time ago.

Still, they seep in through the cracks sometimes, when he is alone or pensive: the mother of five whose husband was mown down in the street in front of her; the old man persuaded to part with every penny he had by a sham insurance clerk. So the young woman whose sister has left a respectable position with no explanation does not visit Frank in his dreams or idle moments. In his twenty-six years, he has learnt that people are unpredictable, inconstant – a mystery, most of all to themselves.

CHAPTER 4

A Roach in the Flour

At Her Majesty's Theatre, Angela has a box that she doesn't use nearly as often as she should. She prefers to offer it to friends, family and employees of the bank, and takes pleasure in the knowledge that it is being enjoyed. Tonight, she has brought her old friend Marjoribanks, his wife, Georgina, and their three granddaughters. Today is his granddaughter Pamela's birthday, and Angela has invited them as a treat to see *The Marriage of Figaro*. She has come without Mrs Brown, as the box is too small for a seventh person.

It is Saturday night, and the theatre is crowded. Heat and steam rises from the rain-soaked bodies in the pit, giving Her Majesty's the atmosphere of a hothouse. During the interval, Marjoribanks handed Angela a glass of champagne and told her that the bank will soon have a new partner, a Mr Templeton, from a rival firm. She is still absorbing this news during the third act, staring in the direction of the stage, wondering why she was not told on Tuesday, when she called in to sign a shareholders' agreement. Her involvement at Coutts & Co. has not been as she would have liked. She is occasionally showcased at parties and dinners, brought out like a lucky charm to meet clients and investors, but her opinion is never sought, her financial acumen never consulted.

Her eyes rove the greased heads and bonnets in the stalls. One or two women glance shyly up at her, offering small smiles; some stare, their eyes burning into her as she focuses on the stage. One of the reasons she does not come frequently to her own box is because it makes her feel as though she is sitting in a frame at the Royal Academy; she might as well be made of oil and pigment, for her audience is just as startled when her eyes find theirs. At the theatre, at parties, she cannot shake off the sensation of being watched, because at any given moment somebody is examining, observing, assessing.

She raises her fan, lets her gaze drift towards the dress circle, and finds suddenly that she is aware of her own heartbeat. Perhaps it's the lights, the champagne – but her body knows better. The tiny hairs on the nape of her neck rise in warning; her pulse quickens in staccato. She swallows, and as vulgar as it is to drink in public, she reaches for her champagne, wondering how she might make her discomfort known to Ballard, who is standing outside the box.

Uneasy, she returns her gaze to the stage but does not see it, keeping the fan to her cheek to shield herself. A wave of amusement breaks over the crowd. Louisa, the youngest Marjoribanks, is partially blocking the door with her periwinkle skirts. Her ringlets bounce as she joins in with the laughter, and she mistakes Angela's glance over her shoulder as friendly acknowledgement. Angela returns the smile and makes quick little peeks over her fan towards the dark mouth of the galleries.

If she rises from the box, she will draw attention to herself. Her skirts will not fit through the gap between knees and balustrade, and the entire theatre will see that she is leaving. Perspiring now, she looks once again into the pit, raking her eyes up and down the rows, raising them to the circle and higher, peering at the pale faces above collars and cravats, but they are all fixed on the gay scene before them, with hardly a care in the world.

And then: a movement at the very edge of her vision. A figure has detached from the dark mass of the grand circle, a tier above where Angela sits. She watches it move across a central row, cutting across the seats, clambering over limbs and layers of tulle and taffeta. It reaches the stairs. In a flash of white cuffs, a hat is placed upon a head, and the person climbs swiftly towards the exit. Very briefly, Angela sees a tall, slim figure silhouetted in the lamplight of the doorway, a stance she thinks she knows – and then, it is gone.

Her heart is pounding now, her skin damp, throat dry. Bubbles pop and fizz in her mouth as she puts the glass to her lips and stares at the dim exit. And still the show goes on: the voices of Almaviva and Rosina soar like birds to the rafters; the audience is in raptures. What was she thinking, putting on her diamonds, ordering her carriage, coming to the opera as though she could live an ordinary life? Her heart slows a little as she reminds herself that Ballard is mere feet away, standing between herself and the theatre with his rattle and baton. Though a showman, Dunn will not attempt anything before a crowd of a thousand.

She has a fleeting image of Ballard on his back in the corridor with a knife through his chest, blood blooming through the dark wool of his coat.

She peers at the grand circle again, combing the rows, knowing that her decreasing pulse, her slowed breathing, means he is gone. Before long, she finds what she is looking for: twelve rows up, eight across. A flash of scarlet – a single seat unoccupied, like a missing tooth.

At the first opportunity, between the third and fourth act, she discreetly alerts Marjoribanks, who steps outside to pass her suspicions to Ballard. The constable returns moments before the curtain falls for a final time, breathless and despondent. 'No sign of him, miss,' he says.

Within minutes, the corridors are choked, and Angela and the Marjoribankses wait for them to clear.

'Are you quite sure?' her friend asks while his granddaughters hang over the balustrade, remarking on the ladies' dresses.

'Not at all sure,' Angela replies. 'I just had a feeling.'

'Only, it might have been some poor chap who remembered he had somewhere else to be.'

'It might have,' says Angela, suddenly weary.

At home, the upper floors are in darkness. She has a cup of warm milk with a dash of honey, and though the log basket is almost full, she rings for it to be filled so that, for a brief time, there is somebody with her. She thinks about calling for Mrs Brown to sit beside her until she falls asleep, as she used to when things were very bad, but decides it would be too selfish.

Before she retires, with the room in darkness, she stands at her bedroom window, peeking out like a child from a two-inch gap between the shutters at the street below. It is almost midnight, and most of the windows in the opposite houses are dark. She thinks of the empty seat in the theatre and how it glared at her. Perhaps she ought to be less public, but on the occasions she had to stay indoors during periods of illness and mourning, with so much life to tempt her on the other side of the wall, she felt as though she was going mad. She had planned to go visiting in the morning, making the rounds of the faces she has not seen since she returned from Paris. But tonight has unsettled her, and part of her does not feel like sitting in airless drawing rooms and talking about art.

Nestling down into bed, her last thought before she sinks into sleep is of Urania Cottage and the girls arranged in their beds like dominoes, and she finds herself wishing that, just for tonight, she was among them.

❧

The next morning is dismally cold, and when Mrs Holdsworth returns to Shepherd's Bush with her basket and a new house-mate, she sends a freezing draught down to the kitchen, where Josephine is putting away the pans.

'Oh, good, Josephine,' says Mrs Holdsworth, unwinding her wrap. 'Would you please give Hannah Parsons her things and show her to her room? I need a strong cup of tea.' She looks with disapproval around the kitchen. Plates of toast crusts litter the table, and a book of fairy stories, a gift to the house from a committee member's daughter, is propped against the coffee jug, stained with jam.

Josephine wipes her hands, removes her apron and finds the latest girl upstairs – not in the front bedroom, where she expects her to be, but in the small room at the back that Josephine shares with Martha and Polly. The new girl is standing with her back to the door, looking at the pictures tacked to the wall drawn by Lucinda, who is the artist of their small colony.

'You're sleeping in the front,' says Josephine by way of greeting.

Without turning round, the girl drops her bonnet onto Polly's bed, which lies adjacent to Martha's.

'I think I'll take this one, if that's all right.'

She begins unwrapping her mantle, made of warm brown wool. Josephine moves to the bed and picks up the bonnet. Her fingertips are raw from scrubbing the pans. 'This one's taken,' she says.

Finally, the girl turns. She is striking, with fair hair, dark eyebrows and a petulant mouth. 'I was told to choose my own bed, and so I have.'

'I will show you the ones that's free.' Josephine holds her gaze with no expression, long enough for Hannah to look resignedly away and follow her out of the room. From the press in the hall, Josephine takes sheets, towels and a dress, stacking them in her arms.

'They don't smell so clean,' Hannah remarks, accepting them.

Josephine piles drawers and stockings on top. 'Laundry day is Monday. You'll alter your clothes this evening, when we sew before bed.'

The girl frowns. 'I don't know how to sew. My mother did all that for me.'

In the front bedroom, Hannah walks to the bed beneath the window and plants her linen like a flag on the mattress.

'I'll fetch your timetable.'

Hannah follows Josephine downstairs.

'We rise at six. Morning prayers and scriptures is at a quarter before eight. Breakfast is after that.'

'What's your name?'

'Josephine.'

'That's a pretty name.'

'Dinner's at one. Supper's six. Evening prayers at half past eight, and bedtime's ten. Where's the timetables, Mrs H?' she yells down the passage.

'In the dining-room bureau,' comes the reply.

The dining room is also the schoolroom. Mrs Holdsworth carries out her correspondence at the shiny wooden desk below the window, where she can keep an eye on the privy and the garden and glance backwards into the hall. Josephine locates the timetables, one of which is marked with handwriting; she makes out a capital *H*.

'Lessons is at half past ten, every day except for Saturday. Each week we work in a different room. There's the bedrooms, living rooms, schoolroom, kitchen, scullery, needlework. Straw-plaiting we do as well. Every Monday, the names of the girls in charge of that room is put up in a frame.'

'So we have plenty of time to ourselves, then,' says Hannah drily.

'We've half an hour between school time and dinner, and an hour after dinner. Half an hour before supper, an hour after.'

The girl studies her. 'How do you find it here? Do you like it?'

'I like it enough.'

'Where was you before?'

'We ain't supposed to talk about that.'

'About what?'

'What came before.'

'Why not?' But Hannah is teasing. Josephine goes from the room, meaning for Hannah to follow, and hears her call: 'How did you get that scar?'

Josephine halts and turns to fix Hannah with a look so blistering that the smile that lives at the corner of Hannah's mouth vanishes. Her eyes grow serious, and she stands straighter, clearing her throat.

'On Saturdays,' says Josephine, 'we clean the whole house top to bottom, including Mrs H's room. Mr Dickens visits in the afternoon. We get our new clothes for the week and take a bath.'

Hannah asks no more questions as Josephine takes her to each of the rooms. She opens drawers and points to jars, demonstrates how the meat screen works, how the copper is emptied, where to find chalk, blue, buttons. When the tour is over and Josephine has helped Hannah to make her bed, the new girl is slightly paler than when she arrived. She sits on her clean counterpane and begins to cry quietly.

Josephine watches from the doorway and sighs before going to sit beside her. She waits for Hannah to stop, which she does after a fashion, hiccupping like a small child and glancing about the room as though the decorated walls are bare bricks and the window has bars across it.

After a while, she wipes her eyes with a glove she pulls from her pocket. 'I want to go home,' she says, bursting into fresh sobs.

Josephine sits quietly, staring at the rug.

'Are they transporting you as well?' Hannah asks eventually.

'That ain't what this is,' Josephine replies.

'How ain't it? Call a spade a spade.'

A knot forms in Josephine's stomach. She thinks of Annie

looking quickly back at her in the oakum room. She did not know then that she was being betrayed. Perhaps she is more naive than she realises.

'Did you come from prison?' Hannah asks, undeterred.

Josephine does not have the energy to deny Hannah again.

'Westminster,' she says.

Hannah sighs gratefully, and something seems to leave her. 'I was at Coldbath. Four months, I did. And then my family thought it best I came here.' She sniffs loudly. 'Ain't it funny what shame does. They'd sooner see me sent round the world than have me home.'

Josephine is hardly listening now. She is back in the stone room with the high window and the broken desk. The top bunk is warm.

'I was trying to help them,' Hannah says. 'We couldn't afford mourning clothes for everyone, so I went to have a look – just a look – at what was on offer. They start taking down all these silks and dresses and laying out the gloves on the counter, and before I know what I'm doing, I'm arranging for it all to be sent home. I set up an account in my mother's name and took a silk mantle and a pair of gloves for her. I knew she'd love them.'

There are footsteps on the stairs, light and slack. They fade towards the back of the house.

'That's all I took from there – the mantle and the gloves. Then I went to another place a few streets away and took some flannel and put some other things on account. Nothing too expensive – it ain't like I took a gown or a pair of shoes or nothing. The last shop was where I spoilt it. I gave my mother's name and then changed it to a false one, thinking there'd be this trail of debt she didn't know about all across London, and the shopkeeper was all shifty with me, looking at me odd.

So I leave, and next thing I know, I'm being grabbed by a bobby in the middle of the street, and the things is all falling in the puddles and getting soiled.

'I'm picking them up, trying to save them, and the bobby keeps on with his rattle and I'm fumbling around on the road trying to stop the silk from getting wet. And then I realised what I done. That I weren't just borrowing these things – I had *stolen* them. I was a thief, and that's what the bobby was shouting over and over, shaking his bleeding rattle.' She sighs. 'I was only trying to make things easier after Henry died, so they wouldn't have to worry about the funeral and all of that. So,' she says, surveying the room differently now, with sad, wet eyes. 'Here I am.'

Josephine takes up Hannah's bonnet, damp from the carriage and smelling of must from the prison storeroom. She brushes it, arranging the folds and ribbons, and hangs it on the bed-post. It is clear to her that Hannah is spoilt, and prison is evidently the worst thing that could have happened to her. Her mind goes once again to how she was shown around by Martha, whose silence was friendly, suffused with warmth and understanding. If Martha had been the one to take Hannah around the cottage, by now she would have put an arm around the younger girl's shoulder. She would probably have offered a handkerchief. Josephine's is screwed into a ball in her pocket, thick with coal dust.

On her first evening, in the parlour after supper, Martha patted the chair beside hers and passed her the sewing box with as much pleasure and encouragement as if it had been a tray of sweetmeats. Martha is able to give without effort, and Josephine knows only how to take. It has been so long since she comforted anybody, so long since she has felt anything except disdain for weeping girls with fair hair who believe the world should turn in their favour.

Outside the room, a floorboard creaks, and Josephine is hopeful that Martha has come to rescue her. But the figure who enters causes her to blink, as she might at the bright sun; she gets to her feet and, sensing she ought to as well, so does Hannah.

'Miss,' Josephine says, wondering if she ought to curtsey. How does one curtsey? Her cheeks feel hot. How long has she been standing there?

Angela looks from one girl to the other, her expression neutral. 'Good day,' she says. 'I am sorry to disturb you.'

Both stare dumbly at her.

'Dinner is ready. Mrs Holdsworth has asked if you would come downstairs.'

Josephine is usually able to read people, but Angela is so far removed from any she has ever known, as though a veil conceals her true self. But then she looks at Hannah, and in her clear, steady gaze is pity and understanding, and Josephine realises that she has heard everything. Their past lives are not to be discussed under any circumstances, and though the two of them have been caught red-handed, Angela appears to be more moved than vexed.

They follow her from the room. Angela offers Hannah a dazzling smile at the top of the stairs, though she does not meet Josephine's eye. Josephine wonders if it is because she offered not a word of solace or comfort.

As she descends the stairs, she feels a touch of guilt and shame – and more than a little envy.

�֍

Martha cannot sleep. She has always been bad at it, even as a child. Especially as a child, for she lay between both her sisters in all the beds they ever slept in. She remembers Emily's sweet, milky breath, how her fair hair spilt across the pillow, smelling of earth warmed in the sun. When Emily was born, Martha was five and Mary seven. She was a perfect baby, with a spray of flaxen curls and bright-blue eyes. It was as though their mother had given them a living doll. She had gone about her work with the baby tied in her shawl at her breast, like the Australian creatures they have learnt about in lessons.

Australia. Martha longs so much for this country that it feels to her like a sunrise, when she has lived so long in the night. Shut inside the dim and chilly schoolroom, she loves to hear about its curious animals, its interesting plants and native people. It is like a place in a storybook and just as impossible to return from, for she knows that once she goes, if she goes, England will be as distant and unknowable to her as Australia is now. There will be no more Mary, Martha and Emily. Martha was not able to tell her sister this at their meeting, for she had already lost one sister, and it would have been too heavy a blow. The notion of them sharing a bed vanished a long time ago, but as soon as Martha's heel lifts from the dock to board the boat, a curtain will draw forever on her old life, never to be opened again. How can she go without knowing that Emily is safe? In her mind's eye, her sisters wave her off at the quayside and stand shivering as storm-clouds gather above them. Martha waves back until she cannot glimpse them anymore.

A whisper flies through the darkness. 'Martha?'

It has come from the foot of her bed, where Josephine's headboard meets the freshly papered wall.

'Why are you crying?'

Martha puts the sleeve of her nightgown to her eyes. 'Sorry.'

'Are you thinking about Emily again?'

Martha almost laughs at her directness. In the bed beside Martha's, Polly does not stir. 'I suppose so,' she whispers.

'What you thinking about?'

Martha feels an almighty sigh inflate her lungs. 'I can't sleep.'

'It's awful quiet here, ain't it?'

'Too quiet.'

'All I can hear is my thoughts.'

After a while, Martha says: 'Why do you think Miss Coutts never married?'

'I dunno. I don't suppose she needs to, she's so rich. She don't need no one.'

'Only Mrs Brown.'

'I don't know why she has that old bat following her around,' Josephine says darkly. 'I shall never understand ladies.'

'I think she is the first proper lady I ever met.' Martha frowns a little. 'It's strange meeting somebody so grand. I hardly know how to be around her. And yet she calls more often than I thought she would. I shouldn't think she cares a jot about us, though she seems to.'

'Perhaps her life is dull,' says Josephine. She is talking at a normal volume now, as if they were scrubbing a floor and not lying in the midnight quiet of a bedroom. Martha is continually surprised by how little Josephine minds what others think of her.

'Why do you suppose Mr Dickens wishes to know everything about us?' Josephine asks.

'I don't know. I shouldn't think we are very interesting.'

'I find it strange, how he gets us on our own and asks us things. And writes it all down in his book. What's it for?'

81

'I suppose he is a writer.'

Josephine says nothing.

'You have heard of Mr Dickens?' says Martha.

'What do you mean?'

'He is a novelist. Rather a famous one.'

Josephine is silent.

'He writes books. Stories. You must know *Nicholas Nickleby? The Pickwick Papers?*'

'I ain't a reader, Martha, to tell the truth.'

Martha feels herself blush.

'I haven't read him myself. My mother had one or two of his books. I don't know why he takes such an interest in us, though. Why he writes it all down.'

'I find myself making up things to tell him,' says Josephine. 'The sillier it is, the more he seems to like it.'

A thoughtful silence descends, and Martha wonders if Josephine has fallen asleep.

But then she says, more softly: 'I suppose you are thinking about how you can't go to the colonies until you know what's happened to Emily.'

Again, her aim is true.

'I think it every day,' Martha replies.

'You must do what's right for yourself,' says Josephine, finally, and the way she says it is heavy with meaning, as though she might be addressing herself, too.

Within minutes, Martha has fallen into a deep and dreamless sleep, imagining the warm weight of her sisters beside her.

The next time Angela calls, Mrs Holdsworth has no time to sit down with her, but when the angel descends upon the manger, her own work must wait. An endless list of tasks are clamouring for her attention, simmering in various parts of her mind like pans put to the boil, and ranging in urgency: the box of books sitting beside her chair, whose pages need cutting and putting away (least urgent); the weekly report she must write for the committee (most urgent); and a score of others in-between.

They arrange themselves in the parlour.

'I mean to discuss with you the girls' religious instruction,' Angela says. 'I was sitting in the little chapel at Albemarle Street, and it occurred to me that the girls are not served in this regard.'

One of the younger girls is losing her hair. Brown clumps are falling out at an alarming rate, and her scalp is showing through in patches. The poor girl has retreated into the book of fairy stories; in her free time, she gazes longingly at the illustrations of girls with flowing hair. There are seven now in the house, and Mrs Holdsworth feels the hours of each day slipping through her fingers like sand.

'It is a concern to me,' Angela goes on, 'that there is little structure to their Bible studies, and I might have a solution. I will offer as many carriages as are needed to transport every-body to St James's, which is the nearest church to the house – a journey of about ten minutes, I should imagine.'

The matter of religion at Urania Cottage is the most prolonged and divisive, and Mrs Holdsworth tries very hard not to sigh.

'Miss Coutts, the girls attending or not attending church is not a question of logistics. You know as well as I the lengths to which we have gone to ensure discretion for the house and for the inmates. A weekly group outing with so many of us firstly contravenes the house's policy that all residents are to remain on the premises at all times, and secondly, won't it draw precisely the sort of attention we wish to avoid? What will it look like, for a large group of girls, known to nobody in the vicinity, to appear each week as if from nowhere? It is a small parish, and people talk.'

Clearly Angela is rarely challenged this way, for red patches begin to glow at her throat. Mrs Brown shifts indignantly beside her. Mrs Holdsworth curses herself for being bullish: her husband's word. She remembers how he used to make horns at his temples with two fingers. He could evaporate her bad moods in an instant.

'My concern is over-egging the pudding,' she goes on. 'They are content with their prayers and the scriptures set by Mr Dickens. Oh, I quite forgot. This is all by-the-by, because we have a chaplain at last.' She gets to her feet and begins rummaging through the correspondence littering the bureau. 'Here we are. A Mr Bryant will commence religious instruction presently, coming out to the house once a week to deliver sermons and lead the girls in prayer.' She attempts to hide the contempt from her voice; the search for a religious leader has evidently been more of a priority than the search for an assistant for her.

'Oh.' Angela seems crestfallen. 'I did not know. Ought there not to have been a committee meeting about the appointment?' But she has seen the pale-blue paper in Mrs Holdsworth's hands.

'He is a prison chaplain, an old friend of Mr Dickens,' says Mrs Holdsworth. She has already come to dread the post boy marching down the path. The letters arrive so frequently and are so long and involved that it is a struggle to find time to read them. 'His schedule does not allow for him being a committee member, but he can spare two sessions a week.'

'I would have written to the Bishop of London,' says Angela in a wounded voice. 'He might have had some suggestions.'

'Or the Archdeacon of Middlesex,' Mrs Brown puts forth.

'Quite,' Angela agrees.

Mrs Holdsworth clears her throat. 'While I have you, miss, I don't suppose there has been progress made on the search for a deputy superintendent?'

'I'm afraid I don't know, but I will endeavour to find out for you, and hurry the search along.' Angela gives an apologetic smile. 'You are doing marvellously, Mrs Holdsworth.'

'Thank you.' Disarmed, Mrs Holdsworth busies herself with tidying up the bureau.

'I know it is the job of two or even three women at times.'

At times! Mrs Holdsworth resists raising her eyebrows.

From the passage: a scream, the smash of crockery, a blistering cry of: 'Mrs H!'

A roach has been found in the flour, and one girl shrieking caused another to burn herself with the iron. Mrs Holdsworth deals with both problems swiftly, applying a poultice to the girl's wrist and instructing her to sit for a while. When she returns to the dining room, Angela and Mrs Brown are in discussion, and Angela is clearly put out.

'If I might make a suggestion for the assistant matron post,' Mrs Holdsworth says, resuming the conversation before she has sat down, 'there was a warden at Bridewell, my previous workplace, whom I might recommend for interview. Her name is Esther Kelly.'

Angela gives a thin smile. 'Very well. And when does the music teacher begin?'

'Thursday.'

Another gripe: the girls must learn strings. How being able to play the guitar and piano will serve them in service, she cannot guess and knows better than to ask. It is the sort of wry, unimaginative question the committee finds exasperating. As well as learning how to manage a household of unruly, uneducated women, she is finding navigating the eccentricities of the committee just as much of an education. They, too, are liable to outbursts, declarations of passion and fury; they, too, can scheme and manipulate. On the whole, she has been more frustrated by them than the inmates.

'And has the pianoforte arrived?' Angela asks.

'Yesterday,' Mrs Holdsworth confirms.

Already, the pots in her mind are threatening to boil over. Order whitewash, check the beer, plan tomorrow's lesson. Last night, she did not blow out her candle until a quarter to one. One of the girls had written in a letter to her family: *The contryside is dull, the work repetitif, and the matron has the idea we are her enymies.* She folded it back inside the envelope, the tips of her ears colouring, refusing to be moved. She can feel her grip slipping as their numbers increase, and yet more will arrive in the coming weeks. All the time, the house is only one difficult inmate away from the balance tipping further from her.

She has no sitting room in the house either, nowhere to gather her thoughts – not that she has time for such things. Frank's infrequent visits, and her hasty walks to the grocer's, the bank, the post office, are the only breaks she has. She wakes with the girls, eats with them, sits beside them in the evenings. Once they are in bed, she does the books, writes reports, attempts to keep up with correspondence. A few nights ago, she fell asleep at her bureau, her hair inches from the candle. The lists lengthen by themselves, and she sees more of darkness than day. The morning passes in a blink, the afternoon in a moment, and then it is night again. The weather has been dreadful, with sideways-slanting drizzle and low-hanging mizzle and icy draughts whistling through the gaps. Surely it would have been better to open the house in summer, when the girls could enjoy the garden and take their own parcel of earth. But here they are, a week from Christmas, the house not even full, yet she at capacity.

'I'm glad to hear it,' says Angela. 'I hope the girls will make good use of it. May I see it?'

Another crash, this time from the upper floor, followed by a muffled volley of cursing. Mrs Holdsworth smiles. 'But of course. After you, miss.'

CHAPTER 5

Curl-papers

Martha is cleaning the doorstep when it begins to rain. She throws the rag in the pail, wipes her freezing hands and is getting to her feet to empty the dirty water into the flower-bed when she sees something out of the corner of her eye. A young man is leaning on the front gate, watching her. He is quite at leisure, chewing tobacco in an exaggerated fashion, working his jaw and looking at her with lazy interest, as though she is a horse to be sized up. Beneath the dust coating his face she makes him out to be two or three years younger than herself. His hands are crusted with dirt.

'Get off the gate,' she tells him.

'Or what?' he returns.

'Shoo! Go on.'

Undeterred by the rain, he ignores her and peers up at the house. 'Been wondering who moved in here. Who's the gaffer?'

'There is none.'

He regards her with suspicion, and she wonders if she has given him licence to torment them now.

'He's away,' she adds, turning to go into the house.

Josephine is standing on the other side of the front door. 'Who you talking to?'

'A boy,' she says.

'What boy?' Already she is pushing past Martha.

'Josephine, it's cold. Come inside.'

But Josephine is standing in the middle of the path, hands on hips. 'What is it you want? Service door's that way.'

'I was only having a look.'

'Well, you've had it. Now move along.'

'Or what?' he says again.

Josephine stands a moment, her silhouette hard, her dark hair bound in a braid at her neck with tendrils coming lose. She is always being told to neaten her appearance, but her hair appears to have a mind of its own.

'Cor, that's a pretty mark you got there,' says the boy. 'Who branded you?'

In one swift movement, Josephine flies up the path, wrenches the pail of dirty water from Martha's hand and slings its contents in a graceful arc. The water hits the boy like a fist to the face, and Josephine cries out with glee.

'You bitch!' He staggers back, wiping his neck and collar, gasping like a fish on land.

'If you so much as step on this path, I'll set the constable on you.'

'Who's your master? I shall seek him out and have you thrown out on your arse.'

Martha takes Josephine's arm, pulls her indoors and closes the door firmly. 'You shouldn't have done that,' she says.

'Why? It's raining – he'd have got wet anyway.'

'Mrs Holdsworth said we aren't to draw attention to the house.'

'Nobody was watching, far as I know.'

'Josephine? Martha?' Mrs Holdsworth stands in the passage to the kitchen.

Josephine hesitates, still holding the pail, and then says: 'Yes?'

'Come into the schoolroom please.'

Martha and Josephine look sideways at each other. Martha feels her neck warm, her stomach turn. Guilt washes over Josephine's face. 'You didn't do nothing,' she says.

Martha leads the way to the schoolroom, where the household is gathered. Some of the girls sit on chairs; others lean casually against the dining table, arms folded, already defensive. Mrs Holdsworth holds one of the laundry bags that hang on each of the girls' bed-posts. Wordlessly, she opens its neck, tips it upside-down and spills its contents onto the floor in a creased heap. Among worsted stockings and yellowing armholes is a streak of dark grey, a slash of claret, and she bends and plucks from the heap an outdoor cloak and bonnet. Then she scrutinises each of the girls in turn, shaking out the cloak, laying it across her forearm like a draper's assistant, and presenting the bonnet besides.

'As you all know,' she says, 'the outdoor clothes are locked in a cupboard, the only key to which exists on my belt. So, how is it that, when sorting through the laundry just now, I came across these items shoved inside a bag?'

Several pairs of eyes rake over the offending items as if for clues.

'I can only assume use of them was intended,' Mrs Holdsworth goes on. 'I shouldn't need to remind you that truth and honesty are cornerstones in this house.' Frowning, she scans their faces. 'Would anybody like to explain to me how these came to be in among the laundry?'

Silence. Somebody clears their throat to hide suppressed laughter, and there is the rustle of skirts shifting against the polished table.

'None of you?'

The silence intensifies, and Mrs Holdsworth appears briefly to diminish, her shoulders sinking.

'Very well. How greatly disappointing. The committee shall hear about this. I shall defer to them for the best course of action, but this is far from the end of the matter. Back to your work.'

The girls file out, furtive, amused, curious. Martha and Josephine are the last to leave.

'Mrs H?' Martha nods at Josephine to go from the room, and with wide, dark eyes, Josephine closes the door on them.

Mrs Holdsworth studies Martha with amazement. 'It can't have been you, of all people.'

'It wasn't,' Martha replies. 'I was wondering if you'd heard back from the superintendent at Reading.'

Mrs Holdsworth goes at once to her desk and begins rummaging. 'Goodness me, I have, and I've clean forgotten what it was he said.'

Martha waits, her whole form tense.

'It was a rather short letter, I'm afraid.' Mrs Holdsworth holds it at arm's length, peering at it. 'No such case has been reported to them. I am sorry.' Mrs Holdsworth tucks the letter inside the envelope and looks at Martha with sympathy.

Martha is overwhelmed with the desire to sit and put her head in her hands. But what was she expecting? A pack of constables set upon the case, combing the streets and knocking at doors, all for a housemaid who left her position?

Mrs Holdsworth begins taking up the laundry. Martha gets to her knees and helps, folding it before dropping it into the bag. The offending cloak and bonnet are draped over a nearby chair.

'I'm sure she'll turn up,' says the matron, more softly.

'I can't leave England without knowing she's safe.'

'You're quite a while off that yet.'

'I really do want to go to Australia,' says Martha.

The matron looks at her, and her gaze is not unkind. 'I know you do.'

Martha puts the last thing in the laundry sack: a chemise with a piped bodice she recognises. She knows whose bag this is. She hesitates, running a thumb along a seam. All the warmth of the body who inhabited it has gone. She folds it neatly and draws the bag closed.

The next morning, Mrs Holdsworth has her answer. A flurry of bare feet on floorboards and urgent knocks rouse her before daylight, followed by the cry: 'Mrs H? Mrs H, wake up!'

She is just getting to her elbows when Lucinda crashes into her bedroom, her desolate tufts sticking up like feathers.

'Hannah's gone! Hannah Parsons.'

In a moment, Mrs Holdsworth is marching swiftly down the landing to the front bedroom, with a gaggle of girls crowding like hens at her heels. Another flight: the second in six weeks. In Hannah's bedroom, the girls clamour to tell her that they heard her get up and dress, thinking her to be starting her work early.

The drama dies down and then erupts again when two of her roommates go to take their gowns and find them missing. Mrs Holdsworth sets about checking the locks and stores, the beer and knives and silverware, finding it all intact except for a curious mound of laundry in the wash-house, dumped beneath the window. It takes a few minutes for her to realise that only the bag is missing, and from upstairs comes the cry that the clothes Hannah arrived in are also gone, along with the dress she was given on arrival. All the cloaks are present, as are the bonnets, and Mrs Holdsworth's first thought is that the girl will freeze to death.

Breakfast is an excitable affair. A plate is dropped and smashed in the chaos, and Mrs Holdsworth is forced to bark instead of speak, admonishing them to eat in silence – to no avail. The new chaplain, Mr Bryant, is to start that morning, and Mrs Holdsworth wonders in what frenzied state he will find them. She abandons the kitchen and a hot piece of toast to go to the schoolroom and write to Angela at Stratton Street and Mr Dickens at Devonshire Terrace, then continues to the parlour to check that the window, through which Hannah absconded, is now locked as it should be, retrieving a fallen handkerchief from the bottom of the stairs on her way. At the parlour window she allows herself a moment of repose, looking out at the bleak front garden, picturing Hannah with her sack creeping beneath the sash, opening the gate slowly, so that it didn't squeak. The frost-hardened lane, disturbed now and then by birds flitting through the hedgerows, is otherwise empty.

Ten minutes later, she is writing at her desk when a series of blows sound down the hall. 'Oh, he's early,' she mutters to herself, and fumbles at her waist for the key.

94

Standing on the doorstep is not the new chaplain but her own son, holding the missing laundry bag, stuffed to the gills, as well as the arm of the person she expected never to see again.

'Hannah! My God.'

She opens the door wider to admit them, and Frank removes his hat. Hannah stretches luxuriantly, like a cat, and rearranges her features into an expression of neutral impassivity. She looks sideways at the girls coming down the hall and appearing in the doorways, but she will not meet Mrs Holdsworth's eye.

'Well, this is quite the turn-up,' says Mrs Holdsworth.

'I saw her on the high street, peering in the shop windows,' Frank says. 'Thought I recognised her. I went to say good morning, and she looked as though she'd seen a ghost. This was a giveaway.'

He hands over the laundry bag and his mother rifles briskly through its contents.

'Take her up to my bedroom,' she says, handing him a key from her belt, and adding almost sadly: 'And lock her in. I'll write to Mr Dickens.'

'You won't tell Miss Coutts, will you?' says Hannah.

'I certainly will.'

Hannah begins to object just as the door-knocker goes again.

'That will be Mr Bryant. Martha? Where's Martha?'

Martha detaches from the small group at the kitchen door.

'Would you please show Mr Bryant inside? Put him in the parlour, give him tea, and I'll be down shortly.'

She follows Frank and Hannah upstairs; the girl flounces ahead of them holding her skirts, more like a debutante than a thief. Inside the bedroom, she looks about with her small nose in the air.

'What were you thinking?' Mrs Holdsworth could cry out with exasperation. She was beginning to grow fond of Hannah, who is quick and funny, a natural leader to the younger ones. She wants to take her by the shoulders and shake her.

Hannah begins to cry. 'I didn't want to be transported,' she sobs, wiping her eyes and nose with a sleeve. She has clearly been crying already.

Mrs Holdsworth closes her eyes and breathes in deeply. The number of times she has attempted to reassure the inmates that they will not be prisoners in a new land now runs to over a dozen, and yet the doubt still blooms like mould. 'And so you stole?'

'The girls can always get new dresses. I seen all the spare ones in the cupboards.'

'Hannah, those dresses don't belong to you or anybody else here. They were paid for by Miss Coutts. By rights they belong to her.'

'I'd never steal from Miss Coutts!'

'Well, I'm afraid you have.'

She cries harder. 'She won't . . . she won't put the magistrate on me? Oh, I feel sick.'

'Here, sit.' Mrs Holdsworth directs her to the chair in the corner, moving a pile of sewing to do so.

'Will I have to go back to Coldbath?'

'That will be for Mr Dickens and Mr Chesterton to decide.'

'I was going to come back, you know. I was mooning about at the shops so I could make up my mind. As soon as I left, I didn't know if what I done was . . . I thought I might come back afore everyone woke, but then it got too late, and I knew I'd be found gone. And then Frank saw me, and he was so kind, asking me what my errand was, and I told him a tale about how you needed some thread and . . . I can't bear you thinking ill of me, not Miss Coutts either.'

There is a gentle knock at the door, and Mrs Holdsworth answers it to Martha.

'Mr Bryant is in the parlour with Mr Holdsworth.'

'Very well – I'll come down. Hannah, I'm going to have to lock you inside until we know what to do with you. You won't have had any breakfast.'

'No.'

'I'll bring you something shortly.'

Hannah sniffs loudly. 'And cocoa, please, if there is any.'

Mr Bryant is a silvery, unobtrusive man in his fifties, with a soft Irish brogue. He sits in the high-backed chair, still wearing his greatcoat, his clergyman's bands just visible, clutching a black felt hat. 'Oh, I am sorry there's no fire, Mr Bryant – we are rather at sixes and sevens this morning.'

'No matter, Mrs Holdsworth,' he replies pleasantly. 'I am quite used to the prison climate.'

Polly arrives with tea and manages to spill it all over the tray while setting it down. Frank, who has been standing by the empty fireplace, leaps to help.

'Goodness me,' Mrs Holdsworth cries. 'Frozen and almost scalded – is there any other way we might torture poor old Mr Bryant today?' She shakes her head. 'I hope your journey was agreeable?'

'Most agreeable, Mrs Holdsworth. There was enough room on the omnibus to revise my sermon, and it came to me somewhere around Holborn Circus which verse I ought to lead with, and so I was obliged to ask a gentleman for a bit of lead to mark the verse in case it left my head on the walk here. What a pleasant lane this is! And the house so well situated for town and country.'

'Yes,' Mrs Holdsworth agrees mildly. 'Mr Bryant, as you may well know already, our governor is a very particular man.'

'Very particular.' He nods and smiles. 'He is an old friend of mine.'

'To be sure. Then I don't need to ask if he has briefed you on the . . . the *temperature* of religious instruction at Urania Cottage.'

'Certainly. Their minds are to be nourished and encouraged. These girls have been badly let down by society; therefore they have no care what society thinks of them. It is only by working in prisons that one comes to understand this, Mrs Holdsworth. By the time I meet my parishioners – because they are parishioners first, prisoners second – they have no room in their lives for God. They feel He has abandoned them. If the church is to be a part of life here at Urania Cottage, it is to be a guest in the house, in every sense. They will receive God if He will receive them.'

By now, Polly has brought a clean tea-tray and sets it shakily down. Mr Bryant thanks her warmly, and she flushes.

'I quite agree with you, Mr Bryant, having worked in prisons myself. The church is mightily off-putting to those who find themselves only judged by it. It has not been a friend to these girls.'

'Mrs Holdsworth,' he says with great sincerity, 'no longer are they friendless.'

She allows herself to be impressed. 'Polly, would you have someone come and make the fires at once, please?' A distant pounding interrupts them. 'What on earth is that racket?'

A rosy-cheeked, gleeful girl named Mary-Ann appears at the door. 'It's coming from upstairs, Mrs H.'

'Good heavens,' says Mrs Holdsworth, regretting it at once. 'Excuse me, Mr Bryant.'

Hannah Parsons is knocking thunderously from inside Mrs Holdsworth's bedroom. 'Let me *out!*' she cries. 'Lemme *out!* You can't keep me in here! I ain't a prisoner! I shan't be transported! I want to see Miss Coutts!'

One of the younger girls stands wide-eyed on the landing, holding a plate of buttered bread and a mug of cocoa. Mrs Holdsworth unlocks the door, takes the tray and ventures inside, to find Hannah red-faced and breathless, stalking the boards like an animal.

'Is Miss Coutts here?'

'No. Harriet, could you please take the two letters on my desk and ask Frank to send them at once to Mr Dickens and Miss Coutts? Their addresses are in the black book in my bureau.'

'Yes'm.'

'And show Mr Bryant to the dining room. Round up the others and make sure everybody has their prayer books.'

'Mary-Ann's is dropped in the sink.'

'I don't want to see Mr Dickens – not him,' whines Hannah. 'I'll see Miss Coutts though – she'll help me.'

'Thank you, Harriet,' says Mrs Holdsworth. 'If anybody needs me, I'll be here.'

By suppertime, Hannah Parsons has been dispatched. Mrs Holdsworth is not privy to where they have taken her, was not involved in the lengthy discussions that took place in the dining room among abandoned prayer books. The next afternoon, just as the light slips away, a note arrives on pale-blue paper. Hannah is once again at Coldbath Fields under the care of Mr Chesterton. There she will remain for two months. There is no mention of her returning to the cottage in Shepherd's Bush. Mrs Holdsworth scans the rest of the note and throws it on the fire.

It is only later, in bed, that she is visited by the dreadful memory of Hannah throwing herself at Angela's feet not a yard from where she lies; the lady's shocked white face; pieces of her pearlware lustre jug scattered on the rug. The jug had been a birthday present from her eldest son, Edward, and was knocked off the dresser in the chaos. When they took Hannah downstairs, Mrs Holdsworth swept the fragments into her hands, her eyes smarting with tears of fury, and put them in the empty cocoa mug. She returned later to find the tray gone, the shards thrown away. She got to her knees and felt under the bed for any more pieces, almost crying out with relief at a sharp pain in her hand, closing her fingers around a fraction of porcelain the size of a child's tooth, with a dab of gold. She added the piece to the locked box of letters she keeps in the cupboard.

She tries not to think of Hannah shut inside her cell for the night, trying to keep warm, used by now to the fires and blankets and warming-bricks, the hot cocoa and buttered toast. She tries to push from her mind the image of her being marched down the path, the final glimpse of the house she took over her shoulder, as if she was drinking it in.

She tries to forget all of it and waits for sleep, that unpredictable visitor, who arrives in the daytime with no warning and sits heavily on her and must be shooed away. She opens the shutters to admit the moonlight and welcome the night, but again she is jilted, and another hour passes before it finally, mercifully, calls.

✤

Christmas Day is the following week. They are all lounging in the parlour, stuffed like birds with food and drink, roasting gently beside the fire.

None of them were expecting presents, but many are given and received, including lengths of cambric from Angela, who called in the morning with Mrs Brown and took a glass of sherry standing up in the kitchen as the girls prepared their feast: a goose and a partridge, with soups, sauces and, to finish, an enormous cream cake. Each were touched to receive journals from Mrs Holdsworth, in which to practise their handwriting and record their memories. 'Your future selves will thank you,' she said wisely, her nose red. And all were astonished to unwrap from Mr Dickens small, glazed frames displaying exquisite butterflies, preserved in time. The girls have spent a long time looking at and comparing them, remarking on their beauty and detail, admiring the strange, furry bodies that without wings would make them dull and ordinary insects. Josephine received a *Vanessa cardui*, a Painted Lady, rich amber and velvet-black. The note included informs her that its lifespan is between fifteen and twenty-nine days.

It occurs to Josephine, who sits dozing with her leg hanging over the chair arm as some of the others play the piano, that Martha has been upstairs for some time. She rouses herself, climbs the stairs and finds her friend sitting on her bed in the dark, her knees bent, examining her *Celastrina argiolus*. Imperfect but cheerful chords sound from below, layered beneath singing and laughter. Outside, the sky is bright and starry, and Josephine perches at the foot of Martha's bed and looks out.

'Isn't it cruel, when you think about it?' Martha says. 'To put a pin through an innocent creature and frame it like a painting.'

'Butterflies only live a few weeks.'

Martha's butterfly was smaller than Josephine's, its wings a dusty blue. The accompanying note from Mr Dickens said that *Celastrina argiolus* was the first butterfly to emerge in spring. 'Just like you was first in the house,' said Josephine. There was a warm ripple of appreciation for her observation, and she felt for the first time in her life that she'd said something clever.

'That makes it worse, doesn't it?' says Martha, frowning at the creature in her hands. 'Why are they made so beautiful when they live such short lives? Surely the most special creatures ought to live the longest.'

'We plain ones have a right to live, too.'

Martha smiles.

'I never did like Christmas,' says Josephine, picking at the eiderdown – a habit that irks Martha, but today she doesn't scold her.

'What was your best Christmas?' Martha asks.

'Never had one.'

'Did you have presents?'

'I don't remember. A sugar mouse, probably. I love them.'

When they woke that morning, before they could get out of bed, Martha gave Josephine and Polly each a pair of bed-socks. Josephine had watched her making them for weeks and thought they were for herself. Martha was pink with embarrassment because of how lumpy and misshapen they were, more like four individual socks than two pairs, for none were quite the same height or size. But they are the best gift Josephine has ever received.

'Do you like Christmas?' Josephine asks.

'Yes,' says Martha, her eyes glazing over with pleasure. 'We'd go to bed in curl-papers, and on Christmas morning

I'd dress my sisters' hair. We'd have fruit and nuts in our stockings, and little dolls and things my mother made for us. After breakfast we would go visiting in the snow. Mary and I went to a ball one year. There were officers staying near our village. Emily was upset that she couldn't come, and so I got her ready as if she could, so she didn't feel left out. I took in an old dress of Mama's.' She gives a half-smile, remembering. 'She kept going to the mirror and wouldn't take it off for bed. She was a vain little thing.'

'Sounds like you had a pleasant home,' says Josephine after a while.

'I did,' says Martha, looking weary suddenly. She spends another moment in her reverie and then visibly returns. 'Are your parents still alive?'

'No. Long dead.'

'Mine too. Do you have brothers and sisters?'

'No. They're dead, too.'

'Oh, Josephine. I am sorry.'

Josephine says nothing. At times, with her gentle, sisterly manner, her quiet authority, Martha reminds her of Angela, though she wouldn't tell her that. Josephine wonders how Martha, with her balls and curl-papers, her Mama and her sisters, came to be sitting opposite her in this room, this house. She expected the others at Urania Cottage to be girls like herself, born in the gutter, picking at the bones life offered them – and certainly, in lots of ways, they are. But not Martha.

In the home for fallen women, it is evident that Martha has fallen the greatest distance. And yet she does not shrink from the depths. When one of the girls, who arrived on a rainy evening a fortnight before, had such weeping sores that they caused her to cry out when she sat down, Martha administered pills, dressed them with ointment and helped her up from chairs until the worst had healed. She does not curse, but when the others do, out of Mrs Holdsworth's earshot, she gives a rueful smile. She makes an effort to smooth disagreements. She darts among them, conspicuous, inscrutable, a rare, exotic fish on a riverbed of eels.

Josephine wants to ask her how she came to be here but senses it is too delicate, like silk in rough hands. If being here has taught her anything, it is that some stories ought not to be told. But it is as though she has disturbed something, unlocked a long-forgotten room and pulled up the blinds, for, holding her butterfly in her hands, Martha begins to speak.

'After my mother died,' she says softly, 'the three of us became untethered. We tried to stay together and keep Emily in school. Papa had died years before, when I was a child. We managed for a while and Mama took in sewing. She was a fine seamstress; she'd even taught herself to make lace. But our village was small and there wasn't the work, so she began taking in laundry. When she died, Mary and I kept on with it, but without Mama at the helm, it all just . . . I don't know what happened. It wasn't just one thing. When my parents were alive we had quite another life altogether. Mary moved to London and sent money home, but Emily and I couldn't manage. Emily would cry at night; her poor hands were red raw from helping me with the laundry. It became too much for me to cope with alone, with her in school, and so we had to give up the house. I knew that was it, that we'd have to separate. We couldn't live together any more.' She swallows. 'And so I found work for Emily at the big house, on the other side of the hill. My grandfather had been the gamekeeper there. And I followed Mary to London. I had no character reference. The number of doors I had closed in my face – it was humiliating.'

'Is that the house Emily disappeared from?'

'No. She wrote to me and said she wanted to leave the village, that it was too small and everybody knew her. She found a situation at Reading. When everybody knows your parents, they look at you a certain way, and it brings back all the sadness. Makes you feel as though you'll never escape it.

'I've been thinking about everything that led me here, because Mr Dickens wants to know. But a *fall* is swift, sudden, when really it isn't like that at all. They imagine it to be a seduction or a moment of weakness, as if we carry this precious thing in a little box on our person. But it isn't a single thing, a single moment. It's more like a series of little deaths. Don't you think?'

The thread Josephine has been picking at comes loose, and she smooths it down, thinking how clever Martha is, and not knowing how to reply. Her opinion is so rarely sought on any topic, let alone one she has barely given thought to.

'I always wished for a sister to do my hair,' she says eventually. 'I never was good at that sort of thing. And even if I was . . . well, there ain't much point to it. Not with this.' Vaguely, she indicates her scar.

'Nonsense,' says Martha, smiling gently. 'I'll put your hair in papers for you, if you like.'

Josephine shakes her head.

'Let me. It can be your Christmas present to me.'

'What do I need curls for?'

'Nothing. It's only to look nice, for yourself.'

'What will the others say?'

'Josephine Nash caring what others think? I never did hear such a thing.'

'All right, then. But if I don't like it, you have to brush them out.'

'Pax.'

The next morning, Josephine works in the back garden, clearing and pruning the soggy shrubs and blackened tendrils left by the previous tenants. She kneels in the earth, enjoying the feel of the cold, wet soil on her hands. Now and then, she lifts a sleeve to push a loose curl from her eye, careful not to muddy them. Martha's curl-papers were a success; her dark hair appears to have doubled, which caused poor Lucinda to cry at breakfast.

The mild winter morning is pierced by a whistle. It is not the shrill hoot of a locomotive, but birdlike, intimate, as though made only for her. There is a gate midway along the high fence that hems the garden, half-covered with brambles, opening onto a bridleway that meets the lane. Josephine looks up to see the same boy from before peering over it, his elbows resting in the same cocksure manner. She ignores him and returns to her task, pulling a thick rope of scrub from the earth, perspiring from the effort. A gardener is being sought, and until one is found, the girls must maintain it; Josephine did not realise the outdoors could need as much work as within. Her knees and back are aching, and the watery sun has disappeared behind a thick gauze of cloud.

'Good morning, miss,' says the youth peevishly.

He is encrusted with the same amount of dirt as before. She has seen similarly dusty people in the lane, going to and from the brickfields and little huts that crouch like molehills on the land. She rocks back on her heels, wipes a wrist along her forehead and scowls at him.

'What do you want?'

'A word with your master, if you'd be so good as to fetch him.'

'He ain't here.'

'I seen him myself, coming and going. He never stays for long, so I thought I'd lie in wait. Trap him.' He grins unpleasantly.

Josephine gathers her tools and gets to her feet. She puts the trowel in her apron pocket and tucks the fork beneath her arm.

'Where you going?'

With Martha's voice in her head, she turns and begins walking to the house.

'You're pretty as a picture today,' he calls.

Martha is in a low mood after a letter from her sister this morning. Mary had written to a childhood friend to see if Emily had been in touch, but to no avail. Martha read Mary's note at breakfast, her face puffy with tiredness. She folded it and tucked it neatly beneath her plate, and Josephine knew from this small gesture that it was not good news.

Josephine feels a stab of envy for Emily Gelder, wherever she may be, with two such devoted sisters. There is nobody for her to write to, and nobody from whom she will hear. Mrs Holdsworth will not sort through the morning post and set a letter down before her at breakfast.

Suddenly, a thought occurs to her. She stands a moment on the path she has trodden through the overgrown grass and looks up at their bedroom window. The shutters are open, and the dull glass reflects the pale sky. She examines the garden-fork in her hand, rubs away the soil. Then she removes her gloves, sets them on the ground with her basket and glances at the window once more.

CHAPTER 6

A House West of London

Angela is in pain. She has been at home for a week recovering from a tooth extraction, and, as though the boredom, discomfort and bread soaked in milk were not tedious enough, somehow the January draughts that trespass beneath doors and down chimneys manage also to permeate her jaw. She has spent the last few days reading and dozing by the fire or looking out at Piccadilly. The toothache prevented her from travelling, and so she passed a rather dismal Christmas at home.

Her sister Sophia sits opposite her now in the warm circle thrown by the fire. Sophia holds up a fan to shield her from the heat, but Angela allows it to gently roast her. Her cheek is so swollen that she can hardly speak and must only nod or make agreeable noises. How frightened she is of living this way, with only herself for company, losing her grip on her usual pleasures. Some unmarried women she knows have slipped into invalidity and spend all their days indoors, visited only by doctors and pitiful family members.

Sophia is twenty years older than Angela, more like an aunt than a sister. Now in her early fifties, Sophia lives a short drive away and prefers to entertain small groups at home. She has brought Angela some coffee and a pint of fresh cream. The coffee is a private joke. Their mother once thought it the cause of Angela's eczema and forbade her from drinking it for two years. When the eczema was undeterred, their mother thought she must have been drinking it in secret. This was a source of great amusement to them, though distressing to their mother, who was more conscious of Angela's skin than Angela was herself. There was an unkind rumour among the children in their circle that Angela had lice. She tried not to scratch in public, and kept her neck and arms covered as much as she could. At home, she bathed in milk and honey and slathered potash lotions beneath her gloves, but the relief was only temporary. Now, she cares less about how it looks. She is no longer obliged to be a thing of beauty, and finds that the condition can even be a topic of conversation at parties.

'Mrs Brown told me the dreadful news about That Man,' says Sophia. 'Has he been bothering you?'

A cold draught finds its way to the pit in Angela's gum. She winces and says: 'Not a stitch.'

'What's that?'

'I said, not a stitch.'

'What, nothing? How marvellous. I told you he would move on eventually.'

Angela frowns. One mercy of being trapped indoors is not having to look over her shoulder in the street, in the park, climbing out of her carriage. But on the other hand, the long days and introspection cause her to feel like a mouse in a skirting board with the hole stuffed.

There was a time Dunn followed her to the coast – Weymouth or Lyme Regis, the hotels and shores all merging into one – and every day pushed a little note beneath her door: *You look splendid in green, my dear*, and *Cream accentuates the ebony lustre of your hair*, and *I so enjoyed watching you on the beach this morning, with your pretty parasol*. She became friends with a young woman from Cheltenham staying at the hotel and made the mistake of telling her about Dunn and his daily missives. 'But how flattering!' this woman said. '*I* shouldn't mind having compliments posted through my door each morning – in fact, I dare say there isn't a better way to start the day!'

Angela never mentioned him in polite company again.

And now, still, each time the letterbox clatters in the hall, it sends a little surge of fear through her.

'It was just a matter of waiting, of sitting it out, which you did so splendidly,' Sophia is saying. 'You didn't rise to it – you went through all that trouble at the courts without so much as a hair out of place. You didn't let him see that it was affecting you. I know you were worried about being in the newspapers, but people do forget about these things. My dear, you do look pale. I so wish you would go to bed. Shall I send for some hot water and wine?'

As Angela shakes her head, Stockton gives a polite knock and enters, bringing with him another cold little breeze. She pulls her wrap more closely around her.

'Beg your pardon, miss,' he announces. 'This just arrived, and the delivery boy said to open it at once.'

'What is it?' asks Sophia.

Angela feels another little spike of fear. At intervals over the years, Dunn has sent bouquets and fussy little gifts: hand-kerchiefs embroidered with her initials and scented soaps, one of which smelt so strongly that, whenever she caught a whiff of lavender for some time afterwards, she was reminded of his nauseating assault. Eventually, Stockton or one of the maids began intercepting these items, presenting her only with flowers and presents from her real friends, which lay unpacked and displayed for her in her sitting room. She does not know what they did with the others: sold them, most likely, or else kept them to brighten their plain rooms and windowsills. She has no wish to know.

Now, she watches the footman place on a walnut table a long, flat package the length of a man's forearm. He unties the string, draws out a sealed note and is about to read it when Angela flaps a hand and tells him to open the gift first. She sits higher in her seat and watches the slow unwrapping of the paper, revealing a great gleam of silver . . .

'A salmon!' Sophia declares.

Like a fishmonger, Stockton proffers the shining beast in its wrappings.

Angela instinctively recoils, but her sister is delighted and claps her hands together. 'It's enormous! Who sent it?'

Stockton reaches for the accompanying note and brings it to Angela, along with the unpleasant odour of raw fish. Angela holds it at arm's length, glimpses *ABC* in the familiar slanting hand. She scans the few lines and finds herself smiling for the first time in days.

'Is it from Lord Sandon?'

Angela shakes her head.

'Who, then?'

Angela replies, but Sophia cannot understand her. '*Ah-ha?*'

Still smiling, Angela passes her the note. 'Ah,' says Sophia, her face hardening slightly. 'How generous.'

'Is there a reply, miss? The messenger said he would wait.'

Angela nods, and the footman disappears to deliver the salmon to the kitchen and fetch her writing things.

'He has invited me to stay with him,' Angela attempts to say, and this time Sophia understands.

'Will you?' she asks. 'Shouldn't you rest here until you're better?' And then, perhaps because Angela is not able to give a fulsome reply, Sophie continues: 'You aren't still mooning after him, are you? I thought you'd put all that behind you.'

Angela rolls her eyes, sighs, adjusts her position in the chair.

'He is old enough to be your father. He is old enough to be *my* father!'

Angela raises a cynical eyebrow, deciding it is not worth the effort to remind her that they have the same father.

'Any man who turns down your hand in marriage is a fool, and I question why he is courting you with gifts and declarations of affection when he has made his feelings more than clear. You ought not to entertain it. You won't go and stay with him, will you? You ought to stay in London, Angie, dear, really. The roads will be treacherous at this time of year.'

Stockton passes Angela her lap desk, and she settles more comfortably, ignoring her sister, for she knows Sophia has made a valid point, if not several. The proposal business was painful and humiliating, but somehow the duke has refused to let it affect their friendship. At the time she withdrew, wounded. The cockatoo remained absent from its perch for some time as she entered another period of mourning, one that no hue of fabric could express. In the end, their friendship survived it. The duke wished to be her friend, her guardian, her protector, but not her husband. And so the cockatoo returned to his perch, the shutters were opened, her evening clothes and jewellery laid out once again.

She asked him to marry her almost a year ago in February, on a cold, clear night at the duke's castle in Kent. Before going down to dine, she took out her diary, smoothed down the page and spontaneously drew a crescent moon, for there was a remarkably pretty one hanging over the dark and wintry sea beyond the castle walls. She thought, walking down the stairs, that she might incorporate it somehow into an engagement ring, would tell people about the sky that night. Later, standing in the dark bedroom listening to the waves crashing on the sands, her face wet with tears and her heart breaking silently, the same moon shone down on the same water, as if nothing at all had happened. Now, when she searches the pages absent-mindedly, chancing upon the little ink moon never fails to bring a prick of pain: a day of such hope and longing, lost among ordinary life.

She finishes her note and hands it to Stockton, who bows and withdraws. Sophia watches her through half-lowered eyelids.

'What answer did you give him?'

'I'll go on Thursday.'

This, Sophia comprehends. She purses her lips in disapproval.

The duke was a friend of their father's, though Angela can only recall meeting him once or twice in her parents' lifetime. Her friendship with him began to bloom two years ago, when she and Mrs Brown, staying at Ramsgate, received an invitation to spend the night at his castle on the beach. What she had expected – indeed, what she remembered of him – was not at all what she found. His Kentish home was an unusual one, yards from the water, battered by wind and salt, like a dungeon on the edge of the earth. She supposed it spoke to the major-general in him. But inside, it was warm and welcoming, even cosy, and she came to realise it was a reflection of the duke himself. That night, she felt as though she was meeting him for the first time and found herself quite shy. He was vivid company, direct, challenging, engaging, asking her all sorts of questions about the bank and her charitable enterprises. He knew architecture intimately, loved history, had strong views on just about everything. He had lived, she realised, in the world, not just in London or Europe, like most people she knew. Afterwards, she wrote *dined and stayed with Arthur* in her diary, and so he became Arthur, and their correspondence began.

A month later, they were writing almost every day, her missives in her messy, careless hand trailing him to his homes in Kent and Hampshire and London. He replied in his trademark brown ink, his handwriting, toppling crazily to the right, winking from silver trays, causing her heart to skip a beat. When he refused to marry her, she carried the box she kept his letters in to her bedroom fire and held a fistful of them over the flames. But in the end, she couldn't do it. The letters returned to the box, the box to the shelf.

He told her she had many decades of happiness left and that she was not to throw it away on a man as old as he. Perhaps he was right about the decades, but she knew there was only so much happiness she could manage without him. A more naive woman than she might have tried harder to change his mind, but she knew him. His will was made of iron, his honour resolute.

Angela straightens, folds the note in her hand, having forgotten, for a moment, the dull, throbbing pain at her cheek, which seeps back into her consciousness like a spilt bottle of ink. She puts the backs of her fingers to it and shakes her head.

'My dear, are you sure you don't want me to fetch Dr Brown?' Sophia says now.

Angela nods, more weakly than she feels.

Her sister leaps at once from the chair and pulls the bell.

Angela's mind drifts guiltily to the cottage, which she has not visited since the Hannah Parsons incident before Christmas: a sorry business indeed. The girl's shrieks haunt her still. Standing in that narrow room with the poor thing clinging to her skirts, begging and sobbing, aware of the dreadful fate that awaited her once again, Angela felt sick to the soul, but the committee were determined to make an example of her and send her back to Coldbath. Angela argued against it, but then where else? If Angela had her way, Hannah would have stayed in the house. After all, it was meant to be a place of forgiveness, of second chances. But not *third* chances, the committee argued, and Angela rather feebly accepted defeat.

The problem was, she thought afterwards, as her carriage pulled away from the house, that her money was only good for so much. If she really wanted to help the girls living at Urania Cottage, *she* ought to help them. She thinks of Martha and Mary, the easy way they crushed themselves together and wiped one another's faces. Her own sister sits at a distance, having only pressed her powdered cheek to Angela's on her arrival.

As the service bell chimes soundlessly in the bowels of the great house, an idea occurs to her, falling into her mind as a ripe fruit drops from a tree.

❦

The evenings are long in the parlour, stretching on like a yawn until bedtime. Supper is cleared away and they are expecting no visitors, so when the sound of hooves and wheels draws to a stop outside, there is a pause in sewing and conversation, a mute tension as they hear the squeal of the gate, footsteps on the path, the door-knocker. Mrs Holdsworth rises with a frown, removing her apron. They are surprised to hear another woman's voice in the hall, muffled by the firm sound of the street door closing.

Martha listens hard, for each time the door-knocker raps through the house, she allows herself to imagine for a moment that it is Emily standing on the doorstep.

'Martha, may I have a word?'

Her heart beating hard, she follows the matron into the dining room to find Angela standing with one gloved hand resting on the sideboard. She is dressed to travel, in a fur-lined cloak and boots. Seated at the large polished table, Mrs Brown is less impressive but just as composed. She raises her head to smile at Martha, who feels disappointment wash over her, but fixes on her face a polite smile.

'I apologise for disturbing you so late,' Angela says warmly.

'Not at all, miss,' Martha replies.

Angela takes a step closer and looks intently at her. 'I have a suggestion,' she says. 'Mrs Holdsworth thinks it an intriguing one, and I wonder if you might, too.'

Mrs Holdsworth, Martha notices, appears wholly displeased. Her mouth is a line, her hands folded stiffly before her.

'I should like to hear it, miss,' says Martha, wondering why on earth Miss Coutts should wish to share anything, least of all an idea, with her.

'I am glad of it,' says Angela, and motions for her to sit.

*

Two hours later, Martha, Angela and Mrs Brown are in an overnight coach, barrelling west. Mrs Brown falls instantly asleep, but Martha is too unsettled, too alert for slumber. She has not travelled at night before, and it is only her second time in a coach. Whenever they pitch to the left or the right, her stomach rolls over. The constant jolting and the dark and silent passengers make her feel as though she is in a nightmare, journeying towards hell itself.

They finally arrive at Reading after daybreak and take breakfast at the coaching inn. Martha is too sick to eat, feeling as though she is still pitching and juddering. She manages a few mouthfuls of strong tea and runs into the yard to bring it up again. Mrs Brown finds her leaning against the wall, shaking, and steers her back inside, sitting her at an ancient table and pushing a stack of buttered toast towards her. Ale has soaked into every surface – the floor, the tables, the benches – and the place stinks of it. Her stomach is so empty it aches, but the toast is very good.

At half past nine, they are moving again in a fly Angela has hired. It is strange passing through Reading after so many years. Here is the railway station, the cattle market, the arms manufactory that exploded, killing a man from their village. The close, smoking streets give way to brewhouses, malthouses, and eventually fields and the river. It seems impossible that this wide, glittering ribbon is the same muddy tide she saw through the narrow windows at the Magdalen. Years ago, when their mother brought them to market, they watched a boat race from the bridge. The four of them hung over the side, waving their handkerchiefs at the lines of sleek rowers, who moved with such grace and swiftness, cutting through the water as though gliding on ice. Emily's kerchief fell from her grasp, floating down to the current like a leaf made of lace. Martha's eyes snag on the spot where it happened as they cross the Thames.

When Emily began working at the house in Caversham, she wrote to Martha. *I have a new situation*, she began. Foolishly, Martha did not keep the letter, but somehow the name of the house has clung to the fibres of her memory. Now, an uneasiness settles over her as they reach the other side of the bridge, passing cottages, a priory and one or two inns before slowing on a wide lane. Spearhill Villa is set back from the road, half-concealed by dark-green clouds of rhododendron. It is a spacious, attractive house, gabled like a cottage, with white-painted shutters on the outside. A carriage drive hints at respectability, but it is not as large as some of its neighbours.

The door is opened by the housekeeper, a woman of perhaps forty, with dark brows and a curling lip.

'May I help you?' she asks, startled and intrigued by Angela's finery.

'Good afternoon,' says Angela. 'I do hope so.'

'I'm afraid the master and mistress are away until Friday.'

'Actually,' says Angela, 'if you are Mrs Garth, then it is to you we wish to speak.'

The dark brow lifts in surprise.

Inside, Spearhill Villa has the chilly air of a house abandoned by its family, though it is immaculately kept and smells pleasantly of beeswax. The three women follow Mrs Garth along a dim and solemn passageway to the breakfast room, where she leaves them to fetch refreshment. Martha looks about at the pictures, the fussy little vases and china objects, the bucolic scenes hanging from the picture rails, trying to imagine her sister dusting in here, humming as she did so, like she used to at home.

Mrs Garth returns, followed a moment later by a maid bearing a silver tea-tray. The maid chances a split-second glance at Angela in her ermine cape before retreating. Martha feels depressed suddenly at the knowledge that she might one day set down the same things in a similar room in a distant country, at the years of service stretching ahead. If only she could explore the house alone and look for some kind of clue. She ought to have come here earlier, as soon as she found out Emily was missing. All that wasted time, when she could have been searching, acting, enquiring.

'Thank you for your hospitality, Mrs Garth,' says Angela. 'Our apologies for calling without notice.'

Mrs Garth hums with anticipation.

'My companion, Mrs Brown, and my ward, Miss Gelder, and I are here on business relating to a servant who worked here until fairly recently. Emily Gelder.'

Mrs Garth's expression does not change, though Martha knows she is surprised.

'Miss Gelder wrote to you some weeks ago enquiring of her sister.'

'I recall,' the housekeeper replies neutrally. 'And I am afraid I have no further information, Miss Gelder. I recall another Miss Gelder—'

'My sister, Mary, ma'am,' Martha interrupts.

Mary, of course, would not have been served tea in the breakfast room.

'I am afraid I shared with your sister all I know regarding the matter – which is to say, not a great deal.' The housekeeper is plainly tired of this particular topic. 'Emily worked here a little under two years and left early one morning last winter with her things. She gave no warning, and we had no knowledge that she meant to leave. She asked another maid which coach went to London, and away she went.'

'She went to London?' Martha asks, sitting forwards.

'I know nothing of where she went, only that she made enquiries of the coach.'

'And was a constable called?'

The housekeeper issues a little noise of mirth. 'Why on earth should one be? No crime was committed. A flighty housemaid is hardly a matter for the constabulary.'

Angela smooths the atmosphere like a knife spreading honey. 'Of course. The very fact that she took her items with her would indicate no misadventure was at play. What were those items, if you don't mind my asking, Mrs Garth?'

Mrs Garth gives a quick little sigh. 'I suppose her purse, her own clothes. I don't inspect the maids' personal items, so I don't know what she had with her during her time here. It was all very sudden. Mrs Bushey was quite put out.'

There is a genteel quiet as they sip from their cups, and Martha's mind races. She looks about discreetly and spies a painted wooden hoop propped against a bookcase.

'Do Mr and Mrs Bushey have children?' she asks.

'Yes,' says Mrs Garth in her matter-of-fact way.

'How old are they?'

'Master Anthony is one-and-twenty, Miss Elspeth eighteen and Miss Veronica fifteen.'

'Do they live here?'

Mrs Garth makes a high little noise of mirth. 'My goodness, so many questions. Only Miss Veronica lives here. Master

Anthony reads at Cambridge, and Miss Elspeth is a student of music in the north of England.'

Martha nods slowly. 'What work did Emily do here?'

The housekeeper purses her lips. 'Maid-of-all-work duties: cleaning, dusting, bed-making, laundry,' she replies in a bored voice. 'She would help the footman serve if there was a party. I am not entirely certain anything I have to tell you will be of help to your enquiries.'

The mood flattens, and then Mrs Brown says, 'You keep a neat house, Mrs Garth.'

There is the first hint of a flush in the housekeeper's papery cheeks, and she hastens to set down her saucer. 'Thank you, Mrs Brown.'

'How long have you been employed by the Busheys?'

'Eight years now. Have you come far today?'

'From London,' Mrs Brown replies.

'What a long way back you must go.'

'We are staying with a friend not far from here,' says Angela.

She told Martha in the coach that a friend had invited them to his Hampshire home and then to Martha's great surprise referred to 'him'. That an unmarried woman might stay with a man surprises and impresses Martha, but the customs and habits of people like Angela remain a mystery to her.

Mrs Garth rises; their meeting is over. They drain their tea and thank her, for though she has not been a great deal of help, the housekeeper has taken half an hour from her day to discuss a former housemaid.

'I do hope you find your sister,' she says, almost as an afterthought, as she shows them out.

Martha asks to use the convenience, and after a moment's hesitation, Mrs Garth directs her to a privy at the bottom of the garden. She sees nobody on her way, but on crossing the lawn back to the house, she notices a face at one of the windows: a small white orb floating behind one of the panes, watching her. Martha raises a tentative hand in a salute, before letting it fall. No gesture is made in return, but the face, belonging to a girl and surrounded by dark-gold ringlets, continues to stare. Martha thinks quickly, and before she knows what she is doing, beckons the observer. The face disappears, and a stretch of time passes, but finally the French doors on the terrace open and a figure appears. Hanging back on the step, the girl kicks one foot shyly behind the other.

Slowly, as though approaching an animal, Martha advances, stopping a short distance from the girl.

'Are you Veronica?' she asks.

'Yes. Who are you?'

'A visitor,' Martha replies. 'My sister was a maid here.'

'Who is your sister?'

'Emily. Do you remember her?'

Veronica brings out her boot and taps the heel on the toe of the other. 'Yes.'

'I've come to look for her.'

'She isn't here.'

'I know that, but I don't know where she is.'

Veronica stares at her. 'Who is the grand lady?'

'She is my friend, Miss Coutts.' Martha knows she has only a minute or two before Mrs Garth will come searching. 'Do you remember Emily leaving?'

Veronica nods. A pink tongue protrudes and pushes at her bottom lip. She is very childish, Martha thinks, for fifteen.

'What do you remember?'

Veronica shrugs. 'Weeping.'

A chill falls over Martha. 'Emily was weeping?'

The girl says nothing and regards her with narrow blue eyes. Her speech is slightly affected, as though she is holding a marble in her mouth. She is like a white paper flower, delicate and angular, and Martha feels a tug of sympathy for this girl left at home with the servants.

From within, footsteps, neat and punctual on the flagstones.

'If there is anything you remember,' Martha says hurriedly, 'I will leave Miss Coutts's card beneath the pot outside the door. You may write to her.'

Veronica nods.

'Anything at all. We are trying to find her, you see, and—'

'Miss Gelder.' Mrs Garth has appeared at the door. Her hands are folded before her. Beyond is the library, a deep, muted space with the suggestion of a thousand books. 'I see you have met Miss Bushey.'

Martha nods.

There is the scrape of sole on stone as Veronica lifts her boot and stands on one leg. Mrs Garth addresses her. 'Was there something you needed from the garden, Miss Veronica?'

'No,' Veronica says in a small voice.

'I'll show you out, Miss Gelder. Your companions await.'

※

In the schoolroom, Josephine sits beside the window, looking out into the garden where Wright, the new gardener, is increasing the height of the fence. The lawn is covered with loose panels, and Wright balances at the brow of an old ladder with a mouthful of nails, hammering posts at intervals.

'Josephine, may I ask what is diverting your attention?'

says Mrs Holdsworth, who stands before the large map of the Empire covering the mirror on the wall.

'Why is the fence being made higher?' Josephine asks.

'The committee has requested it,' is the reply, as she knew it would be.

'But why? So that we can't climb over it?'

'I should hope none of you would try. Now, back to the Empire.'

'Why's there no bars on the windows?' says Josephine.

Mrs Holdsworth gives her a tiresome look. 'Why should there be? You are not prisoners in this house.'

Someone scoffs.

'There is nothing to stop any of you from leaving, as two of your number have so far demonstrated,' Mrs Holdsworth quips.

'Apart from the locked door,' says the bold and inquisitive Mary-Ann.

'And the garden gate,' chimes somebody else.

'Back to the matter in hand,' says Mrs Holdsworth.

'What I don't understand about the Empire,' says Mary-Ann, 'is how Britain just took these countries from whoever was in charge.'

Mrs Holdsworth sighs. 'The process of colonisation is a little more advanced than that.'

'Did they want Britain to rule over them, these conolies? Or whatever their name is.'

Mrs Holdsworth grasps for an answer. 'Not necessarily.'

'So that's like thieving, then, ain't it?' Mary-Ann asks, a genuine frown on her face.

'It isn't *thieving*, no. Colonisation has been around for centuries—'

'Sounds like thieving to me. We're put in prison for taking things that ain't ours. But the Queen's men or whoever are allowed to just sail up to places and say they're theirs, and it ain't a crime? Seems more of a crime to swipe a country than a stocking, to me.'

'There will be time for questions at the end of the lesson. Josephine, is there something other than the fence that fascinates you?' Mrs Holdsworth points her frustration like a musket and fires.

Josephine makes no reply, and Mrs Holdsworth sends her out with instructions to scrub the copper in the wash-house.

Glad to be away from everyone, Josephine puts on an apron, fills a pail and fetches the soft soap. She glances in at the dining-room window as she crosses the garden. Mrs Holdsworth is still standing, hands planted on the table, her head bowed towards an open book. Josephine approaches Wright and wishes him good morning.

'Good morning, miss,' he replies, suspicion in his voice.

'Would you like some tea?'

The gardener is a wrinkled, sinewy man who has the singular appearance of a root left to dry in the sun. He is ill at ease indoors and speaks to Mrs Holdsworth on the threshold of the back door. It is difficult to imagine him living in a house at all.

'I wouldn't say no to a cup, miss.'

'What are you doing today?'

With a grimace, he finishes driving in a nail. 'Extending the fence by a foot.'

'Why's that?' Josephine puts a hand to her brow to look up and down the fence, arranging her expression into one of bewilderment.

'Mrs H reckons she seen a prowler.'

Josephine widens her eyes. 'What sort of prowler?'

'A boy lurking about the place. I shouldn't worry yourself, though, miss. This'll keep out prying eyes. I'll take that tea, if it's going. I take it strong, miss. Brewed like tar.'

✻

'Weeping?' Angela repeats as they journey south, away from the town. Her features are pinched with concern. 'I wonder why.'

They have spent a fruitless afternoon making enquiries at the station house and various coaching inns, but of course nobody can recall a single young girl travelling alone nearly a year ago. Angela caused quite the stir at the station house, and the superintendent was eager to help. Addressing her as 'my lady', he took notes of the case and Emily's description and previous addresses, should she call in and announce herself, which they all knew she would not.

'Mrs Garth said she left early one morning and saw only another servant, the one she asked about the coach,' says Martha. 'So why would Veronica have heard her weeping?'

'And why London?' Angela looks out at the flat, iron sky. 'To come to you or Mary, perhaps?'

Martha shakes her head. 'She didn't know where I was, and she didn't go to Mary.'

Their group falls into a pensive silence, and then Angela says: 'I shall write to Mrs Bushey and enclose a note to her daughter. Of course her mother will read it, but I shall be purposefully opaque and say that she may write to me if she remembers anything.'

Martha is soon brought from her reverie as their fly approaches an enormous pair of gates. Angela waves in a stately way to the gatekeeper who appears at the door to a small stone lodge. He returns her greeting, and they sail up a long, straight drive. A sprawling group of stables and cottages are clustered before a low, honey-coloured main building, surrounded by lawns, and Martha's first thought is that the place is a hospital or asylum. She begins to grow nervous and looks to Angela for an explanation.

Angela merely says 'Surprise,' with a knowing smile. At once, Martha notices she is transformed, suffused with a sudden warmth that causes her creamy features to glow and her eyes to sparkle. They disembark in the centre of the carriage drive, and it is only then that Martha realises that the building is a house, possibly the largest she has ever seen, larger even than a palace. A host of liveried footmen appear to take their things, and a small, neat maid leads them through a splendid marble hall decorated with rich, dark portraits, then through a warren-like corridor to a modest set of stairs. Martha follows like a lost dog, taking in the delicious warmth, the gleaming, waxed furniture, the heady scent of polish all around. The maid leads them swiftly along the upstairs corridor, and Martha is astonished to find herself shown to her own room.

Within is luxury she has never known. She stands in the centre of the carpet, looking at the vast four-poster bed, the yawning fireplace, the soaring ceiling.

'I thought you would like the Rose Room,' says Angela, going to one of the two enormous windows and pointing out a wide terrace, bordered with empty rose trellises. 'It's a pity it isn't summer, when the garden is at its best.'

Martha joins her and sees lawns so smooth they might have been made with a rolling pin. Beyond, a glassy stretch of water glints like a mirror beneath the sun, studded here and there with drifting swans.

Angela tells her that they are to dine with the duke, who has no other guests; she seems pleased that they are to have him to themselves. As they descend into the house, she warns Martha of two things: that the duke is deaf in one ear, and that he should be addressed as 'your grace'. She has changed for dinner into periwinkle silk, and Martha brushes self-consciously at her own plain gown as they travel the length of the house to the elegant dining room, which would swallow the entirety of Urania Cottage. The idea of food makes Martha feel nauseous again; Angela and Mrs Brown shake out their napkins, accept wine, look utterly at home. Martha finds it strange that the duke, who has supposedly invited them, has not yet shown himself, and even stranger that some houses are so large that it is possible not to know where somebody is, or if they are home at all. A trio of footmen have seated them in a row, apparently in order of age, down one side of the table. Mrs Brown sits closest to the head, and to Martha's left is an endless expanse of damask, silver, candlelight. She has the sensation that if she looks directly at it, the room will slide on its axis and she will begin falling.

Just when she is beginning to think the duke is not home after all, the doors are thrown wide and an old man enters the room. He is not tall, but his upright posture gives him the illusion of height, and his slight, muscular figure is elegantly dressed. His skin is browned and weathered, his nose prominent. With his ramrod posture and air of authority, Martha supposes him a military man. He greets the three women with warmth. Angela and Mrs Brown offer their hands, and Martha gets awkwardly to her feet and finds herself attempting a curtsey. The man sits at the head of the table, at the only other place set for dinner, and it is only then that Martha realises that the elderly man *is* the duke.

'Miss Gelder is a friend from Middlesex,' says Angela, causing Martha to sit a little straighter. Angela helps herself to veal cutlets from a silver platter proffered by the footman. 'She is from Berkshire originally.'

'Where in Berkshire?' The duke speaks to nobody in particular, reaching for his wine glass.

Angela turns to Martha, her expression gently inviting, and Martha realises she is expected to reply. She tells him the name of her village, more quietly than she means to, with a scratch in the back of her throat, and Angela repeats it back to the duke, who looks directly at Martha for the first time. Martha finds herself reddening.

She sits silently through most of the conversation, none of which she comprehends, as a constant stream of wonderfully rich food appears at her shoulder. She copies Angela, who serves herself some things but not others, and tries not to be vulgar in her manners. She is thinking again about Veronica Bushey in her pinafore and ribbons, her narrow blue eyes peering as though through dirty glass.

'Martha?'

'Mmm?'

Angela's smile is bright. 'The duke has asked how you like Shepherd's Bush.'

'I like what I know of it, sir. I mean, your grace.'

'Good walking, I imagine.' This is a statement.

'I wouldn't know, sir,' says Martha.

'You cannot walk?'

Martha glances at Angela, whose smile is benign. 'I can walk, sir – your grace.'

'And what is it you do in Shepherd's Bush, if you don't go walking?'

There is a dreadful silence that stretches on and on. Martha looks helplessly to Angela, who for once throws her no rope. The tips of Angela's ears are pink, and she eats in her delicate way and has a sip of wine. Martha burns with shame, not knowing where to look, and eventually the duke returns to his meal. The effect is like a searchlight leaving her.

'I've a new bay filly,' he announces, stabbing a cutlet with relish. 'Cordova is the grandsire. You must see her before you go.'

Martha stares at the decadent food on her plate. The contents of her stomach sit like a stone inside her. Impossibly, more dishes arrive: never-ending plates of fried potatoes and French beans and sweetbreads, all things that ordinarily Martha would find delicious, but instead of eating them, she sits with her hands folded in her lap. A glazed brown wheel of meat is set down before her, and after examining it for some time, Martha realises with disgust that it is a swan, its skin glistening like treacle. Her stomach lurches, and she stands suddenly.

'I am sorry, but I'm not feeling well,' she says.

The others blink at her.

'Oh dear,' says Angela. 'Do you want to return to your—'

'Yes,' says Martha quickly.

With surprising agility, Mrs Brown rises and guides her from the table, past the glittering candlesticks and the shining plate and winking mirrors, past the duke, who is sitting motionless at the head of the table, his knife and fork in hand.

'I'm sorry,' she utters.

Angela has taken her other arm, and together the two women lead her along the tunnel-like corridor that spans the length of the house. In the bedroom, Angela rings for the servants, and maids appear with jugs and towels and hot water. Martha is too embarrassed to let them help her, thanking them effusively and closing the door to undress, peeling off her clothes that smell of straw from the coach and beer from the inn. She stands in her shift, shivering slightly, though a fire has been lit and the bed turned down. The luxury is too much to stomach, like a plateful of violet creams.

She looks about the room at the gilt and the thick, rich canopy. The dizzying ceiling, lifting high above her, causes her head to swim, and the image of the curled dead swan returns to her. She runs for the coal scuttle and arches over it, wiping her mouth afterwards and feeling utterly wretched.

There is a gentle knock. Martha pulls on her nightgown and admits Angela, who has been waiting outside the door, still resplendent in periwinkle. Her face is a portrait of concern. 'How do you feel now?' she asks.

'Much better,' Martha lies. 'I'm sorry.'

'No, I am. Here, get into bed, and I'll send for some hot water and brandy. I know Mrs Holdsworth is dead against spirits, but I'm allowing an exception. Mrs Brown will sit with you tonight.'

'Oh, that won't be necessary,' says Martha, obediently nestling beneath the eiderdown and feeling cold despite the fire. They are silent for a moment, then she shakes her head. 'I didn't know how to speak to the duke. I didn't know if he knows about . . . me.'

'He knows about the home, but he didn't know that I was

bringing you from it, and that's entirely my fault. I ought to have prepared him. I ought to have prepared you.'

'Is he very angry?'

'Of course not.' Angela sits on the bed, looking like such a kind, attentive nurse in the gentle firelight that Martha is overcome with exhaustion so acute her eyelids droop of their own accord.

'This ought to be more comfortable than last night's quarters.' Angela's voice is soft in the dim haze. 'Rest, and don't worry about a thing.'

'Will we leave tomorrow?' Martha asks.

'Yes.' There is a soft rustling as she gets to her feet.

'Miss?'

'What is it?'

Martha tells her about the coal scuttle, and turns on to her side as Angela removes it herself.

❧

Angela closes the door softly and walks towards the stairs. The first floor of the house is used solely for guests, and though theirs is a small party, there is a convivial, friendly feel to this wing, as if many more people are staying and might open their doors at any moment. Heated pipes run along the walls, which are decorated top to bottom with hunting pictures. The duke has always been very good at furnishing, at making all his houses feel like homes.

She finds him where she knew she would: in his private sitting room at the front of the house. He is smoking in his high-backed chair and looks up from his book when she lets herself in. Sitting on a small table at his elbow is the hoof of his favourite horse, hollowed out for his cigar ash, and a glass of brandy, glowing like liquid fire. Opposite him, as though made just for her, is the chair's twin, in which she has sat many times. Now, she lowers herself into it, pushes out her elbows, rearranges her feet beneath her skirts and says nothing.

'Brandy?' Engulfed in a low cloud of pipe smoke, the duke has returned to his book.

'No, thank you. I have rather a painful head.'

Ordinarily, she would be delighted with this domestic little scene on a harsh winter's night, but tonight, she is troubled. One thing that is sometimes unbearable to her is how little she is touched. There is nobody to stroke her hair when she is unwell or give her a kiss goodnight when she is first to retire. Nobody reaches for her when she gets up from the table, and her hand only ever feels the warmth of a mouth for a moment. She has spent years observing Dr and Mrs Brown in their intimacy: a rolled-up newspaper tapped fondly on the head, a pair of tired feet landing on a lap after a long day.

She examines her own nails in an attempt to quell the indignant feeling rising in her throat. It is one she is familiar with in the duke's company. Often she finds herself irritable, her patience worn thin, and knows it is borne of frustration. She sighs.

'My dear?' He turns the page without looking at her.

'Martha is very upset.'

'Who is Martha?'

She clenches her jaw.

Sensing displeasure, he rests the book face down on the chair arm and reaches for his glass. Finally, she has his full attention.

'Martha, my guest. Miss Gelder. She is quite unwell.'

'I'll send my doctor in the morning. He comes at nine for Mrs Cross.'

Angela feels obliged to ask after the housekeeper.

'The leeches seem to be doing the trick.'

Angela grimaces, remembering her most recent application, for her infected gum. After a short silence she says: 'I know you do not approve of my endeavour at Shepherd's Bush.'

The glass is set down again, somewhat wearily.

'I had hoped meeting Martha would allow you to see with your own eyes the young women we are helping. She is a bright girl, an industrious girl who in any other circumstance might be a governess. But it is circumstance that has set her and the others on an unfortunate path.'

'My dear,' he says, 'my thoughts on the enterprise are of no consequence.'

'How can you say that? You know I value your opinion most highly. You were the first person I consulted when it was suggested last year that–'

'And you chose to disregard my advice, which as a woman of business you are well within your right to do. The refuge is a noble enterprise – of that there is no doubt. But I do wonder what your design was, bringing her here.'

'We were in Reading on a family matter.'

'Whose family matter?'

'Martha's.'

The duke cannot prevent a small laugh from escaping, but it is not patronising, only fond. 'My dear, you will wear yourself out with all the care you take for other people. I do wish you would concern yourself less in the affairs of those who are not worthy of your affections, myself included.'

'Not worthy? How can you say such a thing? Arthur, the girls at the home have nobody. Most of them have no parents. Their friends have abandoned them or led them to vice. Some of them don't even know their own birthdays or where they were born.'

'Well, I am very sorry for them.'

'No, you are not,' she says bitterly.

'I am. I should hate to not get birthday presents.'

She smiles despite herself and shakes her head. The fire pops and crackles, and the atmosphere lifts. 'Perhaps I will have some brandy.'

Obligingly, he moves to fetch a glass from the cabinet, but she gets up herself so that she does not have to see him struggle. Beside the cabinet is a secret panelled door, papered to look like a wall, which leads to the duke's bedroom. He showed her the first time she was a guest here, and she was so taken aback that she flushed crimson, like a girl half her age.

She allows him to pour from his chair and settles again more comfortably.

'Another sigh,' he remarks. 'I'm beginning to think you find my company tedious.'

'No more than usual,' she teases. 'We will leave in the morning.'

'I rather hoped you'd stay.'

She is hit with a pang of longing so acute that she is forced to look at her hands. She allows herself to imagine them turning down the lamps and going through the secret door together, closing themselves inside and not coming out until the morning. When she is recovered, she says: 'No. I think Martha is made uncomfortable by it all.'

'Heavens. Does it fall below her standards?'

'Do not be cruel.'

When they flirt like this, it is a physical ache not to go to him and sit on his lap. If they were married, she would do so, and take the cigar from his lips and put it to her own. He would scold her for smoking, and she would move her lips towards his and blow the smoke gently towards his mouth. The image is so clear and strong to her that she feels as though she has woken from it.

And so the rest of the evening passes, with her loving him from her high-backed chair.

❧

Martha is lifted suddenly from a shallow, troubled sleep and placed in a strange bed, beneath heavy warm covers. All around her is deep, utter blackness, and she tries not to panic as she fails to remember where she is.

And then the noise that must have woken her comes again: the light creak of old floorboard beneath thick carpet. She was having a strange dream, in which she and Mrs Brown were walking through a park, and people were coming in and out of the bushes, opening and closing the branches like doors.

At once it comes to her: she is at the duke's house, in the Rose Room. She lies very still, her heart thumping in the impenetrable night, wishing she had a light and remembering also that Angela drew the heavy curtains that enclose her bed, to keep in the warmth. All around is silence now, and she turns over.

But though she means to sleep, some animal part of her is alert, is listening, and after a full minute of remaining absolutely still, the realisation dawns on her that she is not alone in the great pink room. The silence is deafening, and then, so softly, like a bird rearranging its wings: a rustle.

Martha does not know how long she lies there for, waiting. Her mind is absolutely clean of thought, and a high, single note of fear rings in her ears like a whistling kettle, drowning out everything. She swallows, and thinks of calling out, but to whom? And what would she say? *Who's there?* seems too childish, and it might only be a servant replenishing something or seeing to what remains of the fire, or . . .

A breeze softly kisses her right cheek, and all the hairs on her body stand on end as a chink of light appears at the end of the bed. Somebody has parted the curtains and is passing a candle through.

She sits up, blinking, blinded by the sudden flame, and says: 'Miss?'

All she can see is white fire, and black depths all around, and her throat is thick with fear as there is no reply. As her eyes adjust and she begins to make out a hand wrapped around the candle, the light is drawn away, and there is another breath of cold air and a soft sigh of fabric as the curtains are drawn again. Once again, she is plunged into blackness.

Too frightened to move or speak, her stomach swooping and diving, Martha lies frozen beneath the covers. There is another soft creak, and then, very quietly, the sound of the door opening and closing. Just as she knew when she was not alone, she is certain now that she is. The blood pounding in her ears quietens, and her pulse slows.

She knows she will not sleep now. She lies still for a long time, and then, when she feels able to move, crawls to the end of the bed to push apart the curtains. Stumbling across the vast carpet to where she vaguely recalls the window being, she finds the folds of the curtains and pulls, before fumbling blindly at the shutters.

Outside, the moon is so bright she almost weeps with relief. It hangs in the blue-black sky, looking at itself in the clean knife of the river. Martha breathes in deeply and realises she is trembling. She curses herself; she has experienced worse than this. She has known real terror, genuine danger: a thick hand around her throat on a rainy night, a knife held out to her as she foolishly counts her coins beneath a street light. This was merely the suggestion of threat. Nothing happened, and she knows she will tell nobody, because what is there to tell?

Her cloak was taken from her on arrival, and so, to quieten her mind, she makes a fire. Once it has got going, she drags the great eiderdown from the bed, puts it around her shoulders and sits in the chair by the warmth and the light, where she waits for morning.

CHAPTER 7

The Garden Gate

Chickens arrive at Urania Cottage in a crate on the back of a cart. The girls are overjoyed, and Frank builds a hutch and coop for them on his morning off. There is a squabble over what to name them. One girl wishes to name them after flowers. Josephine thinks it absurd to christen things they will kill, and Mrs Holdsworth suggests they draw suggestions from a hat. In the end, they go with Mrs Holdsworth's idea, and the chickens, despite all being hens, are christened Frank, Rover, Christabel and Victoria. Josephine watches them settle, picking over the grass and clucking gently, unsure of their new home and one another, before the cold gets the better of them and they bunch up together in the straw.

In the morning, she goes out to collect the eggs, gathering them in her apron and sitting down on the wet ground. The eggs make a pleasant knocking sound, like billiard balls. The birds have already razed most of the grass, but it has not rained for a week, and the earth is dry and hard. The hens step cautiously around the garden. If Josephine were less preoccupied, she might have laughed to herself at their feathery pantaloons, the way they cock their heads like old women.

Glancing up at the windows, she draws from her pocket a single sugar mouse, wrapped in paper. Her heart quickens, thudding excitedly in her chest, and she does not notice the rain when it comes. It falls lightly at first, as though giving her the opportunity to go inside, and then harder. She only realises she is wet when the mouse's white coat, which has dulled slightly, begins to dissolve, and she hastily returns it to her pocket. She puts down fresh straw and gathers the birds impatiently from the garden, cursing and herding them with her feet before shutting them away. They preen themselves and begin pecking at the potato peelings she has strewn on the ground.

Josephine is about to enter the house when the door opens and two people step outside: Mrs Holdsworth, and one of the most striking girls Josephine has ever seen. Josephine stands aside, and they pass her, going to the wash-house. The girl glances at Josephine and smiles with her lips parted, showing her teeth. Her dark brows are like two question marks. Her eyes are liquid jet, her black hair escaping from the coil behind her neck. Her arms are plump, her waist tight beneath her bodice. Her creamy bosom spills like foam.

'Got caught, did you?' she asks Josephine, who can only stare.

'What?'

'In the rain.'

Josephine says nothing.

'Josephine, get inside before you catch a chill.' Mrs Holdsworth appears over the girl's shoulder, oblivious to her beauty, her soft skin, the red fruit of her mouth.

Josephine's heart kicks up again, and she has a sudden, fleeting image of laying the girl down on the cold stone floor of the wash-house, of peeling back the layers of her skirt like a present.

Mrs Holdsworth's voice rings from inside over the patter of rain. 'Copper. Mangle. The drying racks come down like this. Blue, starch, soap, lye, soda, all in here. Monday is washing day; there'll be two of you in here at a time. Soaking begins on Sunday afternoon. You'll find your laundry bag at the foot of your bed, and they go in these two baskets here for sorting.' There is a pause. 'Frances, are you listening?'

Frances peers into the aqueous gloom. 'Yeah, course. I done laundry before.' She turns back to Josephine, who has not moved, grins wickedly and says: 'You're getting wet.'

'Josephine! What are you doing still standing there? Aren't you on bread duty today? Will you go and see that the dough has risen? Or we'll have none for supper.'

'Yes, Mrs Holdsworth,' says Josephine.

She turns and goes inside, sailing straight through the kitchen, forgetting to check the dough, and feeling as though she has woken from a long and dreamless sleep.

To everybody's surprise, Martha arrives home a little after four, silent and sick-looking with dark smudges beneath her eyes. Angela speaks with Mrs Holdsworth in the parlour before continuing on to London, and Martha is sent to bed with some hot cordial and dry toast. Josephine cannot wait to get her friend alone, and when she has finished her list of chores, she goes to the bedroom, pulls a chair beside her bed and takes out an apron on the pretence of mending it.

'Well, then,' she says to Martha, who is sitting propped against her pillows. 'What did you find out?'

Martha's gaze, fixed on the bedclothes, causes her heart to sink. 'Nothing.'

'Nothing at all?'

'She went to London. That's all they know.'

'I don't believe that,' Josephine says, rage rising to the surface. 'Someone must know something.'

Martha shrugs.

Dismayed, Josephine sits back in her chair.

'What I don't understand,' says Martha, 'is why she didn't go to Mary.'

'It don't make sense,' says Josephine.

In the quiet that follows, she finds herself listening out for Frances, and when she looks back at Martha, her friend is wearing a strange expression.

'What news is here?' Martha asks.

Josephine sits a little straighter. 'Nothing.'

They both jump as the bedroom door flies open. Frances stands in the doorway, her arms piled with towels. 'Oh,' she says. 'I thought this was the cupboard.'

Josephine takes up her needle and begins picking at the apron.

After a moment, Martha says: 'The press is just outside. Towels are on the left.'

'Silly me.' Frances smiles and lingers. 'You feeling better? Mrs Holdsworth said you was taken ill.'

'Much better, thank you. How are you settling in?'

'Well enough. Everyone seems nice.' There is a pause.

'Which room are you in?' asks Martha.

'The front one, with Mary-Ann and Lucinda. I'd have gone for this one, if all the beds weren't took. It has the best view.'

Martha smiles.

'Can I bring you anything?' asks Frances. 'Some tea? I can't believe all this house has. And it's all for us.'

'I know,' says Martha. 'You're very kind, thank you, but no.'

'All right. I'm to do the bath-water now.'

'Oh,' says Martha. 'I forgot it was Saturday.'

Josephine meddles with the apron. 'Did Mr Dickens come today?'

'This morning. He spent an hour with Harriet and then left.'

'What's the matter?' Martha asks, frowning and smiling at her.

'Nothing.'

'Why were you like that?'

'Like what?'

'Unfriendly, just now with Frances.'

'I wasn't.'

Martha pulls a face and puts her head back on the pillow with a sigh. 'I'd forgotten how strange it was to come here and have everything you dreamt of when . . . well, when you didn't have it. Do you know, I feel as though I'm used to it now, but perhaps that's a dangerous thing.'

'What's dangerous?'

Martha closes her eyes. 'Having all this given to us. It's only temporary, after all. Who knows what we will go on to?'

She opens her eyes, looking directly at Josephine, who looks quickly away.

'I haven't really thought about it,' she says, tracing the outline of a rose on the wallpaper.

'You don't wonder what might have happened if you hadn't come here?'

Josephine stares at the wall. 'All the time.'

❧

Josephine is fourth to bathe that night, and the water has all the warmth of tea left too long in the pot. She soaps her knees and shoulders, lost in thought. The kitchen floor is sluiced, the shelves tidy, the range warm and quiet. The others are in the parlour playing the guitar. They have begun having music lessons once a week, and Josephine finds the distant strumming diverting. It reminds her of going to buy beer from the public houses with her father, the golden windows and rain-soaked streets, music and laughter spilling from the doorways, warming her inside. She would think of that happy noise when they were back home later in her cold, damp bed.

A knock wakes her; she often falls asleep in the bath. She stands and dries herself, pulls on her nightdress, tops up the water from the kettle on the range. Polly is standing with her towel behind the kitchen door. Josephine often wishes she had a kind word to say to her, or any word at all, but all efforts melt like gelatin on her tongue. She tries to smile, and Polly returns it and enters the kitchen.

Josephine takes her candle to bed. Martha is already asleep, breathing slowly, one hand tucked beneath her pillow. It is a little after nine. Josephine lies by the light of her candle, staring at the ceiling. Before long, Polly comes to bed, blows out her own candle and is soon asleep.

After a while, restless and impatient, Josephine pushes back her blanket and goes downstairs for a cup of water. From the parlour comes the gentle murmur of voices of those still awake. She treads barefoot over the cold, tiled hall to the kitchen, opening the door without knocking and hearing at the same time a gentle splash of water.

Frances is sitting in the bath, facing the door. A single candle burns on the kitchen table, throwing her wet skin into light and shadow. Josephine sees bare arms squeezing a thick rope of hair, pillowy breasts, a soft white stomach.

'Shit.' Hot wax from Josephine's candle spills onto her hand. 'Sorry. I didn't know you was in here.'

Frances smiles and continues to wring water from her hair, and as Josephine turns to leave, she says: 'Don't go. Sit with me, will you?'

Josephine's eyes slide around the kitchen. Frances lifts from the floor a tin mug and takes a sip. 'Tea?' she says, offering it to Josephine.

'No, thanks.'

She raises her dark eyebrows and offers the cup again.

Josephine takes it and sniffs, then looks at Frances in shock.

'My old man's a smuggler,' Frances says. 'He taught me a few tricks.'

She swigs, feeling the hot, sweet fire coat her mouth and heat her throat.

'I made certain Holdsworth was in bed,' Frances says, grinning. 'Where'd you come from anyway?'

'London,' says Josephine as her stomach burns.

'I hate London,' says Frances. 'I'm from Folkestone. I miss the sea. The smell of it. It makes you feel clean inside.'

'I never saw the sea.' Josephine glances at Frances and

notices a cluster of red veins, like a spider's web, blooming at her collarbone.

'How long you been here, then?'

'Dunno. Not long.' She has not counted how many weeks it has been. She has no wish to know.

'What do you make of the others?'

Josephine lifts a shoulder. 'They aren't bad, I suppose.'

Frances lowers her chin and says in a low, confidential voice: 'You know we have a murderer among us?'

Josephine feels the fine hairs on her arms stand up. 'What?'

Frances grins.

'You're lying,' says Josephine.

'Don't believe me, then.'

'Who is it?'

Frances winks. 'You know we ain't allowed to tell.'

She drains the mug and stands in a great fluid motion. Water cascades over the tub and drenches the floor. She makes no effort to conceal herself, and before Josephine can look away, she has already seen her white thighs and the dark streak of fur between them. Frances meets her eye, and a string of tension, of challenge, of something Josephine cannot define stretches between them, taut and unyielding. Josephine feels the familiar tug, accepts the invitation, allows her eyes to slide downwards.

Voices float towards them down the hall. Josephine throws Frances a towel, and the thread is broken as two of their housemates enter the kitchen to put away their cocoa mugs. Josephine stays a while, listening as the three of them talk, not joining in. Frances downs the rest of the rum, rinses the mug, winks at Josephine. She stands against the counter, feeling the rum burn a hole in her stomach, one hand buried deep inside her pocket, clutching the sugar mouse so hard it almost snaps.

⚘

A few nights later Martha wakes, swimming up from the darkness, opening her eyes to silvery strips of moonlight. She is sweating, her throat dry, but her heart slows at the familiar surroundings. Every night since she has returned, she has dreamt of the duke's house, the intense, black dark, the candle. She listens for the other two breathing, hears Polly shifting in her sleep. Her eyes adjust, lingering on Josephine's bed, which is strangely flat. The frame squeaks beneath her as she sits up, peering hard, and sees that it is empty.

Frowning, she climbs from beneath the covers, ignoring the chill that greets her, and pats the mattress to be sure. It is smooth, and only slightly warm. She gets back into bed and waits for a minute, two, three, listening, thinking Josephine will come back from the kitchen at any moment, but there is no gentle creaking of floorboards, no wheeze of the stair, three from the top, that always protests when it is stepped on.

More time passes. Martha takes the blanket from her own bed and pads hesitantly out to the landing, looking up and down for a chink of light and finding none. The house is utterly silent. She wraps her blanket like a shawl around her and goes down with bare feet, taking care to avoid the troublesome stair, noticing how moonlight floods the hall through the fan-light, making silver fairy-pools on the tiles. The parlour and schoolroom are dark and empty, and there is nobody in the kitchen. The range purrs like a sleeping cat, its orange belly aglow. She checks the cellar door: locked. The

149

pantry and scullery, too, are empty. A note of dread begins to play in her heart.

She moves back into the kitchen and goes to the garden door, trying the handle and finding it unlocked. Martha hesitates a moment, then she steps outside, the soles of her feet pressing into the cold, wet grass as she takes a few tentative steps away from the house and turns to look back at it. The windows are all dark. She wonders what time it is. She forgot to look at the long-case clock in the hall, which meekly chimes the quarter hours.

The garden is eerie, ethereal, like a garden in a dream. Apple and plum trees stand expectantly in the orchard, and the dark privy squats beside the shed. Martha waits, shivering. Her eyes rake over the outermost shadows, searching the deepest black pockets where the ground meets the fence, which seems higher than when she went away, and snag on the gate. The gate is bolted and locked with a padlock, partially covered with shrubbery. But tonight there is something else there, too; Martha walks closer and sees a brown shape hanging over it. Thinking for a moment that it is a dead animal, she stalls and begins to retreat. But looking more closely, she forces herself to approach it, reaching a hand through the brambles and feeling coarse wool. It is a coat.

She looks down: a pail has been placed beneath the gate for a step. Frightened now, she glances back towards the house and wonders if somebody has come in or if Josephine has gone out. She thinks again of the Rose Room, the parting of the bed-curtains, the terrible flame.

She puts her right foot on the pail, and the height allows her to reach the top of the gate and look over. There is a small, indistinct noise, or a series of them, like a scythe cutting through grass, coming from the left-hand side of the gate. On the other side of the fence is a wall, too low to give the garden privacy – the fence was built within its boundary – and it is then that she sees a figure further down the path, ghostly pale, shifting its shape like a supernatural being.

Two bodies move together as one: Josephine and the dusty-faced boy from the brickfields, who has her pinned to the wall, like a butterfly. Her arms reach out like wings, his hand locked around her wrists as he grunts and pants with effort. She is in her nightdress, he in his shirtsleeves, a dark cap pulled low over his brow.

A snap. Martha has misjudged her footing and grasps a handful of bramble to steady herself, falling against the gate. The figures freeze and two white faces turn towards her.

'Who's there?' Josephine hisses.

Martha hops down and begins to hurry back across the grass, ignoring the urgent scrabbling behind her, the *thunk* of the gate as Josephine mounts it like a horse and swings herself over. Josephine is faster and stronger than Martha. In a few strides she has caught her and grasps her right arm, wrenching her round and holding her still beneath the white moon.

'Martha,' she says, her voice flooded with relief. She is panting, gasping, and pulls a strand of dark hair from her mouth.

Martha has seen many things, but now her mind is blank with shock. She begins walking again to the house, and this time Josephine lets her go, following closely.

'You silly goose, what you spying for?' she teases as they cross the lawn.

Martha stops again. 'I didn't know,' she says. 'I wouldn't have come if you'd told me.' She does not understand why she feels hurt.

'It's not what you think.'

'Oh, Josephine, don't take me for a fool.'

'No, it's not that—'

Martha waits.

'He's doing something for me.'

She peers at her friend. 'What?'

'He's – there's someone on the outside.'

Martha stares at her.

'He's been sending messages. Between me and a friend.'

'I don't understand,' says Martha. 'Who?'

Josephine brings a sugar mouse out of her pocket and glances above Martha's head. 'Shit,' she says, and Martha turns to see a light in one of the upstairs windows.

Martha pulls the blanket from her own shoulders and puts it around Josephine's. 'Say you were sleepwalking,' she says.

Josephine nods.

Together they go into the dark kitchen, and Martha closes the door quietly.

'The hairpin,' Josephine says suddenly.

'What hairpin?'

'I used it to open the back door.'

'Where is it?'

'I don't know.'

'You can't have been sleepwalking if you unlocked the back door without a key.'

'My thoughts exactly.' Mrs Holdsworth appears on the kitchen step with a candle. Behind the flame, her face is ghoulish, her eyes hard, assessing the pair of them in their nightdresses. 'And you also had the foresight to put on shoes, I see.'

She steps down into the kitchen. 'I'm tired and must rise in a few hours, so let's get this over with. Where were you and what were you doing?' When neither of them speak, she sighs and sends her forehead skywards, exposing her white throat. 'I should have known this wouldn't be straightforward. But, Martha, you are the last person I expected this from.'

Martha feels Josephine bristle beside her.

'We none of us can go to bed until the door is locked, so pray tell me, where is the key?'

Silence. And then, quietly, Josephine says: 'I didn't use the key.'

Mrs Holdsworth looks unhappily at her. 'I am very disappointed in the two of you. Go upstairs at once. I shall deal with this in the morning.'

As they climb the stairs, the long-case clock dutifully chimes the quarter-hour. Martha forgets again to look, and will wonder, in the coming months, in idle moments, what time it was.

❧

At daybreak Martha cleans the soles of her feet in the wash-basin, and by morning prayers everybody knows what has happened. They dart quick, furtive little glances at Martha and Josephine as Mrs Holdsworth makes her call to arms, rattling off a series of urgent letters to be proffered on silver trays in breakfast rooms across London.

Breakfast at the cottage is strained, punctuated by whispers and splutters of barely suppressed laughter above the bread rolls and marmalade. Martha grows more and more introspective, too nervous to eat, her tea untouched. At last, Josephine demands an audience with Mrs Holdsworth, and because the downstairs rooms are being cleaned before the committee arrive, they go to Josephine's bedroom.

'Martha had nothing to do with it,' she says as soon as the door is closed. 'Don't put her in front of them.'

'I'll thank you not to instruct me on what I ought and ought not to do,' Mrs Holdsworth retorts, looking tired and pale. 'Honesty goes a long way in this house. If you'd told me where you were and what you were doing, as I asked, we might have dealt with the matter quietly and efficiently and been done with it.'

'And not told the committee?'

'Of course they would have to be told. But it could have been resolved and minimised.'

Josephine boils with rage and regret. 'I asked somebody to send a message. Somebody from the outside.'

Mrs Holdsworth's eyes grow large. 'Who?'

'A boy I met in the lane.'

'Which boy?'

'His name's Vincent. He works on the brickfields. I asked him to give a message to a friend in London, and he came back with a reply. That's what I was doing outside. Martha saw me out of bed and came looking for me. She knew nothing about it. That's God's honest truth.'

Mrs Holdsworth glares at her, her nostrils flaring. 'Oh Josephine, why must you insist on making things difficult for yourself? Why on earth would you not send a word the usual way? Or is this acquaintance not merely a friend at all?'

'I didn't know what to put in a letter, and I couldn't have written one anyway!' Josephine knows how rude she is being but is unable to stop, unable to calm herself.

'One of the other girls could have helped you. *I* could have helped you, if you'd asked. But I can only assume there was something you wished to say that you didn't want anybody else to know about. Where is he now, this boy?'

'I don't know. I don't know where he goes.'

'The location of this house is so to prevent association with people of dubious character, who might tempt you to your old tricks. And yet, you have managed to find such an acquaintance and conduct immoral business without my knowledge. I thought you wanted to change – I thought you were beginning to change – but I realise now I was woefully naive.'

Josephine shakes her head bitterly. 'You didn't know me before. You don't know me now. You know nothing!'

She had gone too far. The women fume in silent rage at one another, and a moment later, when the door-knocker rouses them from their quarrel like a magistrate's gavel, Josephine has made up her mind.

Mr Bryant arrives at the cottage at his usual time of ten o'clock, looking rather unkempt, as though he has spent an uneasy night. Mrs Holdsworth bears down on him in the passageway, with Josephine close behind.

'Mr Bryant, thank goodness,' says the matron as the chaplain divests himself of his coat. 'I put a message in the first post in the event you hadn't left yet, but here you are, prompt as usual, so never mind that. I ought to have saved the penny stamp.'

'Mrs Holdsworth, is something the matter?'

'I've summoned Mr Dickens and Miss Coutts and the rest of the committee, not that many of them will be at liberty to come at such short notice. I wonder if you could stay for the meeting? I've asked them to come at once.'

He blinks in surprise. 'Mrs Holdsworth, I am not a committee member. Mr Illingworth represents the church at the monthly board meetings.'

Mrs Holdsworth tuts. 'Right you are, Mr Bryant. I quite forgot.'

He glances at Josephine. 'Has something serious happened?'

'You would think so,' she replies drily.

'Mr Bryant, if you wouldn't mind stepping with me into the schoolroom a moment, we might talk in private.'

'Be direct in my company, Mrs Holdsworth, I beg of you,' Josephine says hotly. 'Mine and Martha's, since it concerns only us.'

Without turning, she knows that Martha watches from the top of the stairs.

'Not another desertion?' Mr Bryant slips through to the parlour and looks about, as though attempting to scent who is missing.

'In a manner of speaking,' says Mrs Holdsworth.

'I heard concerns of a prowler,' says the chaplain, spreading the blinds to peer through the window. 'Hark: who is that?'

Mrs Holdsworth and Josephine crowd him to see Vincent standing at the gate, glancing up and down the road, as though considering entering the front garden.

'Who is that indeed!' cries Mrs Holdsworth. 'Josephine, could you enlighten us? Is this your brick boy?'

'I never seen him before,' she lies, feeling colour spread up her neck.

'The prowler in question,' the chaplain declares. 'I shall see about that.' He flies with surprising agility from the room, and Mrs Holdsworth and Josephine watch from the parlour window as the chaplain hurries down the path, wrestling his hat on to his head. Vincent looks agape at the furious figure and runs away, vanishing from sight. The gate squeals in protest as Mr Bryant unfastens it and sets off in pursuit. In the house, unable to stop herself, Josephine bursts into nervous laughter.

'Will you control yourself?' Mrs Holdsworth is outraged. 'You have no right to find any of this amusing, not with what's coming your way. It will be a miracle if you keep your place here.'

Josephine covers her mouth and tries to stop her shoulders from shaking.

'If I were you,' Mrs Holdsworth goes on, 'I would be very grave indeed. You ought to be demonstrating to me and the rest of this house that you deserve to stay here, not cackling like a lunatic. The committee will be here soon and a reckoning is upon you. Do you know how shocked and disappointed they will be?'

'I shan't stand for this,' Josephine says lightly, half in disbelief, the remainder of a smile still on her face. 'I can't bear it. I shan't stand for it.'

'Josephine?' says Martha, who has appeared in the parlour looking afraid.

'I feel as though I'm being picked apart with needles. Just leave me alone!'

She lurches from the room past Martha and almost collides with one of the girls coming from the cellar bearing a bunch of keys. In a surge of righteousness she snatches the keys from Lucinda's grip and shakes them at the matron.

'See? This place is a prison. It's no better, though everybody pretends like it is. At least there you know what you're about. Here, you pretend it's a house, that we're a family. Yet we're locked indoors, not allowed to write no letters without them being read. We ain't even allowed to make our own beds.'

'Jo.' Martha has come to her and put a hand on her arm.

'Do what you will with me,' Josephine goes on. 'But Martha will come to no harm. She ain't done nothing.'

More faces appear in doorways and through stair railings. As if she is not in her own body but is observing herself from some unknown realm, Josephine watches herself dash the keys to the stone floor, where they crash like glass exploding, and hears herself saying: 'I wish to go.'

There is a deep, astonished silence. Mrs Holdsworth is standing close by her now, and Josephine feels her small exhalation of surprise.

'Now, Josephine,' she says.

'No. I've made up my mind to go.'

'My dear, do not act in haste. There is more for you here than lies out there.'

But Josephine is not listening. She feels giddy, light-headed, just as she did the night she was arrested; there is the sense of things moving very quickly around her, though she is standing still. Frank Holdsworth appears at one end of the hall in his shirtsleeves, holding the little Dutch clock from the schoolroom, whose hands have fallen behind the rest of the house. At that moment the door-knocker bangs through the house: the committee is arriving, but nobody moves.

'I know the rules,' Josephine says, feeling heat creep up her neck. 'Lock me upstairs for a day and I shan't change my mind. I'll tell you the same thing tomorrow. I won't be moved on it.'

'Josephine, you don't mean this,' Martha says quietly. Josephine cannot bear to look at her. 'Come and sit, and we can talk to Mr Dickens and Miss Coutts, and they will–'

'Tell me all about sin, temptation, shame . . . I know it

already. I mean what I say. I'll go in the morning. And Martha
. . . Martha will stay.'

⚜

The committee meeting is pointless. Josephine only repeats
herself and is forced to hear how all that awaits her in the
outside world is destitution. Mr Dickens is bitterly disappointed
in her, and makes it known. She thanks him anyway.

Angela is not here; nobody tells her why, and she does not
ask, but feels deep sorrow at the knowledge she will never see
her again. She has never in her life known anybody like Angela,
with her carriage, her white hands fastened with jewels, her
soft, fine way of speaking. Of course, she will never be
acquainted with anybody like her again. She supposes she is
glad that she does not have to look her in the eye, because she
knows Angela will see through the layers of pride and vanity,
straight to her soul and the ruin within. Angela will know she
is unworthy of grace, beyond redemption. Angela will see that
she has fallen beyond reach.

She pushes everything from her mind and tells the committee
that somebody who wants this more than she does deserves
her place in the house, that somebody else might be saved.

Mr Bryant's pursuit of the prowler has caused great excite-
ment among the girls, who have already decided that the
blemished brick-boy has acquired the mystique of a hero in
a romance; they have not made the connection between him
and Josephine's excursion, though Mrs Holdsworth saw it at
once. The chaplain sends a note that afternoon: he chased
the youth almost to Hammersmith before falling down in the
lane, tearing his coat and twisting his ankle. A kindly cab driver

accompanied him to the omnibus, and he has been seen by a doctor, who kindly posted the letter for him. He will come to the cottage the next morning, if he is able to do so. Josephine is relieved he won't be back to force-feed her salvation tonight.

In their room, Martha sits at Josephine's feet, holding her skirts as though tethering her to the ground, the house, herself. 'How will I go to Australia without you?' she begs, her eyes large and frightened, her lashes dark with tears.

Josephine feels part of her soul splinter and fall away.

She sleeps a final night in her own room, to prove she is certain, shutting out Martha's remonstrations and ignoring Polly, who casts glances of pity and compassion at her, which puts Josephine in a rage. And in the morning, when Mrs Holdsworth asks if she has changed her mind, she cannot look at any of them when she tells them no.

All she has to take with her is the dress and shawl she had at Tothill Fields, and Mrs Holdsworth fetches them for her from one of the locked presses so that she may change. She pushes her head into the neck of the dress, which has been laundered and ironed, as if worthy of sitting among the fine merinos and cottons that fill the shelves and cupboards here. The act of giving back the raspberry poplin and putting on her old dress causes a wave of grief and uncertainty to crash over her, and she is forced to stand a moment at the window, looking at the flat winter garden until she feels level again.

'Are you *quite* sure?' Mrs Holdsworth asks her a final time, hovering at the bedroom door.

Josephine only replies that she was not able to finish refilling the coal the previous day. Then she holds the matron's gaze, which is full of disappointment and regret, and guilt, too, perhaps at involving the committee, at the knowledge that if it was dealt with between the three of them, it might not have ended like this.

But Josephine refuses to acknowledge this, feels only the prickle of her own stubbornness. She is nothing if not a woman of her word.

She looks about for her gloves, remembers she has none of her own, and makes her way downstairs a final time, feeling the cool stair rail beneath her hand, and purposefully standing on the old part of the third stair to hear it creak.

Martha is waiting for her at the bottom. 'Josephine, please don't go,' she says for the hundredth time. She is crying quietly. Briefly, chastely, Josephine puts her lips to Martha's wet cheek, feeling her own eyes blur in response, and hardening herself.

She does not think about Martha's missing sister or how she, too, is vanishing on Martha now. She does not think about the afternoon they made roly-poly pudding and licked jam from their fingers. She does not think about the evening Polly played the piano, astonishing them all with her skill, and how the beautiful music made Josephine feel tranquil inside. She does not think about the words she has learnt, the handwriting that has taken shape like a boat on the horizon, growing clearer day by day. The merry fires, keeping winter from the house; the robins and sparrows flitting in and out of the hedgerows; the first sponge cake she made. Her first happy Christmas, when Martha curled her hair. The chickens in their coop. Her warm bed, all hers. And in the night, the gentle, reassuring sounds of Polly and Martha breathing.

She thinks of none of this as the girls mewl like kittens on the stairs, sniffing and wiping at their faces. Frances is the only one not weeping; she has a sort of hollow look about her, but Josephine will not meet her eye.

161

Mrs Holdsworth unlocks the street door slowly, looking very grave indeed; the lines around her mouth are more pronounced than ever, and her brown eyes are as sad as a dog's.

It is time for her to go. She pauses on the doorstep, pretending to adjust her shawl. There is no warmth to it. The morning is cold, but spring will not be long. She has known many winters away from the parlour in Urania Cottage. She half-turns, meaning to speak, to say a final word, to wish them well or thank them, to tell them not to worry about her, but finds there is nothing that will not catch in her throat.

And so she walks down the path without saying goodbye, opening the gate with its familiar squeak and hearing it clatter shut behind her, and then she is in the road, turning left, away from the house.

CHAPTER 8

Van Diemen's Land

'You're too late.'

Angela feels her face fall, and Mrs Holdsworth turns away from her, retreating into the cool darkness of the hall and going upstairs. Angela stands dumbly on the doorstep in a state of shock. Nobody invites her in; there is nobody to invite her in, for all signs of life are absent. No music plays from the parlour, and there are no bursts of laughter issuing from the kitchen at the end of the passageway.

She has come alone, without Mrs Brown or even Ballard. Her driver waits in the lane. Barely an hour before, at home, she had not unwrapped her mantle when Stockton bore down on her with a silver platter and two urgent notes: one from Mrs Holdsworth, the other from her friend Charles, both relating to Josephine and the events of the last two days. She had stayed a night with a friend in Finchley, and as her cases were being unloaded in the hall she swiftly read both letters and called back the carriage.

Now, in the stark, cold silence of Urania Cottage, it is as though there has been a death. Where has Mrs Holdsworth gone? If the situation wasn't so dire, she would feel offence at being left like a delivery boy on the doorstep. With a growing sense of dread, she goes through to the kitchen and finds Martha sitting alone at the table. Her sleeves are pushed up, her arms folded. She sits quietly, staring into the middle distance, and stirs when Angela appears but says nothing. Angela has the sudden overpowering urge to embrace her but fears doing so would cross a line, and so she stands, with one gloved hand on the door-frame.

'How long ago?' she asks.

'An hour, perhaps,' Martha replies dully.

'There might still be time to find her. I have my carriage.'

Martha's lack of interest causes her to feel embarrassed by the suggestion.

'I am so very sorry, Martha,' she ventures. 'I came as soon as I heard. What happened? Why did she go?'

'It was my fault,' Martha replies.

'Come now, I'm sure that isn't true.'

'Are you calling me a liar?'

Angela feels herself blanche. 'Of course not, Martha. I only meant to say that any hand you believe to have had in Josephine's departure is likely to be grossly overestimated.'

Martha says nothing.

'Did . . .' Angela goes on, treading delicately. 'Were efforts made to prevent her?'

'I shouldn't think so.'

'I should hope that every effort was made to persuade her against leaving.'

'I wasn't privy to their talk.'

Angela frowns a little. This prickly, unresponsive creature is not the Martha she knows. The loss frightens her, and she takes another step into the room.

'You were very dear to Josephine. I know how dear you were to each other.'

'She hasn't died.'

Angela opens her mouth and closes it. Any condolence will be met with fire or ice, and she gropes about for some comfort to give, but all that comes to mind sounds saccharine and unworthy of the young woman sitting before her, solid and real and heartbroken.

'If there is anything at all I can do to help, please do not—'

'Like what?' Martha fixes her with her yard-long stare, and the effect of it is piercing. 'What can you do, other than drag her back here? She does not want to be here. She left of her own accord. And now her bed will be filled with somebody else, her dress altered and worn by another girl. And somehow I'm meant to stay here, for who knows how many more weeks and months, and then go to Australia. And all because I went out of the house looking for her, instead of staying in bed like I ought to have done.'

'Why were you looking for her? Where did she go?'

'It doesn't matter now.' And then Martha adds, more quietly: 'None of it matters.'

'I'm trying to understand,' Angela says, as gently as she is able to. 'So she went out of the house, you found her, and then she said she wished to leave?'

Martha closes her eyes. 'I'm tired of going over it.'

Mrs Holdsworth appears then behind Angela. Her eyes are red, the thin skin below them raw and puffy.

'Sorry to leave you like that,' she says, her voice clear now of the thick emotion that almost drowned it when Angela arrived. 'I was in the middle of something.'

Angela turns modestly away.

'Why didn't you come sooner?' Martha is glaring at Angela.

The two other women look at her in surprise.

'Martha,' says Mrs Holdsworth.

'I only ask because if Miss Coutts had come sooner, Josephine might still be here.' She looks at Angela. 'You might have been able to persuade her, but the committee had no chance. They don't know her like you do.'

'Martha! Miss Coutts ought to be addressed with more respect.'

'It is a fair question,' Angela replies, 'I'm afraid I was out of town.'

'Oh well,' Martha says blandly. 'I suppose she will soon be forgotten by everyone, anyway. Just another girl who left Urania Cottage. I wonder if any of us will survive this place.'

'That's enough,' Mrs Holdsworth barks. 'You will leave the kitchen and go to your room, and when you have calmed yourself you will come down and apologise to Miss Coutts for your rudeness.'

Martha stands swiftly, causing the chair to screech across the stone floor. She makes to leave, before hesitating for a moment.

'Have you written yet to Veronica Bushey?' she asks Angela unexpectedly.

Bewildered, Angela shakes her head. 'I haven't—'

Martha waits.

'Had the time,' Angela finishes pathetically.

Martha looks at her for a beat longer than is comfortable,

then nods and crosses the floor. Angela and Mrs Holdsworth both step aside, and she brushes past them, leaving them alone in the kitchen, where the range, unattended, flickers feebly before them, on the brink of going out.

※

It is early evening when Josephine arrives in Covent Garden. The market is closed, the ground littered with leaves and stems and peelings worn down by feet and cartwheels. She stands for a while on the edge of the great piazza and watches, for though it is quiet, still there is more life here than she has seen in months.

She asks a man loading crates into a cart where she might find the street she is looking for, and he points her in a north-westerly direction, and tells her to look for a public house with the sign of the Lamb and Flag.

She finds it easily at the end of a short, steep road, and turns left. She sees the standpipe, the dusty black door standing ajar. She cuts through a group of children squatting on the cobbles, playing with stones, and pushes her way inside.

※

The weeks pass, winter releases its bite, and the earliest spring buds nudge their way through the ground. By the time the daffodils open in the park opposite Angela's house, people begin to linger on the thoroughfare below, no longer hurrying through the icy fog. Maids cling to railings with their beaus, and clouds of young hawkers gather like gnats, comparing wares and jostling for business, but still Angela cannot seem to shake the winter. A second infection has set in, and she presses her tongue to the tender bed of her gum, tasting the sourness of it. Leeches are applied again, and Dr Brown makes up a tonic of lemon-balm and clove. Tiny, itchy blisters appear on her fingers, and angry red patches circle her eyes.

At home, she is restless, anxious; she finds herself standing looking out at Piccadilly, examining the faces that pass by the house, looking for Richard Dunn and Josephine, often seeing them, and then realising they have the wrong nose, or are too old. And so she goes out, paying calls, going to parties, watching plays, promenading in the parks and gardens, always glancing over her shoulder, with Mrs Brown at her elbow and Ballard a pace or two behind.

It is a Thursday evening, and she is leaving for the opera when she finds a figure on the steps blocking her way. The person is sitting down, wrapped tightly in a cloak. Stockton materialises behind Angela, but she stops him with a gloved hand. There is something familiar, she thinks, in the line of the shoulders, and she picks up the gold-braided hem of her skirts to hurry down, saying: 'Josephine? Is that you?'

The figure flies from her seat, and Angela sees at once that it is not Josephine but a woman all the same, who has stopped to pull off one of her boots. Her foot is bound with rags and newspaper, and she stands unsteadily, reaching for the railings as she does so.

'No, stay where you are,' says Angela. 'I wish to help you.'

The hood has fallen from her cloak. From beneath a shabby bonnet winds a matted brown plait, and as she casts her boot to the ground and shoves her ruined foot inside it, the woman winces with pain, revealing several missing teeth. She might be any age between twenty and forty-five.

'Stop, please. Do not move on my account. You are welcome to rest awhile. Come inside a moment, won't you? I can offer you food, shelter—'

With a final glance of alarm, the hood is drawn back again like a curtain about her face, and the woman limps away towards Piccadilly. Angela and the footman watch her go, and within moments, she is swallowed by the crowd.

On the fretful day that Josephine left, Angela went out with her driver to look for her. They searched Shepherd's Bush and drove as far as Notting Hill, travelling up and down wide roads lined with white villas, circling affluent squares. She often finds her mind drifting back to that afternoon, the gloomy pall over the house, the silent, pale-faced girls sitting mutely in the parlour. Angela spent two hours looking, with no success. She could not persuade Martha to go with her, even though she thought that, with Martha's help, and two pairs of eyes being better than one, they might have found Josephine and convinced her to come back.

The loss of Josephine has affected Martha more than Angela can ever comprehend; she cannot know how loyalties are formed in such circumstances, how friendships, however fledgling, become lifelines. But she does understand that a part of Martha left with Josephine that day.

Once she arrived home, she and Mrs Brown wrote letters to all the prison governors and magistrates she could think of, asking them to alert her if they came across a young woman with Josephine's name and description. She sent a second lot of letters to friends, enquiring of more names she might write to. And then, powerless to do anything else and wanting to be close to the only ones who knew how it felt to lose Josephine, Angela returned to spend the evening at Urania Cottage, where she read a Walter Scott novel to the girls, who listened politely and kissed her before going up to bed.

Martha stayed in her room all evening and would not come down. Angela sat a while beside her, but she lay facing the wall and hardly spoke. Angela left her to sleep, squeezing her hand in an effort to convey so many things, and then sat a long time in the parlour with Mrs Holdsworth, talking until the fire died, and arriving home very late.

But since then, like a coward, she has found herself avoiding Shepherd's Bush, Martha's wrath, the glum atmosphere. Though new faces are arriving, and some of the girls are even flourishing in their cooking and housework, with excellent reports, Angela cannot help but feel a sense of hopelessness about the whole enterprise.

Now, her carriage is waiting to take her the short journey to Haymarket and the opera. She gathers her mantle about her and climbs inside, and as the driver prepares the reins, she stares at the place on the steps occupied by the young woman, wondering where she came from, where she went.

※

Martha and Frank are peeling potatoes when Mr Bryant arrives. Mrs Holdsworth shows him into the schoolroom and puts her head into the kitchen to tell Martha, who has already heard. She sighs and puts down her knife.

With one hand, Frank neatens his pile of peelings into a damp little mound and glances at Martha. 'Lessons going well?' he asks tentatively. It is his day off, and he is spending it at Shepherd's Bush.

'They aren't lessons, really,' says Martha, wiping her hands on her apron and going to the scullery to wash.

'What is it then? Private instruction?'

'Something like that.'

A joint of pork is slowly roasting in the jack, which ticks away in front of the range; every now and then, a jewel of fat falls to the tray beneath it and bursts with a sizzle. Frank picks up a potato, submerges it in the bowl of water, then puts his knife to it gently, as he might a razor at his throat.

'I think I know some of how you are feeling,' he says. 'First your sister and now your friend. Sometimes it's as though life is a balance sheet of who you have in your life and who you've lost. And very often they aren't fairly weighted.'

Martha says nothing. There is an emptiness to her that she has observed without interest, as though she has been scoured of the capacity for emotion. She goes about her chores and lessons, but all she wants to do is sleep. Names and dates, places and numbers she learns in morning lessons take flight from her mind. She retains nothing, is interested in nothing. She struggles to stay awake at her slate. Mrs Holdsworth is patient with her, for now. But Martha knows that this, too, will fade.

'I've lost people very dear to me, not so long ago,' says Frank. He waits, and there is only the sound of the water, lapping gently in the bowl, and the soft shaving of potato. 'My brother,' he says, very quietly. 'And my sister-in-law, and three nieces as well.'

Martha stares at him. Frank swallows, and the knife trembles slightly.

'There was a fire,' he says.

Martha feels the air catch in her throat. 'I'm very sorry,' she says, but her voice has been hollow lately, and she cannot force any warmth into it, no matter how hard she tries. She thinks back to when she arrived in the weeks before Christmas, when Mrs Holdsworth wore grey and mauve and lavender. She had been in half-mourning. Martha swallows and says: 'So Mrs H lost her son.'

'Yes,' says Frank softly. 'And her granddaughters.'

'When?'

'January. A few days after New Year.'

'How dreadful,' Martha whispers. The skin on her face is tight, like a mask.

'It was. It is.'

'How did it happen?'

'They don't know. A candle near a curtain, perhaps. It was late. My brother came home from work and the house was ablaze. The firefighters were there already. He went in to try to save them – they couldn't stop him – but the stairs collapsed beneath him. And then the floors went next.'

Martha has seen too many house fires. At first, she would stand and watch the firefighters' valiant attempts, hopeful herself. But after witnessing two blackened little bodies being carried out of a city tenement, she always left before the fire died, because it always died last.

Another crystal of fat drops with a hiss to the meat tray, and Martha stoops to turn the pork.

'I ought to go next door,' she says.

'Yes,' says Frank. 'I didn't mean to keep you.'

She feels that there is something else she ought to say, but nothing comes to her, and so she hangs her apron on the peg and leaves Frank to his potatoes.

Mr Bryant is waiting, seated at the large table, a small pile of books at his elbow, the Bible open before him. A rare shaft of sunlight illuminates him, and briefly he turns his face to the window and closes his eyes. Martha waits in the doorway, and sensing himself watched, he turns and smiles.

'Martha,' he says, gesturing to the seat before him. 'How have you been since Tuesday?'

'Well, thank you, sir.'

'Did you have much opportunity for religious study?'

'I read the passages you gave me.'

'Martha, religion is not prescriptive. I am no physician. The reading is for your own pleasure. Later this year, you will be ready to emigrate. It may seem a long way off, but the preparation of the spirit can only take place with the proper dedication.'

She makes no answer. Then she says: 'You work in a prison, don't you?'

'I am a chaplain, yes.'

'Which prison?'

'Why do you ask?'

'So you know the prisoners?'

Mr Bryant studies her. 'I do. Some of them.'

'Could you see a list of all the prisoners?'

'I would be granted access to such a list, if access was required. Is there a particular reason you want to know this?'

'Yes,' says Martha, who does not know why she hasn't thought of this before. 'I am looking for somebody, who may or may not be in prison, or in a penitentiary, or somewhere like it. I hope she isn't, but in case she is.'

He raises a gentle eyebrow. 'This person is?'

'Emily Gelder. My sister, sir.'

'Ah.' He nods, moving his mouth delicately. 'Have you spoken to Mr Dickens about this?'

'Yes.'

'Mr Illingworth on the committee might be able to help. He worked for thirty years at Coldbath. I shall write to him for advice.'

'Only if it isn't too much trouble, sir.'

'It isn't.' He smiles. 'And in the meantime, I will write to all the prison governors who owe me a favour.' He leans towards her, a small glint in his eye. 'That's all of them. Emily, you say her name is?'

'Emily Gelder.'

He nods and makes a note in his pocketbook with a pencil he draws from a pocket. 'Anything to lift your spirits.'

Does she imagine it, or does he smile at her for longer than perhaps he intends?

A moment later, he is reaching into his pocket again and saying: 'Of course, the advantage of being a free man is having the occasional afternoon here and there to indulge in my favourite past-time: browsing second-hand bookshops.' He brings out a slim volume bound in oxblood cloth, places it face down on the table and slides it towards her. 'I think you might enjoy this.' There is a hint of mischief to his voice. 'It is not something I would recommend for the house reading list. In fact, it is not something I think the committee would approve at all.'

'What do you mean, sir?'

Mr Bryant nods mischievously towards the book, and Martha opens it. The pages are old and yellowing, and she finds the title page and begins to read. '*Michael Howe, the last and worst of the bush rangers of Van Diemen's Land.*' She pronounces the place wrong, and Mr Bryant corrects her. Haltingly, she continues: '*Narrative of the chief atrocities committed by this great murderer and his associates during a period of six years in Van*

Diemen's Land.' This time she pronounces it correctly. She looks at him. 'A murderer?'

'As I said, not for general consumption,' Mr Bryant says with a genial twinkle. 'I thought you might be interested to read an adventure story, for once, set in the part of the world you will soon call home. Though Van Diemen's Land is enough of a distance from the Australasian mainland so as not to cause undue worry.'

'Thank you,' Martha says. There is a knock at the door, and she slots the book into the space between her thigh and the chair.

'I'm sorry to disturb you, Mr Bryant, but could I borrow Martha?' Mrs Holdsworth asks. 'Frank is in the kitchen, should you wish to join him for a pot of tea.'

'You have a visitor?' Mr Bryant asks.

'Two, actually. Polly's parents. Quite unexpectedly, I must say. Polly has asked if you and I will sit with them, Martha. I explained you were with Mr Bryant, but she was quite certain she wanted you there. Would you mind giving me a hand with the tea?'

Mildly surprised, Martha obliges, slipping the book into a space on one of the bookshelves and following Mrs Holdsworth into the kitchen. Frank has finished the potatoes and is raking out the chicken coop. The back door is open an inch or two, and Mrs Holdsworth closes it to keep out the draught.

They carry the trays through to the parlour and Martha joins Polly on the low settee.

Polly's mother sits before them. She is small and narrow, with a long face and bony fingers. Beside her is a shabby man with his arms folded. He appears thoroughly unimpressed with

Polly, or the house, or all of it. Tea is served, but nobody drinks it. The silence stretches on.

'Have you come a long way, Mr and Mrs Miller?' Mrs Holdsworth says.

'Oh,' says the mother. 'We's Mr and Mrs Collins. Polly's father passed many years ago, God rest his soul.'

'My apologies.'

'We ain't come too far, have we, Harold? Hoxton. Two omnibuses to the Tyburn turnpike and from there we walked. It's a pretty situation here in the countryside, ain't it, Harold? We ain't never been to these parts afore. Harold knew of Shepherd's Bush 'cause of the racecourse near here, didn't you? Said he'd like to have a look later, see what it's about.'

Mr Collins says nothing and stares dimly towards the window, though the blinds obscure the view.

'Polly is a beautiful piano player,' Mrs Holdsworth says. 'Did she learn at home?'

'Oh, no, it was her father what did all that, rest his soul. We don't have a musical bone in our bodies, do we, Harold?'

Mr Collins grunts and does not look at her.

'Polly,' says Mrs Holdsworth, 'perhaps you'd like to tell your parents about some of your accomplishments here at Urania Cottage?'

Polly stares glumly at the floor.

'Your needlework. She really is quite skilled,' Mrs Holdsworth tells the Collinses.

Mrs Collins looks at her daughter with bewildered interest.

'And she has an aptitude for history – names and dates don't confound her like they can the rest of us.'

'Why is your name in that there picture frame?' Mrs Collins nods towards the wall beside the door.

For the first time, Polly speaks. 'This room is where I work for the week. We have our names in the rooms we look after, and they're inspected at the end of each day.' As she speaks, Polly tears off the skin at the side of her nails. 'How did you find me here?'

There is a pause, and then Mrs Collins titters, reddening slightly and saying in her girlish voice: 'Well, that nice lady at the infirmary – the matron was it, Harold? – she made some enquiries on our behalf, seeing as we never heard from you. We didn't know when you was to be released, you see – you never told us. We was going to ask if you'd like to come home, but by the time we got there you'd vanished into thin air. And here you are.' She looks around vaguely and gives a maddening little giggle. 'So, when are you coming home?'

Mrs Holdsworth, who is sitting in a chair pulled out from the wall, looks sharply at Mrs Collins, then her eyes find Martha's and look quickly away.

'Mrs Collins, ' she says. 'The purpose of Urania Cottage is to train the girls for work in the colonies, where they can start new lives. It is not possible or advisable for them to take up their old ones. They themselves have agreed to this.'

Mrs Collins is perplexed. 'The colonies? With all them convicts and thieves and God knows what else? I don't think so.'

'I've already agreed to it,' Polly says quietly.

'And what's so bad about your old life anyway? And us, your family? What about little Thomas? Mrs Fawcett has him today, so we could save on the omnibus fare, but he is desperate to see you. He sends his love and asks all the time when his sister is coming home.'

Martha is sitting beside Polly and can feel her not trembling

177

exactly but spasming gently, her limbs twitching in involuntary little movements.

Mrs Holdsworth is watching her closely, almost fiercely, from her chair.

'What say you to it?' asks Mrs Collins.

'Polly,' Mrs Holdsworth says sharply. 'Be cautious now. Think of all you've learnt here, all there is yet to learn – the opportunity to begin again away from all you have known, the hardships you have faced. Think very hard before you abandon a very different future.'

Martha wishes to speak but can't find the words.

'I'd like to stay,' Polly says.

Mrs Holdsworth breathes an audible sigh of relief.

'Well, I can't say that don't break my heart,' says Mrs Collins. 'What say you to it, Harold?'

But Mr Collins makes no contribution. He avoids the eyes of everybody in the room, and stares instead at the settee leg.

Polly holds herself very still, pressing her wrists together.

'That's that, then,' says Mrs Holdsworth with obvious satisfaction. 'Mr and Mrs Collins, can I pour you more tea?'

'No, thank you,' says Mrs Collins, without taking her eye from Polly. 'I shan't be able to drink it now.'

'Very well. I'm afraid visits with family are limited to a half-hour,' Mrs Holdsworth says, standing and brushing down the front of her skirts.

The Collinses gather themselves, and Mrs Collins takes her daughter's hands. Polly accepts a kiss from her as she might from a stranger, and when the curious pair leave, one murmuring, one silent, Martha takes Polly's hand and squeezes it, and feels the same in return.

THE HOUSEHOLD

❦

An hour before supper, there is a knock at the door. At her bureau, Mrs Holdsworth is arranging the house rota for the coming weeks. She frowns and glances at the clock that Frank has fixed.

Before she can rise, the knock sounds again, though now it is more like a hammer ringing bluntly through the house, as though made with the side of a fist and not the knuckles. It has the unmistakeable air of authority. Mercifully, Frank is still here; she hears the tread of his boots on the hall tiles and gets up as a third thunderous series of blows rains down on the wood.

'Who . . . ?' asks Frank, but she brushes past him and answers it herself.

Mr and Mrs Collins are standing on the doorstep, inches from her. Mrs Holdsworth takes an instinctive step backwards, for at first she does not recognise Mr Collins, who appears to have transformed from a mute, banal man into an ogre. His skin is flushed and mottled; his eyes burn with menace or fierce intent. He is mightily, abominably drunk.

'We've come for Polly,' he declares.

His wife, too, is drunk, her bonnet askance, and she rests a bony hand on the door-frame to steady herself. 'Mrs Holdsworth, we've come for Polly, our daughter,' she echoes loudly.

Frank appears at once behind his mother. 'Who the devil are you?'

'I might ask of you the same question,' Mr Collins barks.

'Polly!' her mother roars. 'Your mother begs an audience, my dear.'

'Mr and Mrs Collins, I will ask you to step back at once,' Mrs Holdsworth says with force.

Obediently, and with some surprise, the man takes a step backwards, and not having prepared himself, almost keels over. His wife takes his arm and hiccups.

'Polly has made perfectly clear her wish to remain at Urania Cottage. Good day to you both.'

Mrs Holdsworth begins to close the door, but Mr Collins has regained himself and lurches forwards to block her with a large hand.

Moving with lightning speed, Frank pulls the door wide and fastens a hand around the man's muffler. 'You heard. Make yourselves scarce, sharpish.'

If Mr Collins is surprised by Frank's strength he does not show it, and when Frank releases him swiftly, he loses his balance again and recovers it at the last moment, righting himself.

'Who are you?' he brays. 'Shouldn't be no men in an house like this.'

'I'll wager it's a Venus house, Harold, and she the abbess,' his wife announces. 'Polly! We thought you was better'n that. We come all the way here across town to—'

From the depths of the house, Polly flies towards them, her face dark with fury. 'Why've you come?' she cries. 'You heard Mrs Holdsworth; I wish to stay. And I wish you would leave me alone.'

'We've come back to get you!' her mother crows. 'We ain't leaving without you. We came all this way, on two omnibuses. It ain't cheap, you know, to the Tyburn turnpike from Hoxton.'

'I told you, I won't come.'

'You' – Mr Collins points rudely – 'are breaking your poor mother's heart. You ungrateful wretch, you don't deserve her forgiveness after what you put her through. You're lucky she still calls you family at all.'

'*Good day.*' Mrs Holdsworth slams the street door, and the three of them breathe hard in the shocked silence.

But it lasts only a moment; Collins takes up his indignant pounding, and Frank steers them into the parlour.

'Let him wear himself out,' he says, helping Polly into a chair. The constable's assertiveness has found him now, and he asks one of the other girls to fetch a blanket, for Polly is trembling violently and has bitten her lip so hard that blood blooms darkly against her white face.

'I don't know why they came,' she says, her face white.

Frank places the blanket around her shoulders. At the window, Mrs Holdsworth splays the slats of the blinds at eye level. The Collinses remain on the path, just out of sight, firing expletives.

'Polly, come here,' Mr Collins bellows, in the manner of a man calling his dog. 'Come here, I tell you. Your mother cares for a word.'

The girls gather around Polly, standing by her chair, putting hands on her shoulders. Mrs Holdsworth notices how they seem affected yet not unnerved by the outburst; most of them wear an expression of resignation and not shock. Frances joins Mrs Holdsworth at the window, sliding her fingers between the slats and peering through.

'Thank goodness we've no neighbours,' says Mrs Holdsworth, half to herself.

Frank is standing before the piano with his arms folded, working his jaw. 'I'll give them another minute,' he announces, his eyes fixed on the clock. The pounding has a brief reprieve and then returns, half-heartedly, before finally ceasing altogether.

A peaceable quiet descends, and everybody's breath is shallow as they wait. The silence stretches on.

'Are they gone?' asks Martha after some time.

Suddenly, Mrs Holdsworth jumps back from the window, pulling Frances with her to the floor as a deafening crash explodes above them.

'He's got a pistol!' shrieks one girl above screams from the rest of them. 'He's shot us!'

Mrs Holdsworth gets shakily to her feet. A scattering of broken glass litters the carpet, and she raises the blind to reveal a violent wreck of a window, grinning with toothy shards.

Her heart pounding, the others crowd around her, their feet crunching glass into the carpet. She puts out a hand to keep them back and looks out. The Collinses are now nowhere to be seen, but the brick they have thrown is, lying like a cannonball in the flower-bed.

CHAPTER 9

To Market

'Martha? This arrived for you.'

Martha is in the scullery washing the breakfast things when Mrs Holdsworth appears with the morning post. Her heart misses a beat as she accepts the heavy cream envelope and sees her own name.

Inside is a folded letter and a second, smaller envelope, sliced open, addressed to Miss Burdett-Coutts at Stratton Street. Martha looks at Mrs Holdsworth, who gives a nod of encouragement. Martha opens the note and frowns at the close, blue handwriting.

'It's from Miss Coutts.' She reads quickly, her mouth becoming drier, her hands struggling to hold the note steady. She hastily casts it aside to tear open the second, which at first glance is longer, though not as long as she would like, and covered with close, untidy writing.

Feeling that she must be outside to read it, she leaves

the gloom of the scullery and leans against the wall of the wash-house.

Dear Miss Burdett-Coutts,

Thank you for your letters to myself and my daughter. Unfortunately, Veronica is unable to read and write very well and so will be unable to enter into any correspondence. I am aware of your charitable endeavours and am in admiration of your work for the Ragged Schools in particular. I have some friends who would be very interested to meet you, who are appointing patrons for the Royal Berkshire Hospital, and—

Martha stops reading. She goes at once to find Mrs Holdsworth, who is in the kitchen, putting on the tea-kettle. She hands her the letter and watches hungrily as she reads.

'What do you make of it?' she asks when Mrs Holdsworth has finished.

The matron sighs, wearing an identical puzzled frown. 'Seems like a dead end to me.'

'She doesn't even mention Emily. It's as if she never existed.' She shakes her head. 'I am sure they're covering something up. Veronica is around the same age as Emily, but doesn't seem at all like it.'

Lydia, Urania Cottage's newest housemate, comes out of the cellar with the ash pail. She is reserved, unobtrusive, and sleeps silently in Josephine's bed. She cried most of the evening she arrived and was comforted by Polly, who took her out the next morning to feed the chickens. The birds allow Lydia to pet them: a privilege they extend to none of the others.

The girl gives a quiet smile and exits into the hall.

'I must write to Mary,' Martha says with great weariness.

'You might invite her here.'

Martha thinks back to the Collinses, how strange and unsettling their visit was, like two cats among pigeons. She looks again at her own name in Angela's elegant hand on the rich cream paper. It does not seem to belong to her but to the sort of young woman who keeps stationery in a desk, dabs rosewater at her neck, has shoes for dancing: a girl she might have been.

The day after Josephine left, Martha and two others did the laundry. She washed Josephine's raspberry dress, plunging it again and again into the hot water, watching its sleeves struggle to the surface like a woman drowning.

'Perhaps,' she says, feeling the dark cloud close in on her once again. She puts both letters in her apron pocket to read again later. In hers, Angela said she would visit soon. Once, this would have cheered Martha, but now she feels nothing.

Mrs Holdsworth goes to the schoolroom, and Lydia puts her head in the kitchen door.

'Martha?'

Martha looks up.

Lydia shrinks slightly and says in her small voice: 'I found something upstairs.'

Wordlessly and without interest, Martha follows her to their bedroom. She stands in the doorway and watches as Lydia pulls out Josephine's bed a few inches from the wall.

'What is it?' She cannot see anything – in fact, she looked herself for an object, a token, anything, the morning after Josephine left, and found nothing. Martha took a few dark strands from the hairbrush they shared, twisting them in a coil and putting them beneath her own pillow, forgetting to hide them somewhere safe before the beds were made in the morning. When she remembered to look later, they were gone.

Lydia is pointing at the wall beside the bed-frame, and Martha gets to her knees on the mattress and peers. With a pin, perhaps, or a nail, a word has been carved into the brand-new paper, patterned with pink roses.

'Street,' Martha reads.

Lydia looks questioningly at her.

'It means nothing to me,' she says, and she shoves the bed against the wall.

✣

Angela cannot remember the last time she entertained. The misery of Dunn's release, the cottage and all her other duties have been too distracting, and it has been long enough since Stratton Street was crowded. She decides she must see the chandeliers blazing, trays circling, arrangements of flowers filling the room. The reception rooms are still dusted daily by the maids, who long for the mistress to permit sheets, but to live in a house with sheets over the furniture would be too depressing. And so Angela invites thirty people to dinner and seventy more for dancing afterwards, and preparations begin.

It refreshes her to see her house set up for a party, with every room dressed and shining, the dining table groaning with silver and crystal and delicious smells floating up from the kitchens. Angela allows herself to look forward to it and feels, on the morning itself, the same bubbling sense of pleasure that she did as a girl waking on her birthday. A quartet arranges itself in the ballroom, and crates of champagne are delivered in a cart, ringing like bells down the street. Constable Ballard attends the street door and keeps a watchful eye for the man who appears to have forgotten all about her, though she knows this is far from the truth. The not-knowing where he is chills her, and she finds her mind drawn to him more than it used to be when he was everywhere.

Angela seats herself in the middle of the table, so that she can look up and down at her guests enjoying each other. Some are old friends, some strangers to one another: actors, singers, bankers, bishops, scientists and scholars and their wives. It gives her great joy to see ladies' feathers quivering, earrings catching the light, cheeks reddening, voices growing louder with humour and indignance. The best parties are like a well-dressed platter: mixed, vibrant, communal.

At a break in conversation with her cousin, Lord Dudley, she butters a bread roll and listens as one of the bank's partners sitting to her right recounts a well-worn anecdote she has heard a hundred times about a clerk, a client and a case of mistaken identity. She smiles and congratulates herself on the seating plan, drinks more wine, moves among her guests.

She dances with her father's friends, her cousin and Dr Brown. She dances until her feet are sore and her back begins to hurt; she jokes about growing older. Her home, she thinks, truly is magnificent. How lucky she is to live in it; what a gift her inheritance has been, but how heavy it is for one person. She drinks more champagne, forgets her back pain, her pinched feet. She has a long conversation with the Earl of Northumbria's daughter, who has recently broken off an engagement, and the pair of them raise a glass.

Shortly after eleven, the waltz she is dancing finishes, and she claps with everybody else and slips from the ballroom, hearing the music and chatter grow fainter as she glides up the scarlet-carpeted stairs to the first-floor drawing room. A pair of young lovers sit on the velvet sofa before a low fire, their dark heads bent as they talk in low voices. They glance up when she enters, invite her to join them, but Angela declines, continuing on her forward momentum. She reaches her private sitting room and closes herself inside.

A street lamp burns outside the window, casting a ghostly glow throughout the little room, and she sits in her father's old chair before the fire and removes first her right shoe, then her left. Once upon a time she danced at five balls a week, rarely retiring before two in the morning. Mrs Brown would sit dozing in the corner, a glass of sherry tipping precariously towards her silks. She smiles at the memories from before she married her money and became a Coutts. Before Dunn even knew she existed. She wonders if Mrs Brown has already made her excuses and climbed the stairs to her apartment.

There is a carafe of water set on the desk for the morning. In stockinged feet, she fills a glass and drinks, looking out at the quiet street where her guests' carriages await their charges, the drivers dozing, the reins looped through their folded arms.

Her thoughts, as usual when she is alone, or at a party, or when she has drunk champagne, turn to the duke. She sits at the desk, takes out a clean sheet of paper, opens the drawer to find a pen. She rubs a finger across her lips, unfastens the ink well, dips in the nib and watches in the half-light as a blue tear gathers, heavy and glistening.

She blots it and, by the light of the street lamp, writes quickly, urgently, with even less care than usual. The duke teases that he needs an interpreter for her dreadful hand-writing, and tonight, fuelled by her giddy head and aching feet, she is more fluid than usual. She signs with a flourish, plucks a feather from her hair and seals it inside with the note. On the front, she writes his name and his address. Somehow, when he is at his London house, just half a mile from her own, she finds it more unbearable than when he is anywhere else. She leaves it in the centre of the desk for Mrs Brown to put in the post in the morning.

When she stands, she trips on her hem, briefly losing her balance and catching the back of the chair. She turns to face her father above the mantelpiece and sighs, feeling more clear-headed beneath his coal-black gaze. They regard one another for a moment, but she cannot decide what he is thinking tonight. She realises that for once she does not care. She has a house full of people, and of that he would be proud.

∗

The next morning, Angela sleeps until half past ten and has pastries and fruit and coffee in bed with the newspapers. It is a bright spring morning, and Mrs Brown throws the shutters wide.

'Can't it be a cloudy day?' Angela groans, holding up the newsprint to shield her eyes.

Mrs Brown is tidying away her jewellery, which is strewn carelessly over her dressing table. Her gown, which she left pooled in a silky heap on the floor, has been rescued by an early maid and put away. Halfway through a news item about the Queen of Spain's visit, Angela has a sudden thought.

'Mrs Brown,' she says, half sheepish. 'In somewhat of a daze, I penned a letter to the duke in my sitting room last night. You haven't sent it, have you?'

'Not I,' says Mrs Brown.

'Thank goodness. Could you see if Stockton has put it in the letterbox? And ask him not to send it?'

'I'll do it now.'

A wave of nausea stills her as she lies there, and to quell it, she eats a pear. The juice seeps through the newspaper, coating her ink-stained hands, and she is wondering whether to ring for a bath to clean off the mess when Mrs Brown returns and asks where she left the letter.

'On the desk, in the middle,' she says. 'You can't miss it.'

'There is no letter on the desk, but Stockton hasn't seen it.'

Angela frowns. 'Would you ask the maids? And Dr Brown? If he's sent it, it wouldn't be the worst thing in the world. I don't want anybody to fret. It was only . . . well. It was only a silly note.'

Her companion disappears again, and Angela wonders for how long Mrs Brown will be able to climb upstairs comfortably. Perhaps in a few years she will move the Browns' apartment downstairs; perhaps in their very old age she will give them a cottage in the countryside. Dr Brown would be happy, she thinks, with the wide skies and birdsong to wake him, though she suspects Mrs Brown would not like the low ceilings or the smell of manure. The notion of it makes her smile and think of her grandmother, Lady St Albans, who in the last months of her life slept in a bed in the dining room at Stratton Street. Like an optical illusion, the plump, lively woman appeared to shrink and grow more lifeless by the day, though she never lost her humour and remarked what a pity it was that nobody could see her new slender figure.

Mrs Brown appears again, almost silent in her silk slippers. 'Nobody has seen or sent a letter,' she says, looking concerned.

'Nobody? But that's impossible. *Somebody* has moved it. Did you ask the maids?'

'They began cleaning at six. Edith did your sitting room; she said there was no letter even at that time.'

'How odd.'

But not odd enough for Angela to think of it again until some days later, by which point it is too late.

❧

'I found us lodgings.'

Annie looks up from the floor, where she is sitting with the baby as the two-year-old crawls over her like a cat. She has made a den between her legs for the infant, who can walk when his hands are held; he bumps along and lands on his bare behind.

'What's that?' she says, smiling.

'I found us lodgings, down near the Hungerford Market. Six shillings a week.'

'In our own room?'

'No, you goose. Shared room.'

The baby pushes himself up on his fat legs, and Annie stretches as he walks towards her feet. 'Back this way, come on,' she says, guiding him.

'So, what do you think? I need to tell the landlady today, else it'll go.'

'Six shillings a week for a bed in a shared room?' Annie says without looking at her. 'That's more'n we pay now.'

'Anywhere would be more'n we pay now, 'cause we pay nothing. And it's sharing with a married couple.'

'We do that here.' Annie is still smiling, and Josephine is not.

191

'I don't like living like this, on your sister's charity. I feel as though I'm in the way.'

'You ain't in the way, and it ain't charity. We look after the children. Where you going?' Annie demands of the youngest, who grips the bedclothes, loses balance and collapses once more. He begins to cry and urinate simultaneously, and Annie makes a soft tutting noise and stands to fetch a cloth.

Josephine makes no offer to help. For several weeks now she has lived in this small room on the fourth floor with Annie, her sister Maud, brother-in-law John, and their five children, who range in age from nine years to eleven months. She and Annie sleep on a mattress in the corner of the room with two of the children; the baby and another sleep in the bed with their parents, and the eldest has a pallet on the floor. The Lamb and Flag public house is their neighbour, opening first thing for the market porters, who leave the piazza at seven in the morning, and closing well after midnight. Between infant limbs and late-night merrymakers, Josephine has not slept more than an hour through since she left Urania Cottage.

The two-year-old squats and lifts an object off the floor. Coins rain down to the floorboards, rolling in all directions.

'Annie, I thought you was going to pawn that.' Josephine leaps to gather them up, finding the last one fastened inside grubby fingers approaching the child's mouth.

'I haven't had time.'

'Shall I go now then?' She lines the coins up on the cupboard. Next to them, out of reach of small fists, she places the pocket-book she stole from a gentleman browsing a bookstall on the Charing Cross Road. It is black kid leather, soft as butter, faded from use. Most of the coins are gone now. She stole it for her and Annie, who told her not to make it known to

Maud, though Maud has asked no questions about how food is acquired and eats what Josephine brings home with relish. Josephine did not realise that her takings would be shared, and with nine mouths to feed, her loot has dwindled swiftly. She has already sold the *Vanessa cardui*, having no idea what a framed butterfly ought to fetch, but knowing that what she got was not enough.

Annie wipes the floor with the rag they use to clean themselves and does not answer. Though it is not yet warm outside, the room is airless. One of the windows has been painted shut; the other jams an inch from the ledge. John has promised to look at it, but each night, he arrives home and collapses on the bed, delirious with tiredness from his work on the railways.

John and Maud are good people who work hard, pay their rent on time and give nobody any trouble. They have been generous with Annie and Josephine, allowing them to share the room in exchange for caring for the children in the day. The three eldest scatter like mice each morning, playing in the courts and alleys, running errands, washing doorsteps, combing dust-heaps. Children of London, they are sharp, keen-eyed, wise to the streets.

On that freezing January evening, when Josephine pushed open the heavy black door and climbed a half-dozen sets of stairs, her heart thudding in time with her boots, she had the strange sense of going backwards in time. The brickmaker, Vincent, had driven a hard bargain in exchange for information about and then correspondence with Annie. She had unlocked the garden door with a hairpin three times to meet him at the gate, where he gave her messages and she gave him herself. It had crossed her mind once or twice to sneak out a pie or a cutlet for him instead, but at Urania Cottage she was not a thief, and had no wish to become one.

She arrived at the uppermost door, listening to the crash and thud of young people, and when she heard Annie speak in a chiding tone, she felt her heart leave her body and found herself opening it without knocking. She stood, unnoticed, on the threshold, absorbing the scene: linen and boots and toys and chamber pots and stockings and rugs and beds and chairs, and at the centre of it, Annie kneeling, still in her smock, with her copper hair falling down about her shoulders.

The racket, the chaos stopped as they looked at one another, and suddenly Annie was on her feet, colliding with Josephine, kissing her face, her hair, her hands, crying out with happiness. Any reservations, any remorse Josephine had about abandoning the cottage, her education, Australia, even Martha, evaporated in that single happy moment.

They left the children and went walking up Long Acre. Josephine listened as Annie told her about the neighbourhood, the baby, the best place to buy apples on the market. The question dragged like a cart between them until Josephine could haul it no longer.

'Why did you do it?' she asked, and Annie stopped walking.

Her eyes filled with tears, and she took Josephine's hands. 'I was a coward,' she said. 'The more we spoke about it, the more I knew I wanted to see Maud, and I didn't know how to tell you. I still wanted to do it – I wanted it so much, Jo. But I didn't know how to tell you any of it, and so I did a shameful thing in leaving you there. I wanted the best for you – I really did – and I knew that house would be really good for you.'

Josephine felt as though she was standing on a very high platform, trying not to fall. If Annie knew how she had paid the brickmaker to find her . . . she might have understood, but she would hate it all the same. Josephine imagined Annie in her place, lifting her skirts against the high brick wall, and felt light-headed with rage and revulsion. Her hands slackened in Annie's, and mistaking her meaning, Annie gripped them tighter.

'I'm so happy you've come to me. When that boy found me, I could have burst. I am sorry for what I did, Jo. But now you're here. You've found me. Some part of me always knew you would. Did you get your sugar mouse?'

'Yes,' said Josephine. 'You are clever.'

Mistrustful of Vincent, Josephine had asked him to ask Annie to send something, so that she knew it was really her. When he tossed the smooth little creature into her palm, she almost cried out with happiness.

After that, she and Annie went arm in arm down to the river, where they sought out a quiet spot by a wharf and found one another.

That evening, as dark as it was, would be forever ringed with gold for Josephine, as though it had taken place on a summer's afternoon. John and Maud had welcomed Josephine and sent the eldest child downstairs for beer. They shared a supper of chops, pickles, bread and cheese, crammed around a small table beneath the window, some sitting on seats, some on the floor.

Josephine thought they lived well, at first. Their room was certainly cleaner than any she had stayed in before Urania Cottage, the light plentiful, with lamps from the street making the walls glow at night. The lodgings themselves were no more tired or dirty than she expected; the other tenants seemed to keep to themselves, save for the occasional crash or shriek after dark.

At first, she did not miss Urania Cottage at all. Her hours were her own; she was at liberty to make a living. She told herself she would find steady work in a laundry or a public house. For two weeks, she helped Annie with the children, and every day she was aware she was contributing nothing. Then, a pocketbook, poking like a tongue from a blue coat, a busy street, an opportunity; before she knew it, she was stroking the leather in her hands, the gentleman none the wiser, browsing the spines with no money to buy them. She turned the corner and flattened herself against the wall, her heart slamming in her chest, the rush of thieving heating her veins, thrilling her. She told herself she would not do it again; she would get work somewhere proper, respectable. Somewhere Mrs Holdsworth would approve of. She stayed pressed against the wall a long time, then removed her shawl from her shoulders, turned it and draped it over her wrists. For a moment, she imagined Mrs Holdsworth standing across the road, watching her, her mouth turned down at the corners.

Now, she takes the pocketbook into the bright, cold day and finds a pawnbroker's on the Strand. Her late father's pocketbook, she tells him, a family heirloom – *look how soft*. She was hoping for more than ten shillings for it – *could you stretch to fifteen, sir? My mother will be heartbroken if I get less than twelve. Yes, sir, very good, sir; ten will do.*

Josephine steps out into the street and begins walking east. She has no wish to return to Coopers Buildings, to the milky stink and shit-stained rags. In many ways, it is worse than prison: the lack of routine, the counting of pennies, the stringent dividing of food. Each day, stretching out not with possibility but with effort and toil. If she said any of this to Annie! All she wants to do is lie somewhere private with her, eating nuts, drinking cocoa, thieving once in a while. She was always good enough at it to not have to do it all the time. Her arrest last year was one of those things: sheer bad luck. A bobby coming round the corner as she fled the grip of another was no reflection of her skill. These things happened.

'Josephine?'

For a moment, Josephine forgets where she is, who she is.

A plump, attractive, dark-haired woman in lustrous brown silk is peeling away from her companion, walking towards her, smiling with a wide mouth and even, white teeth. It takes Josephine several seconds to place her.

'Susannah?'

'You haven't forgotten me?' The woman leans in to kiss her, and Josephine catches the scent of rose talcum. 'I haven't seen you in such a long time. I thought you'd moved on.'

Josephine and Susannah met on Haymarket two or three years before. Susannah is older than most of the whores Josephine knew, but she is stout and healthy, always popular, with her fine, dark eyes and shining hair. She has a Mediterranean look about her and would sometimes put a flower behind her ear. Her clothes have always been a cut above the others, silk or velvet; she moves through the drab streets like a jewel in Thames silt.

'I been away a spell,' says Josephine.

'Was you in Coldbath?'

'Tothill.'

Susannah nods. 'Glad to see you looking well. How you been keeping?'

The roast birds and physical work at Shepherd's Bush have altered Josephine: her old dress is tighter around the middle, her arms and shoulders strong. 'Same as ever,' she replies. 'And yourself?'

'I saved up, like I said I would. Took on the lease of a coffee-house down by Westminster Bridge. I told you I would, didn't I?'

'You did.' Josephine is impressed.

'You must come and see me some time. College Coffee House. We get Members of Parliament coming in for their chops, don't we, Nan? Course, I already know a few of them.' Susannah winks gamely.

Her companion, a pale, rather sour-faced woman, has been standing mutely a foot or two behind. A fleeting compulsion visits Josephine to ask Susannah for work at her coffee-house, but the presence of a third person makes this feel shameful somehow, and so she does not.

'Where you living now?' Susannah asks.

'Up by Covent Garden market. Not far.'

'We used to go to that coffee-stall there, didn't we? He let us stand by the fire long as we wanted. Bread and half a cup of coffee for a penny, was it? Yes, I remember now – he'd bend a sort of clothes-horse around the stall and drape it with blankets, so we was warm. Much nicer, he was, than all the rest. And his wife used to make cake, didn't she? And give him a kiss on his whiskers afore she went home.'

It isn't a time Josephine is fond of remembering. She gives a weak smile and glances at the road, as though she has a mind to hail a cab.

'Remember me, won't you? College Coffee House. Come for your supper one evening, on the house.'

They part ways, and Josephine is swept into the traffic of the Strand. Before she reaches the church by Clare Market, she stops and turns to see how far the pair have gone. Then she crosses the road and leans on the parapet of the bridge, looking upriver at the spires and steeples, the boats and steamers and lighters plunging in a teeming mass on the steely water.

She will not pay a visit to College Coffee House. She tells herself it is too close to Tothill Fields, but it is not that. Susannah's brown silk was expensive, her hair glossy, her cheek smooth where she pressed it to Josephine's. Very few of her contemporaries rise like cream; most sink to the depths. To know one who has risen is to know that one's self is sinking.

Five years ago, she used to copy the older girls on Regent Street, lifting her skirts to the ankle, as though making her way through manure. She looked a gentleman with a tall hat in the eye. He shook his head in disgust and walked on, but another approached her. He was not much taller than her, with closely cropped white hair and the slender figure of a girl. 'Will you come with me?' he said. Fifteen minutes later, she was back on Regent Street, trembling with fear and pride and a little pain, but mainly with relief at the warm coin burning a circle in her palm. Back then, with no family and no home, London seemed like the crush of hell itself, with the thunder of hooves and wheels, the precipice of poverty, the gallows and prison hulks sleeping like dogs on the river. But on that May afternoon when she stumbled from the shadows, leaving the man adjusting his clothes, she felt reborn, wiser than all of them, older than the city itself. Life seemed limitless, opening like a flower before her, blood-red and sweet.

She walks slowly back down the Strand, fingering the shillings in her pocket, and pays a deposit for the room by the Hungerford Stairs. She tells the landlady she will return later with her friend and their things. Annie will be annoyed, perhaps upset. She will ask what she is supposed to do with the children. She *likes* caring for her nieces and nephews, likes being their Aunt Annie. She is disappointed at how little interest Josephine pays in them, asks questions about Josephine's siblings, as if to coax out of her a forgotten fondness for infants.

But Josephine feels little emotion for her long-dead brothers and sisters; too much time has passed, too many things have happened. Each time she rested her forearms against a damp brick wall, settling herself into position, the handful of happy moments she had as a child – stroking a horse with her little brother; a sunny walk hand in hand with her mother, whose face she does not remember; the perfect endless curl of an apple peel springing from her fingers – would shrink further and further until she wondered if she had even been a child at all.

CHAPTER 10

Tin and Iron

Before the candle dies, Martha lights a new one and fits it inside the holder. She extinguishes the stub, leans out of the bed to put it on the floor, and nestles down beneath the blanket with her book. For several nights, she has read *Michael Howe* in the darkness, going through more candles than she ought to. Her progress is slow but steady, like a small boat on a long river. The story is thrilling, frightening in places, and she does not fully understand all of it, but she is gripped all the same. Mr Bryant is pleased, and they talk about it in their sessions. A year ago, she would have found the idea of sitting discussing literature with a clergyman implausible.

'Martha,' comes a quiet whisper from the other side of the room.

Martha holds up her candle. 'Yes?'

Lydia's head rests on her pillow, facing Martha, her eyes bright.

When Lydia does not answer, Martha says: 'Are you all right?'

'I don't think so,' Lydia whispers. 'I don't know.'

There is a rustle as Martha leaves the bedclothes. 'What's the matter?'

Lydia is seventeen or so, around Emily's age, and Martha feels a sisterly protectiveness towards her. 'To be a sister is to be a mother,' her mother said to her once.

She kneels now at Lydia's bedside and holds the candle close.

'It hurts,' Lydia whispers.

'What hurts?'

'My belly.'

Martha peels back the blankets. The sheets are spotted with blood.

'It will be all right,' she says. 'It happens to all of us.'

Lydia nods.

'Wait there.'

She hurries through the dark house to fetch clean sheets and towels. She needs Mrs Holdsworth's key to access the cotton loops they wear beneath their shifts, and she tells herself it can wait until morning. All the girl needs is a new nightdress and something to lie on. She helps Lydia from the bed.

Polly wakes and assists with the bed-making, takes the soiled linen down to the scullery, brings up a warm cup of milk. Lydia sits shivering on Martha's bed, sipping her milk, her bare feet crossed on the floorboards.

'You'll feel better in the morning,' Martha says. Lydia nods. She lights one last candle and puts it on the chair beside Lydia's bed.

A handful of miles to the east, Angela waits on the road outside the Islington assembly rooms. Her friend Frederick Pelham has given a lecture for the Islington Literary and Scientific Society, and Angela has come to show her support. He is delayed by admirers, and she stands with Frederick's wife Viola beside a stuccoed pillar, buffeted gently in the slow current of people flooding the street from the warmly lit doors. She is ready for her bed, and stifles a yawn with her fan as yet another gentleman approaches Frederick to shake his hand. The night is cold, and across the road, on the edge of a triangle-shaped green, vagrants and night workers gather like moths around a coffee-stall. Viola keeps a lookout for their carriage among the crawling cabs, eager to get home to the children.

''Scuse me, miss?'

A small vagrant boy has approached the two women. Angela closes her fan and gives him an uncertain smile, which falters as he hands her an envelope. He has passed it face down, and she turns it to see, in a familiar hand, the letters *ABC*. The pavement bucks and tilts beneath her, and she reaches out a gloved hand to the pillar to steady herself.

'Who gave this to you?' she asks sharply, but the boy is already darting deftly through the canes and skirts.

'What is that?' Viola asks, with an amused little frown.

Angela opens her purse and stuffs her letter to the bottom of it. 'Probably an appeal for the houseless, or something like that.' She tries hard not to glance about her and feels suddenly deathly cold. 'Do we know where we're to be met?'

'I think our carriage is over there. Shall we wait there for Frederick?'

The two of them cross the road. Like a wild animal, Angela is alert to the unlit green beyond, bordered with thick planes and bushes. They locate the Pelhams' carriage and fasten themselves inside.

'I feel that went remarkably well, don't you?' asks Viola, her voice loud in the enclosed space. An oil lamp hangs from the ceiling, casting a dim light.

'So very interesting,' Angela says, forcing enthusiasm. 'I do hope Frederick gets the directorship.'

She knew it was only a matter of time before Dunn appeared again, and she has been proved right.

'Oh, there is Mrs Harcourt. I didn't see her inside. Would you mind if I jump out a moment?'

'By all means.'

The carriage rocks as Viola exits, closing the door behind her. There is no lock or curtain; the Pelhams have no need for protection. Angela sits alone in the feeble lamplight, feeling grossly illuminated. Her palms, hot and damp, leave streaks on her purse, and she strokes the silk, making out the various shapes inside: a bit of lead, the padding of a handkerchief, the sharp edges of her cards and the soft length of the letter. *ABC*. He addresses her in the same way as her closest friends; how he knows they do eludes her, but she does not care to find out.

She takes a shuddering breath in and exhales slowly through pursed lips. The carriage tilts slightly as the driver changes position. One of the horses snorts. It is an unexpected comfort. She is not alone; the driver is feet away and would not allow a strange man to approach her. She adjusts her position, sitting back more comfortably and staring forwards, ignoring the dark void of the window. Several minutes pass.

And then suddenly the handle is seized, the door flung open, and Viola's hat launches first into the gloom, followed closely by her narrow shoulders. Frederick comes next, folding himself inside, and the atmosphere lifts at once.

'Congratulations!' Angela beams, her heart slamming against her corset. 'A triumph of an evening.'

Frederick is relaxed and expansive, and he speaks warmly of his success as they wind westwards, illuminated by lamps passing like torches in the darkness. Angela hangs on to his every word, convincing herself that everything is normal, that she is just a woman journeying home from a pleasant evening with friends.

At Stratton Street, the doorstep stands empty. Ballard had stayed until six, and offered to accompany her to the lecture, but she assured him there was no need. She must have been out on thirty different occasions since Dunn was released, and on twenty-nine of them, with the exception of Her Majesty's theatre, nothing of note had occurred. The constable's protection has been haphazard, and she realises she has been a fool to think Dunn hasn't been watching, hasn't been aware all or at least some of the time of where she was and who with.

The street door opens before she reaches it, and Stockton takes her outdoor things. 'I'll keep this,' she says, pressing the bag against her skirts.

She dismisses the footman for the night and goes to her sitting room, where she pours a small measure of brandy from her father's decanter. The glass, too, is his, and she examines the amber liquid through the crystal, holding it up to the dim lamplight. Feeling a draught whistling down through the chimney, she takes her brandy and purse to her favourite chair, where she opens the letter with cold, stiff fingers, and begins to read.

'Martha.'

The voice reaches her through sleep, and she wakes, bewildered, into pure blackness, afraid for a moment that she is back in the Rose Room in the bed with the curtains, where the light came to find her.

But no, she is home, or what she knows to be home for now, in the little back bedroom, with Polly and Lydia and a friendly flame at her shoulder.

'Martha!'

But Polly's face is frightened, and she pulls roughly at Martha's arm. 'Please, it's Lydia.'

A low, animal moaning issues from the foot of her bed. Martha scrambles from the bedclothes to see Lydia's blankets pulled back, a black pool spreading beneath her. Horrified, she turns to Polly, who has backed against the wall, paralysed with fear.

'Wake Mrs H,' she hisses.

After a second's hesitation, Polly flees, and Martha goes at once to kneel beside her.

'Lydia?'

She writhes in her nightgown, biting down on her own hand. The terrible noise starts up again, a deep, bovine groaning that makes Martha think at once of childbirth, but Lydia's stomach is flat.

'Lydia, how long have you been bleeding?'

But Lydia is not listening or is unable to understand. Martha reaches for her hand to prise it from her teeth and almost gasps at how cold yet clammy her skin is.

Feet pound the floorboards on the landing, and Mrs Holdsworth bursts in with a lamp.

'What in God's name . . . ?'

Their faces appear ghastly in the lamplight, and Martha cannot help but think she is having a nightmare, and might wake at any moment.

'Polly, go and fetch the doctor,' Mrs Holdsworth says in a low, urgent voice.

'Where?' Polly gasps.

'Take this key and go to the turnpike, to the inn there. Ask for the physician.'

'W-what's the turnpike?'

'Out of the house, turn left, all the way to the end, then right and keep going. Bang on the door until someone wakes. Go now!'

Polly grabs her shawl from the end of her bed and disappears. Mrs Holdsworth joins Martha on her knees and puts two fingers to her pulse.

'Elevated heart rate,' she says. 'I'll get the laudanum.'

She, too, disappears, leaving Martha alone in the hellish dark room with Lydia and the deepening stench of blood.

'Lydia,' Martha says, more calmly than she feels, 'Mrs Holdsworth is fetching something to take away your pain. And Polly has gone to get the doctor.'

She eyes the spreading dark stain and draws the coverlet back over Lydia's legs to hide it. Lydia watches her, glassy-eyed and shivering, making the sort of gasping, exhausted sobbing noises young children make. Martha pulls the blankets off her own bed to put on top of her, too, and winds her shawl around her shoulders.

'Lydia,' she says in a low voice, 'have you started a child?'

Lydia shakes her head, her teeth chattering. Martha nods, thinking hard. She has only a base knowledge of illness. When she was seven or eight, her mother gave birth too early to a baby boy, who struggled on for six days. But there had been no blood like this, no fever, no shuddering. Stomach complaints, sickness, influenza – she nursed both her sisters through countless ailments, and they did the same for her. Once, there was a prolonged bedrest for Mary, who had fluid on the lungs, but she made a full recovery. At the Magdalen, she saw far worse. But those cases went to the infirmary, which was closed off from the dorms. Some returned to their beds and many did not, but the suffering was kept from those on the main ward.

Mrs Holdsworth is back with a small glass bottle. 'Fetch more lamps and light the fire,' she instructs, and Martha gets up at once.

As she leaves the little bedroom, the door to the front bedroom opens, and a frightened white face peers out. Two more appear in the shadows.

'We heard voices,' says Frances.

'It's Lydia,' says Martha. But she has nothing else to say, no words of reassurance.

She goes downstairs to find lamps, boil some water, gather some coal. Two of the girls come to help her, all three remaining in the kitchen until they have everything they need, as though they are going together on some great voyage.

By the time they return to the bedroom, Lydia is dead.

The youngest chambermaid at Stratton Street seems startled to find her mistress awake at six, sitting up in bed. Weighed down with a basket of logs and her trusty dust sheet, she almost drops her candle when Angela addresses her directly. Angela supposes the girl mostly sees her asleep.

'Good morning,' she says from the wide snowy bed. 'It's Phyllis, isn't it?'

The girl nods.

'Is Stockton awake yet?'

'I'm not sure, miss,' the maid breathes.

'Phyllis, could you go and wake him? Six is a reasonable time, is it not? Leave the fire for now; do that first, would you?'

'Yes, miss.'

Within minutes, the footman is present, wrapped modestly in a housecoat.

'Stockton, I need you to take a note, urgently and in person. Could you do it now?'

'Yes, miss. Right away, miss.'

The footman gives a deep bow and retreats.

Angela endures an hour and a half of her stomach sliding like eels in a barrel before the duke is announced. She receives him in the drawing room, which she has asked to be kept dim and private. Weak sunlight struggles through the blinds, and she stands by the window with her hands clasped, facing the door.

'I was beginning to think I had offended you,' says the duke, approaching her and looking about in bewilderment. 'Why do you keep it so dark?'

She has not seen him in a while, not since the ill-fated journey to Reading with Martha. Usually, when it has been some time since they met, she feels obliged to close the chasm with a witty remark or, less often, when she craves reassurance, a sense of aloofness that forces him to work for her affection. He does not like it when she does not write to him, and she has barely sent him a paragraph since she saw him last.

'There is something you ought to know,' she says, hearing how cool she sounds. 'Will you take a seat?'

After a brief, intense pause, he obliges, rubbing his hands up the length of his thighs, appearing to brace himself. 'My dear?'

'Last Wednesday evening, I wrote a note to you. A very candid note, typical of our correspondence, with as much feeling as usual – and as much intention.'

He stares at her. 'I received no such note. You wrote to me a fortnight ago and the last was this morning.'

'No,' she says flatly. 'You did not receive it, because it was stolen from my sitting room before it was sent, by Richard Dunn – or by somebody acquainted with him who attended my ball on the night in question. Last night, I received this from a boy who must have followed me.'

She hands him the letter, and he reads it, his expression turning to stone.

'*If you refuse to meet me, you will repent this course, the consequences of which will sooner or later fall on yourself and those who are dearest to you.*'

'Before you ask how the theft might have occurred,' she says, 'there were a hundred people here, not all of whom I knew because guests brought guests and so on. He won't have come in through the street door, because my policeman was stationed there. It's possible he slipped in through the kitchens, as I used agency staff. I suppose he might have posed as a member of staff or had one of them do it for him. Of course I didn't see him – I would have recognised him at once.'

'When you say the note was candid . . .'

'I don't recall the wording exactly. But I wouldn't wish for it to fall into the wrong hands, and now it has.'

The duke sits back slowly, widening his legs. 'And now he is threatening to publish.'

'Naturally, I am writing to every editor I know, every

publisher and journalist, requesting they block such an article, but these things have a way of slipping through. Mr Dickens is helping; he has more influence than I do. But of course he does not know everybody.'

Saying nothing, his brow furrowed, he looks off to the side. She knows he is not annoyed, only thinking.

'Will you meet him?'

'Of course not. Parkinson would call it collusion.' She pauses. 'Do you think I should meet him?'

'No, I don't. *I* should like to meet him.'

'If it were to be published, your reputation—'

'Will not haunt me for much longer. It is yours that matters.'

'I wish you would not speak that way.' She turns and goes to the window, tweaking the lace curtain and looking out. 'I wondered if it was sensible, you coming here, but you can see why I did not wish to put it in writing.'

He shakes his head. 'I despise what this wretched man does to you.'

'Even if Mr Dickens were to keep my name from the circulars, I am not convinced he could save yours.'

'You are forgetting two things,' says the duke. 'The first is that I, too, have friends. The second is that I have endured worse than this. Would you like me to have him shot?'

She laughs, and the sound is like a bell in the gloom. 'No doubt men more noble than he have been slain at your hand.'

She thought he would be angry, but his lightness of touch, the humour with which he has handled the situation, has surprised her. She was awake most of the night, fretting not only for herself but over his reaction, for he can be impulsive and bullish, even with her. Especially with her.

'I think I will go abroad,' she says. 'Perhaps St Petersburg.'

'I think that would be the very worst thing you could do,' the duke warns. 'Remain at the eye of the storm. If you go gallivanting off, it reeks of guilt.'

'But I am escaping something. Him.'

'You must always return.'

'Must I? In truth, Arthur, I have given it some thought. If I left England, I doubt he would follow.'

A knock interrupts her. Irritated, she admits Stockton.

'Mr Dickens is downstairs, miss.'

'I'm afraid I'm otherwise engaged. Tell him to come back later.'

The footman nods; the door closes.

The duke is not a tall man but appears so when he is seated; those meeting him for the first time find themselves deceived when he climbs off his horse. He raises an eyebrow as she approaches and, feeling she should sit also, takes the high-backed chair. From this short distance, she can smell the scent of tobacco clinging to his coat and the soap he has just washed with.

She breathes in, once, deeply, resting her hands on the arms, and says slowly: 'There is, of course, another solution, and I hope you will hear it and understand it as one gravely, and not flippantly, considered. One of the reasons Dunn has been able to continue his campaign of harassment is that I am not married. That is a fact. I am almost certain that he would not persist if I were. And I am absolutely certain he would not persist if I were married to you.'

The duke closes his eyes. 'Angie, my dear—'

'I beg you to listen. Our marriage, if you so wish, would not change a thing between us. We could continue just as we are. I would live here, and you have your houses to yourself. I know

212

you are against the idea of it, but my suggestion is that it could be a marriage in name only, if that is preferable to you.'

'That is not preferable to me. It's an abhorrent suggestion.'

'Why? It would preserve our affection for one another. It would be nothing like yours and Kitty's marriage.'

'Enough!' He leaps to his feet, blazing.

'Why will you not help me?' she cries. 'Why will you not grant me this kindness, this single kindness?'

'Because it is the very opposite of kindness. It is wrong, it is unthinkable.'

'*Why*, Arthur?'

'Because I am old enough to be your grandfather.'

'I don't care.'

'Enough. I have heard quite enough.' He begins to stride away.

'How dare you dismiss me like one of your men?' she barks, white with fury. 'Why are you here, Arthur? Tell me why you came.'

'I am here because you asked me to come. Whatever do you mean?'

'Why do you write to me? And visit me and send me flowers and tell me you are thinking of me when you are alone? I have hundreds, *hundreds* of letters from you. Do you write so often, so ardently, to all your friends? Do you invite them to look at your bedroom?'

'You are being absurd.'

'Am I? Am I so absurd as to be vexed that a man I know to be in love with me will do nothing about it? You say I am better off finding a man my own age. That I will waste the rest of my life with what's left of yours. That is what you say, Arthur, but really I wonder if you are selfish and a coward. You are too comfortable at home with your horses and dogs and weekends hosting regiments, reminiscing and congratulating one another on battles won while good old Mrs Cross fusses after you. You don't want a woman about the house with her things and her friends, interfering with your routines, encroaching on your precious time. You would rather have me live in hope that one day you will change your mind, writing me letters and sending me presents and teasing me when I go away to try to forget you. You want me as a lover in theory but not in reality, and so you string me along because I flatter you too much to be done away with.'

She breaks off and flies towards the window, pausing a moment to compose herself, and then continuing. 'You say you won't do it to protect me but this is not about that. If you wanted to protect me, you would marry me. It will not change your life a jot and still you won't do it, because you are afraid I will dismantle your little kingdom. You are an old man, set in your ways, afraid of starting again. If you are truly the friend you say you are, that you have claimed to be these past years, then do me, your friend, the ultimate charity and absolve me of this nightmare I have lived for a decade.'

She has raised her voice to him for the first time. A strangled silence follows, and she clutches her raw throat.

The duke says nothing, a tendon flickering in his jaw. He wipes his mouth and will not look at her. 'No,' he says heavily.

She glares at him, her breathing ragged.

'I will not marry you to outwit anybody, even a bastard like Dunn. You wish to face him as a duchess? You must find another duke.'

Swiftly, he turns, and in a few strides is gone. Angela does not follow him. She is trembling, too afraid to move an inch in case she screams or breaks something. She has never been in such a storm before, has never shouted at him – or anybody – like that before. She understands that everything has changed now, irrevocably, with the friend she has held dearest of all.

There is a small knock, and Stockton manifests.

'Mr Dickens is still here, miss. He wishes to speak with you urgently. He says it regards the house in Shepherd's Bush?'

❧

Angela and the Browns exchange not a word on the grim journey west. Mrs Holdsworth ushers them into the passage, glancing behind them and closing the door.

'I am so dreadfully sorry, Mrs Holdsworth,' Angela says. 'A terrible thing for you to have to witness.'

'The coroner is coming at three,' Mrs Holdsworth replies. Her face is waxen, her eyes red-rimmed. 'Doctor, if you wouldn't mind?'

'Certainly. Where is the unfortunate creature?'

'In the smallest bedroom. We were using it for storage. Upstairs, second door on the right.'

Dr Brown creaks upwards with his bag. Though the fires are lit, the house feels very cold, and there is the same chilly silence that met Angela when Josephine left. They remain in the gloom of the hall.

'Frank's gone to find a coffin-maker,' says Mrs Holdsworth.

'Is there anything I can help with? Anything at all?'

'A funeral will need to be paid for. And perhaps you could write a letter of condolence to the family? Of course I have already written to her next of kin. Thankfully, she gave her grandmother's address when she arrived.'

'I'd be happy to,' says Angela.

'I suppose her grandmother will have a preference for where she is buried.'

They fall into silence.

'Where was home?' asks Mrs Brown eventually.

'Waltham Abbey, I think. Good heavens, I wouldn't know how to transport a coffin all that way.'

'Leave all that with me. I will ask her grandmother her wishes.'

Mrs Holdsworth sighs. 'I'd offer you tea, but I'm afraid in all the commotion we've run out. The grocer missed it off the list, and I haven't had the time to go to the shops.'

'Leave that with me, too. Mrs Brown and I will go. Would one of the girls like to come for some fresh air?'

'Martha and Polly were with her. Polly washed the body and dressed her. I think they might appreciate a change of scenery.'

They wait in the hall for Mrs Holdsworth to fetch the girls, and a minute later, Polly comes downstairs, wan-faced, and takes a shawl and bonnet off the coat-stand.

At the same time, Frank Holdsworth lets himself into the house, delivering an unwelcome draught. 'The coffin-maker will come in the morning. Handley, he's called.'

'Thank you,' says his mother.

'Is Martha not joining us?' asks Angela.

'She says she'd prefer to remain here.'

A flat silence falls, and Angela turns to Polly and says a little too brightly: 'Shall we go?'

The three women take the carriage to the little row of shops on the Uxbridge Road. Polly, lost in thought, gazes emptily at the various window displays. Once or twice, Angela attempts to make conversation and is then taken aback when the girl interrupts her to speak to Mrs Brown.

'Will Dr Brown know what it was?'

'He will do his best, but there will likely be an inquest if the cause is not obvious.'

'But if she...' Polly stalls, and continues in a low voice. 'If she had started a child, and then...it wouldn't have caused her to die, would it?'

'A conversation for the house, I think,' Angela interjects. 'Is this the grocer's?'

They buy two pounds of tea to take home and more to be delivered, along with a small list of other items from Mrs Holdsworth. It is Angela's first time in a grocer's, and the proprietor is embarrassed when she reaches for her silk purse, and with his ears glowing red, apologises again for missing it off the order, and assures her it will be added to the bill. Their solemn party returns to the house, and Polly goes straight upstairs.

Mrs Holdsworth directs them into the parlour, where Dr Brown stands with his back to the fire. A pot of tea cools, presided over by Frank, who sets out in search of more cups. When they are all five arranged, the hush of anticipation descends.

'I recommend a full inquest,' says Dr Brown, and at once, there are sighs of disappointment from the women. 'I agree with the physician that the haemorrhage most likely originated in the peritoneal cavity, or ruptured into there.'

'The perito—' Mrs Holdsworth stutters.

'The womb.'

She nods. Her mouth is more lined than Angela remembers; she appears to have aged five years overnight.

'There was some swelling to the left-hand side of the abdomen. A tumour is a possibility. It is likely she was in severe discomfort for some time.'

Mrs Holdsworth sighs and closes her eyes. 'Poor girl.'

'And if it wasn't a tumour?' Mrs Brown enquires.

Dr Brown looks grim. 'I have only seen it once before, but there is the possibility of a ruptured tubal pregnancy. It occurs when the foetus and placenta grow in the fallopian tube instead of the uterus. Only a post-mortem will confirm it.'

The others sit in stunned silence.

After what feels like a long time, Angela swallows and says: 'Why do you think this might be the case with Miss Rice?'

'There is a thin, dark line running up her stomach that appears in pregnancy.' Dr Brown says. 'I have not examined Miss Rice before; it could of course be a birthmark or natural discolouration. I cannot be certain, as it is quite faint.'

'Could she have been saved?' asks his wife.

'No. There is no remedy, medicinal or surgical. Unless the body passes or absorbs the foetus, it is always fatal.'

There is another deep silence, and then Angela turns to Mrs Holdsworth, who is standing with her white knuckles pressing into the back of the settee, as though holding herself upright. 'She didn't say anything about—'

'No,' the matron replies softly. 'Naturally the thought occurred, but she passed nothing. Martha asked if she was with child, and she said she wasn't.'

'She likely wouldn't have known,' says Dr Brown.

'All that pain,' Mrs Holdsworth murmurs. 'She must have been so very frightened.'

'A beastly business,' Mrs Brown utters.

Angela's eyes are hot with tears, and she blinks them away.

'Will you stay for something to eat, Miss Coutts? Dr and Mrs Brown? I can't for the life of me remember what we are having today, but you are welcome to eat with us.'

'Mrs Brown and I will cook,' says Angela. 'Or rather, we will attempt to do so. Dr Brown, if you wish to take the carriage home, you are welcome to.'

Mrs Holdsworth blinks in surprise. 'The girls can do it.'

'No, they are in shock. We ought to let them rest, cry, write to their loved ones, whatever it is they wish to do. No house-work or lessons today.'

'If you say so.'

'I do. And if you would be so kind as to show me where the aprons are, we will make haste.'

✤

It is late, and the candle burns low, but Martha is not tired. She sits alone in the bedroom, staring at what was Josephine's bed, then Lydia's. It has been stripped bare to wood and iron, the mattress soaking in salt in the wash-house, where the sheets hang like a bloody tableau. Mrs Holdsworth said they will have to be cut up for rags. Martha's arms ache from the scrubbing; she was determined to wash them herself.

The house is chilly, her blankets warm. Angela stayed for dinner and then supper, clearing away after each meal and insisting the girls did nothing – but industry has become natural to them, and it was strange to sit and mourn. Afterwards, when they expected Angela to leave, she led prayers in the parlour. Mrs Brown dozed, and the girls yawned, yet still she read on as though incanting a spell that might bring the lifeless girl down the stairs.

Polly has still not come to bed, though it must be after midnight. Martha decides to take down the supper tray and with great effort leaves her warm nest. On the landing, light flickers faintly beneath the front bedroom door, accompanied by hushed voices; it is little wonder that sleep has failed to find the house tonight.

She takes her candle downstairs, expecting to discover Polly in the parlour, but the room is shut up for the night, smelling of burnt oil. The kitchen door is ajar, a lone lamp lit within, and she pauses for a moment in the passage, for two people are talking quietly. The long-case clock tells her it is twenty minutes after twelve. She goes quietly to the door and looks in, holding her flame out of sight.

Frank and Polly are sitting opposite one another at the table. Polly's head is bowed, and both their hands rest upon the wood, wrists loose, palms up, inches apart, as though they have been reading each other's fortunes. Polly's sleeves have ridden up, and her scars run like wax down her wrists. She says something, softly, inaudibly, and Frank shakes his head. They appear familiar, intimate, and the scene is so surprising that Martha temporarily forgets herself. Adjusting her grip on the tray, she strikes the door as she does so, causing the two of them to look up.

Frank leaps to his feet, followed by Polly, who glances guiltily at her and pulls down her sleeves. She has been crying.

Wordlessly, Martha crosses the kitchen to put the tray in the scullery.

'I'll be going,' says Frank. He pushes his chair beneath the table and clears his throat. 'Martha?' He comes to the scullery door, where she is washing her things in cold water. 'I don't suppose there's any news?'

Martha does not turn. 'On what?'

'On Emily.'

'No,' she says dully. 'No news.'

She senses him lingering in the doorway before eventually he departs.

Polly is waiting for her in the kitchen.

'Not you as well,' Martha says.

A wrinkle appears at Polly's brow. 'What do you mean?'

'You're leaving.'

'No! Why ever would you think that?'

Martha just looks at her.

'Martha, what makes you say that?'

'I don't know.'

Polly takes her wrist. 'Come, you're shivering. Let's go up to bed.'

The next morning, it is business as usual, and after more prayers and breakfast, the inmates of Urania Cottage return gratefully to their studies. In the break between lessons and dinner, Martha is practising her needlework in the schoolroom to avoid talking to anybody when Polly puts her head in.

'Would you like to come outside with me?' she says. 'It's a beautiful day.'

They pass through the kitchen, where two of the girls are making a Charlotte Russe. The day is bright and blustery, with a breeze as crisp as a starched collar, and Polly leads them to the bench in the orchard and sits down. Martha smooths her skirts beneath her and perches at the other end. A magpie rattles in the bare branches of an apple tree, and they watch it for a moment, admiring its plumage, blue-black and cream against the muted browns and greys.

One for sorrow, Martha thinks. And then she says: 'I told her to go back to sleep.'

'You weren't to know,' Polly replies. 'None of us were to know.'

'She needn't have died.'

Polly looks at her.

'If I hadn't left the house that night to look for Josephine,' says Martha, 'Josephine wouldn't have left. Lydia might not have come. She might have stayed wherever she was, where people might have helped her. Might have saved her. She might still be alive.' It seems a terrible truth when Lydia is still in the house, when they can, in fact, see the window beneath which she lies, open to keep the room cold.

'Frank told me she would have died regardless,' says Polly. 'There's to be an inquest, but what Dr Brown suspects . . . she would not have survived it.'

Martha decides Polly has no reason to lie to her, and she returns her gaze to the glistening grass. A horse and cart travels up the lane and fades once again to birdsong.

Polly leans down to pluck a daffodil from the ground and, twirling it between finger and thumb, says: 'Frank asked me to marry him.'

Martha turns to look at her in astonishment, but Polly does not meet her eye and goes on twisting the stem and peering into the middle distance.

'What answer did you give?'

'I told him no.'

'You don't love him?'

Polly swallows. 'It isn't that. I think I could. I know I could.'

'Is it Mrs Holdsworth?'

'She doesn't know. But no, it's not her.'

The chickens have been let out of the coop before it is to be cleaned. They roam the garden, picking up their wormy claws in distaste.

'I had a son,' Polly says, very softly. 'He was born dead.'

Sorrow spreads like a stain in Martha's chest.

'He was perfect.' Polly smiles, stroking a sunny petal. 'So beautiful. I named him Thomas, after my brother.'

The wind sighs through the trees as Martha's eyes blur.

'There was an inquest,' Polly says. 'They sent me to the workhouse to await the verdict.'

'What verdict?' Martha frowns, failing to understand.

Polly sniffs. 'Infanticide.'

Martha's mouth falls open in shock. 'But how could they—?'

'I was a maid at the time. I had him alone in my bedroom early one morning. Nobody knew I'd been expecting, and when he came . . .' Polly's voice breaks, and when she has composed herself, she says: 'They called the constable.'

'How could they?' Martha breathes.

'I was found not guilty. But by then I had no work and no baby. Nothing, really, to live for. And so . . .'

She traces the eye of the daffodil, circling round and round. Martha recalls the way she shrunk into the wall when Lydia groaned in her bed, the terror in her eyes. Mrs Holdsworth had sent Polly to fetch the doctor, though she was the one who Lydia knew best, and now Martha understands why.

'When it didn't work, I tried again and was taken to an infirmary. Then I heard about this place. I began to see a different way for me. A different life, far away. The other side of the world doesn't seem far enough, truthfully, but I've promised myself I'll try. Frank isn't part of that. And the idea of marrying and . . .' Polly lowers the flower and looks off to the left as the wind rustles the branches. 'They'll send me away if they know I've told you.'

'They won't know.' Martha reaches across the bench and takes Polly's small, cold hand.

'There is one person in here who knows about it,' says Polly. 'Frances. She was at the same workhouse.'

'Pay no attention to Frances,' says Martha, squeezing her fingers.

'What if she tells the others?'

'Then we'll tell Mrs Holdsworth, and she'll be gone. Besides, she won't.'

Polly squeezes back, and together they watch the chickens, who never seem to find what it is they are searching for.

CHAPTER 11

Ink and Water

The constable's whistle pierces the air like a steam train. Ripples of surprise pass through pedestrians hurrying headfirst through the rainy evening, shawls and hats held close against the elements, but the weather is too poor for them to stop and see what the matter is.

Josephine is already changing her appearance in a doorway, pulling the pins from her hair and turning over her shawl, dark green on one side, red and black paisley on the other. She has already cast the pocketbook into the gutter. Swiftly, she steps back into the street and goes downhill in the direction of the Strand.

Still the rain lashes down, gushing in streams and rivulets, and a wet, woolly fog spools down the lanes and alleys towards the river. Josephine pauses on the pavement to cross the wide road, taking care not to show her face, and thinks of the door she will reach in a moment and fasten behind her. No matter that they will have no supper; they have missed it before. And no matter that the pocketbook lies soaking in the road; perhaps it will still be there later, if an eagle-eyed crossing-sweeper has not swiped it first.

She waits for a carriage to pass, careful not to draw attention, to not look as though she is in a rush. In doing so, she glances to the right to check for traffic.

'There!'

In a moment, she is seized roughly, her arms pinned behind her, causing her to cry out.

'Get off me, will you?'

The constable, whistle dangling around his neck, spittle flecking his lips, drags her away from the road.

'Sir, I beg you, let go of me! What is the meaning of this?'

The gentleman she has robbed manifests beside the constable.

'This is her?' The constable pins her arms before the gentleman, who lifts his hat to peer at her.

'Sir?' she says.

Passers-by look but do not stop. Josephine refrains from struggling, afraid the shawl will slip and reveal the green twill beneath. She has stitched the two together, and so far it has served her well.

The man's dark brow furrows as rain pours down his face.

'Please, sir, may I ask who you think I am?'

The constable begins searching her pockets, which are empty save for a few hairpins and a return ticket for the half-penny steamer: her alibi whenever she needs one.

'Oh, please don't tear that, sir, else I won't be able to get home. I was just making my way there now.'

The gentleman appears more and more doubtful.

'*Is this her*, sir?' The constable is drenched and impatient.

'She is bare-headed like the thief, with the same dark hair.'

'There is no pocketbook on her person,' says the constable. 'Lift your arms, girl.'

The gentleman watches anxiously as he pats her skirts and bodice, revealing nothing other than the fact that one or two of the bones in her stays want fixing.

'Nothing there.' The constable sighs, thinking of the report he somehow must write in this weather. He glances at the sky as though telling the time. 'Can you be certain, sir, that this is the girl what robbed you?'

'Sir,' Josephine tries, making her voice softer, 'there has been a dreadful mistake. I have robbed nobody. I am on my way to catch the steamer home.' Her wet hair is flat against her head.

The gentleman is dignified enough to admit he cannot be certain. The constable releases her, and she rolls her shoulders with relish.

'Thank you, sir. I am sorry you was robbed,' she addresses the gentleman. 'I hope you find what was stole from you.'

They are all three eager to be gone, and with no apology from either of them, Josephine takes her leave. Returning to the spot at which she attempted to cross, half-blind with fear and relief, she tries hard to appear calm and pay attention to the traffic in both directions.

She walks slowly, resisting the powerful urge to run, for it was running that put her in Tothill. The idea of going back there now is unthinkable, with all she has come to know on the outside. Already, she feels as though she is losing her grip on things, sliding all the way back to the gutter. She thinks of the Josephine Nash she was at Shepherd's Bush: warm, fed, clean, sitting with a slate in a schoolroom, her mind keen and alert. And now: half-drowned, starving, having robbed a man in the street.

She has reached the door of their lodgings on Villiers Street in the warren of passages between the river and the Strand, but she passes by in case she is being followed, and continues to the pier, where she watches the steamers slide seamlessly in and out like shafts on a loom. Through the mist, she tries to read the names painted on the sides: *Jupiter, Swallow, Marquess.*

Annie will be waiting for her, wondering what she has brought home for them to eat, hoping no doubt for some vinegary cockles, a piece of cheese, a bit of cold chicken. They will have a few hours before Mr and Mrs Frobisher, the couple they share with, stumble in from the public house, shrieking and swearing and fighting and, finally, fucking, as though the two girls aren't there.

The first night, Josephine and Annie found it funny. They covered their mouths beneath the blankets, their foreheads crashing together as they shook with laughter. But when they realised it was a nightly occurrence, it became less of an amusement, more of a pain to endure, especially now that Annie complains of tiredness and more than once has pretended to be asleep when Josephine comes home. Their own consummations are stealthy, urgent in the velvet darkness when their roommates are snoring, with the exception of one exquisitely long, drawn-out afternoon when they had the room to themselves. Josephine used to dream of having Annie alone, away from prison wardens and enforced silence and clinging children. For so long, she fantasised about locking the door and feasting on her, dividing her into courses. But the bountiful banquets she once imagined have reduced to a single, rushed serving, and only when Annie is willing, which is less and less.

She cannot go home again with nothing. She cannot go even further backwards, to the fourth-floor room with Maud and John and the children, carrying slops down endless flights of stairs. But as another day draws to a close, so do her options. The idea of thieving again, of being *caught* thieving, leaves her cold. And so she makes her way home to Villiers Street and lets herself in.

Annie is mending stockings in bed, and before her, on a small table . . . Josephine almost drops to her knees. A knuckle of roast beef, a loaf of bread, butter wrapped in paper.

She cries out: 'You clever thing! How did you get this?'

'I finished the petticoats for the boarding-house lady.'

'You angel.'

They eat slowly in bed, eking out their rations, savouring every mouthful. And when she is finished but by no means sated, she does not think of Shepherd's Bush, where the girls will be setting the table for supper. She does not think of mutton, gravy, dumplings, blackberry jam on good bread; cheese, dripping, porridge with cream steaming on a winter's morning. Best to forget about it, she thinks, licking her fingers, and giving a reassuring smile to Annie, though she is not sure it is Annie who needs it.

❦

Dr Brown finds Angela in her dressing room. The bath has not been emptied, the water is cold, and Angela is sitting on the floor in her robe and nightgown, surrounded by newspapers, pamphlets, periodicals and every manner of journalism she can put her hands on. The spring day is warm, and outside the park is flooded with people. For almost a week, Dr Brown has been attending the newsagent's by the park gates, returning to Stratton Street laden with papers. He tells her he takes a wide selection, but of course he does not, having deemed it unlikely for a society scandal to break in *The Musical World* or *The Gardener's Chronicle*. Angela bathes each morning and then begins reading them cover to cover, which can take all day. By sunset, her hands are like a miner's, her cheeks and nose stamped with ink. She takes a second bath and eats supper in her room, then goes to bed.

'Is *The Satirist* not published today?' she asks.

'Sunday,' he replies.

She is kneeling with them spread about her, swiping through the covers and inspecting them closely, like a punter at a rag stall. Perched on a small table is her breakfast tray, the egg smooth and untouched. A childlike bite has been taken from a piece of toast.

'My dear, how long must this go on?'

'Until I find something.'

'And if you don't?'

She lifts *The Globe* and begins to flick through it, her brow puckered in a frown. With difficulty, his joints cracking, Dr Brown kneels before her and takes her hands in his.

When they retire at night, he and Mrs Brown sit against the headboard, talking late into the night. He is concerned as a friend and protector but also as a doctor. More than once has he seen a young woman's descent into madness, beginning with a beloved cousin in the winter of '98. He was twelve, she eighteen. His recollection of her biting the skin at her nails, the hollow distance in her eyes, haunts him still. Now, nearing her seventieth year, visited by nobody, she has lived in an asylum half a century. The grief killed her mother.

'My dear.' He waits for Angela to look at him, clinging to her fingers. 'Read these later. I think you should get dressed now.'

'Later I might.'

Some days have passed since he received the post-mortem report, confirming his suspicions: that poor Lydia Rice had started a child, and the foetus had grown in the wrong place. He went immediately to Angela's rooms to share the news with her, and she sat in her chair by the window and cried. Mrs Brown came to her and then fetched her things so that she could begin arranging a burial. A reply came back from Lydia's grandmother's house, from the young man who lives there now; her grandmother died some months ago, and so Lydia has no family. The funeral will be a small one, held at a private chapel in Kensington.

Now, he rises stiffly, bearing his weight on her arm. ''Tis a wondrous spring day,' he says. 'Come and listen to the song-birds in the park with Mrs B and me.'

She remains where she is, her robe fanned out around her, and stares at him in disbelief. 'I cannot go to the park.'

'Why not?' he asks innocently.

'Oh, do not be obtuse. If everybody knows my business, I shall be gawped at like a spectacle in a sideshow.'

'My dear, nobody knows your business besides yourself. And this is not Millbank Prison. You may leave the house whenever you like, for as long as you like, by whichever mode of transport you like. If you don't care for a walk through the park, why not take a carriage ride to Highgate? Stay with the Duke of St Albans? You always enjoy the garden there. Or escape London altogether for the coast: Sandgate or Broadstairs?'

She returns to her pages, snapping briskly through them,

and says with bitterness: 'And do what? Sit in a conservatory while the patrons discuss me behind their fans?'

'My dear, you are losing perspective. Firstly, nothing has been said or written about you. Secondly, if it was, do you think people would believe it?'

'Of course they would. I told Parkinson something like this would happen, and yet he was certain Dunn had simply lost interest. It appears I know him better than anybody. Do you know the most curious thing, William? When he wasn't following me, surprising me at every turn like he used to do, I almost missed it. Can you believe that a part of me, a tiny, hideous part was dismayed? I am ashamed to admit it, but it's true. I thought: is it my age? Is it my looks?'

'Now you are being ridiculous.' Getting again to his feet, he gathers up the pile of press into his arms, walks across the room and dumps them unceremoniously into the bath tub. They cascade bodily into the water, before drifting up and floating like a mess of leaves on the surface.

'No!' Angela cries, plunging her hands into the tub, grasping at sheets that disintegrate at her fingertips. 'What have you done?'

'I am saving you from lunacy,' he declares. 'Now, eat your breakfast, get dressed, fetch your parasol and join us in the hall in twenty minutes.'

'I *cannot*, William. Nobody understands how I feel. I am not being dramatic; I am not becoming a lunatic.' She sighs. 'Do you think I ought to write to the people I saw in the drawing room, by the fire that night? They were talking in private; I wonder if they saw anybody come in or out.'

'What would your grandmother say, if she were here now?'

Disarmed, Angela's eyes fill with tears.

'She left all this to you because she knew you could take it on. She knew you could take on anything.'

She gives a deep sigh, and her shoulders sink. They are silent, and the water sloshes gently in the tub.

'Do you know,' she says, 'I have thought once or twice about marrying him.'

'Who?'

'Richard Dunn.'

The doctor is outraged. 'You cannot be serious.'

'Of course I don't want to,' she replies. 'But there would be no more surprises that way. I wouldn't have to live in this dreadful limbo any longer, not knowing where he is or when he will emerge.'

'Marry a madman? Now you have really lost your mind.'

'Perhaps I have,' she says idly.

'Downstairs. Twenty minutes,' he declares.

She glances through the window at the majestic oaks and silver limes. 'Ballard will come?' she asks.

'Naturally,' he says, pulling the bell for the maid on the way out.

⚘

On the afternoon of Martha's next appointment with Mr Bryant, she finds the chaplain standing in the hall, wearing his hat.

'I thought we could take a walk today,' he says. 'Mrs Holdsworth has permitted it.'

They go out into the lane, and he asks which way she wishes to go. She chooses right, towards the open fields, and they begin on foot in silence. Though it is not particularly cold, she wraps her shawl about herself and lowers her bonnet. Mr Bryant remains a pace or two behind and to the left. They walk leisurely, hemmed in on both sides by hedgerows, skirting the occasional pile of horse manure. Though she cannot see him, the tread of his boots relax her somehow, and she senses he will not speak until she is ready.

After a while, she says: 'Will you go to Lydia's burial?'

'I will do my best,' he replies.

'I wish we were allowed to go.'

'What happened was tragic. It would be unwise to expose you unnecessarily to more grief.'

They walk a little while longer, and when they reach the kink in the lane, he says: 'I thought I might have had a lead at the Surrey House of Correction. One of the wardens replied to my letter with information on an Emily *Gerber*. I don't suppose you used that surname interchangeably?'

'No,' says Martha.

'I wrote down both names and can see how one might be mistaken for the other. But I acted in haste; in the next sentence, the warden went on to say she was an old woman.'

Martha is silent.

'The prison population of women your sister's age is small. If she turns up in one of the London correction houses, I am sure we will find her.'

Martha has heard despicable things about the Surrey House of Correction from girls at the Magdalen who came out of it. She is glad her sister is not there.

'And if she doesn't?' she says.

'Then we shall keep looking.'

'I don't know how you find the time to help me, with all your religious instruction,' she says, sounding sour.

Mr Bryant is thoughtful. 'I dislike the term instruction. It's very one-sided. I prefer to think of my work as being more collaborative. Reciprocal, like conversation. Instruction is closed off to learning. I like to learn from people.'

'I doubt you'll learn much from me.'

'I have already learnt a lot from you.'

She scoffs, incredulous. 'Such as?'

'The power of resilience. The value of kinship, whether those ties be familial or social.'

Martha breaks a tall dock at the stem and twirls it pensively.

'She might be lost like I was,' she says. 'In which case, there will be no finding her, until she wishes to be found.'

They walk onwards, and then, feeling the sun break through a cloud and bathe her face, Martha says: 'What made you want to become a clergyman?'

'My mother was a woman of the Protestant faith. It caused her problems, but it never failed her. When she was dying, the curate came to our house every evening. He walked three miles there, three miles back, every night for weeks. His devotion moved me. It brought order to chaos, hope to hopelessness. When she was gone, he came sometimes to speak with my brothers and me. He gave us a prayer book and folded down the pages he thought would offer most comfort. He made our grief smaller. It was the first time I understood what faith could do. I wanted to bring it to people in the same way. I can still picture him coming up the front path, the sound of his knuckles at the door. The feeling it brought us, as though, when he was there, no harm could come to us. Did you know that curate means cure of the soul?'

She says that she did not. When she wishes to turn around and go back, Mr Bryant offers no resistance. They walk down the lane in silence, side by side, and when the house is in sight, Martha notices somebody standing by the hedgerow, looking away from them. As they draw closer, she realises it is Vincent, the boy from the brickfields, and at the same time, he hears them and turns. He looks at each of them and gives an unpleasant smirk. Then he shoves his hands into his pockets and goes on his way.

'That blackguard,' Mr Bryant mutters darkly. 'He's giving you no trouble, is he?'

'No,' Martha replies, watching him grow smaller. Then she turns to Mr Bryant. 'I finished reading *Michael Howe*.'

The chaplain brightens. 'I look forward to hearing your thoughts.'

She squints at him in the bright daylight. She was once a person who lived outdoors, who slept against door-frames and washed at standpipes. Now, it feels as though she has lost a layer of skin.

'How do you feel now at the prospect of leaving England?'

'I still haven't given it much thought.'

'Only I wondered' – the chaplain removes his hat – 'given the extenuating circumstances of your sister's whereabouts… if you might consider remaining here.'

A frown pulls at her eyebrows. 'Here at the house?'

'No. In England.' He hesitates. 'As my wife.'

Martha stares at him.

'Martha, the truth is that I have grown quite attached to you these past weeks. I find myself looking forward to our meetings very much, not only as counsellor and pupil but as something else.' He looks at her intently. 'I have realised I am more invested in your future than I have cared to admit, and the future you have been preparing for is—' He pauses and turns his hat in his hands. 'I began to imagine an alternative one for you, against my better judgement.'

Attempting to comprehend him, numb with shock, Martha speaks the first words that enter her head. 'But you're—'

He waits. 'Too old? A lowly chaplain?' There is humour in his tone.

'How old are you?'

'One-and-fifty.'

She squints into the sun, too dazzled to see him entirely.

'If you truly have your heart and mind set on beginning a new life somewhere else, I will understand. Your life has been difficult. *Is* difficult. I wish to make clear that I have no misgivings about what you have put behind you. None whatsoever. I don't pretend to know about your past, but in the fullness of time, I hope you will entrust me with the parts of it you wish to stay acquainted with. And I promise you are forgiven.

'Which brings me to my true motive,' he says carefully. 'If you become my wife, in your free time, you may devote yourself – and I would devote myself, too – to a matter very close to your heart. The search for your sister.'

She looks up sharply.

'I understand that, while you are here, you are limited in your investigations. I know how dear she is to you, how heavily her disappearance has weighed on you these past months. I have done what I can already, but there is so much more that may be achieved, if only you were able to grant your full attention to the cause.'

Birdsong rises from the woods, and Martha turns towards it. 'May I think about it?' she asks, finding she is unable to look the chaplain in the eye.

'I wish you would.'

That night, she dreams of a voyage. A brand-new ship, smelling of fresh wood; and above and below, deep, endless blue. Emily is at her side, and they walk into the sunlight together.

CHAPTER 12

Flypaper

Josephine peers into the slice of mirror on the bedroom wall and begins pinning her hair, which is still damp from the basin. She has done her best to clean the armpits of the dress she bought from a stall at Petticoat Lane market, but it could do with being let down an inch or two. She hears feet on the stairs, and Annie comes in with her eldest niece and nephew, his fist closed around a handful of nuts. The Frobishers are out, and Alfred, the nephew, sits on their bed and cracks a nut with his back teeth. Josephine says nothing and removes another pin from her mouth.

'When will you be back?' Annie asks, as though they are in the middle of a conversation.

'One?' Josephine replies through stiff lips. 'Two? Depends.'

'What?'

'It depends.'

She feels Annie's eyes travel up and down the new dress.

She has said nothing about it since Josephine brought it home a few days before and hung it on the wall like a painting.

'Why so late?' asks Annie, looking at her fingernails.

'I stay out as long as it takes,' Josephine replies.

'I found some work,' says Annie, combing her niece's hair with her fingers.

For the first time, Josephine turns from the mirror. 'Yeah?'

'Yeah. Making flypaper.' Annie sniffs. 'You know, just till I can find another place in service.'

They have spoken about this. If Annie gets work as a servant, she will most likely be offered a room. The flypaper job will be Annie's third attempt at finding work that suits her. First was mattress-stuffing, and then sweeping up after the packers in a bottle factory; the first caused her to cough, the second hurt her back. Annie is too particular and does not understand why, as a result, Josephine cannot be.

'Where are you going?' asks the niece.

'To the theatre,' Josephine replies.

'Can I come?'

'Not tonight.'

Josephine kisses Annie on the cheek and leaves.

Lately, more has gone unsaid than spoken. Annie is not green. Josephine stays out later and cleans herself when she comes home. The food they can afford is better and more plentiful: mustard, good cheese, fruit. Annie eats the food, makes room for Josephine in their bed and says nothing. Josephine bought the dress to see if Annie would challenge her; if they could hardly afford their board two weeks ago, why now do they have the money for clothes? But the dress remains unchallenged, the truth unspoken.

The wind is biting on Waterloo Bridge, and already,

Josephine feels her mood sinking. She wishes Annie did not have to make flypaper or sweep straw in a factory. She ought to be able to keep her at home, mending for the boarding-house ladies, shopping for them at the markets, with her little basket on her arm. She ought to be a husband to Annie, like John is to Maud, working and sleeping, creating an invisible structure for them to live inside. She thinks of Annie hunched over a work-bench, her hands glazed with fly-poison.

She realises that she is still angry, even now, that Annie did not come with her to Urania Cottage. How short-sighted she was, choosing her sister's family over her own future happiness. If she suspects that Annie would not have lasted a week under Mrs Holdsworth's scrutiny, picking at samplers in the evening and rising for prayers, she does not admit it to herself.

Sometimes, and more and more as she circles the city, she thinks of Martha. She pictures her sewing, writing, chalking a kangaroo on her slate, copied from a picture book, which made Josephine laugh so hard that Martha wiped it out with a sleeve, offended.

When a gentleman tips his hat towards her, she finds she is already smiling. 'Sir?' she asks, but he shakes his head and moves on.

Shortly after nine, she is successful and takes a man to one of the quiet alleys behind a theatre. His breath is laced with brandy, and he takes his time, but thirty minutes later, she is approaching the bridge once again, having given up on Granby Street and its surroundings. A man in a fine green coat asks her age and is disappointed when she tells him; he enquires where he might find young girls, and she lies and says she does not know.

On the bridge, she does not stop to look at the water, for too many like her have done so and have seen something irresistible within.

⚘

One evening, a few days later, Josephine begins at the Star and Garter on Trafalgar Square. Obliged to stand and roam alternately, she is tired before she's even begun. Thieving is easy, less tedious, than this. Swiping a pocketbook, a handkerchief, it's impossible to tell if it's bulging or empty, cotton or silk, and the thrill of success is a gamble. With this, there are very few surprises and sometimes they are welcome.

She is leaning against a partition in the bar, looking about the place, trying not to yawn. A foul-breathed, red-cheeked man has instructed her to wait but has not invited her to sit at his table. She watches the other girls circle, throwing a comment like a fish-hook here and there, seeing if it catches. The man has bought her a drink, a glass of gin and water; it burns her throat and she puts it on the side. The place is busy with clerks, Whigs, reporters; the Star and Garter lies close to Whitehall and Parliament and the omnibuses they take home. But they are talkers by profession, and it takes a tempting offer to peel them from the pack.

Josephine looks about her, catching her own pale face in the mirror behind the bar. To the right of the glass, a woman descends the stairs from the dining room. Josephine only notices her because she wears a dress of striped poplin similar to the one Martha wore at the home. Her face is familiar, but Josephine cannot place her; she stares a moment too long and must have narrowed her eyes, for the girl gives her a strange look and comes over. It is then that Josephine knows her: she is the pinch-faced girl who stood behind Susannah in the Strand.

'Nan,' she says as the name comes into her head.

Nan looks tired, but they all do. She nods at Josephine's drink sitting on the ledge. 'How long you gonna nurse that?'

'Have it if you want it.'

Nan swallows it in one. 'You coming to Susie's?'

'No, I'm waiting for someone.'

Nan raises her eyebrows, and Josephine nods at the grey-haired, red-faced man guffawing in the corner.

'You'll be waiting a while. Why don't you have something to eat?' Josephine is about to reply when Nan says: 'Come with me.'

She follows Nan and her striped dress up the stairs, light-headed with hunger as the smell of roasting meat drifts from a distant passage. The dining-room windows overlook Nelson's Column, Charing Cross and the mall. In the corner, a man is sitting alone reading a broadsheet, and Nan approaches him.

'This is . . .'

'Josephine,' she supplies.

'She's hungry.'

Josephine is not sure what is expected of her, but the man waves a hand at the chair before him, where a bowl of oyster shells sits beside a little saucer of cut lemon. Josephine wonders if she is to pick through the shells, but Nan moves the dishes and drops them on the next table. As if summoned by the sound of china, a pot boy appears to clear the things. The gentleman belches slightly, covering his mouth, and asks for a hot chop, some bread and soup and a glass of wine, then returns to his broadsheet, quite absorbed.

Within minutes, the food arrives and is set before her.

Josephine pushes the mutton towards the man, but he shakes his head and says: 'No, no. For you.'

She eats steadily, mechanically, barely swallowing before filling her mouth again. When she is finished, Nan places a hand on her shoulder, and instinctively she stands.

'Thank you,' she tells the man, who gives a brief smile of indifference without looking up from his newsprint.

She follows Nan from the otherwise empty dining room and, once they are out of his range, says: 'Why did he do that?'

Nan lifts a shoulder. 'He don't like to see girls go hungry. Walk with me to Susie's?'

They have reached the bottom of the stairs. The bar is busier now; the girls have multiplied, the din has increased. Without a glance towards the gentleman in the corner who bought her the gin, Josephine says all right, and they step out together. Her stomach is full and round and satisfied, and the evening sky glows with possibility. Perhaps tonight will fill her pocket; perhaps it won't. Either way, she has eaten, and that is what matters.

Annie is already complaining about the flypaper. Next door to the chemist's where she works is a millinery, and tomorrow she will ask for work there. These days, when Josephine climbs into bed behind her, Annie pretends to be asleep. Sometimes, Josephine finds herself staying out later than she has to, standing at the coffee-stalls, exchanging news and information with other women. There is a coolness, a distance, between them, hardening imperceptibly, like early-morning frost.

They walk down Whitehall at Nan's sedate pace. 'You ever thought about going in-house?' Nan asks.

'No,' Josephine replies.

'They ain't as bad as you think.'

'Some are worse.'

'This one pays the best in London. They're always looking for girls.'

Josephine looks sideways at her. 'Why's that?'

After a pause, Nan says: 'Well, they come and go, don't they? Anyway. Give it some thought.'

Josephine shakes her head. 'I done all that.'

Years ago, Josephine briefly worked at a house off the Ratcliff Highway. The proprietor, a long-faced, angular woman, made her son follow the girls about the streets while she waited in her dank parlour, drinking twice-stewed tea, gnashing her false teeth. She kept all the money they earnt and strip-searched them every night. Once, Josephine kept a shilling beneath her tongue and was beaten so badly she couldn't go out for five days.

At the coffee-house, Susannah is pleased to see them. She fusses over them, arranging a good table, coming over to speak when she is free. They stay an hour or so, and watching her, Josephine is quietly impressed at her propriety, her competence, the deft way she weaves between the tables with her silver pot. Nan and Josephine share a pot of tea on the house, then Josephine says she'd best be going.

'Where to?' asks Nan, standing.

Josephine shrugs.

Nan peers at her, and so briefly she might have imagined it, her eyes fall to Josephine's scar. 'Come with me if you like,' she says.

'Where to?'

'I might have some work for you.'

'What time will Mr Drosselmeyer call?' Mrs Brown asks as they wait somewhere on Cheapside. They are looking out of their respective windows, stuck in a chokehold of carriages and carts as they travel east to west.

This afternoon, Angela has visited an orphan asylum to mark its first anniversary and inspected a site for new housing at Whitechapel. She is fatigued, covered in dust and goodness knows what else from walking around the narrow courts that must be collapsed like a house of cards for the new properties. Stepping back into the weak sunlight, the architect actually removed his hat and jacket to brush them down in the street. Angela handed out pennies like boiled sweets to the shadow-like children who watched impassively from doorways and corners. Not used to being given anything without asking for it, they accepted the coins with suspicion; she even saw one child bite down on it.

The morning was pleasurable, too: a visit to a friend on Belgrave Square and a meeting at the bank to discuss raising the clerks' salaries. And now, she and Mrs Brown have an hour to change and get ready for the theatre with Angela's former drawing master from Germany; she has already arranged for dinner to be served in their rooms.

'He's coming at six,' she replies. 'Do you think I should wear the emerald silk with the black trim? Or the dove-grey silk?'

'The dove-grey is very flattering,' Mrs Brown replies mildly.

On their journey home, she is pleasantly tired and reflective. Three weeks have passed since Dunn's letter, and to her great relief not a word has been written about her in the press, and no rumours have made their way to her. She did not go to Highgate or Broadstairs, but Dr Brown's talking-to has had its intended effect.

At Stratton Street, they disembark, and Ballard climbs down. Angela passes him a small tin of macarons for his wife's birthday and a blush saturates him from his collar to his hairline. He thanks her profusely, clutching the tin like a talisman, and departs.

Just as she is removing her gloves and wondering if there is time for a short nap, Stockton appears.

'Miss, you have a visitor in the morning room.'

Mrs Brown closes the street door, and Angela glances at the calling card tray on the side table.

'No card?'

'No, miss. A Mrs Holdsworth, miss. She says it relates to one of your charitable endeavours. And these messages arrived for you this morning – both marked urgent.'

Angela takes up the letters, frowning, at once recognising both Mrs Holdsworth and Charles's hand, and hurries to the morning room, with Mrs Brown close behind. This room is filled with her grandmother's furniture, still decorated to her taste. The walls are lined with blue silk, and gold damask curtains tumble like gilt waterfalls either side of the enormous window. Among the mahogany and marble sits the diminutive figure of Mrs Holdsworth in her outdoor clothes. Beside her, on a small table, is a silver boat of sugared almonds. Angela cannot think of a less suitable refreshment for the matron, whose very presence makes the room seem pompous, even vulgar.

'Miss Coutts, thank goodness,' she says, rising in her plain cloak.

'Mrs Holdsworth, whatever is the matter? I'm sorry to have kept you. Have you been waiting long?'

'About an hour.' She is pale and fearful-looking, and Angela's heart sinks.

'What is it now? Not another death?'

'No, though this came as a dreadful shock. It did to me, certainly. There was not even a hint of—'

'Mrs Holdsworth, tell me at once, I beg of you.'

The matron looks worn, suddenly, and tired, the lines pronounced at her mouth. She covers her face with her hands and then, recomposing herself, draws herself to her full height, and looks Angela full in the face. 'Martha Gelder has eloped.'

A stunned silence envelopes the three of them, and eventually Angela says: 'Who on earth with?'

'Well, this is the shock. Martha has eloped with Mr Bryant, the chaplain.'

'The chaplain at Urania?' cries Mrs Brown.

'The very same.'

'I don't understand,' says Angela, feeling as though all the air has gone from the room. 'When did this happen?'

'Today, by all accounts. She left this morning before anyone was risen. I found this on the dining table.'

From the depths of her cloak, Mrs Holdsworth retrieves a folded piece of paper. Angela's eyes skim the words, but her brain will not absorb them.

'How can this be?' she asks.

'You say you didn't know they were betrothed?' Mrs Brown asks the matron.

'Of course not! If I had even an inkling of any courtship, I would have brought a stop to it at once. There was no indication – none whatsoever.'

'And you have no idea where they have gone, where they were married?'

'None. That is all the information I have.' She indicates the note, scrawled on the house stationery.

'Have you asked the local churches?'

'I've sent Frank to do just that.'

'But their bans . . .'

'Bryant will have thought of that, no doubt.'

'I am shocked, Mrs Holdsworth. And perplexed. A man of such propriety, a prison chaplain, a friend of Charles, a man of *God*, no less, run off with a girl like Martha? I never heard of such a thing. It makes no sense.'

'I repeat, I was not aware of any wrongdoing, of any impropriety.'

Angela looks at the letter again, as though the truth is concealed somewhere within it. 'But Martha had private interviews with him, on a regular basis?'

'Weekly, yes.'

'Unchaperoned?'

'Well, yes, of course unchaperoned. He's the chaplain. A trusted member of the enterprise. Mr Dickens appointed him himself. He is of course as betrayed and dumbfounded as we are.'

'Who is with the girls now?'

'Mr Dickens and Mr Chesterton. I sent messages to everybody as soon as I knew. I believe they waited twenty minutes or so for you here before continuing to Shepherd's Bush.'

'Her things – are they gone?' asks Mrs Brown.

'The few she had. The clothes she arrived in. She left her house dress.'

'We must go to Shepherd's Bush at once,' says Angela, heading for the door.

'What for?' says Mrs Brown. 'The girl is gone. She is unlikely to call for her wedding breakfast.'

'She might change her mind.'

Mrs Brown shakes her head. 'I imagine it's too late for that.'

Angela cannot bear it – and then, from the depths of the hall comes the elegant chime of the doorbell. 'That will be Mr Drosselmeyer. You couldn't put him off, could you?' she asks Mrs Brown. 'In fact, put him off altogether, with my apologies. Tell him he can have the carriage and take whomever he likes. I'll write to him later. No, wait! I need the carriage. Put him in a cab. Oh, the poor man. If I see him now, though, I shall never get away.'

Mrs Brown slips discreetly from the room, and Angela's mind races. She recalls Martha's sleeping face in the overnight coach to Reading, how like a child she looked. How like a child she *was*: one-and-twenty years old, and already it was as though she had lived twice that. The elegant way she carried herself, the intelligent questions she asked at the Busheys' house, how she seemed to shrink among the carpets and soaring ceilings of the Rose Room.

A fierce, violent sensation rises at once within her, and across a great distance of upholstery and deal tables, Angela wrenches herself around to face Mrs Holdsworth.

'How very disappointing,' she says quietly.

Mrs Holdsworth sighs. 'I agree. I had such high hopes for Martha. She was the first girl in the house, and I'd grown very fond of her.' Her voice cracks, and she closes her hand into a fist.

'I don't mean Martha.'

Mrs Holdsworth is stony-faced.

'Those girls are your responsibility. Lydia's death ought to have been the end of it.'

'The end of what?'

'Mrs Holdsworth, the role of matron at Urania Cottage is

a unique one. It is demanding, exacting, entirely consuming, and I am sorry to say you are not suited to it. Too much has happened: desertion, thievery, a *death* and now an elopement. My God, none of us expected this, but clearly it is too much for you to bear alone.'

The matron reels as if from a blow. Then her pale face darkens, and she says hotly: 'Miss Coutts, I couldn't agree more. I have worked in many establishments and have never been expected to manage alone. I have been asking – no, begging for a deputy *since the beginning*. I don't have eyes in the back of my head. Lydia's death was entirely unpreventable – we know that now. However, she might have been made more comfortable if the signs were spotted sooner.'

'And Martha? And Josephine, and Hannah Parsons, and the girl whose name I have forgotten, who left in the first weeks?'

'Lizzie Hathaway. All were casualties that might have been prevented had I had assistance. I will not take sole responsibility for the failure of this enterprise.'

'Failure!'

'Yes, miss, failure.' Mrs Holdsworth, too, has been brought to the boil. 'If Martha Gelder, a decent girl eager to begin again away from all that she has left behind cannot be reformed, if an offer of marriage from a man thirty years her senior is preferable to all the opportunities we've been preparing her for, the skills and education she has been furnished with so that she may begin again on her own, then what is the point in any of it? Why are we doing it at all, when it is so easily undone?'

Angela shakes her head. 'You ought to have been watching her more closely, Mrs Holdsworth. You lived with Martha – it happened under your roof!' She is trembling now, with shock and rage, and it takes all her strength not to raise her voice.

'It happened under *your* roof,' barks the matron, who does not exercise the same self-control. 'This was not my idea; this was not my project. You think it's enough to pipe money in, buy them books and stock the pantry and teach them to play the guitar? What they need more than any of that is our *faith* in them, love and patience and a foundation upon which they may build their lives. Calling once a week and drinking tea with them only serves to keep the distance between yourself and them. What they need is *friendship*. A real home, a real family, a sense of belonging they've never had before. Not a benefactress paying a royal visit when she has nothing better to do.'

The silence that follows is deafening. The two women glower at one another, breathing hard. Martha's face swims towards Angela once more, and she feels hot tears rise and an unbearable pain in her breast at the realisation she will likely never see the girl again.

She looks away and says in a low, hard voice: 'I will spare you the humiliation of a dismissal and accept your resignation as matron of Urania Cottage. I ask only that you remain until a suitable replacement is found.'

'I will do so if you agree to recruit a deputy at the same time.'

Her lips tight, her jaw clenched, Angela bows her head in a nod. And so, they stand in caustic stillness among the splendour, listening to the muted sounds of Piccadilly, and wait for Mrs Brown.

CHAPTER 13

Celastrina argiolus

Martha has not been to this part of London before. The journey to the church took longer than she expected, first by omnibus, then a walk, then another omnibus across the river. The houses there were large and cream-coloured, and her heart quickened at the prospect of becoming mistress of one of them, but after the wedding, they waited for another omnibus and returned the way they came.

They sit in silence beside one another now, rocking in unison, and Martha smiles at a young girl travelling with her mother. A basket of parcels rests between them, the girl's arm looped through it. Her face clears at Martha's smile, and she looks from Martha to Mr Bryant. None of the passengers notice the gold band on her ring finger, which to Martha seems like a headlamp or a beacon; she cannot stop herself from touching it, thinking how strange it is that she is a wife now. In a year she might be a mother. How remarkable it is that the man who will make her one is the gentle, unassuming chaplain whom she met in the dining room of Urania Cottage on a cold winter's morning, the very same day that Hannah Parsons ran away. That had seemed the most eventful thing to happen to her that day, when really a smaller, more powerful cog, unknown to her, had begun turning. She looks back upon their meeting now with the distance of time, thinking how wondrous life is. Not long ago she was paying a penny to sleep over a rope in a boarding-house; now she is the wife of a clergyman.

At the Magdalen, the girls would talk of their future husbands. Some had been promised marriage. One said she was betrothed to a marquess, and that any day he would arrive to collect her in a gold-crested carriage. The others laughed behind her back, but Martha knew she really believed it, and felt only sympathy.

Mr Bryant is calm and a little withdrawn, glancing every so often at Martha as though congratulating himself on his good judgement. He wore normal clothes for the ceremony, typically unfussy and slightly creased. Martha will see to all that, brushing his coats, ironing his shirts, starching his collars. He will be pleased with the skills she has learnt in homemaking. A year ago, she did not know how to pluck and clean a chicken or make a dress from scratch. She is far better suited to life as a wife than a servant in some distant country. It is as though she has lifted her skirts clear of the ground and jumped neatly across the next five years. There will be no work that does not benefit her directly, no superiors to contend with. Everything she does will be for herself, her husband, their home.

Mr Bryant stands and reaches for the straps on the ceiling, and Martha takes his arm. The young mother sitting opposite smiles. Martha knows she mistakes them for father and daughter, and this makes her smile in return. They dismount on a long, dusty thoroughfare that snakes endlessly in both directions, crowded here and there with shops and houses. They turn off the main street and reach a row of tiny cottages opposite a small, grassy churchyard. Martha has no idea how humbly a chaplain lives, but she is not too disappointed by the sight of cheerful painted doors and potted geraniums.

Mr Bryant leads her past these to the second-to-last house, where a lace curtain obstructs the view of the churchyard and the green-painted door is chipped.

'Mrs Bryant.' Her husband steps back theatrically and allows her to enter the house first.

On the threshold of the dark, narrow hall, she is met at once with the overpowering scent of onions, and beneath it, a more subtle smell of damp. A shawl hangs from a coat-stand, a shabby straw bonnet balances on top, and a moment later she is startled when a woman advances into the passage from a door at the end. She is short, stout, with clear blue eyes, red cheeks and a stained apron. Her arms are raised like an infant's towards Martha.

'We-ell, here she is, the lady of the house! Welcome, welcome.' She takes Martha's bag and begins untying her bonnet, putting her face so close to Martha's that the onion smell intensifies.

'This is Mrs Kenealy,' Mr Bryant offers, removing his own things. 'The most tyrannical Irish landlady this side of the river.'

Martha is momentarily dismayed. She did ask Mr Bryant if he had a housekeeper, and he replied that he had somebody to do his cooking and laundry. He did not mention a landlady.

She tries to push the disappointment from her mind and allows herself to be pawed and welcomed by the woman, who insists on showing the newlyweds upstairs. They have only two rooms: a parlour at the front and a bedroom at the back. The bedroom is sparsely furnished, like a servant's, Martha thinks, though she supposes it should not come as a surprise for a man of the cloth to live simply and modestly. In the parlour, a threadbare armchair sits in front of the tiny grate. The rest of the furniture comprises a small table and single chair. Beneath the window is a large travelling chest, partially obscured with piles of books and newspapers. There is nowhere comfortable for Martha to sit when her husband is home in the evenings.

Mrs Kenealy insists on providing refreshment, but Martha, feeling stifled suddenly, suggests a walk around the neighbourhood. Mr Bryant obliges, warning her there is not much to see, and he is right: only streets and houses, and further, a public garden and the river. He tells her that Lambeth Palace lies a quarter-mile to the north, that another time they may walk to see it, and the idea of this brightens her, for if a palace is built here, it must not be a bad place. All she has for walking is her old dress and shawl, but Mr Bryant has promised a small allowance for clothes, and now that she can sew well, she will be able to shop at the markets for fabric and make one or two new gowns: sprigged cotton for summer, wool for later in the year.

They take their wedding breakfast with Mrs Kenealy, who asks constantly how the food is and if they wish for more gravy. Martha has not been around ordinary people for a long time and finds her a little jarring, though admittedly harmless. Martha tells herself that the old woman only wants for their comfort, and decides she will try harder in the morning, when she is rested.

After dinner, they go upstairs, and she unpacks her things, and Mr Bryant gets out his writing slope and sits at the little table as she looks through the cupboards and examines the shelves. Other than books – the heavy, dry kind with complicated titles – there is not much to see: no pictures or ornaments, nor any of the usual things acquired through half a century of life. She watches him, absorbed in his correspondence, and he looks at her and smiles.

'I doubt Mrs Holdsworth will have you back at the cottage,' she says gently. 'What will you do for work?'

'I have work,' he replies simply. 'You've no need to worry.'

It hasn't occurred to her until now that she ought to worry.

'Will the committee be angry, do you think?'

'I expect they'll have their reservations, but in the fullness of time, they'll understand.'

That evening, she half-expects him to open the Bible, but he shows no signs of fetching it. At nine o'clock, they undress with their backs to one another. She has no nightdress, only her shift. He climbs into bed first and lies facing the ceiling, his bare arms resting on the coverlet, and when she joins him, with no warning he rolls onto his side and clamps his mouth to hers. She kisses him, finding little warmth to his lips. His hands move over her skin like a coarse fabric. Of course, she has known much worse, but she expected it to feel different with a husband. She is not aware of how much he has been told about her and has no wish to give herself away. But when he pushes her down beneath the thin sheet, her heart sinks as she meets his eye and sees the knowledge within it.

When he is finished, he goes to the little ewer and basin and washes himself. He does not speak to her until they are lying beside one another, with the chill of the room pressing down upon them.

'Goodnight, Mrs Bryant,' he says.

'Goodnight, Mr Bryant,' she replies. She knows sleep will not come for a long time; her mind is too full of everything that has happened today.

That she left the cottage this morning seems impossible; that she will not sleep in her bed there ever again even more so. Her stomach churned and knotted as she took out the note she had written by candlelight and unfastened the window she had pretended to lock the night before. Walking down the lane in the dawn chill, she felt only trepidation, not liberation. So clearly could she see the others waking to find her missing, darting from room to room, their raised, excited voices; it was as though she had left a part of herself at the house. She wishes she could have given more of an explanation or talked it through with Mrs Holdsworth and Angela, but because she knew what they would say, she did not.

'You may call me Richard,' says her husband, and he turns towards the wall.

❧

On a warm afternoon, Josephine meets Nan at four o'clock on the south side of Soho Square. The evenings are growing lighter, and the streets are busy. They go first to an address on Meard Street, where a woman with hooded eyes opens the glossy black door and nods them inside. They wait in the gloom of the passage as the woman goes to fetch the person they have come for; as usual, Nan has not needed to ask. She appears a minute or so later, holding a single shoe in one hand, a small hemp bag the size of an orange in the other.

'Ellen, I've mended it!' she yells by way of greeting, and a moment later, there is the thunder of stockinged feet on the old stairs, and a scrawny girl in a shift, her hair in curl-papers, relieves her of the shoe before racing upwards.

Wordlessly, Nan takes the bag, and there is the pleasant tinkle of coins as she pushes it deep into a pocket. 'And the book?' she says neutrally.

The woman makes a face and goes away, returning with a slight, stained little thing with soft covers.

Nan pockets this, too, and says: 'Until next week, Margery.'

'Good day,' says Margery, without warmth.

On the way out, Josephine catches a glimpse of the room overlooking the street. Decorated like a fashionable drawing room, there are comfortable chairs, gilt picture frames, a Japanned screen beside the fireplace. A heavy fragrance, like musk or incense, drifts from within. Above the fireplace is a painting of a white-skinned woman, naked, emerging from a shell.

Josephine and Annie moved out of Villiers Street this morning. All their belongings fit inside a basket and the bedsheet Annie borrowed from her sister, which Annie slung over her shoulder in the street. 'You coming back to Maud's?' Annie asked, as though Josephine really had a choice. The fact that she had asked and not assumed made Josephine's mind up for her.

They had not been able to pay their rent, and the landlady, a black-haired woman with pouches beneath her eyes, would not give them more than an hour's grace. 'I turn away twelve a week, so if there's someone who can pay afore you, they can have it,' she said, clopping down the stairs before them, then herding them outside.

Annie looked on hopelessly as Josephine counted her money; somehow it had become her responsibility. The flypaper job had finished, and Annie had begun to spend her days back at her sister's in Covent Garden, and some nights, too. Josephine would rather have slept on the staircase than alone in their bed beside the Frobishers. But the idea of returning to Maud's room, the mattress, the infant limbs and slop-pails, makes her feel as though she is falling down a well.

Now, Nan leads them to a tall house in Little Pulteney Street, where the door is barely opened before the bag and another book are deposited into Nan's hands. It slams, too, inches from their faces. After that, Golden Square, to a house with a green door. Again, they stand in the passage; again, the house and its occupants are rising, readying, preparing. Through one door, a charwoman sweeps the carpet; through another, a trio of girls sit on cushions on the floor, playing cards and painting their faces. The smell of coffee floats from the kitchen. It is a curious, topsy-turvy world: indoors, it is morning, with breakfast and cleaning and toilette, outside, it is late afternoon.

'Good day, Mrs Jenkins,' Nan announces with more bravado than she has shown in any of the other houses. 'Auction tonight?'

The woman nods and eyes Josephine.

'Who is it?' asks Nan.

'Marianne,' Mrs Jenkins replies.

'Which one's she?'

'You brought her last week.'

'Oh, the redhead. I got one coming tomorrow for the back room. Preston will fetch her about noon.'

'I hope she ain't fair-haired.'

'Dark.'

'I could do with another mulatto as well. I'm having to turn clients away. Annabelle needs moving on soon, so once her room's free.'

'I'll tell Mrs T.'

Mrs Jenkins lifts her head in a half-nod. 'John's getting the book for you now. Will you take some refreshment?'

'No, thank you,' says Nan.

The offer, it seems, does not extend to Josephine.

A door opens into the passage and a very tall man emerges, with ears like barnacles. 'How many chairs?' he asks, stooping beneath the frame.

'Twenty should do it, Larry. Make some of 'em stand. It excites them – they'll feel as though they're at the derby.'

She does a forced sort of jig, looking directly at each of them, and Nan laughs nervously. Footsteps trip lightly down the stairs, and a girl of sixteen or seventeen wearing a nightdress, and with russet hair falling about her bare shoulders, appears at the half-landing by the street door. She pauses at the sight of Nan, and stares.

'Marianne, my darling,' says Nan, suddenly animated. 'Good luck tonight. Just be the same as you was at Threadneedle and you'll be our star girl.'

'What is it, girl?' asks Mrs Jenkins. 'I'm sending your bath up in a minute.'

'I wondered if I might have something to eat,' says Marianne.

'Yes, yes, I'll send something up. John!' Mrs Jenkins cries in the direction of the passageway. 'How long you be?'

At the far end of the passageway, a young, attractive man appears with a small, battered-looking book and a coin-purse.

His shirtsleeves are pushed up, revealing smooth, brown arms. 'Finished,' he says. 'All in order.'

He hands them to Josephine and winks.

❧

When Frank finishes his shift at two o'clock, he changes and dines quickly at the section-house, passes up an invitation from one of the constables to play cricket, then goes on his way. Wandsworth police station stands on a quiet country lane off the high street, surrounded by fields and orchards, and he heads south, towards the main parade of shops and businesses.

He walks east, aiming for a speed of four miles per hour, enjoying the brisker pace and the views afforded by the market gardens and pastures of Battersea and Chelsea. Momentarily, he is distracted by a beautiful new church with a clocktower, sitting amid young lime trees and neat lawns. He has never been a religious man, and yet under the pretence of admiring the simplicity of the architecture, he allows himself a brief fantasy: himself and Polly bursting from its doors, hand in hand. The image coaxes him into the sort of introspection he takes care to avoid, and so he cuts purposefully through a more salubrious neighbourhood.

Approaching the Regent's Park shortly after four, he finds the prominent house easily, for it is larger than the police station, with more windows and chimneys than a single family could possibly need. The iron gate stands ajar and he slips into the courtyard. His knock is answered promptly and he waits in the yard until he has what he needs, hearing the occasional carriage pass on the other side of the wall and marvelling at the unlikeliness of it all.

Twenty minutes later, he is consulting his trusty folding map and walking east, towards the city. Sherborne Lane is exactly where it is supposed to be, tucked behind the back of a church. It is a respectable neighbourhood, with boot scrapers on the steps and fan-lights above the doors. He seeks out the house he is looking for, raps the knocker smartly and steps back. The housekeeper who answers speaks briefly with him and waits while Frank scrawls a note. He hands it to her, thanks her and is soon on his way, shrugging off the chill that has set upon him.

He reaches Cheapside in time for the last post and hesitates on the pavement, wondering what to do. The answer he seeks is almost within grasp, yet still elusive. He wonders if, perhaps, the course of events will advance him to the relatively new and alluring detective branch, and then he remembers Martha, whom the world has let down so badly, whom he has let down so badly. He might have tried harder to help find her sister; he might have written to the constables he trained with in their various districts, asking them to keep their eyes peeled. The chances of finding Emily were almost nothing, but better to have helped Martha then, when he could, when she asked him to, instead of now, when it is far too late.

Mrs Holdsworth has not taken a half-day's holiday since she moved to Urania Cottage. She makes the arrangements with Dr Brown, who agrees to watch the girls for an afternoon. But only when dinner has been served and cleared and she has dealt with a bill from the coal supplier does she realise the day is getting away from her. In the hall, she listens to the low voices sounding from the parlour, the gentle strum of the guitar.

She has no more excuses to delay her: her bonnet is on, her shawl fastened; an umbrella is fixed in her palm against the threat of rain.

She walks to Shepherd's Bush-green to catch the Bayswater omnibus, changing in the city and alighting at the Borough. She has not been to this part of town in some time, and notices a new chop-house on the corner with a gold-painted sign. A few doors down is the galleried inn where she took her grand-daughters to watch the horses being changed. She stands at the mouth of the cobbled entryway, observing the chaos of ostlers and carriages and travellers, remembering how they would make up stories about the tall coaches and their passengers, laden with trunks and carpet-bags. The girls would ask the names of the mail coaches, trying to imagine their destinations, when all they had known was the Borough: the market, the river and the tangle of streets they called home.

The forget-me-nots she brought from the front garden look dry and tired after their journey. She pinches the bottom of their stems and, after a moment's hesitation, steps inside the yard and enters the inn. She finds a low table by a window, orders tea and a little cup of water. She drinks the tea as the flowers revive in the water, and from her bag she draws out her notebook, turns to a blank new page and fishes in her purse for a pencil.

She writes the word *prisons* and underlines it with a sigh. Listing them from memory, her mind travels down dim corridors, where sunlight lives behind bars. Next, she writes *infirmaries and dispensaries*, pausing to sip her tea before putting down as many as she can recall. She looks out of the steamed-up window, trying to remember the name of an old acquaintance who went to work as the matron of a hospital for eye disease.

She notes down the name of another, who helped set up a mother and baby ward at one of the larger London infirmaries. She will write to both of them tonight.

Closing her notebook, a great weariness settles over her. She pays her bill and steps back outside, readjusting her shawl and laying the flowers in the crook of her arm. The churchyard is less than ten minutes' walk from the inn, on the boundary of the old Marshalsea prison. A vast oak tree provides shade and shelter for the graves huddled beneath it, but Edward, Sarah and their children are in an outermost corner. Mrs Holdsworth walks slowly towards them, glancing at the few slabs decorated with wreaths and flowers. She removes her shawl and lays it on the ground, then kneels before them.

'Good afternoon, Edward,' she says. 'Good afternoon, Sarah, Philippa, Isobel. Baby Laura.'

She sets the forget-me-nots against the stone. Their floppy heads rest across Laura's name, bright blue against damp grey.

The fire destroyed everything: every book, baby gown, blanket. She had nothing of her son's to keep. Sarah's wedding ring had gone to her mother, whom Mrs Holdsworth had exchanged a few letters with. They broached the idea of meeting, but in the end nothing came of it. Sarah's mother had no other living children; at least she has Frank. 'There's no at least about it,' Frank told her.

The boys had been so different. Edward was a large man, soaring above six feet, reserved and tolerant, with a gentle humour. Frank she finds more difficult to define, as he is still alive, still evolving, still only a young man himself. His spirit is restless and lively; his brother was happiest at home with his girls.

When Charlie was alive and the boys were young, they

would sit on each of his knees and he would bounce them until they screamed. Charlie was a doting father. In the early years he danced about the kitchen hanging up washing, his arms and shoulders draped with linen as she fed the boys in the easy chair she brought from the farmhouse. When they could walk, he took them to see the great masts on the river, and when they could help him in the garden they grew potatoes, runner beans, onions. How dearly she missed him when Edward died, her grief for Charlie layered among that for her son, as fresh and keen as it had been eight years before. How different, how tender it would have been to have her husband by her side as she mourned their son.

'I'm sorry I haven't been in a while,' she says.

She is yet to tell the girls at the cottage that she is leaving. From the beginning, the committee agreed that drastic change, anything at all unsettling, should be avoided. They appear to have forgotten it now. With two new staff members, she is doubtful some of the girls will stay, not because they are loyal to her in particular but because they are bolters and need almost daily encouragement. The phrase *tempted to virtue* springs to her mind; it was in a letter early on and has stuck with her.

A single mercy brought by Martha's sudden departure is that a deputy superintendent is finally being sought. Tomorrow, she will meet two candidates at Urania Cottage. Her own replacement will be interviewed elsewhere, without her involvement. She is pleased to know that all the applicants so far do not have her experience, and the committee is unimpressed.

'I'll be moving on again soon,' she tells Edward. 'It's a shame, truth be told. I'd grown quite fond of the place.'

She begins to cry.

The tears come thick and fast, beginning somewhere in her

throat, coursing down her cheeks so quickly her gloves are soon soaked. She rummages for a handkerchief and presses her face into it as her shoulders heave. She has not cried like this in months, but it feels good. She cries for her son, her daughter-in-law, her granddaughters asleep in their beds. She cries for the lost souls at Urania Cottage, swept like waste into life's hogwash. She has worked so hard to bring order to their lives, to ensure that their routines are cast in iron, that their days are predictable and dependable, and she herself is reliable, though at times it is like driving a runaway coach with unbroken horses. And she cries for herself – for having to start again at her age: new faces, new lodgings, new systems to learn.

But then, nothing lasts forever, other than death. And at least she has Frank.

It begins to rain, gently at first, but by the time she reaches the oak tree, the heavens have opened. She left her umbrella propped beside the table in the inn. She stands beneath the ancient branches and watches the gravestones turn darker, the grass greener, and waits for it to stop.

✻

That evening, in the dining room at Urania Cottage, the small hand on the little Dutch clock is almost at nine. Mrs Holdsworth, Angela and Mrs Brown are gathered at the large rosewood table as the girls sew and read to one another in the parlour next door, their muted voices passing through the wall. In the dining room, though the curtains are drawn and the fire lit, the atmosphere is icy, the conversation stilted, until Dr Brown comes in from treating a sore throat upstairs and sets his bag heavily on the table.

Mrs Holdsworth has been occupied with various tasks: copying bills into the household receipts book and planning her lesson for the morning. Ordinarily, in the present company, she would have set her duties aside, but she has decided the veneer of pretence may slip now, with things being as they are. She arrived home at suppertime to a letter from Frank, saying he would call that evening, and thought little of it. It was only when she answered the door to Angela and the Browns, looking troubled and expectant, that she found out they'd received a similarly vague note, with the directive to hurry to Shepherd's Bush.

When they eventually hear a knock on the street door, there is a surge of relief and a flurry of anxiety. Mrs Holdsworth goes out to meet Frank, expecting to find him alone, and finds instead that he is accompanied by a small man with cropped dark hair and a clean, round, pleasant face. He shakes her hand warmly, but he appears resigned, almost grim, and she turns at once to Frank.

'Who is our guest?'

Frank's own expression leaves her cold. He indicates the dining room. 'Are the others here?'

'Miss Coutts and Dr and Mrs Brown.'

'Not Mr Dickens?'

'He was here this morning. Were you expecting him?'

'I sent a message. He must not be at home.'

Frank brushes past her and stalks along the passage, glancing into the parlour on his way. A hush falls over the girls assembled; they peer through the open door at the late arrivals, and on seeing Mrs Holdsworth pounce on their needlework and books.

In the dining room, Frank closes the door behind his mother.

'Will you have tea?' she asks their guest.

At the same time as the man begins to reply, Frank holds a hand up to stop her. 'In a moment,' he says with authority.

She has not seen her son at work, and now, with a glimpse of Frank the constable, feels a little jolt of pride.

'This,' says Frank, putting out a hand to the gentleman, who has been standing unobtrusively all the while, 'is Mr Bryant.'

Angela gets to her feet. 'Sir, how could you?' She rests a many-ringed hand on the table, and the jewels shine in the firelight. 'In eloping with Martha, you have well and truly betrayed not only my trust but the trust of—'

'Wait, wait,' Mrs Holdsworth says loudly. 'This is not Mr Bryant.' Though she addresses Angela she does not take her eyes from man.

'I assure you, ma'am, that I am,' he replies, bringing his fingertips together. 'Your son explained to me the sorry circumstances. I was quite alarmed to—'

Mrs Holdsworth presses her fingers into the tip of her nose, feeling a pressure build behind her forehead, and shakes her head in an attempt to clear it. 'I'm sorry to interrupt you, sir, but, Frank, what is the meaning of this?'

'Yes, Frank, what is the meaning of this?' Miss Coutts echoes.

'Hold on,' says Frank, staring at Angela. 'You think this is Mr Bryant?'

'Isn't it?' she replies, looking from one to the other. 'I have met with you before, haven't I? At Mr Dickens' home?'

'Indeed you have, miss,' says the man.

'This is not Mr Bryant,' Mrs Holdsworth insists.

'Are there two Bryants?' asks Dr Brown.

'Good heavens, will everybody stop talking!' cries Mrs Holdsworth. 'Frank, who is this man?'

Frank nods at the newcomer, who gives a cautious smile to each of them in turn. 'Please, sit down. I shall do my best to explain myself.'

Dumbly, they each make their way to a chair and land on it.

'My name is Mark Bryant. I hold the chaplaincy at the New Prison, and I also provide out-relief work for Clerkenwell Workhouse, for widows and the aged and infirm living within the parish. I have known Mr Dickens for some years now.'

Mrs Holdsworth opens her mouth to speak, but Frank motions for her to stay silent, and reluctantly she obeys.

'In October, Mr Dickens approached me and asked me to take on the chaplaincy at Urania Cottage. He invited me to come and see it, and so we ventured out here one morning when the decorators were still here. I had told him my plans to go to Europe – I have a cousin in Switzerland – but he was insistent I saw it. He was very persuasive, but my travel arrangements had already been made. I took leave from both my roles in November and returned to London last week.'

'How can that be possible?' Angela asks. 'Charles said you accepted it, he told me so himself.'

'I assure you, miss, I never did. I have been out of the country these six months.'

'But . . .' says Angela, a frown darkening her brow. But she is too preoccupied to continue and falls silent.

'This afternoon, I found my housekeeper quite flustered. She said a young man had called, a constable off-duty, asking of my whereabouts. She told him I was only lately back from Zürich, and he left quite puzzled.'

Frank has been standing in the corner with his arms folded, wearing a dismal expression. Now he speaks, and everybody turns to face him.

'I knew something wasn't right,' he says, and when they think he might not continue, he steps forwards into the room. 'I looked in my mother's address book the day Martha left, to find where Mr Bryant lived, thinking that would be a good place to start, and found that there was no address at all; he collected his letters at a post office. I made a note of it, and then today after work I went to Devonshire Terrace, to Mr Dickens's house. He wasn't home, but Mrs Dickens fetched his address book and sure enough, there was a note beside Bryant's name that from November of last year any mail must be sent care of the Kennington Road post office, and not his home address of Sherborne Lane in the city.'

The man Bryant nods in agreement.

'It would have been easy for an imposter, who knew Bryant was away, to have anybody involved with Urania Cottage send letters to a post office convenient to him. Sure enough, I went next to Kennington Road.'

'Good heavens,' says Dr Brown.

'The postmaster there said that a man had indeed been collecting mail several times a week for a Mr Bryant.'

'But who?' says Angela.

Mrs Holdsworth stares at her. 'You have never been at the house when Mr Bryant was here?'

'No,' says Angela, blinking. 'Are you saying this man is not the same Mr Bryant who has been coming to the house? *You* have not married Martha?' she asks the man standing helplessly before them.

'I have not,' he replies, holding up his hands.

'Then who has?'

'That is the question,' says Frank. 'Who would pretend to be Mr Bryant, and why? Because the fellow as was here these past months sure as hell ain't him. Sorry,' he adds, glancing at the chaplain.

'Honestly, this sounds like the plot from a sensational novel,' Mrs Holdsworth declares. 'The most plausible explanation is that there has been a mix-up. Could there have been a confusion of identities? I don't see why anybody would pretend to be a prison chaplain in order to – what? Work here? Seduce Martha? It makes no sense. There must be some mistake. I'm sorry you've come all the way here, Mr Bryant, and I don't mean to sound rude, but how do we know that you have not got the wrong end of the—'

'Miss Coutts, are you all right?'

Frank has leapt across the room to where Angela is sitting, for she has gone quite white and is holding the edge of the table as though she might fall away from it. She is staring at the other Mr Bryant. 'At which prison did you say you were chaplain?' she asks faintly.

'The New Prison.'

'Where is that?'

Mrs Holdsworth stares at Angela, for she looks quite mad, leaning towards the man with a frightening sense of urgency and desperation.

'Clerkenwell, miss. Also known as the Clerkenwell House of Detention.'

'Clerkenwell prison,' she whispers, her features distorted with anguish.

'My dear?' says Dr Brown.

Mrs Brown has got up from her chair and is kneeling before her.

'It's him,' Angela says, her eyes darting over things unseen. 'It's him – I know it is.'

'Who?' asks Mrs Holdsworth, failing to understand.

They are all surrounding the lady now, gathered around her skirts like presents beneath a tree. Angela is quite transformed, from the cool, smooth and polished lady to a trembling, child-like creature, who grasps Mrs Brown's papery hands in hers as though she might disappear at any moment.

Frank glances uneasily at her before continuing. 'I mentioned the postmaster. He said Mr Bryant's son-in-law had been collecting his mail for him at Kennington Road. He said his father-in-law lived with him, but was too infirm to leave the house. Nice chap, the postmaster said. Well, the same man had his own parcels sent there of course. Name of Richard Dunn. I wrote it down.' He scrabbles in his jacket. 'I haven't had time to look him up yet, but – Miss Coutts?'

For Angela has folded in her seat like a draw-leaf table, and fainted clean away.

CHAPTER 14

Dean Street

'Dunn, you say?' The real Mr Bryant frowns. 'Richard Dunn – why do I know that name?'

Dr Brown is rummaging in his bag for salts as Angela murmurs in his wife's lap.

'Hush now, dear,' says Mrs Brown. 'Don't try and get up.'

'Richard Dunn,' says Mr Bryant, suddenly enlightened. 'He was an inmate at the New Prison. The inmates are mostly awaiting trial, but there are a handful of convicts. He was convicted, if I remember correctly?'

'Three years ago in February, for perjury,' says Mrs Brown darkly, stroking Angela's hair.

'Remarkably intelligent fellow. A barrister, I believe. And you say it was him who pretended to be me?'

'I don't know for certain, but that's the name I have.' Frank glances at the figure wilting in a pool of silks on the carpet. 'And Miss Coutts appears to have some acquaintance with the man.'

'It's the very opposite of an acquaintance,' Mrs Brown admonishes. 'The man has made her life a living hell. He has sued her, harassed her, subpoenaed her, bothered her everywhere she has gone for nigh on ten years. He has been imprisoned more than half a dozen times. The last time – this time – he made out that she had promised him one-hundred thousand pounds using forged correspondence.'

'Hence the perjury,' Mr Bryant says, nodding.

'Are we talking about the same Mr Bryant? Sorry, I mean Mr Dunn.' Frank is beyond perplexed. 'The Bryant we had here is Irish. Is Richard Dunn Irish?'

'From County Fermanagh,' Dr Brown mutters darkly.

'Who else could it be?' asks Mrs Brown.

'Before we get carried away with ourselves,' Mrs Holdsworth interrupts, spreading her hands, 'may I propose we do nothing until a committee meeting has been arranged and the matter discussed? We have very few facts and far too many theories about who this man is or isn't, when there might be a simple explanation.'

'Mrs Holdsworth, please.' The salts have roused Angela, and at once Mrs Brown helps her into a chair. She sits weakly and rubs her temple. 'You have no idea what this man is capable of.'

'I'm sorry, but I find it too far-fetched. Isn't there a possibility that Mr Dickens knows another chaplain of the same name who was able to accept the post at the last minute?'

'It's possible,' says Mr Bryant. 'But I know of no other Bryant working in London. The Church is *un monde petit*, Mrs Holdsworth. Chaplains move institutions – we most of us are familiar with one another, particularly among the prisons.'

'Then perhaps he embellished his experience. I just don't

see how the man who has been coming here these few months can be a . . .'

'A madman,' says Dr Brown. 'He is a madman, Mrs Holdsworth. A dangerous, vile blackguard who ought to be locked up and the key thrown in the Thames. It surprises me not at all that he has swindled this outcome, and hoodwinked everybody in the process.'

'The policeman who comes with you,' Mrs Holdsworth says to Angela. 'He is protecting you from Dunn.'

Angela nods.

'But *why*? What would the man do to you?'

The Browns and Angela look unhappily at one another, and Angela gives a great sigh. 'I don't yet know, but his only design can be to hurt me, to punish me. Martha is a pawn in a very cruel game of his own making.' She shakes her head and closes her eyes for a moment. 'Dunn thinks of himself as my suitor. His campaign has lasted – oh, years. He appeared when I inherited. He wrote to me a few times, proposing marriage, and I threw away his letters, thinking him mad. He followed me to the north and wouldn't leave me alone. He was sent to prison for a month. But on his release he took rooms near my father's house in St James's and began accosting me and my family. He called at the house day and night, pushing his demands through the door. He appeared everywhere: in the park, where I walked; in the street, in the time it took for me to get to my carriage. Sometimes, he took a room at the hotel opposite my house, so that he could watch me. He has followed my every move for years now.

'I would travel to escape him, and he would pursue me. Not every time, but enough for me to always be looking over my shoulder. Only when he is in prison am I free of him. And he has been imprisoned several times – but he knows the law, you see. He is a barrister. I have been obliged to face him in court on many occasions. He is jailed for intruding upon me, then he appeals on the grounds of some tedious loophole, arguing his own case and often winning. I think he believes that, if he is successful in wearing me down, I will give in and either marry him or pay him to leave me alone. I have thought about both, let me tell you. But whatever I gave him, he would always come back for more.'

She looks at her hands in the lamplight. 'I should have known he would follow me here. But I'd never imagined he would . . . the idea of him being in the *house*.' She shudders and closes her eyes. 'I hope I am wrong, but I know that I am right.'

There is a deep, shocked silence. And then, grasping desperately for it not to be true, Mrs Holdsworth says: 'But Mr Dickens! He can't have been hoodwinked. He would have met this . . . this person.'

'Would he?' says Frank. 'What if he received a letter, claiming to be from Mr Bryant, saying he had changed his mind about travelling and was able to take the post after all? Wouldn't he have been delighted that his friend had a change of heart and could begin at once, having already seen the house and the way of things? You said yourself, Miss Coutts, that the man has forged letters.'

He glances at Angela, who nods.

'What's not to say he stole some correspondence of Mr Bryant's at the New Prison, in order to copy his hand? He then wrote to Mr Dickens, telling him his plans had altered, accepting the post, and asking Mr Dickens to write to him at Lambeth for some reason, I don't know: staying a while with a friend, perhaps. Why wouldn't Mr Dickens believe him?'

'It's plausible.' Dr Brown nods.

'But *very* involved,' says Mrs Holdsworth. 'The chances of him being found out—'

'Were quite slim if Miss Coutts, Mr Dickens, myself and Mrs Brown were never here at the same time as him,' says Dr Brown, closing his bag with a snap. 'He wasn't on the committee. He had no cause to meet with the governors.'

'But one of you is often here. It would be too much of a risk.'

'Perhaps he had an accomplice. Somebody helping him on the outside. Or the inside.'

'Come, now, Dr Brown. You're beginning to sound like a novelist yourself,' says Mrs Holdsworth wryly.

The look he gives her causes her to shrink slightly.

'What I mean to say is, it's late,' she goes on. 'We are all tired. We've had a shock. Frank, I admire your efforts in attempting to seek the truth, but I think we are all putting the cart before the horse.'

'Perhaps you are right, Mrs Holdsworth. I certainly hope so,' says Mrs Brown, who looks thoroughly worn out.

'Not least because, if is true, and the imposter is Dunn,' says Frank slowly, 'what does that mean for Martha?'

The silence that falls is a heavy one.

Long after Mrs Holdsworth goes to bed, she cannot put Angela's story from her mind. Angela seemed terrified, for herself and for Martha. Mrs Holdsworth has seen expressions like hers before, on the faces of haunted women in the places she has worked. And if Angela is right, and the man Dunn has infiltrated their little world, *her* little world, the very idea of it is appalling. A convict, a madman, drinking tea from her own willow-patterned china, being left alone with young and vulnerable women. She swallows, feeling colder and colder beneath her old blanket, and by the time the chill has spread to her bones, she is sick to her stomach.

The reproachful figure of Angela in that grand, gilded room on Piccadilly returns to her: *desertion, thievery, a death*. And now this, which could be the worst of all, for a young woman in danger with no knowledge of it and no way of being warned is too, too frightening. Martha has walked directly into a trap he constructed under her own nose, in plain sight. Her responsibility has been to keep the girls safe, and on that account she has failed utterly.

⚘

Josephine is back at Coopers Buildings. She waits for Annie in the mouth of the court, and watches her approach, swinging the hand of a child, the baby balanced on her hip. When she steps from the shadows, Annie stops. Josephine asks to speak with her, and Annie leaves the children with a neighbour on the first floor.

Together, they walk out into the brightness of Covent Garden, and Josephine finds herself leading Annie to a churchyard, where they might have a slice of peace. The clatter and buzz of the market falls away, and they sit side by side on the steps before the church doors, slightly turned away from one another.

'I found new lodgings,' says Josephine.

'I supposed you had.' And, after a pause: 'Where?'

'In Soho.'

'With her?'

'In the house she lives in.'

'With her, then.'

'Not in that way, Annie. I told you.'

Annie sighs. 'I thought you might go back to that house out west.'

'I can't do that.' And then: 'Maud and John have been so kind, letting me stay, but——'

'I know.'

'I wanted us to live together. To be together, like we said at Tothill.'

'I know.'

They sit a moment, and Annie moves her knees from side to side. 'I worry about you, Jo. I don't like what you're doing now.'

Josephine stares at the neat grass and the ancient gravestones. She wants to say that she doesn't like it either, but she also wants Annie to feel guilt, and so she says nothing.

'I wish you'd find work doing anything else,' Annie says.

'Like what? Making flypaper? Sweeping floors?' She regrets it instantly, for Annie looks ashamed.

'There's other things you could do.'

'Not to me, there ain't. And I ain't doing that now anyway.'

Annie looks sideways at her. 'What are you doing then?'

'Something else. Something . . . you wouldn't understand.'

Annie shakes her head. 'No, I don't think I would,' she says quietly.

'Don't get all holy on me. You been in prison, too.'

'My mother was sick, Jo, and I made a mistake.'

'I need to live somehow.'

'Some living that'll be.'

Josephine leaps to her feet and turns on her. 'It's you I left that house for! Do you not think I'd rather be with you than anything else?'

'You can be with me——'

'No, I can't,' she roars. 'Not in that poxy room with your family. Why am I not enough for you?' Hot, furious tears blur her vision. 'I was doing all right without you. I was beginning to see another way for myself. I had an opportunity to go far away from here and start a new life. What a fool I am for throwing it away, and for what?'

'Then why did you?'

'Because you asked me to!'

'No, I didn't, I *didn't*,' Annie cries. 'I asked for your forgiveness – I never asked you to come. I knew that place was good for you, I would never have asked you to leave it. You have no family, and I thought they might be a family to you. It pains me that you left there for me – I wish you hadn't done it. I thought I was doing you a mercy.'

'Some mercy, Annie. Some mercy!'

'Don't blame me for your choices. I won't be blamed. I didn't want to move to Villiers Street, and I did that for you.'

'Because I wanted to be alone with you. I wanted us to be together. I realise now that you never did.'

'I did, Jo.'

'No, not really. I was only good for Tothill, for the time you was locked up.'

'That ain't fair.' Annie is weeping now.

'But it is true,' says Josephine. Tiredness overwhelms her. She feels slack, soft, clear-headed. Empty. She wishes only to climb the stairs to her comfortable bed at Urania Cottage and nestle down inside.

After a moment, they stand. Annie wipes her face and says: 'Can you let me know where your lodgings are, so I know you're safe?'

Josephine laughs and leaves the churchyard.

THE HOUSEHOLD

✼

Nan lives in a tall black house on Dean Street belonging to a woman called Mrs T. The moniker initially made Josephine think of a large, benign woman the shape of a teapot, like a character in a nursery rhyme. But Mrs T is stately, resplendent, with fine silk gowns, bronzed skin and black hair, like a Spanish woman, though she speaks without any trace of an accent. Her teeth are white and straight. She does not eat bread or sugar and drinks only hot water, though her gatherings go on all night and into the morning, when the house is like an abandoned ship, festooned with empty bottles, stained maps, topcoats and even, once, a pair of grey parrots, nestled atop the dining-room shutters. The house, too, has a queer, nautical sense to it, with tilting floors and dimly lit staircases; on the first-floor landing is a painting of a shipwreck, with pale, half-clothed bodies vanishing beneath the foam.

Josephine has not asked how Nan came to be here, nor Mrs T, though she can hazard a guess. Mrs T took barely any notice when Josephine arrived with her few things, as though she habitually took in strays. Josephine wondered at first if Nan was interested in her in the way Annie is, or was. But Nan showed her to a bedroom on the top floor and does not seem to hold a candle for anybody.

When they return from collection, she and Nan unburden themselves of the bags and books and put them inside a black metal deed-box that is left unlocked for them on the dining table. They go out on foot three nights a week, covering Soho, the city and Whitechapel. In the last two districts they are followed at a distance by various men, all of whom Nan acknowledges as they set out and then ignores. In Soho, they

283

have no protection; when Josephine asks why, Nan replies simply: 'No need.' The next morning, somebody calls at the house to return the shabby little books to their homes. Somebody else comes to take away the deed-box.

Nan appears to be several things to Mrs T: housekeeper, minder, assistant. There are no staff other than a cook, who does not live in and is seldom seen, leaving meals for them in the warm nooks beside the range. A charwoman comes a few times a week, tidying unobtrusively; Josephine and Nan often sleep late and do not see her at all. Josephine has the sense that Mrs T's kingdom is a vast, powerful clock made up of many cogs.

On the days they do not go on collection, Nan sets out alone. Where she goes, she does not tell Josephine, but again Josephine can speculate. Occasionally, she comes home with the ones who are harder to persuade, the ones who are more suspicious; she can hear their chatter as they drink tea in the sitting room, and once, coming down the stairs, she met with a girl in the hall. A single threadbare carpet-bag sat patiently by the front door, and the girl walked towards it and picked it up. She heard Josephine on the stairs, turned and made a little sound of surprise, her wide eyes fixing at once on her scar. Nan lurked in the parlour doorway, looking annoyed. 'I will go to my uncle's house first,' the girl said to Nan in a northern accent, holding her bag closely. 'He'll be expecting me. But thank you for your kind offer of a place to stay. Could you tell me the way to Albemarle Street?'

'It's your scar,' Nan said afterwards, gesturing vaguely to her own face.

Since then, Josephine has stayed upstairs whenever she hears voices.

Mrs T has two sons, with the same bronzed skin and smooth heads. Occasionally, they stay at the house, and Josephine walks into the dining room to find them reading their morning newspapers, immaculately dressed. Around them, Nan turns slightly fawning, even servile, bringing them coffee and polishing their shoes. Josephine never learns their names and does not speak to them directly. They stay a night or two, dining privately with their mother if she is at home, and leave without fanfare.

When Nan falls ill with a fever, Mrs T calls Josephine to the dining room. This room, at the front of the house, is always gloomy, thick with a haze of tobacco, the light shut out from the street through impenetrable blinds. Mrs T smokes a pipe on occasion, filling it with long, elegant fingers, studded with rings.

'You will go on collection,' she says, in her smooth, accentless voice. She blows pipe smoke considerately to one side.

Josephine nods, her mouth dry.

'Preston will go with you.'

Preston is one of the heavies, as Nan calls them.

'Do you have any questions?'

Josephine shakes her head, knowing it is expected. She gets up, her stomach sliding down to her feet, and leaves Mrs T in her fragrant fug. She takes some bread and cheese and a few slices of cold ham from the larder and leaves a plate by Nan's bedside. Nan appears to be in a fever dream, murmuring about a pond and a child named Sidney.

Josephine eats alone in her room, sitting by the small window and looking out at the backs of the houses on the next street. She sees, dimly, a man shaving at a mirror, and wonders where she would be now had she not met Susannah

285

in the street all those weeks ago. She would not be sitting in this cabin-like room in this large, quiet house, watching the man shaving. Would not be about to go on collection, walking around Whitechapel with what she knows to be hundreds of pounds. What if she misses a bag, forgets something? What if she is robbed on the Ratcliff Highway? Would Preston himself steal from her, beat her, leave her half-blind in the gutter? Mrs T has eyes everywhere, cogs everywhere, turning in her mighty clock; if Josephine were to run, she would be found. She shakes these unpleasant thoughts from her mind, finishes her crust, makes her bedclothes like she used to at Urania Cottage. She lives now the way she did before, day by day, with no past and no future.

She puts on her shawl and bonnet, then looks in on Nan, who sleeps calmly now. Mrs T's large marmalade-coloured cat is crouched at the plate by the bed, eating contentedly. She goes downstairs, unfastens the intricate series of locks on the heavy street door and finds Preston waiting there. They share a neutral look, and she begins walking east with Preston behind her, following like a curse.

Just as Martha suspected, Mrs Kenealy is a busybody. Mr Bryant does not take a sit-down breakfast, preferring to leave for work with a morning roll, and when he has gone the landlady brings Martha's tray upstairs. She has told Martha that married ladies take the first meal in bed, but Martha prefers to be dressed around her, and waits in the chair by the window, looking out. Mrs Kenealy makes a high, satisfied noise and sets the tray on the table: pink, trembling bacon with ribbons of fat, a watery egg with a weak yellow yolk, nothing like the strong gold colours of her childhood. Martha's appetite vanishes at once, and she thanks Mrs Kenealy, who insists on pouring the tea, which is the grey-brown of rainwater.

'Settling in well, are you?' she asks, leaving Martha no option but to say yes.

'I wondered,' says Martha, after she has attempted a bite of the egg white. 'If I might repair the curtains? Only there are small holes letting in the light. I expect it's moths.'

Mrs Kenealy is delighted. 'Oh, certainly! How industrious of you. I'm sure I'd do it myself if I had the time.'

'And I will clean our rooms myself, if that is agreeable to you.'

'Will you? Well,' says Mrs Kenealy, astonished, 'what a wonderful tenant you're proving to be. I'm bad with my hands these days. Rheumatics, you see – gets all of us Kenealys one way or another. I can't keep up with the house, I confess. I'll keep you company as you work, after your breakfast, mind. Got to be keeping your strength up for what's to come.'

Mrs Kenealy looks meaningfully at Martha's stomach. Martha says nothing, moving the miserly produce around the plate. Meanwhile, Mrs Kenealy has eased herself into Mr Bryant's chair. She removes her shoes and places her stockinged feet on a small footstool.

'It will be a blessing to have a little babby in the house,' she says.

Martha removes the curtains and asks to borrow the sewing box.

'You've no sewing box?' Mrs Kenealy scoffs. 'You'd not get far as a new wife where I come from. Downstairs, underneath the side table in the sitting room.'

Martha fetches it and sits at the table. Mrs Kenealy has not appeared to notice the untouched breakfast, or is not offended. With something to do with her hands, Martha's mind quietens, though the landlady watches from beneath her mobcap.

'How long has Mr Bryant lived here?' Martha says, for the sake of saying something.

'Now let me think. It'll be five months on Thursday.'

'Only five months?'

The frilly cap bounces as she nods.

Martha returns to her sewing.

'And where was yourself before?'

'Middlesex. Shepherd's Bush.'

'You in service?'

Martha nods.

'I thought as much. Strong back, good hands. You'll be well equipped for an infant. Not like these fragile little daisies you see these days. General housework?'

'Yes.'

'I thought as much. Was a chambermaid myself, a hundred years ago.' She grins, revealing slick brown teeth.

That evening, when her husband is home and they have eaten supper, Martha asks Mr Bryant if she might accompany him to work in the morning. He gives a baffled little smile and shakes his head. 'Why would you want to do that?'

'I realised today that I don't know which prison it is that you work at,' she says.

After a pause he says: 'Clerkenwell.'

There is nothing for Martha in Clerkenwell, but she would accompany him to Seven Dials if it meant getting out of the house. 'I might travel with you, and walk about a bit. I can come home alone.'

He laughs, as though she has said something outrageous. 'Alone? I'm afraid that wouldn't be appropriate. You're a clergyman's wife now, Martha, not a whore.'

And that is the end of it. Stung and winded, her heart sinks at the prospect of another day with Mrs Kenealy.

He asks her to iron his collar as he opens his post with his dinner knife. Something in one of the letters displeases him, for his mouth turns down at the corners, and to Martha's surprise he puts it in the fire. Later, he pushes Martha beneath the bedclothes and then climbs on top of her. He keeps his eyes closed. At one point, opening them briefly, he finds her looking at him and tells her not to.

The days and nights pass in much the same way, with Mrs Kenealy watching her from the chair until she falls asleep, snoring, and the wind pushing the glossy branches in the churchyard outside. Mr Bryant sleeps soundlessly beside her in the old wooden bed. They don't talk as Martha expected a husband and wife to. He does not consult her on domestic matters, does not enquire about her day, though she has little to tell him. Nor does he recall his own in any detail. She asks him questions about the prisoners, the widows and sick infants he visits in the workhouse parish, but he does not seem a fraction as devoted to his work as he did when they first met. He does not pray at home; the Bible remains buried in the pile of books on top of the chest. Martha thinks this is perhaps because he prays all day, and home is another type of sanctuary for him. She supposes that a cooper would not wish to mend barrels when his work is done.

Though it is a little strange, perhaps, that his faith has so little bearing in their life and marriage. She imagined that it would be the central pillar of their home, the maypole to which they are tethered: she pictured them reading Bible passages in the evenings, giving thanks at breakfast, going about the parish with everybody knowing them. As she is so often alone, she finds herself drifting into a reverie of how things could be if, instead of a London chaplain, her husband was a country reverend. They'd have a rectory, wreathed with climbing flowers, and children tumbling in and out. These small rooms, she tells herself as she sits looking out at the sinking gravestones, are temporary. She must tell herself this, for she feels more of a prisoner here than at Urania Cottage or the Magdalen. At those places, she had no care to leave, for within was work and company and conversation. But here, she finds herself without meaning, incurious about her new neighbourhood. She has no need to go anywhere, as it is Mrs Kenealy who calls at the market, the baker's, the public house for their beer, and so she knows no neighbours or shopkeepers or anybody with whom she might forge a friendship.

Living with Mrs Kenealy is like having another matron, but one with none of Mrs Holdsworth's qualities. Mrs Holdsworth would never sink down into a chair, remove her shoes and resort to idle chit-chat. She would never sleep in the daytime, mouth open, chin glistening with drool. Catching flies, as her mother used to say. Martha has never missed her mother as much as she does now. She has not yet written to Mary, to tell her she is married. And Emily. Emily. Despite his promises, Mr Bryant has not once brought up her sister.

On a rainy evening during supper, Martha suggests going again to Reading to try to speak with Veronica Bushey. She shows her husband the strange, dismissive letter from Mrs Bushey, and he reads it and seems uninterested. There is not, he says, any money for her to go to Reading.

Mrs Kenealy begins taking all her meals with Martha. For dinner, they have watery broth with stale bread; she saves the meat for Mr Bryant. While Martha cleans, Mrs Kenealy sits by the fire in Mr Bryant's chair. She is such a frequent fixture in their rooms that, when she is elsewhere and the chair is empty, Martha finds herself glancing at it, as though the old woman might appear any moment.

The laundry is taken each week by a neighbour and returned two days later. Martha goes downstairs to replace a clothes brush and finds Mrs Kenealy sitting in the kitchen, sifting through her soiled clothes. 'Next month, perhaps,' she says, nodding again at Martha's stomach.

Martha is so incensed, so defiled by this invasion of privacy, that she decides she will take a walk in the rain. She sets off blindly, still fastening her bonnet, with no route in mind. Hunched against the weather, her shawl wrapped tightly around her, she walks until she is soaked through.

CHAPTER 15

Mrs Bryant

The bath-water laps gently against the side of the tub, cooling rapidly, but Martha has not yet undressed. She is standing in the middle of the floor with her hands on her hips, looking about the room, wondering what she might use to ensure she can bathe in seclusion, when she sees the great chest beneath the window. She walks hesitantly towards it and kneels, putting a finger to the brass padlock and wondering not for the first time what lies inside it.

Piles of books sit on top of it; Martha is permitted to dust around them but not move them. She made the mistake of doing so once, tidying them away onto a shelf, and Mr Bryant complained before returning them to the chest. One afternoon, lifting the covers of the uppermost tomes, she discovered them not to be studies of religion or theology, but law. *A History of English Law; or an attempt to trace the rise, progress and successive changes of the Common Law; from the earliest period to the present time* by George Crabb Esq of the Inner Temple; *The Criminal Law and its Sentences in Treasons, Felonies and Misdemeanours* by Peter Burke Esq of the Inner Temple. Where was this mythical Inner Temple? Layered between these heavy books are articles that are just as dry and solemn: Parliamentary reports, torn papers from legal journals.

She sets them carefully on the floor in their stacks. With difficulty, she manoeuvres the chest towards the door to use as a barricade, straightening and dusting off her hands, satisfied. Finally, she undresses and lowers herself into the water. The noise in her head quietens slightly; the stiffness in her neck softens.

But within a minute, she hears Mrs Kenealy's clogs on the bare wooden stairs, and notices how her jaw tightens in response. She waits, and when the door refuses to open, there is a pause of surprise before the landlady tries again, and then again a third time.

'What's the matter with this?' she mutters. 'Martha, the door's stuck.'

'I'm bathing,' Martha says.

Another pause. 'Och, there's no cause for shyness. I've a letter arrived for Mr Bryant.'

'It can wait until later.'

'I'll give it to you now if you'll open the door.'

Martha says nothing and puts back her head.

'Will you not be wanting it?'

If the water were deep enough, Martha would sink below it. There are so many letters; Mr Bryant has an astonishing volume of correspondence. He spends most of his evenings writing, reading over what he has scribed at regular intervals with an expression of mild contempt. On the two occasions

Martha enquired about whom he corresponded with, his replies included a sister in Kildare and a deacon in Manchester. Martha can only assume he means a sister-in-law, for she remembers the tale of the brothers and the visiting pastor. He had not mentioned a sister.

When they are in bed, Mr Bryant has begun uttering a strange, strangled cry. It is a sound or perhaps a word she cannot make sense of, which erupts almost involuntarily from his mouth. He draws himself urgently from her, gasping, and spills on her thighs, her back, her stomach, crying out this noise; it sounds, she thinks, like *Hanji*. Each night, at the same time, they put out the lights and draw the curtain Martha has repaired, and Martha does not know what version of her husband she will get. Sometimes he is tender, almost loving, though his eyes are screwed tightly shut. Sometimes he is rough, moving her about the room with surprising strength, pushing her face against the wall, hinging her over the bed, grabbing her by the hair. She realised some weeks ago that the creaks she could hear during these times were coming not from the bed but from outside the room: Mrs Kenealy, coming upstairs in stockinged feet to listen to them. When they have finished, the landlady creeps quietly away.

Now, like at night, the footsteps recede, but they will be back. Martha realises she has not spoken to anybody other than Mr Bryant and Mrs Kenealy in a long time. How long? She does not know the day of the week, the date of the month. She has no use for them. She thinks of Lydia, gone. Josephine, gone. Emily, gone. Perhaps now they are all dead, and Martha is the only one left alive, though she scarcely feels it.

A scene visits her again, of Lydia with her broom, rosy with life, showing her the word scrawled into the wallpaper by Josephine's bed. *Street*. She showed Martha the word, and then she died.

The water is almost cold now, and Martha's skin is covered in gooseflesh. She tries to picture the wallpaper in their bedroom at Urania Cottage. Pink roses, blooming from golden sconces in the shapes of fleur-de-lis, on a pinstripe background. *Street*.

Suddenly she freezes, then sits up straight. The water sloshes in protest, splashing onto the rug.

'Rose Street,' she says aloud. 'Is it Rose Street?'

Her skin tingles in response. She leaps from the tub, hurrying across the room and crouching naked at Mr Bryant's chest, for she has seen him fold a map and store it inside here. She prods at the lock, wondering where he keeps the key, then remembers he puts it inside his pocket. She curses, for he won't be home for hours, and besides, she has no wish to involve him in her discovery. He will be suspicious, exacting. She has not allowed herself to admit what a disappointment he is to be married to, because the idea and its implications are too lonely and frightening.

She looks about the room for something else to use, remembering Josephine and her hairpin. Fetching hers, and ignoring the chill that has found her bare, wet skin, she crouches again at its mouth and fiddles, gazing at a spot on the mould-speckled wall to listen to the mechanism. It has been some time since she last picked a lock, but within a minute or so she hears the welcome click, and the padlock yields. She sets it gently on the floor and heaves open the lid, resting it against the door-frame. Distantly, reassuringly, she hears Mrs Kenealy clattering pans in the kitchen.

Martha does not know what she expected the trunk to hold – perhaps old clothes, blankets, more books – but she finds herself quietly astonished. The trunk is free of miscellany, containing only a single category of item. It is filled, halfway up the sides, like Martha's bath, with paper. Sheets and notes and envelopes; newspapers and magazine pages, torn at the centrefold; folded, unfolded, tossed in carelessly, tied neatly with ribbon. Mr Bryant is a tidy man, who hangs his coat on the peg, aligns his cutlery and smooths down his side of the bed after rising, but here is a chaos of correspondence, perhaps a lifetime of it. She is breaking the surface, searching for the map she knows he has, when a word catches her eye.

It is not the word itself but the shape of it, familiar somehow, like a name Martha used to know. She brushes it clear and frowns, realising it is the handwriting she recognises: untidy, negligent, even, as though the author had no inclination to write at all. The bottom of the paper is concealed by another, which she swipes off like a fly, and the writer is revealed to be Miss Coutts. She smiles, feeling a pain inside her, and is briefly consumed by regret at the loss of their friendship. For it *was* friendship, despite the dizzying chasm between them; she is sensible enough to know that Angela's affection was genuine.

Before she can prevent them, a series of hideous remembrances visit her: the night at the duke's house, and the raw hatred in her voice when she shouted at Angela in the kitchen at Shepherd's Bush. The hurt look on the lady's face, when she had done so much for Martha, and none of it was her fault.

She gathers herself and begins rummaging again, but the map continues to evade her, and what she finds instead is ream after ream of correspondence from Angela to her husband, which in itself is not strange, but the letters themselves are unfinished, incomplete, the same words repeated as though she were practising her handwriting. When she looks more closely she realises they are not letters at all, but lines and lines of the same thing. *My dearest Richard. Marry me, Richard.*

She takes them out and splays them like a deck of cards on the floorboards. Her mind, thick and drowsy with dust and neglect, clunks into action, attempting to understand why a great lady like Angela Burdett-Coutts would write such things to Mr Bryant. There is poetry, too, about Angela, in her husband's hand, bawdy and shabby in its execution. Her stomach plummets: were the two of them in love? Having an affair?

And beneath all this, to add to Martha's bewilderment, a hundred envelopes and just as many letters addressed to Richard Dunn Esq, at various addresses, some of which, she is disturbed to read, include prisons and detention houses: Clerkenwell, York, the Fleet. Some are soft and yellow with age, like the newspaper cuttings that date back five, seven, nine years, carefully folded and otherwise intact. At first, Martha does not understand what connects these reports of balls and royal sightings and country houses and charitable dinners, until the same name fires like a pistol into the noise in her head. Her brain hurts with the effort of understanding why her husband has collected dozens of news articles about Angela, why this man, Richard Dunn, is named in some of them, and why Mr Bryant has his correspondence. On examination, their handwriting is the same. She stares at a note in Angela's hand to *My dearest Arthur*, signed *Your devoted Angie*, and finds beside it an envelope, carefully steamed open, for there are no cuts or tears, addressed to the London residence of a duke.

As well, there are dozens and dozens of letters from editors at newspapers and magazines, *The Illustrated London News*, the *Public Ledger*, *The Satirist*, tossed together in a swamp of rejection: *Sir, Regrettably, we politely decline*; *Sir, Miss Coutts is one of our eminent supporters and friends*; *Sir, while the note you sent purports to be authentic, we, as a publication, would need irrefutable proof—*

She feels giddy, as though she is falling or the room is tilting, as a single, high-pitched note pierces her eardrum and then recedes, for another abrupt realisation has dawned on her: the utterance Mr Bryant makes each night is a word, the same word that appears dozens of times before her, on almost every one of these letters and pages and notes and cuttings.

Angie.

❦

Nan is unwell for a fortnight. Mrs T has a nurse sit with her in the daytime, and a doctor visits twice. The nurse is built like an armoire and can barely manage the stairs, but she brings Nan elegant little tinctures and brews medicinal teas of camomile and liquorice, which scent the house with their pleasant aromas. Each night, when Josephine gets home after collection, she takes the nurse's chair beside Nan's bed and shows her the books before putting them in the deed-box. Propped against pillows, Nan's eyes travel hungrily over the columns of names and figures as she sips her herbal tea. On some of the pages, names are struck out like items on a grocery list.

'What do they mean?' Josephine asks.

'Killed by pirates,' Nan replies, mocking her. She turns the page.

Josephine gives a hollow laugh. 'What do they mean really?'

Nan shrugs. 'Moved on, thrown out. Gone to a better place.'

She says no more about it, and Josephine doesn't ask.

The first night she went out alone, Josephine had to tell each house that Nan was indisposed and was met with narrowed eyes. But a glance at the bulky shadow of Preston beyond her shoulder assured them, and they handed over their bags.

One house in Whitechapel gives Josephine the jitters. It is dark, intensely fragrant, and she is met at the door by an impassive Chinaman, who glides like a swan through the gloom. From the depths of the darkness come low, nightmarish moans – the sound of men immersed in pain or horror. Josephine cannot leave quickly enough, and each time finds herself shivering on the street, her head foggy, gulping at fresh air.

Not all of Mrs T's properties are clean, tall houses filled with art and expensive furniture. There is a place by Leadenhall Market that is narrow and shabby, leaning crazily into the street as though the slightest nudge might cause it to collapse. Josephine knocks on the door one evening and hears shrieking, followed by the cruel, hard sound of a smack. The bawd there is a pockmarked woman, shrewd and callous, and she answers the door breathing hard, her pox-scarred face aflame. Behind her, a young woman sits on the bottom of the staircase, holding her cheek and sobbing. The bawd glances about her, ushering Josephine inside. Josephine says nothing to the weeping girl, and when the bag and book are safe inside her pocket, she leaves gratefully.

The only house she does not mind visiting is the one at Golden Square, where the girls are full-cheeked and seem content. It reminds her, in a way, of Urania. The man with sun-browned forearms, John, brings her the things himself, always with a wink and a smile. While the mistress is indifferent to Josephine, he is friendly, even flirtatious; he takes his

300

time putting everything together at a narrow, blue-painted desk in the kitchen, where Josephine waits. Once or twice, a girl has come in to make some toast or heat some cocoa. They tease him, ruffling his hair, perching in their shifts on the large, scrubbed table, waiting for the milk to warm. Josephine has the sense he is like a brother to them. He makes her think of Frank, putting up a shelf, fixing a clock, painting over damp in the scullery.

Leaving the light and warmth of the Golden Square kitchen for the cold, cluttered streets and the other doors that must be knocked on, she feels entirely untethered to her body, as though she is examining herself from a great height, like a bird perched on a rooftop, and it is only this that allows her to keep going. As her skirts grow heavier, her mind empties, and she pictures herself winged, in flight, free.

Dawn comes early, and the curtains are thin. Mr Bryant is exasperated when Martha moves too often, so she has taken to making tea as quietly as possible on the little fire in the sitting room. She sits by the window to drink it, beside the chest, looking out at the churchyard and the graves. There is peace and privacy in the early morning; it feels as though she is the only person awake in the street, Lambeth, the world. Even her husband's snores do not reach her.

Martha has always liked this time. At home, her mother would rise early to begin her work, and Martha would sit on the doorstep as the day hung about the garden like a question mark. She thinks of home more than ever these days, now she knows what goes into making one. Perhaps it is the gravestones that cause her to be morbid. But nobody ever visits them, and she has never seen anybody go inside the church, as though nobody remembers it is there.

Mr Bryant leaves at eight o'clock. She watches mildly as he puts on his coat, fastens his collar, pats his pocket for the chest key. A sheath of freshly written letters sits in the crook of his arm. He smiles wolfishly at her, and she returns it. She hears Mrs Kenealy pass him his morning roll and a bag of biscuits in the passageway and listens for the sound of the street door closing. Then she takes her shawl from the peg and her shoes in the other hand and goes barefoot down the stairs. She lets herself out quietly and fastens her shoes on the doorstep. Mr Bryant has turned left, towards the high street; she sees his slim black coat vanishing around the corner, and proceeds.

It is a gloomy day, with the sort of high wind that precedes a storm. It makes the horses skittish, and playbills whip from one side of the road to the other. Martha follows her husband up New Bridge Street, past Vauxhall Gardens, towards the river. He leads her through Westminster, where sewage chokes the gutters and maids emerge from black-painted railings to throw dust into the road. Several times, he turns his head to cross the street, and Martha covers her face but keeps walking, once or twice purporting to cross herself, then falling back again. Among all the tall hats, his wide brim is easy to spot.

He leads her in front of the Queen's palace, towards park-land. Here, he is more conspicuous, but she is less so; the park is full of women walking with their children and servants, and she leaves the path to dart between the trees, where the cool green light is soothing. She watches him pass through large iron gates onto the busy thoroughfare of Piccadilly. He walks into the road, slipping between a removals wagon and a phaeton, and she almost loses him, but then his hat appears on the opposite side.

Martha stands behind the tall gate, watching through a gap as he approaches a side street and stares up at a very large, brown-bricked house, towering like a great ship over Piccadilly. He waits, looking thoughtful, and then buys a paper from a nearby newsagent's, leaning against the railings by the area steps to read it, as though waiting for somebody to come out. His face disappears beneath the wide brim of his hat.

Astonishingly, he remains here for almost two hours. In that time, the street door opens, and Martha is shocked to see Dr Brown descend the steps to the pavement, which is tucked down the side of the house. He walks out onto Piccadilly and turns left, towards St James's. Only then does Mr Bryant move, not towards Dr Brown but away from him, pulling down his hat and tucking the newspaper beneath his arm to stroll languidly in the opposite direction.

When the doctor is some distance away, he returns to the railings, and there he stays. Martha is wondering how Dr Brown came to be here and if it is his home and, at the same time, how much longer she can watch her husband before he will notice her, when a coal-delivery boy approaches the house with his cart, and Mr Bryant stands aside to allow him to pass. They exchange a few words, the boy squinting up at him, and then the boy puts out a blackened palm, and Martha sees a flash of silver. The boy hauls his coal down the stairs, making two more return trips, then takes up the handles of his cart and speaks again to Mr Bryant, who nods and, to Martha's horror, begins walking in her direction.

She spins on her heel and hurries into the park, moving quickly down the path away from him and veering off behind an oak. She stands with her back to the tree, waiting. A minute or so passes, and her pulse gradually slows. When she looks out again, there is no trace of him. She returns to Piccadilly, glancing among the carts and barrows and carriages and bonnets for the black brim, cursing silently, but she has lost him.

She stands awhile, thinking hard, and then approaches the newsagent.

'Can you tell me, sir, who lives in that house?' she asks, pointing at the mansion.

'That I can, miss. The great lady of Stratton Street, Miss Angela Burdett-Coutts. Very pleasant she is, too. Her man buys all her periodicals from me. Books, as well. She's very well read, I'm sure.'

Martha thanks him, feeling sick. She stands a moment, thinking what to do, and then crosses the little side street to approach the black street door. Its paint is glossy, no doubt cleaned of dust and dirt that morning, and she hesitates a moment before ringing the bell. A pale, smooth footman answers within seconds.

'Yes, miss?' He sneers down at her.

'Is Miss Coutts at home?'

'The mistress is away, miss.'

'Oh.' Martha swallows and glances behind him into the dim, cool hall, catching the scent of beeswax and fresh flowers. 'Do you know when she will be back?'

'Afraid not, miss. Shall I leave a message?'

'No, no. I'll try again another time.'

'Very well, miss,' he says.

He shuts the door in her face.

She stands at the foot of the steps, her heart thudding against her chest, wondering how she could have been so blind. She thought she had her wits about her. But the signs were always there: the books on law, the vague way he spoke about his day, that time several weeks ago when she opened his pocketbook absentmindedly and found pages of curious shorthand: *21st March Dorchester House 2 p.m. stayed 30 mins. 2nd April Royal Academy 11 a.m. left 12.15. 13th April walked Hyde Park with HB 45 mins.* Perhaps she did not want to know the truth, had brushed it conveniently from sight.

She feels a weight at her thigh and remembers the map she has brought with her. And then she remembers Rose Street, and the idea of seeing Josephine again is like the sun bursting through cloud. With a new lightness in her step, she hurries east towards Covent Garden, pausing on Long Acre to consult the map and realising she has gone too far. She has almost run here, and arrives breathless at the lip of a narrow court by a public house, looking up and around at all the possible doors and windows Josephine might call hers. She resists the urge to shout her friend's name, and knocks instead at the first door, but nobody of her name lives there. She approaches the second door when it opens, and a young woman comes out into the street with an infant on her hip, the hand of another fastened in hers.

'Excuse me,' Martha says. 'I'm looking for Josephine Nash.'

The woman blinks. She is round and pretty, with skin like cream. The curls framing her face are the handsome hue of wet autumn leaves. 'She ain't here no more,' she says, to Martha's astonishment, and it takes her a moment to compose herself.

'She was here? Where is she now?'

'I dunno,' the woman says guardedly. 'She left not long ago.'

Martha closes her hands into fists, tips her head back and sighs.

'I'm sorry,' says the woman. 'Are you a friend of hers?'

'I was, yes. I am.' Martha looks up and down the court, feeling hopeless. 'I haven't seen her in some time.'

The woman peers at her. 'You ain't from that cottage?'

'Yes! Do you know it?'

'Are you Martha?'

'Yes!'

Her pretty face clears; she appears relieved and shifts the child more comfortably.

'Were you the person she was sending messages to on the outside?' Martha asks.

'Guilty as charged.' The woman gives a shy smile. 'I'm Annie, by the way. Have you come to bring her back?'

Martha pauses. 'No. I'm afraid I left myself.'

'Oh.' Annie's forehead creases. 'I thought you was all to move to Africa or Australia or somewhere?'

'We were.'

There is an awkward silence. Then Martha says: 'If you see her, will you give her my address? Only, I don't know how long I'll be there.'

Annie recites it back to her and promises to remember it.

Martha wanders through the market, with no money to buy anything. Mrs Kenealy has insinuated twice that Mr Bryant's rent is late. For all her faults, Martha thinks she would not put them out onto the street. Not yet.

She drifts among the fruit peel and cabbage leaves and wonders where she ought to go, for their rooms in Lambeth feel menacing, the air thick with lies. Briefly, she thinks of Mary, living above the pastry-cook shop near Oxford Street.

She shares the rooms with the shop owner and his wife, and does general housework for them; there is no room for Martha. Besides, Mary does not know she is married. Now Mary has had both sisters vanish. Martha feels the persistent drip of shame and guilt like rain down her collar. Mary deserves a better sister than her.

It is strange to think, as she walks the streets of London, that Emily could be here, too – caught in the same rain shower, taking the time from the same street-clocks, one of her coins, glowing like an ember, nestled in a toll-taker's box as Martha passes by. The city is enormous, and yet it should not be impossible to find somebody within it, not if she looks for long enough.

She knows she will never think of London as home, will never truly think of anywhere as home again. Home was a whitewashed cottage with sheets in the kitchen, hollyhocks in the garden, three sisters in a bed. Home is only a memory. And she is grateful for it, because to have had it and lost it is better than never having it at all.

CHAPTER 16

The Light Beneath the Door

The garden at Holly Lodge is one of the prettiest Angela has ever known, particularly on a warm late spring evening such as this. Angela and Mrs Brown sit on the terrace, clutching glasses of madeira, overlooking the lawns and glades, the bustling beds of lilacs and chrysanthemums. The house was her grandmother's, and now belongs to her grandmother's husband, William, the Duke of St Albans, whom Harriot married six years after the death of Angela's grandfather, when Angela was thirteen. A screen of glossy rhododendrons blocks the lodge from the road, and the skill of the gardener means there is no obvious boundary, no sign of a wall or fence anywhere, so that London appears as a little town at the bottom of the lawn. There are glasshouses, fishponds and even a small farm, where her grandmother once kept pigs. Some of her horses are still alive and have grown fat in the stables, loaned now and again to the village children for rides.

Angela loves this house. Harriot and William lived very happily here, and William has kept things mostly as they were. Harriot's lucky horseshoe hangs on the porch, and her grandfather's maps decorate the shady hall, where his musket, too, hangs on display in a nod to the previous century, when highwaymen dwelled in the shadows of the road near the house. The seashells and bell jars crowded with exotic birds live on in the bathroom, and Harriot's tropical flowers cast their heady perfume in the conservatory, watered by William himself. Her rich, musky fragrance still lingers about her bedroom, escaping in an opulent draught down the corridor, and on her first night, Angela stood in the doorway, breathing it in.

It has been years since she last stayed at Holly Lodge, but William was delighted to welcome them, extending his warm invitation after receiving a concerned letter from Mrs Brown. They arrived after nightfall, shaken from the turbulent journey up the hill to Highgate. White and silent, Angela refused supper and went straight to bed, and Mrs Brown and William talked long into the night. The next morning, waking to birdsong and the undeniable canopy of spring, Angela began to feel a little better, and a long walk around the grounds with Mrs Brown further improved her mood.

The Browns had all but carried her home from Urania Cottage that night, where she fell into a sort of nervous breakdown, a lucid fever dream of grief and rage and terror. And guilt: the guilt is crippling, like an anvil on her chest.

For two days, she cried like a child. Mr Dickens visited her at home, sitting in her bedroom for the length of an afternoon. He was distraught to have unknowingly colluded in Dunn's deception. He said he thought little of it when his friend informed him of his cancelled plans, and that he'd decided to stay the winter in Lambeth with an ailing friend as his house in Sherborne Lane was being redecorated. Dickens had made the relevant note in his address book and continued to communicate with his friend, who admittedly he had not seen in some months, which was unusual. But it was not for wont of Dickens trying; over the winter and early spring he had suggested meeting on several occasions, but Bryant had a ready excuse each time. And with the chaplain being so busy with his parish and prison work, his house renovations and sick friend, Dickens thought little of it. He assured Angela that nobody was more shocked than he to find out the chaplain had eloped with Martha: his friend Bryant was a proud bachelor whose moral compass never wavered.

Angela was sympathetic, and reminded him that Dunn's mind worked like nobody else's – except, perhaps, for Dickens'. He is hopeful that they will find Martha and bring her back to Shepherd's Bush. Angela is not. She knows that Martha will not be found until Dunn wishes her to be. She cannot help but picture Martha tied like a witch to a stake, flames licking at her feet. Only laudanum tempts her to sleep, and each night Dr Brown brings it to her room, the tinkle of his bottles registering his arrival.

The duke – her duke – has written several times. His letters with their brown spidery scrawl were brought to her in bed at Stratton Street, but she did not open them, and so they were taken away. The cockatoo was removed from its perch some time ago.

At Holly Lodge, all the doors and windows are thrown wide, and they take their meals in the dining room, the setting of so many of her grandmother's parties. As a girl, Angela sat here late into the night, dazzled by Harriot's friends in their silks and tails, singing songs and playing the pianoforte. Even now, she half-expects her grandmother to sweep onto the terrace in a cloud of patchouli and pearls.

In the daytime, she wanders the house as though searching for her, touching her things and wondering if William might let her have some of them to put about the house like talismans, for Harriot had such extraordinary luck throughout her life. Or did she make the luck? Only her final years were difficult, when she had lost her looks and her figure and the newspapers were unkind. The more ill she grew, the more she shrunk into the enormous bed downstairs at Stratton Street. There, propped among pillows, she spoke wheezily of her early life as a child-player. Angela loved to hear about the long coach journeys, the strange little theatres in anonymous towns, the costumes darned together between scenes. In her later life, when the periodicals were harsh, the caricatures grotesque, Harriot stopped going to the theatre at all and was content riding on the heath with Angela, wearing her purple ermine cloak, which gave them the appearance, from a distance, of a queen and her handmaid.

As the evening draws in, Angela leaves Mrs Brown and walks once more around the grounds, stopping now and again to put her nose to the flowers or talk with the gardener, who is loading his barrow in the walled garden. They return to the house together, talking of his baby son. They agree that the duchess would have adored him; nobody loved babies more than Harriot, who had none of her own, though she treated Angela as such, taking her down to the south coast and up to the highlands, supervising Angela's trunks herself and holding up gowns to her each morning. She filled scent bottles with water and allowed Angela to mimic her at her toilette, draping her like a plaything with stones and jewels and furs. Angela always felt very small in the enormous mirrors festooning the house at Stratton Street, and ridiculous in everything Harriot put her in. She had the plain face of a servant, made all the more ordinary by the opulence of Harriot's things.

Coming back through the house, she brushes a hand across the grand pianoforte, where her sisters sang as Harriot played, while Angela sat on the rug, too small to take part. She presses a single note, as if summoning her, listening for her silk shoes in the hall. But the house is silent, and a gentle breeze flows through the open doors, carrying the mellow aroma of cut grass. When William dies, Holly Lodge and everything in it will be hers: the parrots in the bathroom, the horses in the stable.

Before she goes to bed, she looks back at the handsome instrument, silent for so long, wondering how it is that, though everybody has left her, she is the ghost.

❦

The staircase at Dean Street is bare wood, and Josephine presses herself against the walls as she creeps quietly down, carrying her candle. It is after three in the morning, and the house is silent. Nan is asleep in her bed; Josephine could hear her light snores as she passed her doorway. Mrs T is not at home. At the bottom of the stairs her bare foot lands on something soft and warm. She gasps, clapping a hand over her mouth, a split-second from crying out.

There is a loud, serpentine hiss, and the marmalade cat trots reproachfully towards the cellar. Josephine curses, breathing hard, collecting herself.

The deed-box sits where she left it, at the centre of the

dining-room table, conspicuous as a cask of gunpowder. She does not know where Nan keeps the key. Approaching it cautiously, she loosens her grip on the hairpin in her palm and silently pulls out a chair from the table, holding her breath. She sits for a moment, her mouth dry, her heart beating hard, and then she takes the pin to the lock.

Nan was waiting for her when she came home. She is almost recovered and some days ago moved from her bed to the chaise in the sitting room, where she forces Josephine to play cards. She is thoroughly bored of being indoors, and the boredom makes her sour and peevish. She turns her nose up at the food Josephine brings up from the kitchen, wrinkles it at the bitter coffee Josephine brews. By the next collection, things will be back to normal, and Josephine will no longer have to go out alone.

The lock gives way with a little click. Slowly, Josephine eases the lid open and pushes aside the bags of money, which have been sorted by Nan into bank notes and coins. There are bags of sovereigns, half-sovereigns, half-guineas, crowns, but it is not these that Josephine's fingers seek; they search for the black books, stacked against the uppermost right corner of the velvet-lined box and, trembling, withdraw them.

She sets her candle on the table and, taking a deep breath, opens the cover of the first. An L, two Ts, an E…Little. Little Pulteney Street. She returns the book to the corner of the deed-box and opens the next, frowning until the letters bloom into words. Poland Street. Silver Street. The candle gutters as she opens the fourth, and she waits for it to settle, and sees the word Square. Golden Square. She swallows and listens a moment, imagining the creak of a foot on a floorboard, but the tall house is silent. The first page has numbers at the top, a two and a three, and the word January. At the beginning of every lesson Mrs Holdsworth chalked the date on the slate propped against her bureau; at the end she rubbed out the numbers and left the month.

Josephine turns the thin pages, marked in lead with columns of words and numbers. All the words are names, some of which she can read more easily than the others. Ann. Mary. There are six or seven per page, sometimes more, sometimes less. When a new name is introduced, a V is often marked beside it. Occasionally a name is struck through. Ann disappears from the book in March. A name beginning with M appears the following week, a V beside it. She stares at it as it slowly reveals itself to her, the two Ns, the first part like Mary but not. Marianne. Miss Virtue.

Josephine knows it is all a sham, that the girls brought in to have their virginity auctioned off are often only new faces, brought to Soho from Whitechapel or Cheapside or somewhere else they will not be recognised, and moved on again. V for virtue. For virgin. She turns the page to May, and pauses.

Tucked inside her sleeve is a piece of paper with her own muddled handwriting, copied from another of the slim black books. She smooths out the page in the flickering light and reads.

❧

The night in Highgate is like a shroud thrown over the lodge, falling blackly across the window, which Angela has left open so that she may fall asleep to the gentle rustle of the rhododendrons. A little after eleven, she puts down her book and turns down her lamp, but she has left at home the laudanum and the paste of potash and zinc Dr Brown makes for her eczema, which burns in rough patches on her neck and in the crooks of her arms, and so she drifts in and out of a fretful sleep.

When the night is at its darkest hour, and the house has finished issuing its little creaks and sighs, Angela wakes to the sound of light footsteps in the passageway.

They pause down the hall, near Mrs Brown's room, and Angela remembers the time, several summers ago, when the line of propriety between her and William blurred. She was staying at Holly Lodge to assist with the inventory of Harriot's estate. She and William drank a lot of very old brandy from the cellar, and she went to sit at the pianoforte, playing and singing quite unselfconsciously, surprising and delighting him with her knowledge of popular music. William is only thirteen years older than Angela; he was Harriot's junior by twenty-three years. When they said goodnight, he regarded her with unguarded affection, kissing her as though she was a sister and, in the act of doing so, became aware that she was not. His lips lingered a moment too long, and she felt his breath warm on her cheek. Though she drew back, it stirred something inside her: not a dormant passion for him but a glimpse into an alternative life in which the kiss might go on. The next morning, though, he was quite ordinary with her, and she was grateful.

Her door opens quietly, and somebody carries a candle inside.

'William?' she says as her eyes adjust. 'What is it?'

But it is not William. She feels the ground lurch sickeningly towards her as she stares into his face, illuminated like a death mask in the candlelight.

'My darling, you have nothing to fear from me.'

She is too shocked, too frightened to scream. Her voice is strangled in her own throat.

'I beg you,' he says, his voice like silk. 'Do not be afraid. I want only to talk.'

Cautiously, he approaches, with the flame dancing before him. A pathetic little whimper leaves her mouth. He draws closer in the darkness, treading lightly on the floorboards, and lowers himself to sit on the bed, by her feet. If she couldn't feel his weight sink into the mattress, she might believe it to be a nightmare. But Richard Dunn is here, solid and real, and she is utterly, completely alone.

He regards her tenderly, and she feels her skin crawl. If she were to shout out, to attempt to run from him, he might kill her at last. Yet for her to die in this moment – she has never felt more fiercely, powerfully alive. Blood pounds in her veins; every nerve hums, lit like touchpaper. She tries to unstick her tongue from the roof of her mouth, but it will not come.

'You need not look so afraid,' he says, almost fondly.

And then it comes to her: if she can keep him here, talking, somebody might hear them or see the light beneath the door. Mrs Brown is a disturbed sleeper herself; she might already be awake.

Angela swallows. 'How did you get in?'

'A window was open downstairs,' he says amiably. 'I'm no housebreaker.'

Another loophole that he will use in court if he has to. If she makes it that far.

'What have you done with Martha?' she asks, trying to sound clear and unafraid.

'Done with her? Why, she's asleep at home. Where else would she be?'

'Why? Why her?'

'Come now. Are you envious?' His smile leaves her cold. 'My darling, I had to get your attention somehow. I had no other choice.'

She recalls the letter marked *ABC*, pressed into her hand in Islington. *If you refuse to meet me, you will repent this course, the consequences of which will sooner or later fall on yourself and those who are dearest to you.*

'You can't say I didn't warn you,' he says. 'I offered to meet you and you declined.'

'I didn't decline.'

'You failed to respond, then. Don't let's get drawn into semantics.'

Can she scream yet? She isn't sure and doesn't want to try until she is certain it will not die in her throat. She pictures him lunging at her, pressing her face into the pillow.

'I'm no villain, Angie.'

'What is it you want?'

'I told you. I just want to talk to you.'

She waits, listening hard for the creak of floorboards in this old house: a servant upstairs, or Mrs Brown. But there is only silence.

'How did you do it? Become Mr Bryant?'

He seems pleased she has worked him out. 'He was the chaplain at the New Prison. I saw him carrying *Martin Chuzzlewit* and struck up a conversation about literature. Imagine my surprise when I found out he knew Mr Dickens himself. Of course, *I* am familiar with Dickens, who has flatteringly taken an interest over the years in our various trials and tribulations. I hope to meet him properly one of these days, man to man.'

'He would have recognised you.'

'Which is why I arranged my visits around his.'

'How? You have caused him much anguish. He blames himself for not seeing the truth.'

'Nobody ought to blame anybody. We are all of us free agents.'

'Apart from Martha, who did not know the truth. Does she now?'

'I didn't force her to marry me.'

'But you did trick her.'

He says nothing and shrugs carelessly.

'How did you do it?' she says again.

'I found out from Bryant that Dickens had asked him to take up a chaplaincy in a private institution, which he was obliged to turn down as he was going to Europe for a spell. He wouldn't say what or where this place was, of course, but one day I had a scratch in my throat, and kind man that he is, he fetched me a glass of water. While I waited, I didn't go searching for anything in particular, but my eyes found a well-known signature, quite a famous one, and I leant down to tie my shoe and the words Urania Cottage caught my eye, as did, to my great surprise, your name. What a stroke of serendipity, I thought. I was curious about the terms of the role and so thought that I ought to write to Mr Dickens to clarify some things.'

'Pretending to be Bryant?' Her voice is thick with contempt.

'I told him what I thought, that it was a wonderful endeavour: a refuge for fallen women, who are not looked upon kindly by society or indeed their fellow creatures. Inspired.'

'And you evaded him.'

'He wrote back to me, saying that he was satisfied that,

having shown the cottage already, and him being a man with many demands on his time, I could begin right away. He desired a final meeting to talk through everything, but I was sure to only give my availability on the days he said he was away. I followed him for some time, to learn his habits and what days he typically went out to Shepherd's Bush. Once I knew he generally visited on Saturdays, I was able to structure my own calls accordingly.'

'And you corresponded in such a way that he suspected nothing. You lied repeatedly.'

'We corresponded about my instruction. He gave his preference on sermons and so on. He insisted on full reports on all the residents and I was happy to oblige.'

'You told him you – Mr Bryant, that is – had decided not to travel, but that your house was being decorated and you were staying with a friend in Lambeth.'

'I do live in Lambeth. But not with a friend. With my lady wife.' He smiles, and her stomach coils.

'Have you harmed her?'

'Harmed her! My goodness, what must you think of me? Martha is very well indeed. Very well. She keeps a nice home for us. She was taught by the best.'

'I don't believe you.'

'Then don't.'

Angela takes a trembling breath. 'What is it you want? You haven't said.'

He gazes levelly at her. 'You're an impressive woman, Angie. What is it that your friend the duke said about you? That you are made of gold?'

She glares at him. 'You stole my letter. You broke into my house.'

'I did no such thing.'

'Then you had somebody steal it from me.'

'An item of correspondence fell into my possession. Again, I did not housebreak or trespass.'

'How did you get it, if it wasn't you?'

He smiles. 'I'd be more stringent about who you let into your house, if I were you. You are far too trusting, though it is one of your most endearing qualities.'

'The agency staff, then, the night of my ball,' she says. 'My servants would do no such thing.'

He says nothing and goes on giving his infuriating little smile, as though she is a petulant child. Every exchange with him is like a dance in which he draws closer and then moves further away.

'How did you avoid me at the cottage?'

He glimmers with mischief. 'I had a lookout.'

She waits for him to elaborate.

'A boy from the brickfields. He'd stand in the lane and signal to me if you or the Browns were there. There were a few close calls, but he never failed me.'

She shakes her head. 'You still haven't told me what you want,' she says. 'I know you didn't marry Martha because you care for her.'

'What is it *you* want, Angie?' He speaks slowly now. 'I'm so glad we have the opportunity to talk like this. After all these years.'

'I want you to leave me alone.'

He scowls, mock offended.

'What will it take for you to leave me alone and release Martha?'

Now she has him. He lowers the candle, and the light plays

eerily upon his features. 'Pay off my debts,' he says softly, 'and I shall release you.'

'How much?'

'Fifty thousand pounds.'

She stares at him, breathing hard. 'You shall have it.'

He grins. 'You are forgetting something, Angie. I know you. I know how that fine mind of yours works. As soon as the money has left your account, you'll have a warrant for my arrest – one of your bewigged horsemen bearing down upon me, when I have only ever been your humble servant. Only ever shown you the utmost devotion.'

'Is that all?' she breathes. 'Fifty thousand pounds, and no arrest?'

'Fifty thousand, in notes, so that it can't be traced. Leave it at the Kennington Road post office for Martha Gelder. When it's done, Martha is yours. And then you leave *me* alone. No more solicitors. No more barristers flaying me alive in the public courts.'

This is the moment that Angela realises that he truly sees them as equals, both guilty parties, each as bad as the other.

'There is one more thing.' He grins again, and her stomach drops. He lifts a hand, and stopping two inches short of her face, with a finger traces down her cheek, her lip, her jaw. 'You're even lovelier close to. But I am a married man now. I must resist temptation.'

Her heart is thundering in her chest.

'Don't be afraid, my darling. I want only to look at you. Dearest Angie.'

His eyes drink in her hair, her skin, the place where her nightdress meets her throat as she trembles with fear and revulsion.

And then two things happen at once. He moves to reach for her hand, and the candle, which he holds in his left hand, falls from its holder. It topples to the bedclothes, igniting them immediately, for the heavy counterpane is so old it might well be made of straw.

He leaps at once from the bed, and she scrambles from the blankets. Panic registers on his face, rendering it innocent, almost childlike, and there is a single, solitary moment where they look at one another, and she feels something like sympathy for him. It is clear he did not mean for this to happen, and the flames begin licking over the bed, devouring the ancient fabric with such ferocious intent that nothing can be done. Inside of a minute the bed is roaring like a furnace, and she is shouting: 'Fire! Fire!' more loudly than she has ever shouted anything before, until her throat gives out, and though the household descends with thick blankets and sand, she shouts still, like a woman in mania, and it is only when the fire is extinguished and the room thick with smoke and coughing and noises of concern and relief that she realises he is gone, vanished, as though he was never there at all.

CHAPTER 17

Golden Square

It is a little after six in the morning when Frank returns to the section-house at the end of his shift, light-headed with tiredness and aggrieved that breakfast will not be not served for another hour, by which time he will be asleep. He is cleaning his boots in the brushing room, where weak morning light spills feebly through the high window, when the inspector – the stern, jet-whiskered Clark – finds him.

'Sir,' he says automatically, setting down his brush.

'There's a woman outside asking after you,' says Clark.

'Sir? Do you know her name?'

The inspector shakes his head. 'She wouldn't give it. Or any other detail, for that matter. Said she'll only speak to you.'

'Yes, sir.'

Frank has never had a visitor before. It could be any one of the waifs and strays he encounters on shift, many of whom know him by name. But he had no dealings with any women last night; it rained for all but one of the eight hours, and people stayed sensibly indoors. A few nights ago, he caught a thief knocking at the door of a marine store by the dyeworks with a case of stolen copper nails. The thrill of it carried him through the rest of his shift and the following one, but last night had been dreary. He took to his old habit of trying shop doors and windows to see if they were secure, looking like a thief himself.

He allows himself for a brief moment to imagine that it is Polly, and follows Clark through the section-house with a spring in his step. Frank knows the rules state that a woman may not enter the premises, but this is generally taken to refer to sisters and sweethearts. Beside the inspector's office, a door opens onto the stable-yard, and from there Frank can see across the road to a small parade of shops. At first, Frank does not notice the scant cloaked figure standing before the black-painted frontage of a cabinetmaker's. When he does, his heart almost flies from his chest. But as he approaches, a pale hand lifts the hood, and he is astonished to see the fine, dark eyes that meet his own, and beneath them a thick, silvery scar, running almost from nostril to chin.

'Josephine!' he exclaims, hurrying towards her.

But she shows none of the same delight. 'I didn't know who to come to,' she says, her tone as dull as her expression. 'I hoped to find you here.'

'How long have you been waiting? Where have you been?' Frank glances over his shoulder at Clark, watching impassively from the stable-yard.

'Can you come with me?' she asks, her dark eyes troubled.

Frank has not seen her in months. It is surreal to find her here in Wandsworth. He realises he has come to think of the Urania girls like dolls, existing only in their little kingdom.

326

'Where?'

'Do you know where Miss Coutts lives?'

Frank is surprised but does not show it. 'Yes,' he says. 'Now?'

She nods, and at once he agrees, all traces of hunger and tiredness extinguished. The way she glances at Clark tells him to be cautious, so he relays to the inspector that she is an old friend in need of help.

'What sort of help?' Clark growls.

'She won't say, but she is trustworthy,' Frank replies, though he isn't sure of this.

Frank has a good reputation in V division: bowler in the cricket team, conductor in the band. He once carried for half a mile a fellow constable who had been kicked almost to death by a drunkard on the high street. Clark sees him off with a curt nod and a note in his pocketbook, and when he returns to Josephine, she nods at his uniform and says: 'You can't wear that.'

Frank is about to remind her that Angela knows he is a Metropolitan police constable but something prevents him, and he hurries inside to change as Josephine waits, looking up and down the road as though expecting someone. She leads him north towards the river, at a pace much quicker than a constable's, but knowing what a distance they have to cover, Frank stops an empty cab and gives instructions to the driver. They sit opposite one another, and Josephine looks impatiently through the window as if they are stuck in traffic, though due to the early hour their journey is smooth.

'Where have you been living?' he asks, once the driver has paid the toll on the bridge and they are picking up speed again.

'Here and there. Covent Garden. Soho. Wandsworth is a long way from Soho.'

'Yes,' he says.

The driver drops them at the corner of Piccadilly and Stratton Street, where Frank asks him to wait. There is no mistaking the grand Coutts mansion. The shutters and curtains are still drawn against the gentle morning. Frank and Josephine approach the street door, and he knocks smartly. After a delay, a footman answers in his dressing gown and slippers and, with great disdain, informs them that the mistress is away.

Josephine makes a fist and holds it to her forehead. 'Do you know where?' she says.

The footman pretends not to hear the desperation in her voice and addresses the air a foot above her. 'Miss Coutts is visiting a relative and is expected home tomorrow.'

Josephine turns to Frank as if to ask what they ought to do. Of course he has not a clue what they *are* doing, but he draws out his pocketbook all the same. 'We shall leave a message,' he says, turning to Josephine. 'What – what do you want it to say?'

'We'll have to do it another way,' Josephine says quietly, almost to herself, her features drawn. She tells Frank what to write, and he takes it down as the footman waits dispassionately.

When it is done, the footman snatches the note and closes the door firmly, and they return to their cab, giving the same address and rolling onwards, to Soho.

❧

They climb out at the south-west corner of a square, and Frank pays the driver. But when the cab draws away, Josephine walks towards a narrow side street and stands on the corner, looking towards a house on the eastern side of the square with a painted green door.

'What'll we do now?' Frank asks, slightly helplessly.

'Emily is in there,' she says.

Frank sifts through his memory, wondering why he has heard that name or ought to know it.

'Emily Gelder. Martha's sister,' Josephine adds.

'In there?' And then, looking around at the shabby square, the once-grand houses given over to tenanted rooms: 'Is it—'

'We have to get her out.'

He stares at her in astonishment. 'You and I?'

'But first we wait for Mrs Jenkins to leave.'

'Mrs Jenkins?'

'She goes out looking for girls most days.'

Frank is utterly out of his depth. 'We ought to involve F division,' he says. 'I'm a constable – I can't go strolling into a bawdy house.'

Josephine looks at him and laughs, not unkindly, and he is instantly chastened.

'F division is already well acquainted with Mrs Jenkins,' she says.

They watch the house for almost an hour. In that time, a young man with greased, dark hair comes out, dancing down the steps with a basket and reappearing fifteen minutes later with the basket filled, a cloth lying neatly over his produce. Frank looks at Josephine sideways for a reaction, but her eyes are narrow, her gaze fixed.

Another forty-five minutes pass, and then Josephine stands straighter, drawing her chin to her chest as a woman of around fifty sashays down the steps to the pavement, wrapping her fringed shawl about her and looking left and right before heading north. They watch her, and Frank is amazed once again at how it is always the ordinary-seeming ones who are the most dangerous, the most evil, who burn their children where nobody will see the marks and who snare girls who are scarcely more than children themselves, lending them a shawl, offering a bed for the night.

'That's her,' says Josephine. 'She's gone.' She rolls her shoulders back and sighs, like a soldier on the brink of a battle.

Suddenly, it occurs to Frank that Josephine does not know about Martha. The moment to tell her presents itself and then passes just as swiftly by. He tells himself it is because she is already marching towards the house with the green-painted door. He could pull her back, tell her to wait, for they have stood here almost two hours now, but he shakes the truth from him like a cobweb and follows, convinced he will tell her later, when the time is right.

As they wait for Josephine's knock to be answered, Frank imagines he is wearing his uniform and arranges his face as though he is.

The door swings abruptly open, and the handsome young man breaks into a smile.

'Josephine,' he says. 'To what do I owe the pleasure?'

'Mrs Jenkins at home?' she asks, her tone light and business-like.

'She ain't.' He leans against the doorpost and folds his arms in rather a proprietorial way. 'New bully, is it?' he says, looking directly at Frank.

'He's doing some bookkeeping for Mrs T. It ain't Mrs Jenkins I was here for, anyway. Nan's sent me to speak to the girl what arrived last week.'

The man's brow creases, and there is a pause. 'Come in, then.' He leads them into a square-shaped hall, which smells of perfume, sour wine and something more febrile, and nods towards the staircase.

On the first floor, all the doors are closed except one, at the end of the landing. A girl with bright, brassy curls is asleep facing the door, her bare arms and shoulders thrown over the bedclothes. The bright daylight streaming through the window behind her washes through the dimness, revealing plain, dusty floorboards and grand plasterwork on the ceiling, acorns and grapes, from days long gone. A pair of ladies' shoes wait outside one of the doors; inside one is a single stocking, beside it a half-drunk glass of red wine.

They go up, winding further into the stuffy air, all the way to the top. The stairs are narrower here, more precarious, with loose, dry boards that snap beneath their feet. Frank follows Josephine to the front of the house, where she knocks lightly at an unvarnished door and puts an ear to the wood.

There is no response, and a moment later she opens an adjacent door, which leads into a garret-cum-cupboard next door to the bedroom. It is empty, with a sloping roof thick with cobwebs, drifting like spectral curtains. The connecting door to the bedroom is unlocked, and Frank follows Josephine through. It is large, sparsely furnished with cheap, old pieces; one of the drawers in the chest will not close, and the shutters over the window hang at an angle. In the middle of the bed, beneath crumpled sheets, lies a girl in the process of waking. Her expression is all mistrust as she props herself on her elbows, but it clears at the sight of Josephine, who says softly: 'This is Emily.'

She is perhaps sixteen or seventeen, creased with sleep,

wearing a sleeveless nightdress. She wrinkles her nose, which is the same as Martha's, speckled with freckles.

Frank looks at Josephine in wonder. 'You found her. How did you find her?'

Josephine's dark eyes have none of the awe or amazement of his. She looks upon Emily almost resignedly, and he knows at once, knew when he saw her outside the station, that she has lost some fundamental part of herself along the way.

'Who are you?' Emily asks him.

'My name is Frank Holdsworth. I'm a constable. Don't worry, you aren't in trouble,' he adds hastily, seeing her face. 'I am a friend of Josephine's. And of Martha's.'

'You know Martha?' she asks.

'Yes.'

'Is she vexed with me?'

There is a pause of disbelief. 'Not in the slightest. She has been desperate to find you. She has been very worried.'

Emily watches him for a moment. 'Why didn't she come?' she asks.

'She thought it'd be best if we came to get you.'

'And they know that's what you're doing?' She indicates the rest of the house.

Josephine glances at Frank.

'Not exactly,' he says.

Emily is petite and childlike, but there is a hardness to her. The look she gives them now is challenging, half-amused. 'You think Larry will let us walk out of here?'

Frank looks anxiously at Josephine, who says: 'Larry's the bully.'

'Unless you got a few bob, I shan't be going anywhere.'

'How much?' Frank asks.

Emily's features soften. 'Too much for them to ever tell us. They make it impossible. They say we have to buy our way out, but how can we when they don't pay us? And if we leave, they have ways of finding us. One of the girls got brought back here from Deptford, wherever that is. She didn't leave her room for two weeks.'

'How long have you been here?' Frank asks.

'A week or so.'

'Where were you before?'

'Some other house. I don't know where, exactly. I could see the cathedral from the window, though.'

'Leadenhall Market,' says Josephine, and Frank looks at her. 'They're shifted around.'

'How did you find her?'

Josephine sighs. 'I'll tell you how I got to be there later. But I was at the Leadenhall house, and when I knocked at the door I heard the bawd shout her name before she smacked her. When I went in, Emily was weeping on the stairs. I hardly took no notice, but after, when I was thinking about how sorry she looked sitting there and how I done nothing about it, I was picturing Martha. I couldn't get straight in my mind why, and then I realised they looked similar. I remembered that horrible woman had called her Emily. I went and looked for proof the only place I knew how, and there she was, in lead, on paper. Emily G. If your mother hadn't learnt me to read, I'd never have saw it.'

From beyond the room comes the noise of a sluggish tread on the stairs. All the hairs on Frank's arms stand on end; for a moment, he had forgotten where they were and what they are about to do. Their time for talking is over, and Frank can only guess at what's ahead.

The door to Emily's bedroom opens, and in comes Mrs Jenkins, bearing a key. There is a dreadful silence as she looks at each of them in turn and says: 'Visiting hour, is it?'

Noticing how Josephine appears to shrink slightly, Frank squares himself towards the woman, saying: 'Our business here is not done.'

She regards him, and a cold trickle of fear descends inside him. 'I thought *I* conduct the business in this house. Perhaps I'm mistaken. What's this message from Nan, then, eh?' She asks this of Josephine, who appears both frightened and full of loathing.

'She wants Emily to come to Dean Street,' Josephine says.

'Does she? Funny, that, 'cause I seen her just now on Brewer Street, and she never mentioned nothing about it. She did say, though, that you'd left the house at Dean Street without saying nothing. Like a thief in the night. And here you are. She'll be very interested to know you've paid us a visit, I'm sure. So what is it you're doing here then, the both of you?'

'Mrs Jenkins, Emily has been missing from her family for months,' says Josephine. 'They've been searching for her. She wants to go home, don't you?'

Emily nods uncertainly, and Frank sees at once how afraid she is.

'Ha! They won't want her back,' Mrs Jenkins crows. 'We're her family now. And family sticks together. She ain't going nowhere.'

'Mrs Jenkins,' says Frank. 'You will not hold her here against her will.'

'Who are you?' She peers at him. 'I ain't seen you afore.'

'My name is Frank Holdsworth. I'm a constable with the Metropolitan Police.'

At this her eyes widen sardonically. 'Are you now? Where's your stick then, Mr Peeler?'

'We've been looking for Emily, to reunite her with her family.'

'Right, that's enough.' She claps her hands together as though silencing a room full of people. 'Get gone, both of you. You shan't disturb my girls at their rest.'

'Mrs Jenkins—'

'You heard me! I don't believe for a second you're with the police. I know constables, and you ain't one of them. I want you gone afore you go upsetting my girls.'

Frank turns and begins rifling through the broken wardrobe for some clothes for Emily, but there are no outdoor things, only fussy, frilly nightgowns and cheap satins, nothing she might keep warm in. Josephine sees what he is doing and removes her own cloak from around her shoulders.

'Ha!' Mrs Jenkins cries again. 'You do mean business. Larry!' The name is bellowed with such velocity it is anyone's guess if Larry is within the house or several streets away.

But soon there are heavy, pounding footsteps on the stairs, and a man almost a full head taller than the door-frame lowers himself into the room. He appears to Frank like a giant, stitched together from several men. The nose is out of proportion with the face, which is at odds with the large eyes and the ears of different sizes. His hair is cropped closely to his uneven head.

Frank eyes him levelly and then addresses the proprietor, his heart thudding in his chest, his hand reaching automatically for his truncheon and finding nothing. 'Mrs Jenkins, be reasonable. We are Emily's friends, here to take her home.'

'Funny, that, Mr Peeler, as I was under the impression that this was her home, me being the one what clothes and feeds and keeps her. And I believe I've asked you twice ever so politely to leave now, so if you have trouble understanding me a third time, Larry here speaks the language.'

'How much do you want?' Frank addresses Mrs Jenkins, who blinks in astonishment.

'Who said there was a price on her?'

'You as good as did. How much, then?'

'You'd have to take that up with Mrs T.'

'Who?'

Mrs Jenkins makes a noise like a bark. 'Who is this queer fellow? He don't know a lot, does he? Where did you find him?'

Frank looks meaningfully at Josephine. 'How much do we have?'

She gazes blankly at him.

'All of it?' he exclaims, as if she has spoken.

She opens her mouth and closes it as he takes from his pocket a small purse, in which he keeps coins for the toll roads and bridges. He crosses the room towards the bawd, who holds out a flat palm, her eyes flashing hungrily. He sets the purse onto it. As she sets about unwrapping the knot, with Larry as absorbed as she, Frank turns very slightly to look at Josephine, then gives an imperceptible jerk of his head in the direction of the door.

And then two things happen at once. A cascade of pennies rains down on the floor in a racket, and Frank darts towards the door leading into the garret.

'Larry!' Mrs Jenkins screeches. With more agility than seems possible for a man his width and size, Larry hauls up a spindly chair from beside the door and appears in the hall, blocking Frank inside. Mrs Jenkins appears at the other entrance, red-faced with glee.

'O-ho, no you don't, Mr Peeler,' she cackles, her beady eyes livid with hatred. 'You'll do well to get past Larry.'

Frank is aware of the breeze from the chair on his cheek before Larry makes the first blow. It is not unlike the breath of wind on a pleasant summer's day, and he feels his legs fold out beneath him as his head fills with lead or wool, or something like it. Lead and wool are very different, he recalls as he loses his sight temporarily, and his right shoulder and collarbone burn white with pain.

He hears footsteps on floorboards, and when Mrs Jenkins kicks him, he realises he is on all fours, in the process of getting up or down, and his right ear is ringing. He puts a hand to it, and his fingers come away scarlet.

Mrs Jenkins looms over him, her musty skirts almost brushing his lips, as she says: 'Thought you could fool me, did you? You have no idea who you cross, Mr Peeler.' A boot jabs into his sore shoulder, and his right arm collapses, sending him into the wall. The garret really is very small, he thinks, as his teeth close on the skirting board, and rather a pointless space. That musty smell again, and now a large black boot blocks his vision.

'Now, pick up every last one of your pitiful pennies and be on your way, else it'll be the last thing you do,' Mrs Jenkins says, and Frank thinks again how astonishing it is that such horror can exist so quietly behind ordinary, green-painted doors, and how this ought not to surprise him anymore, and yet it does.

He drags himself upright against the wall, holding the heel of his hand to his ear. 'How much is Emily worth really?' he gasps. Through Larry's tree-like legs, he can see into the narrow hall.

'More'n you can pay on a Peeler's pittance – I can tell you that, my boy. You ain't in no position to negotiate. Now get up

337

and stop dirtying my floor. And take that poxy jade with you.
I knew that Josephine were up to no good the first time I laid
eyes on her. A girl with a scar like that ain't trustworthy.'

'You're a slave-driver, Mrs Jenkins,' Frank says, with effort.
'You're only missing a crop.'

Larry swoops like a bat from the eaves and lifts him by the
muffler, pinning him against the whitewash and breathing
unpleasantly into his face.

'You heard her.'

He is a man of few words, but they are effective ones, and
before he can take in what has happened, Frank is set unsteadily
back on his boots. Then comes a cry from the bedroom.

'Where've they gone?'

Larry thunders into the room, and Frank rights himself
against the door-frame. A chair is overturned and cursed at,
and Mrs Jenkins flies into the hall.

'Where are they?' she cries.

Frank's guts grow slippery as Larry fixes his dull gaze on
him.

'You done this, ain't you?'

'What? They can't have. They've left me?' Frank cries,
looking blankly about and wondering if he is overdoing it,
just as Mrs Jenkins appears again and lets out a roar of rage.

Briefly, he wonders if he might yet escape, with the two
of them circling through the garret as he flees through the
doorway to the hall. But Mrs Jenkins appears before him, hands
planted on hips, while Larry solidifies at the other door like a
giant phantom. He is, as his colleagues say, blocked at both
ends. He quickly calculates the distance from the window to
the street and discounts it, then remembers the window at the
end of the garret, leading, he thinks, to a sloping roof. There

338

are two exits, then, and two obstacles to those exits. Only in the unlikely event of Larry and Mrs Jenkins uniting at one will the other become free.

'John!' Mrs Jenkins hollers down the stairwell. 'John, see where them two strumpets went.'

A male voice makes a query from another floor and is screamed at. Then she returns the blaze of her rage to Frank, moving slowly towards him. Frank feels real fear then, knowing full well what she is capable of, what she has already done.

Before he has even decided to do so, Frank rushes at Larry headfirst with all his might. His skull meets with the brute's stomach, but it is like running into a wall. He falls to one side, stunned, barely feeling the fist that sends him sprawling into the bedstead. He pulls himself upright, wondering how he did not notice before how tilted the room was, for surely everything must be sliding down it continually, like he is now.

He forces himself to remember the exits, the stairs and the window, but they seem so far from him now and so unappealing; the floor here is soft and warm, like a feather-bed, and he sinks down, down as a great pair of legs comes striding towards him. His vision narrows, and the room appears to darken as they grow closer, and he notices a stain on the trousers: mustard or sauce, a day or two old.

Another blow is dealt somewhere on his body – he does not know where because it hums as one entity, like a beehive; in fact he barely feels it. Last night on the beat, he was bored, so this serves him right for always craving danger, seeking adventure, like in the penny bloods he and Edward used to pass back and forth.

Wait till Edward hears about this, he thinks with a smile, and then a face disturbs his thoughts, serene and pale and familiar, floating in the doorway like a memory or a dream. The attic door is too narrow for the dress, which is black-and-white striped, like the peppermint-flavoured sweets he remembers from childhood. Edward loved those, too; perhaps he will buy some and give them to the girls, his nieces, though the baby is too small yet for sweets.

Their pretty faces are his final thought as he sinks into oblivion, and the stripes flicker and go out.

CHAPTER 18

The Night Watch

On the fourth day, Martha is beginning to think he isn't coming home at all when there is a sudden hammering at the street door. She scrambles up from her position on the floor, wondering what to do about all the papers surrounding her, and decides there is no use in tidying them up. She hurries down the stairs to find Mrs Kenealy already fumbling at the lock.

'Good morning, madam,' announces the thick-set man standing on the doorstep. 'Mr Powell of Brotheridge, Taylor and Powell Removals, collecting for a Mr Richard Bryant.'

Martha steps forwards as Mrs Kenealy makes a small noise of disbelief.

'Collecting what?' says Martha, seeing the horse and wagon taking up most of the narrow street and a lean young man sitting behind the reins, eyeing her.

Powell consults a piece of paper. 'A travel-chest, a collection of books and small items including a watch, linen and a cast-iron pan.'

'The filthy blackguard,' the old woman exclaims. 'He ought to be ashamed of himself.'

Powell is wholly uninterested. 'Is one of you able to show me where they are?'

'I should think not,' Martha says, drawing herself up to her full height. 'If he wants his things, he can show his face and fetch them himself.'

'He has employed our services, miss.'

'To take them where?'

Powell looks shifty. 'That I'm afraid I can't say, miss. Customer confidentiality.' He pronounces the word with effort, and then nods, satisfied.

'I'm afraid, sir, that we will not let you in this property unless you tell us where these items are going.'

'I told you, miss, I can't do no such thing.'

'It's Mrs Bryant. Or perhaps Mrs Dunn . . .'

'The man's her husband, who has abandoned her, the cowardly, low-down piece of—'

'Mrs Kenealy,' Martha warns.

Powell's face opens with surprise. 'Oh, I see,' he says. He glances at his companion, who shrugs with disinterest. 'There must be some type of misunderstanding. We'll be on our way, madam. Sorry to have troubled you.'

They pull away and, watching them go, Mrs Kenealy covers her mouth with her hands and cries out. 'Oh, Martha, what else will the Lord send us to bear?'

Glowering with rage and confusion and a dose of panic at the confirmation she has been abandoned, though in a sham marriage to a convict, Martha retreats up the stairs.

'What'll you do now?' Mrs Kenealy wrings her hands in the hall. 'Oh, what a mess, what a God-awful mess he's left us in.'

Martha slams the door and shoves the chest up against it.

For the last few days, she has been sorting through every scrap and piece from within the black chest, putting together a picture-puzzle of the kingdom of lies Richard Dunn has single-handedly erected, maintained and now deserted. She takes up the hand-drawn plan she was examining when the removers arrived and peers at it, wondering where it could be. It is a hastily drawn lead sketch of the floor-plan of a large house, and though Martha doesn't know it, something about it seems familiar, particularly the long ground-floor corridor, with the staircase at the end—

It dawns on her that she does know this plan, this house, because she has only ever stayed in one like it, and unless all such grand places are designed to be identical, it is the very same one, with the dining room where it ought to be and the bedrooms all overlooking the terrace, as hers had. And then: she remembers the silent visitor to her room, holding the candle aloft through the bed-curtains, and she knows, with utter certainty, that it was Richard Dunn.

There is a mark on the drawing at the window of the room she stayed in – but what would he have wanted with Martha then? She thinks back to that dreadful day, and remembers how the first person to go to the window there was Angela, to show her the rose trellis; he must have been watching to see where they were put and mistaken her room for Angela's. She knows she has been used, but this must have been the moment he decided, having watched Angela closely to see who she brought under her gilded wing.

Martha is so numb from the series of shocks and discoveries

she has made over the previous days that this registers as just another fact to be stored and examined later. She moves on, and after a moment, as though one revelation has lit the way to another, something else becomes clear to her: the duke, Arthur, was the recipient of Angela's letter Dunn has stolen, and Angela is in love with him. When they went to stay at his house, Dunn followed them. Why? To find out if Angela was alone in her bed? She remembers the warmth in the lady's voice when she spoke to the duke, the way her features softened as their carriage drew up the long drive. Dunn must have known of her affection for the old man, and planned to use it against her.

There are love letters to himself from Angela, composed for his own amusement, as well as promises of cash and even rude little poems. His obsession with Angela, she has learnt, goes back a full decade; the first time Dunn was imprisoned for disturbing the peace, Martha was a child. Hand-drawn maps, St Valentine's Day cards, declarations of love and chastity, newspaper-clippings of *R. V. Dunn* at the Middlesex Quarter Sessions – there are hundreds and hundreds of items, the breadth and depth of which Martha is only beginning to comprehend.

For the last few nights, she has shut herself inside her rooms, wading through paper by candlelight, barely eating, reading and reading and reading as the full extent of his deceit grew if not clearer then less muddied, for it is so involved, so complicated, she cannot get the measure of it all. He appears, too, to have used aliases, taking rooms at hotels in far-flung places. At least his attempt to sell Angela's private letter to the duke has been thwarted by what appears to be every editor in London.

But the remover has startled her, and she knows she cannot go on like this. If Dunn were to come back, she knows he would overpower her, perhaps even harm her. She puts down the plan of the duke's house and at once begins collecting up all the papers within her reach and throwing them back into the chest in no order whatsoever, for there isn't time, and she has seen all she needs to. When they are all shut inside, she sits on top of it and tries to clear her mind. She knows what she will do next, for it is the only thing she can do.

When she has finished writing, she goes downstairs and hands the letter to Mrs Kenealy, who looks at her in surprise. 'Please go now,' she says firmly, before the old woman can begin her lamentations again. 'I would take it myself, but I must stay here in case he comes back.'

The landlady's rheumy eyes flit fretfully across Martha's, and Martha wonders if the old woman has finally gone mad. But she puts on her raggedy old shawl and leaves, and Martha goes to the passageway and fastens all the locks, knowing that to do so is futile, but doing it all the same.

※

There are two policemen now stationed outside Stratton Street: Ballard, who was regretfully detained on a housebreak callout during the sorry incident at Highgate, and at night-time, a senior constable named Peppard. Josephine looks out of the window for reassurance ten times a day, and one evening thought her heart would stop when she saw a young woman in a bonnet like Nan's speaking with Peppard by the light of the gas jet. But when she turned her head to thank him, she saw it was a stranger.

She has been at Stratton Street three days, sharing a room with Emily, who suffers from nightmares and wakes often, murmuring that somebody is coming. Perhaps in their proximity her dreams are contagious, because Josephine's are the same: elusive, shadowy, with a prevailing sense of menace. Though they have been assured of every measure of protection, Josephine is made uneasy by their proximity to Soho and the tall black house on Dean Street.

Oddly, and despite the nightmares, Emily is less so. She showed no distress at being brought into the grand, gilded surrounds of Angela's mansion. How like a child she looked in her nightdress and cloak, climbing the scarlet staircase – and as trusting as a child, too. For more than a year, she has been shunted from one place to another, and Josephine supposes this is just another house to her.

For somebody who has no home to go to, she has made herself quite content here, leaving orange peel on the pillow, her clothes on the carpet. Josephine realises that Emily is used to having her things picked up after her at the bawdy houses by churlish maids and charwomen. Here, the maids are sleek and inconspicuous, as they themselves were taught to be at Urania Cottage. Though all that was a long time ago, Josephine cannot help but make the bed neatly when they get out, for they have no things to tidy or look after, only each other.

This morning, she washes with the porcelain ewer and basin, dresses in one of the gowns brought for her and Emily from Urania Cottage, then goes up two flights of stairs to sit with Frank, who is staying in Dr and Mrs Brown's apartment, in an invalid's cot before the fire. He shuffles upwards at the sight of her.

'Don't,' she says, filling the chair beside him, which is usually occupied by somebody or other, generally Mrs Brown or Angela. Mrs Holdsworth has come to see him most days. The first time, the matron wept uncontrollably, to nobody's surprise, because where Frank's skin had been white it was now mostly blue and purple and green and yellow, and one of his eyes was sealed shut. Dr Brown has advised it will be too harmful to move him, and so he will stay at Stratton Street until he can walk and eat again. All he can manage now is blackcurrant jelly, and more than once, Josephine has come upstairs to see Mrs Holdsworth feeding her son from a spoon like a kitten. The last few months have decayed Josephine; she feels like a plum left to the flies. But this sight is like a balm to her soul. She is moved by it, and knows now that witnessing love can be as nourishing as experiencing it herself.

'You can stop feeling sorry for me now,' says Frank, regarding her with his one good eye. 'Why would you anyway? I'm living in a palace, getting my meals brought to me. Pigeon for dinner today. And I can stay in bed all day.'

She smiles reluctantly.

For days, he has tried to alleviate her guilt for leaving him in the house on Golden Square. 'I told you to!' he keeps insisting, but she has not shed the tarnish of blame. She escaped the doors of hell, but in doing so left him within.

'Will he be all right?' Emily had asked as they left, glancing worriedly at the uppermost windows.

'Course,' she lied, her stomach churning. And then Angela passed them in her sleek black carriage, and had Josephine not looked at the window and seen her face peering out, frowning up at the tall houses, looking for the one Josephine had described in her note, they would have missed one another.

She put the girls in the carriage and sent them to Stratton Street, where they passed a constable on the doorstep and were shown to a very large, grand room to wait in anxious silence. Josephine was so preoccupied, listening for the sound of the door, of the heavies forcing their way in, that she barely registered where she was. Twenty or thirty minutes passed this way, and her heart almost stopped when finally they heard a commotion in the hall and hurried out to find two footmen carrying a crumpled Frank across the threshold.

She knew from the careful way they held him that he was not dead, and she almost wept with relief, though he looked very bad indeed and was crusted with blood. There were bloody smears on Angela's black-and-white dress, and a streak across her cheek where she had wiped her hand, and Josephine realised she had gone into that house alone to save Frank, not knowing what or who she would find. If Angela had not cut short her family visit, come home at breakfast-time and found their note, he would almost certainly be dead.

But Frank was only unconscious, and when they laid him out like an offering on the enormous dining table, Dr Brown put a little bottle to his lips before they cut off his clothes. Josephine and Emily were sent to the kitchen, where the cook gave them bread and milk, as if they were infants, and some strong beef tea. There, they waited until Angela came to find them.

Emily told her about the heavies, Larry and Preston and the others, and Angela reassured her they had a constable at the house night and day. Josephine wondered why Angela needed a policeman at her house, then Angela's eyes found her own, and she looked quickly away. Angela, too, was frightened of somebody.

'Josephine,' Angela said, covering her hand with her own. 'Who is it you are afraid of? Is it the people in the house at Golden Square?'

Josephine shook her head.

'Somebody else? Somebody you worked for?'

She imagined Nan scoring through her name as Mrs T smoked silently in the drawing room. The smooth-headed sons, who regarded her vacantly and only when she moved, as though she were a stray cat.

She nodded.

More policemen came to the house: Inspector Clark with his coal-black whiskers, and a constable from Wandsworth. They sat with Frank an hour or so before leaving, as grim and impassive as when they arrived.

With the Browns, Frank, Angela and her many servants, there are so many people coming and going at Stratton Street that it has the atmosphere of a fine hotel. Each morning, Emily and Josephine wake to a merry little fire in the grate, and before long, the maids bring a silver tray of breakfast for them: porridge with cream, with a rack of toast and a pot of tea. But Josephine cannot enjoy any of it and declines to walk in the park with Dr and Mrs Brown. More than once, she has entered their apartment and disturbed a solemn conversation between Angela and Mrs Brown, and occasionally, a smooth, scentless man named Mr Parkinson is shown upstairs and leaves looking as grave as the policemen.

'I need to leave London, Frank,' Josephine says now, putting a glass of water to his lips. His hands are bandaged; several of his fingers are broken.

'You and me both,' Frank says. 'I don't fancy a transfer to F division.' His face softens. 'Don't look so worried. We got the old boy on the doorstep, and about a thousand rooms in this place. If they come looking for us, we can just play hide and seek.'

There is a gentle knock, and Emily enters. She is wearing a green poplin dress, and Josephine thinks she recognises it as one

Hannah Parsons used to wear. Nobody has told them how long they will stay at Stratton Street. Nobody has told her where she will go afterwards.

'How do you feel?' Emily asks, sitting down by them.

'Never better,' Frank says cheerfully. His gaze grows more serious and does not leave Emily's face. 'I've been meaning to ask you, and please, say nothing if you wish.' He swallows. 'But I've been meaning to ask you what happened at Reading. Why did you leave, and how did you come to be at that . . . in Soho?'

Emily's face darkens, and she looks towards the window.

Josephine has already heard the story and rearranges herself in the easy chair.

'The Busheys' youngest daughter, Veronica, she's . . . she's only a year younger than I am. But she isn't the same as girls her age. She's like a child. Her brother and sister are away at school, and she doesn't have a governess, so she would sort of follow me around. I suppose she was lonely. She'd sit and talk to me while I worked and show me things she'd made or found. She was always collecting things: flowers and plants from the garden, and insects that she put inside jewellery-boxes. She always cried when they died, as if she wasn't expecting it. She'd come up to my room at night if she had a bad dream, or if she couldn't sleep. The master and mistress – they were away a lot of the time, in Europe or London, so it'd just be her and us. We felt protective of her, in a way. She never bothered us. She'd sit in the kitchen all day long sometimes. The cook would give her things to do: she'd help make biscuits and do her painting at the table, things like that. Mrs Bushey didn't like it, but she was hardly there.'

Emily picks at Frank's blanket, her mouth set in a line. 'The winter I left, everyone was home: the master and mistress and the children. Master Anthony had two friends staying, from Cambridge.

'She took a liking to one of them. She started following him about, mooning after him, going up to talk to him all the time. Master Anthony was gentle with her. Patient. But they were all amused by it, and this friend, Stanhope his name was, seemed to brush it off. But the way she was around him – it seemed to come out of nowhere. I knew something wasn't right.'

She narrows her eyes and looks towards the window. They are at the very top of the house, and there is only sky. 'And so I waited, one night. On the back staircase. Shortly after midnight, he went to Veronica's room. Crept across the landing like a thief and let himself in. I don't know how many times he'd done it, but suddenly it made sense. She'd shown him no interest at first, and then . . .' She swallows. 'I faced up to him. The noise brought the master out of bed, and then the mistress, and then everybody else. He accused me of telling tales. Said he'd only been going to get some water and I attacked him. Veronica said nothing, but nobody asked her. He'd been taken red-handed, and yet it was me it all came down on. Mrs Bushey – I know she believed me. I could see it in her face. And yet she was the one to send me away the next morning.'

'And then what happened?'

'And then I came to London. I didn't know where Martha was – we hadn't heard from her in months – and so I went to find Mary. I had her address, but I'd never been to London before. I took the mail coach and got out somewhere with lots of people – I don't know where. I wandered about, and I suppose I lost myself, though I never knew where I was to begin with. I thought somebody would tell me how to find

Orchard Street, but nobody seemed to know it. I must have looked hopeless, because a woman came to speak to me, and when I said I was new to London and looking for my sister's pastry-shop in Orchard Street, she said, *Ah yes, let me take you to somebody who will know it.* And she took me to a house in Soho, a tall black house where a young woman lived. The woman called herself Nan.

'She gave me some wine and water and some food, and I was grateful, for I'd travelled a long way. She told me she knew my sister, that she was a friend of hers, that they used to live by one another. She said she hadn't seen her in a few months. But she said I was quite a way from where she lived and asked me if I needed lodgings. I told her that I did but that I'd no money, and she said I could stay with her aunt until I found work, and that she'd take me herself to Orchard Street in the morning.'

Emily laughs bitterly. 'She was so convincing. I knew London was a big place, but I believed her. And so I was taken to a house close by and given a nightcap, which was laced with something, because when I woke up, there was a gentleman with me and . . . well. That's what they do. They take girls, young girls from the country looking for work, and girls coming to London to stay with family, and girls who have nobody, and they auction us off. And before we become too familiar with their clients, they move us to another house and do the same thing there. Some of the girls just disappear altogether, nobody knows where they go. Sold onto ships, perhaps. Or they're sent somewhere to have babies. There was a girl I made friends with, at one of the Whitechapel houses. I knew it was Whitechapel because I saw a letter once. Her name was Lily. We knew when we were going to be moved; we were usually told a few days before. But Lily hadn't said anything about it. And then suddenly she wasn't there. Nobody would tell me where she'd gone. I like to think she ran away, but the ones who ran away usually were found and brought back. They were made to work twice as hard and fed half as much. You'd hear them crying through the walls.'

She sits back, sighing, and Frank looks at the bedclothes, absorbed in a troubled silence. 'I'm very sorry that happened to you,' he says eventually.

'Do you think Martha will come today?' she asks him.

Josephine watches Frank closely. There is something he is not telling them about Martha, because any time she is mentioned, he grows furtive and slippery and asks for a sip of water or his pillows to be moved.

'You'd have to ask my mother,' he replies. He clears his throat. 'I don't suppose one of you would open the window just an inch?'

Emily gets up to do it. She has not suspected anything is wrong. Josephine has not yet asked Frank about it and is wary of doing so, because she is afraid of the truth.

She offers to make cocoa, and closes the door on the two of them, standing in the passage a moment to gather herself, closing her eyes and pressing her hands against the cool wallpaper. This house, this haven, is only a hotel, just as she thought. People don't live in hotels, she tells herself. They must leave eventually.

❦

'Mrs Cridge? Mrs Cridge!'

Mrs Holdsworth hurries from one room to the next,

353

putting on her bonnet. She finds the deputy superintendent taking an inventory of the larder, her broad back hunched over the jars of tapioca and oatmeal. She straightens up with a groan of effort.

'Mrs Cridge, can you man the ship for a while? I must go at once to London. I shall be home for supper.'

Urania Cottage's newest staff member lowers her pencil and blinks with concern. 'Is anything the matter?'

The deputy super has been there a little over two weeks, and as the saying goes, the addition of her hands has made Mrs Holdsworth's work feel considerably lighter. Mrs Cridge has come to Urania Cottage from the House of Charity, where she spent a year arranging beds, food and medicine for the houseless. She is placid and capable with a tireless, ox-like energy, and Mrs Holdsworth is thoroughly pleased with her. Whomever the committee decides to hire for her replacement, Mrs Holdsworth knows that, with Mrs Cridge as deputy, the girls will be in good hands. This knowledge causes her to feel lighter in herself, too, now she knows her son is on the mend, and despite the fact she is soon to begin all over again, as one of the ward matrons at the General Lying-in Hospital on the York Road. She looks forward to the role and the uncomplicated nature of babies. Their mothers might be challenging, but she will have a team of nurses beneath her and need not shoulder everything on her own.

'No, no. Don't worry about me.' Mrs Holdsworth can hardly keep still, so anxious is she. She finishes tying her bonnet. 'We need more arrowroot, and the rice is low,' she calls, already halfway out the kitchen.

'Mrs H?' A voice floats from the parlour. 'What should I use for—'

'Ask Mrs Cridge,' she interjects, flaring out her shawl and wrapping it around her shoulders. 'I shall be back later.'

She trots down the garden path, feeling once again for her purse in her pocket. The gate makes its little squeak before clattering back into its cradle, by which time she is already away from the house, scurrying headlong up the lane.

CHAPTER 19

The Summerhouse

'How did you get your scar?'

Emily's face lies inches from Josephine's. Her breath stirs the air between them, sweet and mild. A single candle gutters on the dressing table, almost burnt out.

Josephine smiles.

'What?' says Emily.

'People are always wanting to know.'

'Oh, sorry.'

'No, I don't mind.'

Emily blinks in the darkness.

'My dad done it. People suppose it's something terrible, like a fight, or he tried to kill me or something. He was a grave-digger. He was breaking the earth with a pickaxe, and I went up behind him. He didn't know I was there. It weren't his fault. He used to say only approach a gravedigger like you would a horse, from the front, and never from behind, and I clean forgot.'

'I bet you remembered after that.'

They laugh and talk a little more, and then the candle goes out.

In the darkness, Josephine feels the fear creep in. She might be anywhere: in the bunk at Tothill or the narrow bed at Dean Street. She tries to imagine that she is at Urania, with Martha's bed to her right, and Polly in the corner.

Most nights, she and Emily have stayed awake for hours, talking. She has told Emily all about Urania, which to her is inseparable from Martha, so that every story or anecdote or description involves her somehow. She knows in her heart that Martha is not there anymore. She can see it in the faces of Frank and Mrs Holdsworth and Angela, who avert their gaze or mumble something to change the subject when Emily speaks of her. She knows they will not tell Emily until she is safely at Urania Cottage, because there is too much of a risk she will flee and be swept back into the bleak river that almost consumed her.

Josephine cannot help but imagine the worst, and even the thought of it causes her to feel as though she is drowning. So, when the darkness comes and the fear and worry set in, she thinks of Martha, who is everywhere at Urania Cottage: in the samplers on the wall, in the eiderdown, which she would clutch to her neck in bed at night. She is in the garden, where the peas and broad beans she planted will grow; she is in the kitchen, her care and effort sealed inside jam-jars, in the proud gleam of the saucepans. She is in the faded velvet of the armchair, where she sat so often with her sewing.

She knows Emily will find her sister, even if she is not there.

In the morning, a maid knocks as they are dressing and tells them Miss Coutts would like them to join her for breakfast. Feeling as though they have been summoned by the Queen, they traipse downstairs and find her in the vast breakfast room, sitting alone. They take chairs opposite her and are served their usual porridge. Angela is brought a single egg in a silver cup.

'Today, you will go to Urania Cottage,' she says, looking at both of them.

'Me?' says Josephine.

'Yes.'

'Will they have me back?'

Angela is bemused. 'Of course.'

Josephine feels as though the sun has flown in through the window, so blinded is she by relief. Her eyes sting with tears, and she laughs, a sound so light and warm it causes the others to smile, too.

'Did you not think you would go back?' Angela asks her. 'Where else would you go?'

'I don't know,' she says, truthfully, feeling as though she might weep.

It is the work of a minute to ready themselves, for they have nothing to take with them. They tidy the bedroom as best they can, and before they leave, Josephine opens the window a fraction, as though to let something out: perhaps the fear and doubt that dwelt in there with her. Going upstairs behind Emily to bid farewell to Frank, she feels weightless, though she reminds herself there is grief ahead.

They journey west with Angela and Mrs Brown, taking the same roads she took all those months before with Mrs Holdsworth. Josephine feels trepidation about meeting again with the matron, who she is sure will feel the same way about meeting her. She is not proud of the way she left Urania Cottage, and had never expected to see Mrs Holdsworth again.

But as the pedestrians thin out and Westminster gives way to countryside, the anxiety lifts further and is almost released altogether. Mrs T, Nan, Mrs Jenkins, the tall, shabby houses: they are so far removed from these wide skies and flat pastures, it seems impossible that they exist at all. She imagines them vanishing like smoke in sunlight, and allows herself to exhale. Emily is excited, peering from the carriage window, and she thinks that the girl is too trusting; they might be taking her anywhere, to somewhere worse than that horrid house in Leadenhall Market. Then she feels gloomy again and falls into a sullen mood, and by the time the carriage turns left down the lane and slows outside Urania Cottage, she is sick with nerves, her hands as cold as ice, for it has dawned on her, too, that she is reluctant to share Emily with anybody.

The horses stop, and the driver gets down and opens the door. Josephine is caught between staying here in its leather interior and taking flight, running away down the lane. But both notions are ridiculous, and Angela is looking at her curiously, with a knowing smile, as though she can read Josephine's mind.

The gate makes its familiar squeak, and Emily cries out, tumbling like a sack from the carriage, because standing there, waving and smiling, is Martha.

She is wearing a checked lilac dress, and her hair is curled neatly, and Josephine looks on in astonishment as Emily collides with her sister. They are a tangle of limbs and hair and hands reaching for one another's faces, and over Martha's shoulder, a tall third woman who looks like each of them appears and wraps them both in her arms, and it is not clear where one ends and another begins.

⚶

The park at the duke's country house is at its best in early summer, when the light makes a mirror of the river, and the trees sway like ladies at a ball. Angela arrives at lunchtime and asks to alight at the stables, telling the driver she would like to walk first.

It is a bright day, and she strolls up the drive into the park, seeing in the distance his scarlet jacket above an Arabian mare. She puts up her hand to shield her eyes and waits for him to notice her, which he does, pausing for a moment before trotting neatly towards her and arriving in a cloud of dust.

'To what do I owe the honour?' he asks, climbing down to get to her, but she says: 'Shall we walk?'

Disarmed, he agrees, and she waits for him to take the horse to the stable before leading him down to the river. They talk of nothing – her journey, the weather – as they amble along the bank and stand a while on the pretty bridge, before walking through cool woods to the summerhouse. This pleasant little chalet is always clean and ready to receive whomever may come upon it, with fresh logs stacked in the grate, paper in the desk and the shelves filled with books for afternoon reading. On a clear night, the duke sometimes has his camp-bed and telescope set up here for a night of stargazing, and sends her sketches he has made of the constellations. They have sat here many times, too, with the doors open, like pioneers on the prairie, watching deer and pheasants. It makes her realise

361

how pleasant life is when it is simple, and how complicated her own is.

He opens the doors and sets out two chairs on the painted wooden porch. 'Should I send for coffee?' he asks.

Standing at a distance from him, she lowers her parasol, closes it and leans it against the side of the house.

'You seem changed,' he remarks, looking closely at her.

She says nothing and does not sit.

'What became of that man? Have they found him?'

'No,' she says. 'I have a feeling it will be a while before he bothers me again, but you never know with him.'

'Oh?' says the duke. And then, in a mischievous tone: 'What did you do?'

Angela gazes at the uppermost treetops, swaying calmly. 'I gave him something. And I took something away.'

There is a beat of silence. 'How much?'

'Enough to pay his debts. The amount would mean different things to different people.'

The duke lowers himself into his seat. 'You can't let him win.'

'On the contrary, I feel I have won this round. Time shall tell.'

'Won't you sit?'

But she does not and, remaining very still and clutching the back of the chair, says: 'I respect your decision not to marry me. I shan't propose to you again.'

He lifts a bristling eyebrow and says: 'To what do I owe the honour?'

She smiles, despite herself.

'I don't know whether to be disappointed or not,' he says. 'I think I am.'

'There is one condition under which I shall agree to it.'

'And that is?'

She unsticks her tongue from the roof of her mouth and swallows. 'I want you to show me something.'

He looks inquisitively at her.

'I want you to show me how it feels.'

His face clouds with confusion, and when she does not elaborate, he says: 'My dear? How what feels?'

'It,' she says. Her mouth is dry, and her breath comes shallow. Her heart is beating hard. 'I am asking you,' she says, 'to show me.'

'I don't understand.'

She moves slowly towards him, her eyes bright, her head giddy, as if she has drunk too much champagne. He waits for her, almost glaring with surprise and disbelief and, she is relieved to see, desire. She takes his hand and lifts it to her mouth and kisses it gently. Then she puts her lips to his ear and kisses there, before moving her mouth slowly along his cheek to the corner of his own.

'Angie,' he says.

'Don't.'

They kiss gently at first and then with greater thirst, their hands at each other's faces, waists, backs, until they are so urgent something else must be done. She leads him into the summerhouse and closes the door.

CHAPTER 20

The Calcutta

JANUARY, 1849

The day could not be wetter. It is afternoon when the train
slides into Gravesend, and the rainstorm that burst over
London has followed them east, soaking roads and hats and
umbrellas, though a temptingly pale sky can just be glimpsed
above roiling clouds. They disembark from their various
compartments and jostle to find one another and their luggage
on the crowded platform. When everybody is assembled and
thoroughly soaked, they go out on the boats.

There is a journalist among their party, battling valiantly
with paper that turns to gelatin, holding his coat over his notebook as they are rowed out to the *Calcutta*, before eventually
giving up and surrendering it to a deep pocket. Somebody
makes a comment about missing the English weather, and
everybody laughs, for nerves are running high. Lack of sleep
plus a gallon of coffee as the house fell into and emerged from

chaos that morning has caused them to take on a wide-eyed, anxious appearance, and those sitting with their backs to the ship look constantly over their shoulder to see that it is still there and growing closer.

Today, Martha, Emily and Polly leave for Australia. Josephine is the only inmate at Urania Cottage allowed to see them off, and though in a few hours she will be shaking her umbrella and hanging her rain-soaked things in the passageway at Shepherd's Bush, she appears as excited and anxious as the others. Martha is glad her friend is here, that she has come with them on the very first part of their journey, though it feels more like an ending than a beginning. Mostly, she is glad that they have not yet had to say goodbye, though Josephine will join them in a few months' time.

They are led on board the ship, where the visibility is even poorer, like stepping into a cave or a tunnel. A dark crush of bodies gather like moths beneath lanterns to check their papers. The four girls are accompanied by Mrs Holdsworth, Frank, Mr Dickens and the journalist. When the throng clears, the latter two stride off to explore, while those remaining go in search of the 'tween deck. The ship smells clean, of shaved wood and other, more exotic things: a hint of salt and spices, new rope, a fragrant note of sandalwood, a memory from a distant shore. The rest is barrels and crates, bunks and sheets being shaken out, claims made on berths and floorboards, chests and parcels and luggage of every kind taking up space, blocking the walkway, tumbling from towers at the slightest tilt. The *Calcutta* is holding herself steady, making room for the life growing inside.

The women locate three bunks in a quiet corner at the front of the ship, set down their things and look about their new home for the next six weeks. Their fellow travellers range in age from seven days to seventy years: farmers, draughtsmen, salesmen, maids. Some are alone, others together, in pairs or bands formed as recently as twenty minutes ago on the dock. Everybody is animated, cheerful, harried, relieved to be there or anxious to go. A young girl weeps as she says goodbye to her grandmother; a man with curling whiskers stands thoughtfully at a window, but all there is to see is fog.

They set to work. Polly is quieter than usual and unpacks her chest as Mrs Holdsworth takes from a carpet-bag their bowls and cups and plates. Frank is silent, too, his mouth set in a line as he shoulders their trunks and helps hang sheets for curtains. Emily and Josephine stack dried goods in a crate that will fit beneath the bunk. Martha is adjusting the rags separating the medicine bottles when she feels a tap on her shoulder. Josephine is standing over her, her expression unreadable. She gives a silent jerk of her head.

Martha follows her to a walkway, where Josephine takes both of her hands.

'I'm going with you,' she says.

Though her voice is so soft, so quiet among the chaos, Martha hears her as clearly as if the deck had been empty. 'What?' she says, despite this.

'Polly isn't going. I'm going instead.'

'What do you mean?'

'She's going to stay, for Frank. To be with him. To marry him. She's changed her mind.'

'But—'

'She's given me her papers. I'm taking her place.'

'Did Frank agree to this?'

'Of course not. He doesn't know. He thinks she's going.'

'Mrs Holdsworth will never——'

'I know, which is why we won't tell her. When we say goodbye, I'll pretend to leave with them and get lost in the crowd. They'll think I've taken another boat. Polly will sneak out after them and find them on the dock when it's too late to do anything about it.'

'But your things——'

'I don't need them. I'll have Polly's.'

Martha's heart is beating so hard she fears it might give out altogether. 'Mrs Holdsworth . . . she'll feel betrayed.'

'You know we can't tell her.'

Blood hums in Martha's veins as she looks across the deck at Polly, who is shaking out sheets and pillowcases to dress the beds, inscrutable. How mousy she had seemed when she set down her canvas bag on the bedclothes at Urania Cottage. How broken she was. Now, though she is still slight, she is lean with muscle, her face brown from working in the garden. Martha realises how transformed she is from the girl who came from the infirmary.

A few yards away, Frank stands with a rope from one of the crates held loosely in his hands, gazing at her.

'You can't pretend to be somebody else,' says Martha.

Josephine shrugs. 'I'll be Polly Miller on the boat, then. And when I arrive, I shall be myself.'

'And what will Polly do? Where will she live?'

'I doubt Mrs Holdsworth will evict her daughter-in-law.'

'But what about——'

'Martha.' Josephine squeezes Martha's hands and smiles. 'It's done. We've agreed it. I was coming out soon anyway.'

The committee decided that, after everything, Martha, Emily and Polly should be the first to emigrate. Josephine would follow after some more education, with two or three more girls. Privately, though she would miss Josephine, Martha was relieved to find out she would be in the first group. After all that has come to pass, even the other side of the world does not feel far enough.

Mrs Kenealy took her letter for Mrs Holdsworth to the post office on the morning the removers arrived. Martha kept close by the chest, as though without supervision it might take off like a hot-air balloon, and that evening Mrs Holdsworth came to the little house in Lambeth. Martha knew that what she had found was too enormous, too dangerous to ignore, and that Mrs Holdsworth would know what to do.

She did. She fetched a cab, and the pair of them took the black chest to Stratton Street, where it was hauled down the area steps and locked inside the wine cellar. Martha waited in the cab, looking up at the golden windows, thinking for a moment that she saw a familiar silhouette playing with the blinds.

Mrs Holdsworth did not tell her at first that they had found Emily, so relieved was she to have Martha back, and so concerned about her health. For though Martha felt well, when the reality of all that had happened sunk in, she fell into a deep depression. She was nursed in her old bed at Urania Cottage by Polly and a succession of new girls – or new to her at least; some of them had been living there weeks and knew the place as well as she did. She was pleased to see that Lucinda's hair had grown into a handsome, boyish crop. Frances had discovered a talent for baking, and Mary-Ann wrote the first letter of her life to an aunt, and burst into tears on receiving a reply.

She did not know where Richard Dunn had gone to, but she knew he was not gone for good. Angela came to see her at

Urania Cottage while she recovered and, with Mrs Holdsworth, they talked into the night. Angela was hopeful he would hide for a long time, faced with a conviction for arson and a trunkful of evidence of his deceit. They went over everything and both of them cried.

But that was all months ago now, and since then, Martha has freed herself of the identity of Mrs Bryant, though it was false to begin with. Frank found the church in which they married at Lambeth and discovered that Dunn had signed the marriage registry as Richard Bryant, who did not exist. Angela dealt with it, setting her lawyer upon the matter, and just like that, Martha was never married. Somehow she found that she was able to put it all behind her, eventually throwing herself into the routine and work at Urania Cottage and the distractions of her sister and friends.

Last night, their final one in England, Angela called with Mrs Brown and an armful of presents: a trousseau of linen, as though they were three new brides, luxury cocoa, thick and creamy writing paper. Mrs Holdsworth tutted and sighed that they would have to find room for it all, as the trunks were packed without breathing space, but later, Martha discovered her crying over the parcels and persuaded her to keep the cocoa for the house.

The matron had turned down the job at the hospital when Angela begged her to stay. The girls gathered at the cottage windows, which were thrown wide so they could eavesdrop on the conversation outside. They heard Angela say that she and Frank had shown such loyalty to the home and the people within it that she could not imagine finding anybody more dedicated. Mrs Holdsworth had pretended to consider it, but in under a minute agreed, and the pair of them came into the parlour for a celebratory cup of tea. While they made pleasant talk, a quarrel broke out in the scullery, which Mrs Holdsworth broke up without leaving her seat or even putting down her teacup.

Martha is dumb with shock as they return to their party. A thousand doubts and questions clamour at the forefront of her mind, but when she looks at her friend and her sister laughing and talking so easily, any hesitation she has melts to sheer delight. She embraces Polly fiercely, and Frank, too, who is slightly bewildered, and soon, the time has come for them to leave.

All around the 'tween deck, friends and family kiss and cling to one another. The journalist arrives with Mr Dickens, who bears down on the girls with his usual force and energy, pumping their arms and kissing them as passionately as if they were his own daughters. Mrs Holdsworth takes each of their faces in her hands, as though committing them forever to memory, as tears cascade down her soft cheeks. The final farewells are administered in a blur and tangle of hands and cheeks and lips, and not a single face is dry as the group tenderly divides.

With the press and crackle of paper at her ribs, Martha watches the departers leave along the walkway, past the barrels and beams, the pails and packages. When they are gone, she takes out the envelope that she has kept a secret for months, folded inside her copy of *Van Diemen's Land* on the shelf in her bedroom and now worn against her skin. It contains fifty-thousand pounds in bank notes. She has told nobody about it and perhaps never will, though she won't keep the money to herself. Perhaps they will find work; perhaps they won't. For now it doesn't matter.

When Mrs Kenealy handed her the plain envelope that was waiting for her at the post office, Martha took it in surprise, thinking Richard Dunn had perhaps confessed everything. She managed to conceal from the landlady its contents and closed herself inside her rooms, dizzy and shaking.

All this time, she has expected somebody to come calling, to claim it as stolen, for who could have left her a fortune? Not Richard Dunn, who spent his life running from debts. Only Angela could spare such riches, but she has never mentioned it to Martha – and why would she leave it at a post office in Lambeth? She hasn't dwelt for long on who might have given it to her, because however it came, it had her name on it, and so it was meant for her.

When everything is put away, Martha, Josephine and Emily take their cloaks and go up to the top deck to wave farewell to England. The floor rises gently to meet them as the ship strains at its anchor, eager to be gone. The weather has worsened, and they walk towards the hatch, where a sheet of rain teems down the staircase, appearing like a portal to another world.

Martha takes the rail in one hand and her skirts in the other. She puts her face to the sky and climbs.

Historical Note

In 1847, at the peak of stardom, Charles Dickens established
the Home for Homeless Women with his friend Angela
Burdett-Coutts. Though the project was Burdett-Coutts' idea,
the driving force behind it was Dickens, who was thirty-five at
the time. He combed jails, workhouses and hospitals housing
reformed prostitutes for the 'experiment', found a house in
Shepherd's Bush – rural but close enough to London to visit
regularly – and furnished it himself, choosing everything from
the clothes the inmates wore to the pictures hanging on the
walls. Burdett-Coutts, the heiress of Coutts bank, footed the
bill, and in November 1847 Urania Cottage opened its doors.

A halfway house between a refuge and a social experiment, it
took in women living on the margins of society. All were poor,
many were destitute, and some convicted criminals. They were
to be handled with caution, 'tempted to virtue', away from
the bleak futures that awaited them. Dickens' rigid routine
trained the inmates – all in their late teens and early twen-
ties – for domestic service, teaching them basic housekeeping
and cooking and providing them with an education. Once the

governors were happy with their progress, they would emigrate to the colonies, where they could begin new lives.

Urania Cottage had mixed success. Many of the girls left of their own accord or ran away. Some were thrown out for thievery and drunkenness, or ended up back in jail. Several were successful and emigrated to countries including Australia, Canada and South Africa. For its duration, the house and its subjects were top-secret. Dickens was careful to keep all mention of it, and any connection with him, out of the press. He devoted a decade of his life to the project, hiring and firing matrons, directing the committee, liaising with Burdett-Coutts for funds and befriending – and often despairing at – the girls.

Most of what we know about Urania Cottage comes from Dickens' letters, but the story of *The Household* is influenced by *David Copperfield*, the first full-length novel Dickens wrote after the inception of his Home for Homeless Women. In *Copperfield*, a character called Martha 'falls', leaves her rural community for London and eventually emigrates to Australia. Urania's first group of emigrants set sail for Australia in January 1849 – the same month Dickens began writing *Copperfield*. Among them was a young woman named Martha Goldsmith, who provided the basis for my Martha Gelder, and perhaps Dickens' Martha Endell.

Dickens and Burdett-Coutts' friendship cooled with the breakdown of Dickens' marriage, and Dickens withdrew his involvement after 1858. Urania Cottage appeared in the 1861 census with ten inmates, and wound down operations the following year. There is one photograph of Urania Cottage, taken in 1915, before it was demolished.

Acknowledgements

At Bonnier, I am very grateful to the following people for seeing The Household through to publication and beyond: Ellie Pilcher, Rob Power, Holly Milnes, Justine Taylor, Francesca Russell, Eleanor Stammeijer, Vincent Kelleher, Stuart Finglass, Mark Williams, Kevin Hawkins, Jeff Jamieson, Jennie Harwood, Robyn Haque, Alan Scollan, Andrea Tome, Stacey Hamilton, Laura Makela, Jenny Richards, Lucy Dundas and Alex Riddle. Special thanks to my editor Sophie Orme, who never wavers in her support and enthusiasm, and who I feel very lucky to be published by for the fourth time. Thanks also to Margaret Stead, Katie Lumsden and Michelle Bullock.

I am grateful to Jenny Hartley, Claire Tomalin, Edna Healey and Diana Orton for their work on Dickens, Urania Cottage and Angela Burdett-Coutts. I drew from their books for research and inspiration, and am always astonished at the energy and effort required for non-fiction writing.

With thanks always to my husband Andy for his endless support, encouragement and culinary skills. And especially to my mum Eileen, dad Stuart, Karen, Jon, Keith, Caroline and Victoria, who all looked after my baby so that I could write this book. I dedicate this novel to my late father-in-law Keith, who I miss very much.

Reading Group Questions

1. The women who come to Urania Cottage do not conform to gender expectations in Victorian society. Discuss the ways in which this is explored.

2. Angela and Josephine come from two very different backgrounds. What impact does this have on how their lives are contrasted and unfold in the story?

3. Richard Dunn has stalked and harassed Angela for years. He also been imprisoned many times. How does the justice system in nineteenth-century England compare to the present day?

4. Many of the characters in the novel have lost loved ones. Discuss how loss and grief have affected various characters and led them to their present circumstances.

5. Martha talks about her sisters Mary and Emily often, but she also develops a strong bond with Josephine. How important is sisterhood in the novel?

6. There are many female characters in *The Household*. Discuss how the few male characters are portrayed.

7. Mrs Holdsworth is an important figure as the matron at Urania Cottage. How would you describe her relationship with the girls and how they view her? And with Angela?

8. Josephine mentions that the girls who come to Urania Cottage are not allowed to talk about what came before. Why do you think this rule exists?

9. There are courtships between Angela and the Duke, Polly and Frank, and Martha and Mr Bryant. What do these different relationships demonstrate about the perceptions of marriage and patriarchy?

10. Lydia is the only character at Urania Cottage to pass away. Why is her death significant and what does it symbolise?

11. Martha eloping with Mr Bryant is a shock to those close to her because of the skills and education she was being offered. Why do you think Martha made this decision?

12. Even though Mr Dickens co-founded Urania Cottage, the readers never meet him in the book. Why do you think this is?

Dear Reader,

I hope you've enjoyed reading *The Household*. If you'd like to receive more information about it, and about my previous three novels, *Mrs England*, *The Familiars* and *The Foundling*, you might be interested in joining my Readers' Club. Don't worry – it doesn't commit you to anything, there's no catch, and I won't pass your details on to any third parties. You'll receive updates from me about my books, including offers, publication news and even the occasional treat! You can unsubscribe at any time. To register, all you have to do is visit **www.staceyhalls. com**.

Another way of reaching out to me is via Twitter @Stacey_ Halls or Instagram @StaceyHallsAuthor. I hope to hear from you soon, and that you continue to read and enjoy my books.

Thank you for your support,
Stacey

To save her child, she will trust a stranger. To protect a secret, she must risk her life . . .

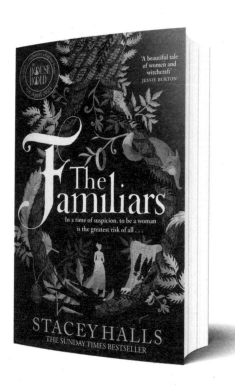

Discover the original break-out witch-lit novel, in Stacey Halls' *Sunday Times* bestselling debut.

The anniversary special edition is available now in paperback.

Read on for an extract from
The Familiars

CHAPTER 1

I left the house with the letter because I did not know what else to do. The lawn was wet with late morning dew that soaked my favourite rose silk slippers, for in my haste I hadn't thought to put on pattens. But I did not stop until I reached the trees overlooking the lawns in front of the house. The letter I had clutched in my fist, and I opened it once more to check I hadn't imagined it, that I hadn't drifted off in my chair and dreamt it up.

It was a chill morning, misty and cool with the wind racing down from Pendle Hill, and though my mind was in turmoil, I'd remembered to take my cloak from its place at the end of the wardrobe. I'd given Puck a perfunctory stroke and was pleased to see my hands weren't shaking. I did not cry, or faint, or do anything at all except fold what I had read back into its old shape and go quietly down the stairs. Nobody noticed me, and the only servant I saw was a brief glimpse of James sitting at his desk as I passed by his study. The idea that he might have read the letter himself crossed my mind, as a steward often opens his master's private correspondence, but I dismissed the thought quickly and left through the front door.

The clouds were the colour of pewter jugs that threatened to spill over, so I hurried across the grass towards the woods. I knew that in my black cloak I'd be conspicuous among the fields from servants' prying eyes at the windows, and I needed to think. In this part of Lancashire, the land is green and damp, and the sky wide and grey. Occasionally you see the flash of a deer's red coat, or a pheasant's blue neck, and your eye is drawn swifter than they can disappear.

Before I reached the shelter of the trees, I knew the sickness was coming again. I pulled the hem of my skirt away from where it splattered the grass, then used my kerchief to wipe my mouth. Richard had the laundry-women sprinkle them with rose water. I closed my eyes and took several deep breaths, and when I opened them I felt slightly better. The trees shivered and birds sang merrily as I went deeper, and in less than a minute I had lost Gawthorpe altogether. The house was as conspicuous as I was in these parts, made of warm golden stone and set in a clearing. But while the house couldn't keep you from the woods that seemed to draw ever closer and were visible from every window, the woods could keep Gawthorpe from you. Sometimes it felt as though they were playing a game.

I took out the letter and opened it again, smoothing out the creases that had formed in my tight little fist, and found the paragraph that had left me reeling:

You can divine without difficulty the true nature of the danger that your wife has been in, and it is with solemn regret that I impart on you my professional opinion as a physick and expert in matters of childbed: that upon visiting her last Friday sennight, I drew the deeply unfortunate conclusion that she can not and should not bear children. It is with excessive importance that you understand if she finds herself once more in childbed, she will not survive it, and her earthly life will come to an end.

Now I was out of sight of the house I could react with some privacy. My heart was beating furiously and my cheeks were hot. Another surge of sickness overcame me, and I almost choked on it as it burnt against my tongue.

The sickness came morning, noon and night, wringing me inside out. At the most, it was forty times a day; if it was twice I felt lucky. Veins burst in my face, leaving delicate crimson stems around my eyes, the whites of which turned a demonic red. The awful taste in my throat would last for hours, sharp and choking as the blade of a knife. I couldn't keep food down. I had no appetite for it anyway, much to the cook's disappointment. Even my beloved marchpane lay in broad, unsliced tablets in the larder, and my boxes of sugar candy sent from London gathered dust.

The other three times I hadn't been this ill. This time it felt like the child growing inside me was trying to escape through my throat instead of between my legs like the others, who announced their untimely arrivals in red rivers down my thighs. Their limp little forms were grotesque, and I watched them being wrapped like fresh loaves in linen.

'Not long for this world, the poor mite,' the last midwife said, wiping my blood off her butcher's arms.

Four years married, three times in childbed, and still no heir to put in the oak cradle my mother gave me when Richard and I married. I saw the way she looked at me, as though I was letting them all down.

Still, I could not fathom that Richard knew what the doctor had said, and had watched me fatten like a turkey at Christmastide. The letter was bundled in among several papers from my three childbeds, so it was possible he could have missed it. Would he have done right by me in withholding it? Suddenly, the words seemed to fling themselves from the page and wrap around my neck. And written, too, by a man whose name I did not recognise, so wreathed in pain was I when he visited that I could not recall a single detail about him: his touch, his voice, or whether he was kind.

I'd not stopped to catch my breath, and my slippers were truly ruined now, soaked with greenish mud. When one of them got stuck and came off, sending my stockinged foot into the wet ground, that was more than I was prepared to take. With both hands I made the letter into a ball and threw it as hard as I could, taking a brief moment's satisfaction when it bounced off a tree several yards away.

If I had not done that, I might not have seen the rabbit's foot a few inches from where it landed, nor the rabbit it belonged to – or at least what was left of it: a mangled mess of fur and blood, then another, and another. I hunted rabbits; these had not been slain by a hawk or a falcon making a neat little kill before circling back to its master. Then I noticed something else: the hem of a brown skirt brushing the ground, and knees bent, and above them a body, a face, a white cap. A young woman was kneeling a few yards away, staring at me. Every line of her was alert with an animal tension. She was shabbily dressed in a homespun wool smock with no pinafore, which is why I did not see her straight away among all the green and brown. Flax-coloured hair spiralled down from her cap. Her face was long and narrow, her eyes large, their colour unusual even from a distance: a warm gold, like new coins. There was something fiercely intelligent, almost masculine, in her gaze, and though she was crouched down and I standing, for a moment I felt afraid, as though I was the one who had been discovered.